D1106068

SPIES
AND
TORIES

SPIES
AND
TORIES

A Novel
by
Rita Cleary

SUNSTONE
PRESS

SANTA FE

The lines of verse at the beginning of each chapter come from pro-British poems published in the loyalist paper, *Rivington's Gazette,* 1779–1781. They are recorded on microfilm Reels 2 and 3 at the New York Historical Society. *Rivington's Gazette* is the paper that published the commentary of the spy, Robert Townsend. One passage comes from the writings of Jupiter Hammond, local slave, poet and religious leader, who belonged to the Lloyd family of Lloyd Harbor.

Sunstone books may be purchased for educational, business, or sales promotional use. For information please write: Special Markets Department, Sunstone Press, P.O. Box 2321, Santa Fe, New Mexico 87504-2321.

FIRST EDITION

10 9 8 7 6 5 4 3 2 1

Library of Congress Cataloging in Publication Data:
Cleary, Rita, 1941-
    Spies and Tories / by Rita Cleary.—1st ed.
        p. cm.
    ISBN: 0-86534-275-X
    I. Title.
PS3553. L3916S7   1998
813'.54—dc21   98-7720
                                          CIP

Published by   SUNSTONE PRESS
                    Post Office Box 2321
                    Santa Fe, NM 87504-2321 / USA
                    (505) 988-4418 / *orders only* (800) 243-5644
                    FAX (505) 988-1025

Appreciation and thanks for their resources and help:
>   The Oyster Bay Historical Society
>   The Friends of Raynham Hall
>   The Lloyd Harbor Historical Society
>   The Society for the Preservation of Long Island Antiquities
>   The Townsend Society of America
>   The Cold Spring Harbor Whaling Museum
>   The New York Historical Society
>   The South Street Seaport Museum
>   Mr. Thomas Kuehhas
>   Mr. Stuart Chase
>   Mrs. Cynthia Kendall Morrongiello
>   Mr. George W. Campbell
>   Mr. John Hammond

For the efforts to preserve the trappings of history: Raynham Hall, Wightman House, Benjamin Thompson House, the Joseph Lloyd Manor, Rock Hall, Fraunces Tavern, Old Bethpage Village, Old Mystic Seaport, St. George's Church in Hempstead, and more. So very little is left.

Thanks to my many friends and neighbors who contributed the stories of their ancestors.

Special thanks to those ancestors who created this great experiment we call democracy. Their efforts have taken root and flowered.

1

Sorrow and terror seize the Yankee race
When the brave Briton looks them in the face.

The dawn was fiery red. The Flatbush Road was dusty and dry. The line of militia crouched behind jagged earthworks along the plain. Determined and grim, farmer and fisherman rallied to the cause. They knelt in granite stillness, muskets primed, targets sighted, sweating, waiting. Behind, on the heights above them, a second line, a bright glistening stubble of bayonets, wavered in the summer heat. The two colonial lines dominated the plain below and watched the enemy advance.

The 17th Light Dragoons, the 42nd Black Watch, the 71st Highlanders, guards and grenadiers and twelve more regiments, marched toward them on the horizon's rim. The British rose like the sun from the southern shore. The red of their coats shone like the sun's own fire. The clamber of artillery and tramp of feet rumbled like thunder over the ground.

Robert Townsend rode down from the heights, reined in his horse and swallowed hard. He was on his way home. It lay beyond the plain and the field of fire, beyond this last line of men and weapons. He had cut the first line. He had tried to cut the second twice but the crush of refugees had driven him back. From his seat atop his horse, he stared down on the soldiers' backs, on grimy, sunburned necks, dark bands of sweat where shoulder blades poked holes through linsey shirts. Bleak profiles turned briefly to bite off charges, pour black powder down musket barrels and ram the lead balls home. Artillerymen stood by cannon in the forward redoubts, tompions and matches at the ready. They were young men, old men. Some of his neighbors were here, merchants like himself. And some marched in red with the other side. Robert Townsend stood apart from both.

The distant red line fired a smooth volley. The noise was deafening; the smoke blinding. He heard an eager captain shout, "Fools! They be not yet in range!" Suddenly the captain looked back at Robert, "Do ye come to join us man?"

"I would go to my home." Robert had to shout. He pointed east down the road toward the advancing red line.

"To the King's men! We'll not let you pass to join the enemy! They are tyrant's rogues! We unhorse cowards like you but I'll not now call my men from their labor!" He reached out, seized Robert's rein and shouted, "Fire!" An earsplitting volley split the air. Robert's horse leaped back, jerking the captain off his feet but his iron grip held the rein. The red line swelled and advanced relentlessly. The captain cursed and looked enviously at Robert's bay. "General Stirling needs a good horse! We need men in the line!"

"I am neutral, Quaker!" Robert tried to loosen the captain's hold.

The man screeched with laughter, tightened his grip and shouted for help. "Bloody Quaker shirker! A horse for the general! A horse for our baggage! Horsemeat for dinner! A man is neutral but not his horse!" Men left their posts and circling, began to close in. Desperate, Robert took a knife from his belt and swiped down on the rein. It snapped. The captain drew his hand away quickly as Robert spurred the frightened horse forward. The beast lunged through the line of battle, running madly down the length. Men leaped out at him in an effort to catch the prize.

Robert Townsend steered the racing horse north to the end of the line. The colonial volley crashed behind him, and another volley rattled from somewhere off to his right. Robert looked back once to see white surprise in the eyes of the commanders, glassy fear in the open mouths of the militiamen. Another red line had emerged from behind hills in the east. The soldiers forgot the horse. He slowed and blinked his stinging eyes. They ached in the glare of the dawning sun and the parched smoke of battle. His heart thumped wildly. His hands groped for wounds about himself and his horse. He was unhurt. The precise

British fire, the rhythm of their marching feet, echoed in his ears. With his single rein he turned his terrified animal. They plunged into the sheltering woodlands and cover.

He stopped there and turned to watch the battle lines converge. The line of colonials faltered and the ragged Americans ran, first a few, then groups. Then the whole line crumbled. The Americans were flanked! Musket fire, shouting officers, the scuffle of running feet, the crash and boom of the guns continued, and the colonials broke into headlong flight up the Flatbush Road to the heights of Brooklyn.

Flames licked the well-tilled fields. Livestock ran in panic. The colonials felled trees, broke storage cisterns and dikes, flooding the low-lying areas to slow the British advance. But the redcoats came on like the ancient red plague that turned the waters to blood.

Robert Townsend dismounted to walk his lathered horse. He cut a strip from his belt for a new rein and moved farther into the wood. Gradually, his breathing slowed. He knew what had happened. General William Howe had sailed his army east, marched through a gap in the Jamaica hills and come at the Americans from the side and rear. Sullivan was to blame. He was new to the command, had no time to consult Putnam and Woodhull, did not know the territory, had fortified the Bedford and Flatbush passes but had forgotten Jamaica. Nathaniel Greene would not have forgotten. Now it was too late. The island had succumbed.

Robert Townsend pushed on through the brush to the road and a tangle of frightened humanity. He rode with them to Bedford, where they came within shouting distance of British sentries. He turned north again, crossed the Jamaica Road minutes ahead of the advancing British and galloped madly for the thick forest of Queen's County.

He was not alone. It was midday. Frightened residents dribbled into the sheltering trees: a farmer with his wife and babe in arms, his sheep and goats and the milk cow on a tight tether; a boatman in straw hat and bare feet with his meager possessions tied in a rude cloth; a smithy, his huge muscles bulging with the weight of his tools that he carried on his back. Robert dismounted, set the farmer's wife on his horse and tramped on. Her husband simply turned, grimaced and kept going. The woman was pale with fear.

The afternoon turned hot with the itching, penetrating wetness that seeps into pores and spells an oncoming storm. They slashed their way through heavy undergrowth. Few spoke, but Robert did learn their names. Jacob Crosswell was the farmer and the boatman's name was Muirson. The smithy scowled suspiciously when asked his name and turned away from their path deeper into the anonymity of the wilds.

The little group trudged on through the stout vines and heavy greenery of late summer, over great fallen trunks and glacial outcrops, through swamps and across rills of clear water. Robert had faint glimpses of the noon sun through the leafy canopy. Gradually he realized that they did not know where they were going. They were running aimlessly in a frantic rush to the shoreline. No one had thought of what they would find when they got there.

In the afternoon, the sun darkened and it began to rain, small spitlike drops and then heavy pouring streams that churned the earth to bog. But the rain killed the awful heat. It washed the blood from Muirson's feet. It ran down Robert's clothing into his boots and sloshed like great puddles around his feet. He wrapped his cloak around the woman and finally spoke. "There is a meeting house at Flushing and another at Manhasset where you will be safe for the night and sheltered from the elements. I will contact a friend who will take you across to Connecticut." The woman's eyes widened in disbelief.

Her husband was suspicious and questioned, "The meeting house? Are you Quaker? How do you come by such friends?"

Robert answered forthrightly, "My father owns ships and can send a launch.... Muirson here can man an oar. So can you." The animals would not fit in a launch. He added as an afterthought, "Yes I am Quaker, neutral."

The farmer grumbled in his beard. "They will not let you be neutral! Who is your father?"

"Samuel Townsend of Oyster Bay."

"The same who was delegate to the Provincial Congress?"

"The same. I am his third son, Robert."

The farmer's dark eyes softened and he held out his hand. "I am in your debt, Robert Townsend."

They reached Flushing that first night and found shelter under a hay-stack. It rained all through the night. They arrived at Manhasset the next. The rain had stopped but a dense humid mist hovered over the water. Muirson found a skiff hidden in the salt marshes of the bay. They did not wait for the promised launch but in their haste turned the animals out to range and piled into the skiff with whatever they could carry, two men a woman and a baby, rowing hastily, desperately, for the Connecticut shore. Robert watched them disappear into the fog. They had left their dog, a brown mastiff, panting on the shore, with the milk cow. Robert took up the tether. He could not leave the cow who would become prey to roaming wolves.

Alone again, Robert Townsend led the weary animals to the wagon road and started once more for home. The dog followed. The cow slowed his progress. At the Parrish farm, he learned how Stirling had surrendered and how the greater part of the Colonial Army had escaped. They had built up their blazing camp-fires even in the rain to distract and deceive the British. Stout fishermen from Marblehead, Bay Colony men, had manned oars against time and tide and shuttled the ragged army to the temporary safety of the tiny city of New York, at the tip of Manhattan Island. Soldiers had swarmed like insects over the cliffs of Brooklyn into every saucer of a boat that could carry them. It was not good news. Farmer Parrish would not speak his fear but Robert could read his eyes. An invading army was coming. Robert Townsend felt icy fingers of fear invade his chest and squeeze the blood from his heart. But Washington, his army and many of their neighbors, had escaped. Their absence would betray their alle-giance. Their lands and their livestock would be forfeit.

He had delayed warning his family by two days. Had they heard? Was his father, Samuel, prepared to protect himself? Possibly to flee with the others? And what would become of his mother and sisters and the slaves and the house called Raynham Hall, and the fields and orchards and animals and the Townsend ships in Oyster Bay? What would become of him, Robert Townsend? He was an affable young man, twenty-six years old, broad-shouldered and brown-haired, blue-eyed and handsome. He would be expected to join up and fight.

At Jericho, he looked back and saw that the dog had disappeared. He jogged down the familiar South Road through the tall, sweet-smelling pines in the hollow just beyond the town. All was quiet. The smell of fresh earth permeated the air. He passed the Underhill Farm and the Weekes' house, homes of his closest neighbors. Animals grazed behind sturdy rail fences. Wheat and corn yellowed in neat fertile rows and apple trees dappled the higher hills with shade. A swift stream coursed through the hollow and cold springs spouted pure, potable water. The land was kind.

Robert Townsend turned into the lane toward the quiet of Raynham Hall, his family home. The hall faced south. Two tall maples stood in front, to the right and left of the craggy locust called the whipping tree. The trees speckled the white shingles with welcome shade in the humid warmth of late summer. A picket fence defined the yard and small garden on the west side. Beyond the garden, lay an orchard. Nothing was disturbed. He had come in time.

Robert tied the horse to a post in the shade and handed the cow to Cob. Cob was the slave who tended the animals. The dogs jumped up to greet their master. He leaped over the gate, flung open the door and stomped into the hall. The door bounced back noisily against the wall and rattled the clock which promptly struck noon. Carelessly, he dropped his dirty coat on the wide plank floor.

A cane rapped the floorboards in the gloomy interior and a brittle voice called, "Gently, Robert, you'll break the hinges.

"I've brought us a new cow, mother!" Robert Townsend ignored his mother's rebuke and looked past her at a lithe female silhouette emerging from behind the stairs. "Sally, is that you?" His hair was disheveled; his face flushed with the summer heat. Sweat stained his linen shirt which hung over his belt. He rubbed his eyes. They had not adjusted to the shadowy interior.

"Surely, Rob, you recognize your own sister! Audrey's in the parlor. I'll hang your coat." Sally Townsend stooped to pick up his soiled garment. Loose red hair fell gracefully over the pale skin of her neck. Even here in the dark hall, the sheen of her hair dulled by the shadows, his sister was very beautiful. Robert stomped the mud from his boots. "Sally, where's father?" There was a sharp urgency in the tremor of his voice. "You've heard the news?"

Sally's voice was calm. She cocked her head knowingly, "That His Majesty's fleet is off Brooklyn and the British are coming ashore...." She leaned forward to embrace him, "What, no hug for your favorite sister! You've been gone a week!"

Sarah Townsend, a large woman leaning on a silver-tipped cane, appeared at the parlor door. She turned a demanding cheek toward her son. "And a proper kiss for your ailing mother, Robert!"

Robert Townsend brushed his lips lightly against her cheek. He was not a tall man, the shortest of the four Townsend brothers and the same height as his sister, but intelligent eyes danced happily in his rosy face. His usual expression was a broad smile, his demeanor open and friendly. He possessed an inner warmth that Sally and everyone who knew him, loved. It marked the upturned creases at the edges of his eyes and the smoothness of his brow. But now the muscles of Robert Townsend's face were tight, his lips drawn thin and blue, and his eyes narrowed and bloodshot.

Sally studied him more closely. In all her nineteen years, she had never seen him so grim, but his anxiety did not dull her cheerfulness. "William and David have joined the loyalists." She added with hesitancy, "To fight..." William and David, their brothers, were not practicing Quakers. "The Katherine and the Weymouth just dropped anchor. Father's on the beach, overseeing the landing."

Robert's words broke loose suddenly in short staccato breaths, "Sally, mother, Putnam is routed! Sullivan is taken! The British came ashore at Gravesend day before yesterday, fifteen thousand of them, enough soldiers to equal the entire population of the city! They will not leave us to life as we know it." When the women stared unbelieving, he rattled on, "They come like a horde, with muskets and cannon, cavalry and foot! Washington's entire army is scurrying to Manhattan Island. Weapons, powder, cannon, valuable animals, they abandon all in the road and jump into the river with only the clothing on their backs!"

Sarah Townsend punctuated his speech with rap of her cane, "Surely you exaggerate, my dear boy.... The British shall restore order."

Robert gagged. "Mother, they are invading the island! They'll arrest father as a member of the Provincial Congress!"

Sarah's composure shocked Robert. "What an imagination you have, silly boy! Your father has never gone to Philadelphia, did not join those foolish Livingstons in signing that outrageous declaration! Your father only wants to be treated as a proper citizen of England and he supports His Majesty and so do I! Come, help me to my chair." She leaned her heavy bulk on Robert's strong arm.

"Mother, you are mistaken. You cannot speak for father." His mother chose not to hear. Robert Townsend clamped his jaws together and helped his crippled mother to her mahogany armchair. His fists balled tightly; the veins in his temples throbbed. Two tiny vertical lines carved worry in the smooth skin over the bridge of his nose. In his mind, vivid as flames that danced against a fireback, he pictured the ranks of redcoats piling onto the Jamaica Road. He pictured the flight and the panic of his countrymen. It was a scene he would never forget. This quiet parlor, the ample chairs, the desk with its books, his great grandfather's sword hanging over the hearth, were diminishing in his mind's eye with every advancing step of each British soldier. Siege, invasion, arrest, escape - it had come to this! A rebellion, the British called it. He had not intended it. Samuel Townsend had not intended it. The Continental Congress had not intended it, until the first shot was fired. Now armies were on the march and Sarah Townsend sat arranging her voluminous skirts about the claw and ball feet of her chair!

Sally lingered at the parlor door. Micah Strong, to whom she was to be married, was fleeing with General Israel Putnam's army.

Robert read her thoughts. "Sally, Micah is hardy. Don't fear for him.... Fear for this village as we know it! Fear for father who is old. He will rue the day he put his quill to paper and signed his name in public protest!" All the elder Townsends, Robert's father and uncles, had openly supported the Philadelphia Congress against the injustices of Parliament.

Robert Townsend pushed past his sister, through the kitchen and out the back door. He ran across the orchard and emerged on the gravelly shore of Oyster Bay. Sally hiked up her skirts and ran after him.

Twin sloops, square-rigged and triple-masted, rocked peacefully at anchor. On the near ship, the Katherine, seamen were busy furling the canvas and unloading the cargo. The Katherine and her twin, the Weymouth, had been 22-gun fighting ships of the Royal Navy. They had been decommissioned and sold to Samuel Townsend as transports. Now they plied the West Indian seas, not for war, but for profit. Casks of rum groaned against the gunwales as the hefty seamen hoisted them into wherrys and rowed them ashore. Rum, indigo, coffee and sugar were the stuff of Samuel Townsend's profits. He was a rich man. As a Quaker, he did not deal in slaves or the materials of war.

Robert scanned the shore frantically for his father. He was not there. Finally, he spotted Samuel aboard the Katherine, reviewing bills of lading with her Captain, James Farley.

Robert ran to the nearest boat, heaved the last cask up onto the beach and seized the hapless oarsman by the collar. "Back out to the Katherine on the instant!" He shouted to Sally, "Go home Sis! See to mother!"

Sally did not easily take orders from her brother. She came after him, skirts trailing across the beach through shallow tidal pools. "You'll not dismiss me so easily, Robert Townsend!"

The stubborn oarsman grimaced at Robert. "Only a damn lubber would ask a sailor to put back to sea when he has his Captain's leave and four month pay!"

Robert clenched his fists, swallowed a curse and shouted, "A guinea to the man who'll row me to the Katherine!"

A black-bearded whaler overheard the plea. He smelled heavily of rotten fish. "It's Rob Townsend with a harpy on his heels!"

Robert splashed to his boat. "Brewster, by God!

Sally Townsend reached the waterline as Robert jumped in the boat and Brewster pushed into the shallows. She screamed after them. "I am not a harpy, Caleb Brewster! Robert Townsend, come back here or I'll swim to the Katherine!" It was a vain, threat. When she was a freckle-faced girl, she would have swum like a mermaid across the bay. Now she was a woman ruled by the constraints of her sex. She stood frustrated, angry, oblivious to the appraising glares of the sailors.

Brewster eyed her with admiration. As he rowed swiftly out beyond her reach, he shouted back, "A woman aboard's bad luck, Miss! Unsettles a lusty crew! And you're not a harpy! You're a siren! Yours are the irresistible charms that can lure a good seamen onto the rocks to spend an inglorious night upon the dry land!" He stood up in the wobbly boat and bowed. Brewster was a whaler salty in his speech, flamboyant in his actions.

Sally's eyes spouted fury as fiery as the sun's reflections on the red sheen of her hair. "Pull in your horns, Caleb Brewster, and save your insults for your scurvied crew! Dry land couldn't stand the smell of you!"

A sudden wave struck the boat and Brewster fell back in embarrassment. He turned his attention to Robert and shook his shaggy head. "I'd swim ashore if I thought she'd give me a care! Damn her insolent soul! You've a beautiful sister, Rob, far above my station. With your permission, I'll admire her from a distance." His eyes lit up with glee as he winked at Robert, "But that's a foul mouth in a pretty head, Rob! She's been cavorting with sailors to speak so bold!

"She has four brothers, Caleb, who taught her language."

"And a mother who would wash her mouth with lye if she heard....I apologize, Rob, if I've offended your sister!"

Robert Townsend laughed. Caleb Brewster picked up the oars and heaved. The distance increased between boat and shore. The two men watched the girlish form as her feet sunk farther into the muck with each ebbing wave. When he was almost out of earshot, Brewster bellowed again, "I'll tell Micah you're contrary as a shark on the hook." Satisfied he'd had the last word, he turned his black-whiskered face to Robert in the stern. He had a mellow voice when he wasn't shouting. "It's a lively time Micah will have with that one."

Robert shrugged. "My mother ordained the marriage. She thinks Micah will subdue her." He loved his little sister. Boisterous, impetuous, daring to flaunt convention, that was Sally. Quiet, studious Micah Strong would need the patience of a tortoise and the endurance of an ox if the marriage ever came to be, neither of which traits would keep Sally leashed. Brewster would have been a better choice, but the bearded whaler, who butchered and boiled smelly blubber to earn his living, was not a suitable match for a Townsend.

Samuel Townsend stood amid the clutter, midships, beside the Captain, checking each cask against its bill of lading as it came up from the dark, damp hold. He was surprised to see his son, Robert, who did not like the sea. Robert was happier with two feet on solid ground, than on the rolling, pitching deck of a ship. Robert avoided traveling by ship except for the short trip, to and from their warehouse and small house at Peck's Slip in New York City. He preferred horseback.

Robert loved horses and human companionship. He had many friends from city and country and was a successful journalist and shopkeeper at 41 Peck's Slip near Pearl Street. There he minded the Townsend warehouse and store from the house across the street. For diversion he rode to hounds over the vast acreage of the Hempstead Plains or raced horses around the Jamaica beaver pond. Samuel loved him as he did all the members of his diverse family. Everyone loved Robert, rebel and Tory alike, except his mother, who preferred his fawning brother William.

Robert raised his voice in alarm. His left eyelid flicked spasmodically. "Father, the island has fallen. Putnam is in full flight. He has crossed the river to Manhattan! General Howe, the British and Hessians, rule our island!"

Samuel Townsend's face went white as the snowy hair on his head. He was not young, in his mid-sixties. His hands shook and he dropped his ledger. He spoke weakly, "I did not think it would happen so soon." The on-shore breeze scattered the loose papers across the deck and into the sea.

Captain Farley scrambled quickly to pick up the papers that were left. "Sir, if I can be of service."

Samuel placed a hand on his son's shoulder to steady himself. He was a lean, arthritic man, stooped with the beginnings of age. The lines in his face etched deeper and his whole form shook and seemed to deflate, except for his doleful blue eyes which expanded against the pallor of his face. His jaw fell open as if to speak and his lips quivered involuntarily before the words came. "Georgius Rex! Doesn't he comprehend that our quarrel is with Parliament and not the Kingdom?... Captain Farley, please to carry on here." He accepted the crumpled bills from Farley with a trembling hand. "And please to summon Moffet with the launch."

The Captain nodded obediently.

Samuel motioned Robert wearily to the ladder and glanced at his watch. "They will be here soon. Come! We must see to more important matters."

The mate helped him down the ladder and drove the launch forward on the northwesterly breeze, to shore. As they struck the beach, Robert jumped into the shallows. Samuel followed, slipped and went down on one knee. Robert caught him before he fell forward into the water. "Thank you, child." For a moment, a familiar smile brightened the old man's face but he walked ashore woodenly, as a prisoner to a gallows.

2

Go summon Trumpeter, yon haughty town,
Bid them surrender to the British crown.

Sally met them at the high water mark. The son and daughter supported the father like a withered stalk. When they reached the shadows of the orchard, they stopped. "Sally, go to the house. Fetch father dry stockings."

Sally had not shed her resentment at being left on shore, and her reply bordered on insolence. "I'll go at father's bidding, Robert Townsend, not yours!" Then turning to Samuel, "You'll not go concocting any schemes without me, father!"

Samuel revived at this, "That's my girl, my Sally! Red hair and a sharp tongue do make a daring and tempestuous woman!... Sally, I need my stockings and a blanket and my brown coat." He turned to Robert. "You go for my brace of pistols... and my flask. I'll wait here to consider.... And say nothing to your mother or Audrey." He added as an afterthought, "And some beef and biscuit. I'm hungry."

Pistols, Robert could not remember when Samuel Townsend had last used his pistols, not here in the quiet hamlet of Oyster Bay. He disappeared with Sally beneath the maze of apple trees.

Their green leaves shaded the yellow grasses in the even light of the afternoon and cast changeling shadows across the path. The trunks were mature with smooth grey bark like silk to touch and broad shade-giving branches. Cob, the Townsend slave, had trimmed them carefully each year before the bud and they produced rich juicy fruit. The apples were ripe now and shone brilliant red, like British coats, against the green. The smell of apples baking with brown sugar wafted from the kitchen.

Beulah was testing them with a fork as they broke into the kitchen. The hefty slave woman planted her large body squarely in their path. "No you don't! No sandy feet in my kitchen! You clean 'em before you track my floor!"

Sally spoke up. "Beulah. Father is on the beach!"

"And he sired a lady and a gentleman, not two galley scrubs! Shoes covered with mud, dripping water like a mange-dog drips fleas! A bar maid dresses better! An' Mr. Robert soaked to the hips like a common swabber! The Mrs. will rave like a caged coon!"

The Mrs. did rave. Sarah Townsend was a puffy difficult woman. She had broken her hip years ago. It had mended poorly and now, in constant pain, she hobbled around the house with the help of her cane and Beulah to support her considerable weight. She passed hours sitting regally on a velvet cushion to ease her hip, in the tall, mahogany chair in the front parlor, and ruling her household with the order and rectitude of an absolute monarch. Samuel Townsend deferred all household responsibilities to her. She had always been a consummate housekeeper and now required stiff perfection of those delegated to perform duties she was unable to accomplish herself. The duties usually fell to Sally or Beulah. Audrey, her elder daughter, was pale and consumptive.

Sally brushed her hair back while Beulah dried and straightened her skirt and Robert wiped the seaweed from his boots. They walked through the hall to the parlor.

Sarah Townsend complained loudly, "Sally, bring Robert here! He comes home from the city and ignores his mother! Your brother William always remembers his courtesies!"

Sally changed the subject. "The apples are ripe, mother. We will be baking and churning tomorrow and pressing the cider next week. I've asked Beulah to bake pies for supper but she's run out of sugar." Sarah Townsend brightened momentarily.

"Tell her to use molasses."

Sally curtsied politely and backed out of the room. Robert was already on the stairs and they climbed together to Samuel's bedroom and opened a large sea chest against the wall. The pistols lay in a black leather case at the bottom of the chest beside a pouch of guineas. Robert wrapped both in a blanket and checked that the flask was full. Sally lay her father's stockings and coat neatly on the bed. She placed all the personal articles in a stiff canvas bag.

Audrey peered through the doorway as they were about to leave. "With the new cow, Rob, we can make cheese!... Are you coming to Reverend Pryor's sermon, Sally? Rob, if you would come, we could drive the gig." She already knew that Robert would not come and they would have to walk. He detested the ravings of Reverend Pryor, Rector of the upstart New Light Baptist Church. The New Light Baptists were inspirationalists who breathed dragon fire one moment and oozed sticky sweetness the next.

Sally and Robert were Quakers, like their father, like the Townsends before them. It was a rational, tranquil faith. Townsends had all been Quakers until Sarah Stoddard married Samuel. Quakerism was why the first Townsends had come to Oyster Bay - to practice their religion in the Dutch Colony of New Amsterdam because the Dutch were more tolerant than the Puritans of New England who had expelled them.

Sally paused a moment trying to remember if she had already agreed to go. "Rob is home, Audrey. We should spend the evening with him."

Audrey's smile faded to a pout as she backed away. "I shall have to ask Phoebe." Phoebe, the third sister, had married and lived nearby.

They slipped down to the kitchen. Sally snatched one of Beulah's fresh loaves and a leg of mutton.

Robert grinned mischievously, "And a bottle of madeira, Beulah... for father."

Beulah's granite frown silenced him. "No strong spirits will leave this kitchen!" The slave would have to explain the missing wine to Sarah.

Robert added dutifully, "I'll replace it before she knows it's gone."

Samuel sat dolefully on dry ground at the far edge of the orchard, his back against the prickly bark of a locust sapling, his white-stockinged legs protruding like two fence poles before him. Sally bent to set the basket beside him.

Robert handed him the guns but remained standing. He gazed down upon his father and sister. Samuel's buff breeches were stained with grass, his boots wet and his wig, askew. He was hunched and feeble. He had aged in the last few days. His sixty years looked eighty. And Sally looked more like some disheveled serving girl, not the vivacious Sally Townsend of Raynham Hall, prettiest girl and best dancer in Queen's County. Sally's skirts still held the stain and fishy smell of the sea.

Samuel straightened his wig and brushed the facings of his coat in a vain effort to restore decorum, but his voice cracked when he tried to speak. His deep blue eyes were liquid, near tears. He lay his hand across Sally's bare arm. Robert noticed how the bones protruded at each joint and the veins pulsed blue under translucent, patchy skin.

Samuel tucked a napkin into his shirt, bit into an apple and munched nervously as he spoke. "It's worse than I thought, Sally. Farley told me young Ferguson's troops are busy rounding up rebels, anyone who will not recite a loyalty oath to His Britannic Majesty." As a Quaker, Samuel Townsend did not believe in the taking of oaths, any oaths, nor did he believe in armed rebellion. But liberty and justice were dear to his soul. As a member of the New York Provincial Assembly, he had voted to ratify the Declaration of Independence and had signed the letters of correspondence to the Congress in Philadelphia, protesting the closing of the port of Boston and the arbitrary and abusive treatment of the colonies by the British Parliament. The old man wiped apple juice from his chin and tossed away the core.

Robert's sharp tenor intruded, "Cousin George Townsend is arrested and John Kirk and Elias Baylis, and Dan Cox sailed to Connecticut last night on the ferry from Huntington Harbor and George Weekes...." He stopped abruptly, shocked at his own words. The Oyster Bay meetings protesting the Coercive Acts had been held at George Weekes' house and Samuel Townsend had attended, had witnessed with Weekes the offending papers. A tic in Robert's left temple began to throb and he continued, "They say it was DeLancey that took poor blind Baylis and they say he struck Squire Woodhull after he had already surrendered his sword but I cannot believe that of Oliver DeLancey!" Oliver DeLancey was one of Robert Townsend's close friends.

Sally fidgeted as Robert continued, "...and Jonah Coe and Thomas Thorne and William Lawrence pulled from his sick bed..." Samuel sank deeper into the grass.

"Rob, stop!" Sally's voice was so soft it was doubly intense. Her eyes met his and directed his glance to Samuel. Samuel was staring straight ahead, trancelike, his face drained of all color. His hands were shaking, his lips groping for the unspoken words. "Father, where can you hide?"

Samuel put a broad arm around his daughter's shoulders. He continued to stare glassily at the yellowed, trampled grass beneath his feet, at some particular slender blade that his own step had pressed flat. "Maybe nowhere, Sally... The British have offered a cash bounty to any civilians who enlist. Do you know what that means? Criminals will run from their lairs, the greedy and the shiftless will flock to the army for the bounty, for a guinea, for the love of gold. They will make an unruly and careless army. Sally, Robert, we must be very careful where we place our feet." With his fingernail, he scratched up the downtrodden grass and mused, "We are fragile, like the thin, dry blades of grass." He combed his long fingers through the stems. His children listened in awe as the wise old man continued his musings. "Heels walk over us, trod us down, deny us water, suck the lifeblood from our veins, but they will not kill our roots." He broke off a yellowed stem, crushed it between his thumb and forefinger and held it up. "This was lush and green only last month and now it's dead, but its roots are there." He pointed to the grey earth. "It will spring up again...after the winter has come and gone. You are young. Have faith; endure. I am old.... That is why I love the spring and the budding plants the most." A grasshopper jumped on to his hand. "Don't bounce about like the thoughtless, cowardly hopper. Live with integrity and persevere." His blue eyes turned mournfully to his son then locked on the beautiful face of his daughter, "You who have your lives ahead of you! Don't let them trample you into the ground like these thin blades of grass!" He wiped the dirt from his hands and placed them in his lap.

Robert saw tears forming in the old man's eyes, "You can flee, father, take the launch to Connecticut! British ships are not yet in the harbor!"

"Not in the harbor, but their ships have entered the Sound....Captain Farley told me....Flee? And leave my family, leave my lovely Sally and poor Audrey and your crippled mother and my beautiful Raynham Hall to Hessian mercenaries! No!" Samuel Townsend's eyelids drooped and the worry lines pulled at the edges of his eyes like cruel weights. He shook his weary head, "The British are not monsters. British law is good law. We only protest the evasion of that law. It is thugs and blackguards who loot and burn. We will stand by what is ours and trust His Majesty's troops will defend our property and treat us fairly." He stopped as if doubting his very own words and repeated faintly. "We will not resist. Our God will see they treat us justly." It was a fatherly lecture. Samuel Townsend abhorred violence. Even now, even after the ratification of the Declaration, even with British troops at his doorstep, he could not envision a complete separation from Mother England. He could not bring himself to think of bloodshed and plunder and the bitter scourge that is war. His final words fell like stones from his lips, "If we suffer, our father in heaven will grant us relief." He was a religious man. He believed in the justice of the Lord. He forced a stiff smile. Samuel Townsend was also a brave man.

Robert eyed him with concern. "Father, why should Britain suddenly act with justice toward you, when for years you have complained of her injustices?"

Samuel Townsend looked up. Robert, his most intelligent son, put the predicament so plainly. Samuel Townsend stammered a thoughtless answer. "Because I am old, Robert."

Sally interrupted, "Father, please, at least, board the ship!"

"Hide? If it will allay your fears, child, I will board the Weymouth. Captain Markham is trustworthy." The old man smiled. It was the same sweet smile as Robert's but without the flash of resolve. "Robert, you must see to the warehouse and our city businesses at Peck's Slip. Your mother and the girls will be safe here. Raynham Hall is our home, Sally. You must care for it well."

Samuel Townsend rested that afternoon and well into the evening under the shade of the wide apple branches. The sunset cast pink streaks over the brown surface of the bay and the tide turned from flood to ebb. The Katherine and the Weymouth unloaded. The seamen came boisterously ashore. Only skeleton crews were left on board. Caleb Brewster brought a boat - it was only a skiff. He would row Samuel secretly to the Weymouth. But the wind had turned by six o'clock in the evening to a strong northeasterly blow which whipped the ebbing waves back upon themselves and turned the water's surface into jagged chop. A storm was coming, another wet pelting onslaught from the eastern ocean that would flog the sandy shore like a cat o' nine tails. There was no jovial banter now. Brother and sister watched Brewster's broad shoulders strain at the creaking oars. It was a hard pull for the hefty whaler from Stony Brook, harder now in the evening, against the indomitable northeast wind.

Sally hugged a cloak around her as the wind picked up and the rain dripped from the canopy of leaves. Robert stood next to her like a statue, in his waistcoat, shivering, wet, stark and stoic. He shocked Sally by the intensity of his stare at the thunderclouds that hovered over the bay. Two new wrinkles were there in his brow, above the long straight nose that they both inherited from their father. They gave him a stark, manly look, distinct from the cheerful young man she had always known.

Robert took his sister's hand in a gesture of reassurance and squeezed until it hurt. He released it and she rubbed the pain from her fingers. They watched the rocking boat as it slapped dangerously against the mainchains, until Samuel Townsend was safely up the ship's ladder.

Sally turned to go but Robert held her back. "No one must know, Sally, only you and I and Captain Markham. Mother must not know."

"Caleb Brewster, he knows and Beulah."

Robert thrust his wet hands into his sleeves and turned his face windward into the rain. His eyes were cold, his face frozen in a deep frown. Raindrops spattered his cheeks and he wiped them away like so many tears. He was holding some powerful force tight within the cloister of his heart, like an imprisoned beast, shackled and barred. The look on his face struck worry in his sister's heart more than any of his accounts of lootings and arrests. He was far away in his mind, and she could not follow.

Robert snapped off an apple and bit into it to relieve the tension in his jaw. The onrushing clouds streamed across the sky. His thoughts coursed with them into a fearsome unknown that loomed like a long and untrodden distance before him. The wind at his back pushed him forward involuntarily. His nostrils dilated as if he could smell the rush of storm, the scent of danger. As he chewed the fruity pulp, his keen eyes narrowed and he peered out at the maelstrom of waves. Raindrops thickened. Finally, he spoke, "Brewster and Beulah, they can be trusted." His voice echoed dryly as if it had come from far across the bay. Sally watched him and shivered.

Black clouds blew in from the east and raindrops fell sparsely, then more steadily when Caleb Brewster returned with the skiff, jumped ashore and slung the boat's line over a nearby rock. He spoke with emotion through his black mat of beard, like a man in mourning who has just closed the coffin on his dearest friend. "I sail across on the next flood, Rob and Sally, to Connecticut. You'll not see me again." The mischief in his eye returned and he took Sally by the shoulders and planted a whiskery kiss on her cheek, before extending a massive palm to Rob. "Good-bye to you both....I will miss the banter, Miss. It was a privilege matching wits with you."

Robert seized Brewster's huge hand eagerly, "Good-bye, Caleb, and good luck. I'd go with you but...."

"You'll do as well to stay here. I know." Caleb Brewster nodded grimly. Sally saw him touch his brow with the fingers of his right hand. To dry the rain from his brow? To flick away a tear? Not Caleb Brewster. It was a deliberate gesture of respect, directed at her brother.

When Sally took Robert by the arm to walk back to Raynham Hall, their clothes were wet to the bone. Robert ignored the discomfort and explained. "Brewster goes to fight with Putnam...." He did not face her but stared down, at the dark thick slime in the path. "Sometimes I am half tempted to enlist myself...." He paused pensively. She did not interrupt and he lifted his gaze. "Can you see to Raynham Hall here, Sally, you and Beulah, while I look after our spot in the city?"

"Of course." Sally tightened her grip and leaned on her brother's arm. She drew strength from him and he drew confidence from her. "Will Caleb Brewster see Micah, Rob?... I should have remembered to send Micah word."

"Will you make Micah a dutiful and loving wife, Sis?" The question did not intrude. Brother and sister had always been open with each other.

Sally shrugged and mused, "Maybe I don't love him enough."

Robert paused at that, then shifted her attention. "Look at you, Sis, Beulah will have to scour you clean twice in one day before mother gets a look at you!" His effort at forced humor fell like a rock in the mud.

Sally smiled back wanly, "Look at yourself, Rob, what will you tell mother? That we had dirt fights like two six-year-olds!" They had endured their mother's reproach during good times and bad, innocent and guilty, big brother and little sister. Robert had taught her to swim, clam, fish, ride a horse. Sally was seven years his junior and even as a small girl she trailed after him like a puppy, imitating, worshiping, more daring than their brother, David, who was older than Sally by a year but timid, and more reckless than their brother, William, who detested the sight of mud.

Sally had always been unusual for a girl. She would run faster, throw harder, climb higher, fire a musket or row a boat with the devilish energy of defying the conventions of her sex. Her mother would have despaired of ever seeing her suitably wed, except for her beauty and a spontaneous exuberance that men found incredibly attractive. Like Robert, most men liked and admired her. But unlike Robert, whose brotherly love was honest and innocent, most men desired her carnally.

As for Robert, he was thinking how much, for the past adventures they had shared and for the trials that were sure to come, he wished that she could have been born a man or could have remained a fearless, freckle-faced little girl. He did not understand this impetuous, strong-willed, eminently attractive, young woman.

3

What held the town of beauty, wealth and power
Was all devoured in that cruellest hour.

Sally Townsend's figure had lengthened and filled, in a graceful, aristo-cratic carriage. Her rich red hair fell in folds over the creamy complexion of her brow and beneath it all, expressive blue eyes, so like her father Samuel's, peered out from an intelligent oval face.

She loved her brother Robert best of all her six siblings. It was no longer the hero-worship of little sister for older brother. She and Robert shared many experiences of roots. They shared the deep attachment to the beautiful harbor, to the grassy plains and the virgin forests of their native Long Island. They shared a fascination for the fishes of the sea and wild creatures of the land.

Robert had not gone to sea like Solomon, or joined the Loyalist units like William and David. He had remained home, or nearly so. He lived in New York City much of the year, in quarters opposite the Townsend warehouse and store at 41 Peck's Slip near Pearl Street. He kept accounts and wrote a column for his friend, Jack Rivington, who had established a bi-weekly gazette. He fre-quented taverns and coffee houses, attended hunts and horse races and cock fights and balls. He knew the DeLanceys and the Murrays and the Philips, the Livingstons, the Schuylers and the Buchanans.

When Sally visited New York, Robert escorted her to all their homes. He was her escape from the confinement of a small colonial village and a capri-cious, demanding mother. She was his excuse to stay single despite their mother's efforts to find him a wife.

Sally was sleeping soundly the next morning, when Robert suddenly seized her by the shoulders and shook her violently. She jerked up to protest, but he held his hand to her mouth.

"Sally, I must leave. Captain Youngs has brought word that the city is in turmoil. The Sons of Liberty expect an invasion and are destroying everything of value. They have set the city on fire! The property of known loyalists is their target! We who are Quaker and have not taken sides are suspect! They may descend upon our own at Peck's Slip! Pray for a southeast wind to drive the flames away from us and into the river."

Sally blinked. "Rob, you'll wake Audrey! It's dark! Light a lamp." Audrey slept in the bed on the opposite wall. Sally fell back to her pillow.

"Sal, did you hear?" Robert lowered his voice to a whisper. "I've saddled the bay! I cannot wait.... Hessians are coming here! You must do here as I will do in the city.... Hide our wealth! Preserve what is ours! The silver, candlesticks, father's tankard, great-grandfather's sword with the emerald stone in the hilt that he took from the Spaniards, secure them, Sally, bury them deep, now while they sleep!" Robert sat on the edge of the bed. Sweat oozed over his linen collar. He breathed the word, "Please." The softness of his whisper accentuated the urgency of his words. "The Kings American Regiment, Fanning's men under Captain Grant, have sacked Henry Carpenter of every last farthing! They are out of control. The Carpenters have not a candlestick left!"

Sally sat up. "I'll ask Cob to dig a trench."

"No Sal, do it yourself! The Brits have offered freedom to any slave who enlists! Cob may not be here tomorrow." His brows knit together and a throbbing in his temples distorted the smooth contours of his face. "We who do not take sides may become the targets of both sides!" He frowned. His sharp blue eyes narrowed. "Our own neighbors will accuse us! For every rebel denounced and delivered to the Jamaica Presbyterian Church, the Brits will pay one guinea."

The implications of this last statement were not lost on Sally. Dishonest men would lie for a guinea: many an innocent man would be denounced. Samuel Townsend would be denounced. "Rob, Cob is no use to the army! He's deaf!... Who has excited you so? How do you know?"

Silence. She watched the furrows form over his long patrician nose. "I am a journalist, Sally. It is my business to know. They came with torches lit, for Jack Rivington and his presses, but he escaped. He saw honest people run for their lives! Trust me. Unburied, the Stoddard silver will end up in some officer's mess or worse melted down to the last sou...to be won or lost when the soldiers cast their lots."

Sally didn't answer. She stared at the set of his jaw, at the newly-etched furrows between his brows. The rest was a dark grey blur that melted into the last shadows of night.

"Please, Sally." He rubbed an eye to stop a nervous twitching. "The British have hired mercenaries, Hessians, brutes." His square jaw trembled involuntarily. "They hardly speak English.... You must watch mother, and Audrey...and guard yourself. Jack Rivington and Captain Youngs do not lie."

Raw fear struck Sally Townsend's heart, like a hammer on an anvil and it sent sparks swirling in her brain. That Britain would send foreigners to govern her own colonies, her own people, seemed incomprehensible! Hessians would not comprehend British language and law; they would heed the denunciations of thieves and malcontents. They would not respect the property and privacy of a quiet colonial family, of a simple colonial maiden.

Robert was talking again in a monotone hum, "I will try to convince the British authorities of our loyalty and good will and I'll seek protection for father. I shall see Buchanan and Oliver DeLancey. Perhaps he can send his Provincial Brigade. They can at least speak intelligibly!"

Sally stared back silently at her brother in the grey cold dawn. The drip of rain in the gutter beat to the throb of his temples. He was repressing something he could not reveal, a tension buried deep within the crypts of his consciousness. And he was not going to confide in her.

"I'll do as you say, Rob." Her answer barely stirred the quiet air.

He turned and bounded out the door and down the stairs to the bay horse that Cob held under the giant locust tree in front of the house.

Sally's last words were lost in the clatter of his boots on the hardwood stairs and in the suck of hooves trotting away in the mud. She uttered them anyway to the sleeping form of Audrey, to calm the anxieties welling up within her like some heaving demon from the vastness of the ocean. "Where are you going Rob? It is still night. And what shall I tell mother?... And Audrey?" Audrey, the weaker sister, slept on.

There was a slender moon, almost new, still shining just before dawn when Sally rose and lit the lamp. She took the blanket from her bed and the lamp and descended the familiar stairway. She collected tankard, candlesticks, fruit bowl and sword that hung pretentiously over the hearth. Its green emerald was the symbol of family strength and pride, of continuity and honor. Her hand trembled as she lifted it down and wrapped it in the blanket.

She stood over Samuel's desk and pulled open the center drawer and swept what guineas were there into a chamois which she tied tightly and placed within the tankard.

It was drizzling lightly. An owl hooted, the slow mournful cry of the great horned beast. It was a lonely sound intended to drive away all others of his species. In Massachusetts, the Puritans feared the owl because he heralded witch-craft and death. Sally imagined she saw his giant almond eyes, watching, staring, intruding upon her secret. She felt akin to the creature who stood guard in the blackness until the faint rays of dawn seeped through its cracks.

The rain stopped. The air smelled of sea and salt and the sweet growth and decay which was the life of the shore. A damp morning mist blew in over the shallows, dense clouds of grey moisture that shrouded her movements. She found pick and shovel, and crept like a specter to the orchard. But the orchard was rutted with roots, its ground hard. She found softer soil in the cow pasture, under the soft round droppings of the animals. Here she dug easily, a trench the size of a child's grave. She lay the sword diagonally and the other pieces in a sack on top and shoveled the damp earth back in. She smelled of the muck of the barn when she was finished. Dirt layered her shoes and muddied her arms. Sweat stained her dress. She wiped her muddy hands on her apron and walked to the spring behind the house to wash away the grime. And then she remembered. She had not marked the spot.

Dawn was breaking. The owl hooted again. Now he was the invader in the realm of the day. Sally straightened and listened. The rays of the rising sun splayed over the eastern horizon beneath an iron band of cloud. A cool breeze chilled the sweat that dripped down the small of her back. She walked back to the ditch covered with new earth like a freshly-dug grave. The owl hooted a third time, a slow trailing blast from out of the remnants of darkness and she thought of the Apostle Peter and his denial of the Savior but that was a cock, not an owl. The eerie song haunted her. She too, would have to deny her actions of the night. One last sweep with the shovel to smooth the bare earth; a few handfuls of grass and the animals would trample the scar. The owl was silent. The cock crowed. She paced off the spot from the pasture gate and counted her steps back toward the spring. She stood for a long moment, looking back, fixing the place indelibly in her mind. A light flickered behind her.

The slave, Beulah, who slept by the hearth, had roused with the first chirp of dawn. She stood squarely in the doorway, holding a single candle, black against the blacker backdrop of the interior. "Who there?" Her gruff voice echoed on the still mist as Sally emerged from the shadows. "Miss Sally, you out with the witches! I hear them calling in the middle of the night!"

"It was an owl, Beulah!"

Beulah snorted disapproval. "Or Mr. Robert, I saw him leave, sneaking out like a thief from his own house!"

Sally stared into the sharp white eyes of the slave. Beulah had raised her after her mother had broken her hip. "Tomorrow or the next, Beulah, soldiers will come.... I have only tried to protect what is ours."

Beulah met her mistress' gaze with full knowledge written in the white pools of her eyes, "A bad omen, Miss, the owl, a creature of the devil! The master and Mr. Robert, I heard them talking.... You lied to me! You gonna lie to your mother!"

"I have not lied, Beulah, but I shall tell my mother nothing, neither truth nor falsehood, and you shall tell her as you just told me, that the owl wakened you and that I came to comfort you, and that meddlesome ghosts were parading all over the orchard last night."

Beulah glared back, her massive hands on her hips. "There's mud on your skirt Miss, and blood on your arm. The sword is sharp...."

Sally locked her eyes on Beulah's in shared understanding. "Say nothing of Robert, Beulah, until after the soldiers have come and gone." Beulah would remain silent because Beulah loved Robert Townsend like the son she never had and Sally like a daughter. Beulah and her husband, Cob, had two daughters of their own and Sally remembered their safety. "And keep Josie and Melly in the yard. Guard them. It will not be safe in the lane."

Beulah hauled a bucket from the spring and Sally washed off the offending blood. The cold water stung like the bite of a wasp and reddened her skin. Beulah took the clothes to the spring and scrubbed out the stains. As the morning sun skimmed the horizon and shimmered across the dark waters of the bay, slave and mistress watched from the kitchen. Waves inched up the beach, submerging first a rock, a clump of saw grass, a rotted cask, until water lapped the seawall at the edge of the salt meadow. Beulah broke the enveloping stillness, "It's coming, Miss, trouble creeping in, sure as the tide. I can smell it!"

It was a beautiful time of day, cool with steam rising where the water was warmer than the air and the pink rays coloring water and sky a pale rosy hue. The Katherine rocked evenly at her anchor beside the Weymouth. But two more ships had entered the harbor on the flood during the night. They stood in deep water, out from the shore, twice the distance of the sloops. They were large ships, frigates, whose bows would slice a swath of sea and cast the white foaming wake far astern as they pushed their massive hulls through the water. Their decks were spotless, their masts, lofty. The sun gleamed on the fresh paint of their bowsprits and glimmering brass guns flashed golden from the open ports of their twin decks. They dwarfed the smaller sloops.

Sally studied them and felt a tightening in the pit of her stomach. They were tall and stately and graceful and rocked evenly at their moorings like large predatory birds on the surface of the bay. They were massive, murderous weapons.

"They are warships, Beulah. That one is the Rose of forty guns." She stared and lifted her arm to point. The other is the Jackal - I do not know how many guns."

"An' Mr. Samuel is out there with them like Daniel among the lions! The owl hoots for a reason, Miss!"

There was a shuffling upstairs and the rapping of Sarah's cane. "Beulah!" Sarah screeched in pain.

Beulah jumped at the summons. Sally ran to bar the doors. Navy men must not know there was no man in the house.

The naval crews came ashore later that morning. They were rough, colorful men impressed from ports worldwide, swarthy Moors, slant-eyed Turks, Italians, Spaniards, English, Scots and Gaels. They hovered near the Weymouth and the Katherine like vultures over carrion. To them these were American ships, prizes of war and sources of wealth to the crew who could claim them, but only if their owner was in rebellion against King George. And they were a source of replacements for the warships' tired crews. The British Navy recruited regularly from merchant vessels at the point of a gun - the rebels called it impressment, a theft of human talent and effort. But the Katherine and the Weymouth had disgorged their cargo and dispersed their crews only yesterday. Casks of rum still littered the beach and the crews had melted into the countryside. The Navy men swarmed drunkenly over the casks and filled the local taverns. No merchant sailor dared show his face.

Sally, her mother and sister and the slave children remained locked indoors. Only Beulah went out to bring lunch to Cob in the stable.

At noon a horse clattered into the lane and came to an abrupt halt under the locust tree outside the yard gate. Sweat lathered its shoulders and beaded its flanks. Sally recognized the rider and so did the dogs who licked his hands eagerly. He was awkwardly built, a short, slim man who walked with a peculiar bow-legged gait and was clearly more adapted to riding than walking. His dress was plain, dull homespun except for his boots whose shiny black was coated with a layer of mud. He was one of Robert's hunting friends and a fine horseman - Austin Roe.

Sally had unbarred the door before Austin had a chance to knock. "Austin, how good of you to come. What news of Setauket?"

"Where is Rob, Sally? I come with an urgent dispatch."

Silence. Sarah Townsend thumped into the hallway. "Austin, you'll stay for lunch." It was more command than invitation. Sarah Townsend could sniff a desirable match for her daughters like a bloodhound on a scent. Austin had a handsome Saxon face, was well-bred, educated in England and the only son of a wealthy squire, albeit a shabby dresser and short and unattractive, built like a jockey to perch atop a racing horse, not to walk upon two legs on solid ground.

Austin bowed. "Mrs. Townsend, Madame, I am at your service. Is Rob at home?"

Sally interrupted, "Rob is with father, in the city." It was a lie.

Sarah Townsend broke in. "Your horse is winded. Come with me to the garden, Austin. Audrey will join us. Beulah has pie in the oven!" It was an obvious pretext. Sarah took Austin's arm and directed him toward the garden. "Cob will saddle you a fresh mount." He stumbled along like a trained spaniel but Sally's knowing glance absorbed his attention.

Sarah Townsend was aware of Austin's attention to Sally, but misconstrued his reasons. "Beulah will bring lunch to the garden."

The garden was a small square of land at the west side of the house, walled with stout fencing and carved geometrically with boxwood and privet. Woody lilacs grew at the south end, screening it from the lane.

Sally took Austin's arm and when they were out of earshot, she spoke, "Father has gone aboard the Katherine, Austin. Mother does not know. We cannot fetch him except under the eyes and guns of twin men of war! And Rob has gone to New York!"

"Then you must give him this, Sally. It's from Solomon." He thrust a small packet into Sally's hands. Solomon Townsend, Sally's eldest brother, had captained the 300-ton Glasgow, and was moored in Portsmouth, England, when last they had news. "Solomon has left his ship.... He is in France." and he added as if Sally knew the significance, "and has thrown in his lot with Franklin!"

So Solomon was a rebel. Sally thought of families that had divided, the Lloyds, the Franklins: the father, Benjamin, in France, negotiating on behalf of the Continental Congress; the son, William, appointed His Majesty's loyal Governor of New Jersey. Such was her own family; Samuel and Solomon, her father and oldest brother, firmly on the side of rebellion; William and David, younger brothers, enrolled in Loyalist brigades. Her mother's leanings were also strongly Tory as were her sister, Audrey's. As for herself, her loyalties were more personal than political. And Robert? What to make of Robert, the brother dearest to her heart? Robert concealed his deepest feelings.

"Austin, you must deliver the dispatch yourself." She held it out to him. "I cannot leave - the harbor is awash with seamen." She sat demurely on an oak bench under a heavy arch of lilac, more to please the scrutiny of her mother than her own inclination.

Austin did not argue. He shoved the billet deep into the pockets of his coat and remained standing. "Sally, tell your father that Solomon is safe in Paris." He shifted his weight self-consciously as if he, too, felt the eyes of Sarah Townsend drilling into his back.

Beulah arrived with cold meat, cheese, apples and a bottle of wine. Sally turned to Austin. "When you see him, tell Rob please to come home."

"Sally, you know Rob will not listen to me if he has pressing affairs in New York...." His voice faded as if he could not phrase the remainder of his thoughts. He clamped his teeth shut and muttered, "You are a resourceful woman, Sally. I've admired you for it. You will do what you must. For help, you can look to Captain Youngs. He is an honest and able man." He blushed, seized an apple and a wedge of cheese, rose and bowed to Sarah Townsend. "My regards to Audrey. And thank you for lunch, Mrs. Townsend." The pie remained in the oven.

He hurried out by the garden gate, leaping nimbly astride the tired horse that Cob held waiting and spurring it to a gallop down the lane toward Poverty Hollow. The animal had rested only briefly and Austin whipped it cruelly. At other times, he always carefully considered an animal's stamina and strength.

Sarah Townsend was ready with reproach for Sally's curt dismissal of the eligible young man, but her daughter's defiant eye and lift of jaw silenced her. Sally walked proudly back along the pebbled path to the house, past the glaring stare of her mother, who stood leaning her stout form on the brittle cane, frowning a deep, angry purple.

4

Sore sighed the mother, for her babes afraid;
And anxious for herself the blooming maid.

*A*udrey was sitting by the parlor window stitching, when Sally Townsend stalked into the house. Audrey, five years older than Sally and innocent of the world, seemed younger, more naive. She was a tall, colorless, angular girl. Brown eyes, not blue, set deeply into their sockets and contrasted with the pallid bony expanse of her face. Wide bones spread her cheeks horizontally and she wore her dark hair pulled severely back, tied tightly in a square knot at the nape of her neck, accentuating her facial width even more. Her brows were delicate, almost non-existent and arched, not over the long, straight Townsend nose but over a pointed, concave piece of cartilage which made her look birdlike. She always complained of the cold and knotted her woolen shawl tightly around her skinny arms, pinning them closely against a flat chest like the wings of a chicken dressed for roasting. She suffered from poorly-functioning lungs and rarely went out except to church. When she coughed, the shawl dropped down about her elbows as she gripped her throat painfully. But she had beautiful hands, slender, graceful fingers, trained to execute complicated stitchery and this was her daily occupation. Her experience of the outside world derived only from apocalyptic sermons and from the occasional visitor to the Townsend home.

News of a visitor excited her now, "Sally! Austin was here and you didn't call me?" She anchored her needle in a pincushion, and looked up with childlike eagerness.

"Austin sends you his regards, Audrey."

"He gave you a package!" Visitors often brought packages for Audrey. Her eyes settled on Sally's hands.

"From Solomon for Rob."

At the mention of Solomon, Audrey jumped up, "Presents from Solomon! He never forgets!"

The words were barely uttered when the dogs started to bark and a rumble of hooves sounded in the lane. There was a clatter of metal, slam of gate, and a yelp of pain as a dog ran for cover. The clomp of heavy boots echoed on the cobbled walk and a loud, insistent fist banged the door.

Sarah hobbled with Beulah to answer the door. She opened the top only of the Dutch door, and stood like a gate-keeper, effectively blocking any unwarranted intrusion.

A muscular red-coated officer stood outside. One hand rested on the hilt of a sword, the other adjusted the crested helmet of a loyalist dragoon.

"Major Edmund Fanning, Madame, Kings American Regiment. I would speak with Mr. Samuel Townsend, the gentleman of the house." His clipped English was courteous in word only. He barely tilted his head to the ladies.

"He is not here. He has gone to the city." The wide bodies of Sarah and Beulah, barred any view Sally and Audrey could glean of the officer.

"Then I would speak with Mr. Robert, Mr. William or Mr. David Townsend." He read from a parchment. His voice gained a sharper edge. He placed a gloved hand on the rim of the lower door.

"Mr. William and Mr. David have left to join His Majesty's forces. Mr. Robert is away. I am in charge." Sarah rapped her cane like a gavel against the hardwood door. "We are not peasants, sir! Would you kindly remove your hand from my door and step back, until you are invited in." It was a command, meant to be obeyed.

Major Fanning did not move one finger of his gloved hand. The rebuke sloughed off his shoulders like the dry skin from an old snake. "Colonel Cunningham orders me to speak with heads of households, Madame, - as a woman you do not qualify - and to inventory all effects of possible rebel sympathizers. You are aware, are you not, that your husband was a member of the New York Provincial Assembly? That your eldest son has fled to France?" He drew back his lips in a false smile exposing yellowed horselike teeth. "You will forgive me if I conduct a search." He did not wait for an answer but lifted his hand to signal two subordinates toward the stable. Uninvited, he reached over to the inside of the lower door, unfastened the latch, pushed it open and marched six soldiers into the hall. He removed his helmet and bowed, in cursory recognition of the ladies present. He directed two men to the parlor, one man to the kitchen and one upstairs to the sleeping quarters.

Sarah Townsend's anger erupted. "You are an outrage to the civility and good name of an Englishman, sir!"

Fanning turned an icy stare in her direction, and uttered with oily disdain, "I am not English, Madame. I was born in Ireland... and I am a loyal subject of good mother, England, as are my men. We do not abet the churlish rabble in Boston or the salacious accusations that leak interminably from Philadelphia... as has your husband and your son. I obey my orders, in the honorable and faithful service of His Esteemed Majesty, King George Third."

The soldiers in the parlor escorted Sally and Audrey into the hallway. Major Fanning bowed obsequiously a second time as if the gesture justified his effrontery and let his eyes feast if only for a moment, on the curving bustline, pinched waist and flaming hair of Sally Townsend. "The Misses Townsend, I presume." He did not wait for an introduction from Sarah Townsend and addressed only Sally, without granting Audrey so much as the blink of an eye. "Edmund Fanning, Major, Kings American Regiment, at your service, Miss."

Sally smiled graciously at Fanning and deliberately anchored his steely grey eyes with a welcoming smile. Audrey smiled too, like an eager barmaid, at his subordinates.

Another officer marched up beside Fanning and kicked the tall clock that stood by the door. The pendulum clanged like a cracked bell against the stiff wooden casing and the clock stopped. He held sheaves of paper, an inkwell and quill.

Fanning ignored his brutish conduct, "May I present Captain Grant, my adjutant." He added with condescension to Mrs. Townsend. "We will need a writing desk, Madame, if you please."

Sarah Townsend did not please. She stared speechless at Fanning and summoned her slave. "Beulah, I shall retire." She exited like a dowager queen, thumping her way to the staircase and oozing offended superiority from every pore.

Sally reacted to the cold leer in Fanning's eye, "Father's desk is in the parlor, Major."

The Major's lips parted in his round pink face. His head turned sideways and his eyes narrowed to slits as he followed the receding back of Sarah Townsend. He flung his next sentence like a well-aimed dart, "I am ever amazed Miss Townsend, how fair blossoms spring from foulest dung."

Sally glared back at Fanning's self-satisfied smirk. She waited, lips sealed in angry silence until Fanning dropped his eyes, then unleashed her reply. "A man who can so easily combine compliment with insult, Major, must have risen precipitously to topgallant from out of the bilge."

She had chosen her words well. His smirk shrank and his eye narrowed but he was an army man and did not know the language of the sea and she said it so sweetly that he smiled back. But he paused before admitting, "Miss Townsend, you are very...perceptive."

She motioned him pompously to her father's desk.

Major Fanning tilted his crested head like a cock to his houseful of hens, sat himself at Samuel Townsend's desk like a lord counting tithes, and proceeded to spend the afternoon with his men inspecting every cupboard, closet, drawer and dusty corner of the house. Even the beams overhead did not go untouched.

Fanning could not help but notice the wall over the parlor hearth. He addressed his question to Sally. "A sword, Miss Townsend, it appears from the outline on the wall that a sword has hanged here. I have been instructed to list, in particular," and he drew his thin lips back over his teeth, "all weapons." He enunciated the last consonant so harshly that his saliva spat into the still air between them.

Sally wiped the front of her dress with an end of her shawl, "The sword was my grandfather's. My brother, David, took it when he enlisted in Colonel DeLancey's Brigade." She issued a very accommodating smile with a very agreeable nod that let her red hair fall gracefully onto the creamy skin of her neck.

The Major gloated. "Colonel Cunningham, my superior, will be most disappointed."

For the rest of the afternoon, Sally sat stiffly by Audrey and watched the rape of Raynham Hall. The soldiers turned out the contents of every container from the kettle of stew that Beulah had boiling on the kitchen hearth which they threw into the yard, to the pie in the pan in the oven, which they ate. They even pulled apart the bread dough set to rise under a cloth in the sun on the back doorstep.

When they left, mayhem was everywhere. Fright clouded the brown eyes of Audrey but the white eyes of the slave glowed with angry fire and Sarah's voice thundered offended pride. "Major, he calls himself! He has the manners of a galley slave and the language of a whaler!"

Only Sally was unmoved and rallied the others. "Beulah, see what has happened to Cob in the barn. Audrey and I will restore order here."

Beulah returned with Cob muttering incomprehensibly and shaking his head. He usually avoided the ill-temper of Mrs. Townsend but today he feared her less that Fanning's soldiers. "Mrs. Townsend, they've taken Horace to pull a foraging wagon!" Horace was the old plow horse that the women used for driving. Once Cob had begun to talk he could not stop. "The others, the two mares and the bay, I took to the south kettle on the neck." The kettle was a glacial depression, where stock could be hidden away from the lookouts' eyes on the mastheads of ships. "I would have taken Horace too....Horace won't last the winter pulling weight." Cob loved his horses, especially old Horace, who was docile and deaf, just like Cob.

Sally calmed the old slave, "It's none of your doing, Cob." She put her hand on his and he responded to the touch. They set about putting the house to right and worked long into the night.

It was Audrey who voiced what Sally was thinking, "Those were Loyalist soldiers, not Hessians. Fanning is Irish and Cunningham is an English name! I wish Rob would come home." Audrey's eyes blinked in pain and doubt like a child slapped for some petty offense that he did not commit. She coughed from the excitement and began to wheeze.

Sarah offered little consolation. "They were Americans, Audrey, but the basest sort, greedy, untutored, uncivilized Americans!...They would pillage the property of good Tories in the name of the King if it meant money in their filthy pockets. Proper British regulars will put them right!"

5

Hopeless yourselves, yet hope you must impart,
And comfort others with an aching heart.

Proper British regulars never arrived. The Townsends were not the only family to have lost livestock to Major Fanning and the King's American Regiment. The Youngs' grey pony had disappeared; the village blacksmith, George Weeke's sorrel horse was taken from the hitching post in front of his house; six of Powell's cows and the Conklin's entire herd of sheep had disappeared from the meadow. Conklin's slave, Primus, had gone with the soldiers who had offered him his freedom in exchange for enlisting. A barge was missing, assumed taken at flood tide from the side of Young's sloop, Prosper. This the Townsend women learned from Mother Youngs who had it from Hannah Blackwell whose slave, Jesse, had heard it from the kitchen girl at Tredwell's Tavern.

More news arrived with Captain Markham of the Weymouth who came ashore at two bells of the morning watch. Beulah admitted him and fed him breakfast. He ate ravenously. He sat wide-eyed, talking incessantly and stuffing chunks of bread and cheese into his mouth. The women, still in their nightrobes, hung on his every word.

Markham was a commanding presence aboard ship. On land he was gangling and self-effacing. Now he bowed his balding head over his bowl, slurped noisily and looked about as if there were listeners at every keyhole and what he had to say was heresy or treason.

"He would not go, Mum. We should've sailed for Connecticut last night on the flood - Mr. Sackville had come with a skeleton crew to hoist the sails and the Connecticut shore was within an easy reach on the southerly puffs.... but he would have none of it. Says he cannot leave his girls alone with no man to look after them, cannot forfeit his property, like Mr. Lloyd and Mr. Conklin.... Mr. Joseph, him of the Lloyds, left two days ago and is safely ashore on the other side." He hesitated then, looked up at Sarah who frowned down like the lord in Judgment. He clamped shut his jaws in an effort to stop his tongue, but the torrent of words continued unabated, "He would forfeit his freedom and maybe his life! Aye Mum, it's a blessing we did not sail, for Captain Layton of Youngs' Prosper tried and they boarded her, forty swift marines from H.M.S. Panther with blackened faces, pikes and cutlasses - like devils from the bowels of hell!... And they pressed her crew to serve their navy and stole her spars and rigging and struck down her masts. They need wood and lines and able seamen. And molasses and rum! How the bloody British love their rum!" He stopped to sop the last glob of porridge from his plate. "Shipped it off, the rum they did, in Prosper's barge for their messes - drank most of it first. 'Tis a wonder they could steer the barge." He pointed a bony finger at the harbor. "The Prosper lies to there....She is no more than an empty hull."

When the women stared in disbelief, his voice rose in affirmation. His syllables flowed in cadences then crashed down like breakers on a rocky shore. "Their Navy is the greatest in the world!... Never have I seen so many ships in our waters, sloops, cutters, fire ships, frigates of 44 guns, 49 ships of the line of 74 guns apiece, triple-decks and more guns on the quarterdeck and forecastle! They are monster men-of-war!" He went rigid suddenly. "Do you know, Mum, what the broadside of a 74 could do?" He answered his own question with lips quavering and pale staring eyes. "Sink my poor Weymouth in the wink of an eye as surely as the tides rise and fall twice daily."

It was Sally who summoned the courage to interrupt. "But you do not have to fight, Markham. You command a merchantman."

Sarah Townsend objected too. "Markham, surely you exaggerate. These are not proper tales for young ladies."

But Markham's fears billowed like smoke from a wetted fire. "'Tis true, Mum, the H.M.S. Revenge, Captain Marbury, took a French merchantman off

Hispaniola only last month. Do you know what they did to her? Shredded her canvas with grape, canister, chain; killed half her crew and shipped the rest in neck irons to Bermuda. All but five died of the yellow jack!"

"Markham, stop!" A flush of anger colored Sally's cheeks. "What has become of father?"

Markham blinked, pulled a handkerchief from out of his sleeve and wiped the saliva from his mouth. "He is in the orchard, Miss. He did not want to bring you harm in case you were searched."

Sarah Townsend answered in crisp staccato syllables, "Thank you for your consideration, but we have already been searched. Please see to your ship."

Markham bowed feebly and exited by the back door like a hunted fugitive scared of the sound of his own boots on gravel.

Sally reached her father first, ahead of Audrey, far ahead of Sarah who thumped painfully out to the orchard leaning on Beulah's strong arm.

Samuel Townsend, with Sally on the right and Audrey on the left was already walking toward his home. He smiled calmly like a man who had settled his conscience and his soul. "Come Sarah, back to the house! This damp ground will ail your hip. We must have a meet, decide what is to be done when they take me." He grinned more widely as if what he said was in jest. "And we must send for Rob." He replaced Beulah at Sarah's side. "They will arrest me, but the Lord will protect his own."

When they entered the house, Samuel sat first at his desk and penned his legacy and a writ of freedom for his slaves. He moved to the table and took his seat at the head. His family sat in rows on each side. Beulah set out fresh bread, cheese, apples and smoked ham with brown sugar and vinegar. They bowed their heads in thanksgiving. Samuel Townsend recited the prayer, ending with Matthew 5:10. "Blessed are they which are persecuted for righteousness' sake: for theirs is the kingdom of heaven." He looked wistfully from one member of the household to another, naming each in succession and finished with the deaf slave, Cob. "War brings with it persecution and injustice....God has blessed us." After dinner, he scratched a message for Rob.

"And now Sarah and my girls, it is time. Sally, obey your mother, make a list of all our friends and acquaintances of loyalist persuasion - the Murrays, the DeLanceys, the Buchanans. Sarah, I ask you to shed your pride, get down upon your knees and beg them to do whatever is in their power on my behalf. Audrey, sustain your mother. Give a hand in the house. Beulah, Cob, work hard, without complaint, bear with us now and your children, Josie and Melly, shall be free." He breathed in deeply and exhaled. Total silence engulfed his listeners. His voice fell to a whisper. "And now I shall give myself up to the proper authorities."

Sarah blanched. Audrey gasped. Only Sally arched her proud neck in a gesture of obvious agreement. Samuel continued, "We shall trust to the mercy of God in heaven, and Georgius Rex and his army. We are British citizens. They are not ghouls." He pushed his arms wide and his shoulders up, a gesture that seemed to double his size. As he spoke, his grey eyes settled for a moment on each person present. "The British require every man who would retain his property to swear allegiance to the king. I shall explain that I belong to the Society of Friends, that Friends do not sully the sacred name of the Almighty by speaking that holy name in oath, that my witness shall be as the Bible dictates. There is no need to swear oaths. My word is my bond." He stopped as if realizing the full impact of what he was about to do, like an animal about to pounce, quivering, mustering all its strength before descending to the kill. "Nor do Quakers take up arms. We want only peace and order."

"Will they believe you father?" Sally's brows drew together fearfully.

The slave, Beulah, was more direct, "They'll whip you, Mr. Samuel! They'll take the cat to your shoulders to spite your courage, Mr. Samuel!"

"The cat o'nine tails tears skin, not spirit, Beulah."

"It'll lift your skin in strips from one rib at a time!" The outspoken slave bore the scars of whipping by former masters. Whipping had not silenced her.

Sally squared her shoulders. Her knuckles were white where she gripped the rough edge of the table. "I will go with you father."

"No! You will stay home." He raised his voice emphatically. "You are strong. Audrey and your mother cannot subsist alone." He patted her hand. Secretly, he loved and trusted Sally most. She understood the unwavering conviction, the abhorrence of violence, the reverence for learning and the unshakable honesty that was her father's creed. Samuel Townsend was no coward like

Markham. He was not afraid to suffer. He stood tall and spare as the hardwood trees of the forests. His beliefs ran deep as their roots which sucked at the bedrock of the island. Would the British commanders, would Hessians or loyalist Americans or Colonel Fanning understand that Samuel Townsend would honor his promise like a sacred covenant, unto death?

Samuel was smiling. "And now eat, my children, this good food which God has provided and for which we will be forever thankful and which Beulah has so faithfully prepared...." He placed a palm gently over Sarah's, leaned and whispered in her ear, but everyone at table overheard, "God will put it right, my love. I do only what I must. I do not mean to give you another trial." Sarah Townsend straightened at this display of affection, pursed her lips and rose from the table before embarrassing tears shook her frame. Her cane clattered to the floor. Beulah caught her before she fell and took her to bed.

Later that morning, the women and slaves, lined the hallway to bid Samuel Townsend farewell. He donned his finest black coat, yellow suede britches and silver buckled shoes. The family stood as one, in a solemn rank, to bid him farewell. He bowed proudly, shook each hand earnestly and walked out into the lane, where the soldiers had passed earlier on their way to Cedar Swamp. He carried some ship's biscuit, two apples, a bottle of cider and a blanket. He turned left toward Richbell's store where Major Fanning had his headquarters.

Major Edmund Fanning seized him according to his written orders. Samuel Townsend went quietly and George Townsend, John Kirk and Jonah Coe went with him, four prisoners in the open back of a spring wagon, across the dusty Hempstead Plain to the Jamaica Presbyterian Church. This was the collection place for all prisoners from eastern Queen's County. Tomorrow or the next day or the day after, they would each be brought before a magistrate, newly appointed by the British occupation force, who would decide which prisoners should go free, which should go to the holding pens at the Sugar Warehouse and Bridwell Prison in New York City, and which should go to the death-ridden hulks.

6

He stands - he mocks, unconscious of a shame,
The voice of Clamour and the lies of Fame.

*R*obert reproached himself for not having stayed in Oyster Bay. In the city, he helped Stewart, his caretaker, wet down the warehouse to deter fire. So far they had preserved 41 Peck's Slip from the bands of thugs who burned and looted any property that might fall into British hands. In the end, rain ended the threat of fire and Robert distributed bribes to insure the safety of his property. Stewart, a tight-fisted Scotsman, could be trusted with inventories and accounts.

It was Austin Roe with Captain Farley of the sloop, Katherine, who brought Robert news of Samuel's arrest and delivered the letter from his brother, Solomon. Robert left immediately, boarded Farley's sloop for Oyster Bay, but the easterly blew hard and prevented the ship's departure. Finally he departed on horseback with Austin Roe for the ferry to Brooklyn and British-held territory.

Sentries questioned them at the Brooklyn dock and let them pass. Robert remembered the road, how it snaked down from the heights to the fertile wheat fields below. Now, the road was rutted, the fields trampled and brown. The dead were buried, the battlefield cleared, but devastation lay all around. Broken fences, tree stumps, the charred skeletons of dwellings, littered the landscape. He remembered farmer Croswell and his wife and a hollowness filled his soul.

They rode across the plain. Robert's head fell forward on his chest as his tired horse plodded obediently behind his friend's. Only then did Robert pull

Solomon's letter from his pocket. It was a single yellow page. He read with effort in the sunlight. Solomon had written the message in French. Robert blinked at the combination of syllables and struggled to remember what French he knew.

Solomon believed that France would send weapons and ships to aid the rebellion. He told of a wonderful ally he had recruited, a playwright, Count Beaumarchais, and others in high places, who could sway the sympathies of Louis XVI and his court. He encouraged Robert to work for the rebellion. The English, he asserted, were harsh masters.

Robert laughed at his brother's innocence, "Beaumarchais, a playwright?... To intercede with King Louis XVI? Preposterous!" But France was a hotbed of libertarian thought. The French adopted all sorts of bizarre philosophies and champions. Rousseau. Diderot. Solomon said they had invited Benjamin Franklin, that bumbling old tinker from Philadelphia, into their salons and to court! And Solomon was confident that France would enter the war on the side of the Americans.

Solomon signed the letter, "*Votre bon ami et frere libre!*" Robert handed the letter to Austin Roe who rode beside him. Austin lifted an eyebrow wistfully, "Solomon," he asserted, "is a dreamer."

They arrived in Oyster Bay the next afternoon. The house was funereal in its silence. They had been on the road for hours. It was a hot day. Sweat dripped from beneath their hats. Robert ran his hand over his brow, onto his neck and around the rim of his collar. They passed wearily through the shuttered town to the barn beside the Townsend home. Austin Roe changed mounts and rode on to his home in Setauket. Robert approached the house.

Dust had invaded every crease of his linen coat. His white collar was grey; his pupils showed red from lack of sleep and grime lined the crevices of cheeks and the sockets of his eyes. Only his dogs came out to welcome him and licked the sweat from his hands. By the kitchen door, bushels of apples sat in wide baskets, like sleepy sentinels, on either side of the door. He picked up an apple and polished it on his dirty sleeve. Through the doorway he could see the bare brown backs of the two slave children. They were shucking clams on an old piece of sail canvas and tossing the empty shells into a wooden bucket. Sally stood at the end of the table, bare-armed, an apron covering the front of her

workdress, scraping the scales from a large striped bass. Beulah was peeling potatoes to add to the stew. The kitchen smelled strongly of fish and the two house
cats meowed in chorus for a share of the entrails. There was no human sound, as
if any meaningful note would disturb the fragile peace. But the click of clam
shells one on the other, the buzz of black flies and the mewing of the waiting
cats created a cacophonous symphony.

Sally was first to look up. When she saw Rob, her knife slipped and cut
her finger. "Rob, I'm glad you came." Her hand went to her mouth to suck the
offending blood.

Rob said nothing, but sensed her relief. He offered her his handkerchief.
His eyes locked on hers.

She reached out to take the apple that he held. She spoke from duty, not
from any prompting of her heart. "Rob, I'll polish that for you." Beulah reached
for Robert's coat. Their actions were shallow, barely skimming prescribed courtesies. Sharper feelings ran turbulently and much more deeply, below the surface.

Robert Townsend bowed his head. "I heard. Austin brought the news...
I should have been here to stop them." He could find no other words to lift the
heavy pall that had fallen over the house. He placed a dry kiss on Sally's cheek,
tousled Josie's stiff hair and reverted to the immediate present. "Wrap your finger tightly, to stop the bleeding." She nodded. They were all bleeding in ways
that it was impossible to staunch. "Where's mother... and Audrey?" His question filled the awful void.

The slave children resumed the shucking and the click of the shells resounded. He sensed the need for his presence.

Sally answered haltingly. "Mother has taken to bed. Audrey had an attack last evening.... She is mending stockings by the fire in the parlor." He smiled
at that - Audrey loved warmth like the kitchen cats loved the smell of fish. They
were mewing again outside the door. Sally dipped the apple in a clean bucket of
water and handed it back to him with a brave smile. "Rob, how long will you
stay?"

Robert's breathed in the damp air of the kitchen. His words fell from
his lips like stones into a well. "I'll not go back to the city until they release

father." His voice was thin; his blue eyes, bloodshot. His whole body sagged with fatigue. "I've had a letter from Solomon, from Paris."

"Austin told me."

"Solomon says there are many Whigs in England that sympathize with the rebellion."

Sally answered derisively. "Solomon has lived too long at sea. The salt air has addled his brain."

"Read for yourself." Robert handed her the letter.

Sally glanced at the letter and handed it back. "He waited six months for the British convoy to assemble in Jamaica, before he could sail."

"Six months, with the Glasgow manned, loaded and collecting barnacles and every sort of tropical parasite on her bottom! Six month's money lost. Six months is time enough for two crossings. At when he arrived in England, he had to overhaul the ship at exorbitant rates."

"He says he is afraid of American privateers."

"Sally, Solomon wants to turn a profit. The delays, the overhauling, will cost him more than any American privateer. What is frustrating him is inertia and greed..."

"Are you saying he is going to rebel?"

"It is to his advantage, he already did. He has gone to France."

Sally studied her brother. "I thought he was more principled....And what will you do, Robert Townsend?" Robert usually followed the lead of his older brother.

He shrugged casually and changed the subject. "I called on the DeLanceys and Jack Rivington, John Aspinwall and Thomas Buchanan." Buchanan was an ardent royalist and owned the Glasgow that Solomon captained. He was married to Almy Townsend, their first cousin. "They will do what they can to intercede for father. I sent word to David and William. They will approach Colonel Ferguson. You do remember Patrick Ferguson, the one who invented the gun?...But Thomas Barney has denounced father."

Beulah and the children stopped what they were doing. Denouncement could mean disaster. For the slaves, loss of their master, a prison sentence, could bring sale, separation, a new and cruel master. Samuel Townsend had been a good master and had promised them their freedom but the mistress, Sarah, was another matter. She had little sympathy for pain, physical or emotional. She would sell a slave in the wink of an eye. Silence again, like a shroud. A bird twittered in the thick, heart-shaped leaves of the lilac bushes.

Robert hunched his shoulders. "William and I should have been more attentive to Miss Hannah and Miss Esther." Hannah and Esther were the two daughters of Thomas Barney, both thirtyish, stout and tedious old maids, given to giggling and pointing fingers at less well-dressed and well-appointed individuals than themselves. Robert and William had always chosen other less socially prominent but more friendly partners at balls, to the intense indignation of Mrs. Thomas Barney. Her husband, Thomas Barney, was a large landowner on Hog Island, the spit of land that formed the northern shore of Oyster Bay Harbor, and separated the bay from Long Island Sound. Thomas Barney and John Hulet were village magistrates and dedicated Tories who had no love for Samuel Townsend, even less for Robert and Sally, his irreverent children.

Sally's voice fluttered. "They are disagreeable ladies. No one blames you, Rob."

Beulah spoke next, "There's stew in the kettle, Mr. Robert, and pie in the oven and good fresh cider." Apple pie with molasses, brown sugar and nutmeg was the favorite dish of Robert's from the time he was a small boy.

"Thank you Beulah but I'm not thirsty or hungry." His mouth was dry but he refused the refreshment as if by depriving himself, he could make up for his absence. But they all knew what vindictive testimony Thomas Barney would bear against Samuel Townsend. Robert's presence and Beulah's cooking, the endless repetition of kitchen chores, could not dispel their despondency.

One year ago, Samuel Townsend, George Weekes and John Kirk had called a meeting of the freeholders of Oyster Bay to support their Boston brethren and correspond with the Philadelphia Congress. Thomas Barney had objected violently. He had raided the meeting and threatened its participants. And now Major Fanning had appointed Barney the new Magistrate of Queen's County. The appointment boded ill.

And there was another instance last January when Samuel Townsend had stood in Quaker Meeting and read aloud from Paine's pamphlet. The words were as true in England as in the colonies, a simple affirmation of every Quaker's belief in the equal value of every human soul. But they flew in the face of the hierarchy of British aristocracy where a peer was always promoted before a commoner, and title and privilege bore honor and merit. In the colonies the system had degenerated further so that ambitious men scrambled, like mosquitoes to the smell of blood, for political and economic favor. Such was Thomas Barney.

Barney was jealous of Samuel Townsend. Samuel's uncle, for whom the Townsend Acts were named, was a peer of the realm, and his cousin, a member of Parliament. Barney had no such lofty connections and sniffed at the very scent of a title. The loss of the Battle of Long Island and the advent of the British occupying forces facilitated the full venting of Thomas Barney's envy. He voiced it from the judge's bench and the pulpit of the Anglican Church.

They sat down to dinner. Beulah served a steaming stew. Sally pursued conversation. "Was it a difficult journey?"

Robert ripped off a slice of bread and dipped it in the gravy. He talked while he ate. "It was a hungry one. We rode past sentries at Brooklyn and Jericho.... Beulah, is there any beer?"

Beulah shook her head. "Only your father's madeira."

Sally's thoughts reverted to Barney. "The British will discount the comments of a pompous little man as Barney?"

"The British command is as open to presents as the next man, Sal." Robert smiled wanly. "Like the brigands who roam New York....They left our warehouse alone, not out of any respect for father or for any thought of our welfare or that of the city. I paid them...in gold.... This war may impoverish us all." His shoulders sank. His lively blue eyes clouded and he added softly, "I have enlisted Tom Buchanan's help for father. He has Cunningham's ear."

"Who is Cunningham?" None of the women remembered the name.

Beulah poured a glass of madeira and Robert took a long swallow. He wiped his mouth with the back of his hand. "Colonel William Cunningham, Keeper of the King's Provost and organizer of the foraging efforts on this island. Fanning is under his command. Colonel Cunningham controls the assignment of prisoners and the provisioning of prisons." Robert's dark brows came together ominously..."And the execution of punishments."

"You mean father is to be imprisoned?"

"Unless Tom Buchanan can stop it." Robert bowed his head and sucked the flesh of his cheeks between his teeth. The action gave him a peculiar skeletal look that had the effect of narrowing his expansive face and drawing down the edges of his eyes. It made him look older. He sopped the last of his stew with more bread.

"Does mother know?"

"She would only reproach me for bringing bad news."

"Father will need food and a change of clothing."

"And soap and clean water and a candle to light."

"How is this Cunningham in league with Barney?"

Audrey exclaimed, "Rob, you look sick!"

"Sick like the news I bring, Audrey." He returned his worried gaze to Sally. "Cunningham and Barney and Fanning and George Hangar, the brutish Hessian, they are all in league to plunder what wealth we have. I have been told that Cunningham can be bribed." When no one reacted, he repeated, "Cunningham and also Loring, especially Joshua Loring, the British Commissary General." He repeated the name with lips that moved mechanically as if his horrible words were somehow disconnected from his thoughts, "Loring, you know him, Sally and Audrey, Elizabeth Lloyd's husband, lately from Boston. You met him and his wife three summers ago at the Manor at Queens Village, when we visited the Joseph Lloyds...Mrs. Loring is Theo Lloyd's first cousin. Loring took a whip to one of Mr. Lloyd's stable boys for eating a carrot that was meant for his horse. Mr. Lloyd protested all too politely..."

Audrey looked puzzled. Sally shook her head. "Theo's cousin? I don't remember."

"Elizabeth Lloyd, Mrs. Loring, is the daughter of old Mr. Lloyd's brother, Nathaniel, who drowned crossing the Sound...." Still Audrey looked confused. He explained further. "Mrs. Elizabeth Loring, batty blue eyes, blond, attractive in an churlish sort of way. Interrupts a conversation and bats her brown eyes around like a spaniel on a leash, at every man present."

Audrey brightened suddenly, "Panting voice, so many rings on her fingers she can't hold her fork and bosoms that overflow her bodice like pudding in a pan!"

"You have a gift for description, Audrey!"

Sally was laughing heartily. "When she danced her pearls bounced off her chest like billiard balls." They laughed harder.

Robert was not smiling. "News from Halifax has it she is General William Howe's mistress."

Audrey reacted eagerly, "Oh Rob, how delicious! And I hear the general is a round sort of man! Two fat ponies make a fine matched pair!" Audrey could not stop giggling.

Robert's somber stare cut her short. "You won't laugh so heartily when father rots in prison!"

Audrey stared in disbelief. The truth seeped through like black oil rising to the surface of a clear pond. Sally looked up in alarm.

Robert continued, "Cunningham will make all requisitions for the prisoners from Loring...blankets, clothing, food and fuel." He stopped to let the revelation penetrate. "That is why Loring was appointed, as a reward."

Audrey's innocent face clouded. "What are you saying Rob?"

"My sisters,...Cunningham and Loring will not feed and clothe the prisoners. They will accumulate blankets and precious fuel and food. They will sell the same blankets, fuel and food to whomever will pay the highest price, while the Army command looks the other way. In the end, they will enrich themselves."

Sally voiced the awful truth. "Cunningham and Loring will let their prisoners starve...and Joshua Loring shall grow fat in payment for his wife's loyal services in General Howe's bedchamber!"

Audrey gasped. "But they are Englishmen, Rob!"

"It does not follow that they are virtuous....Greed is the failing of too many men, Audrey."

Silence. Audrey's mind pushed to another conclusion. "The General is a shameless lecher!" Audrey was slow but perceptive. "And our father is to be held hostage to the whims of a harlot and a panderer!" She sucked for breath and started to wheeze. Robert passed her his handkerchief and a glass of madeira.

Audrey took a long drink of wine and calmed. Sally enunciated what they were all pondering. "Cunningham and Loring are worse than Fanning and

Hangar. Why does General Howe permit this?"

Robert spoke with derision, "You forget, General Howe was a Whig when he was in Parliament and favored independence for the colonies. Howe doesn't really wage a war. Britain's mighty army should wash over the colonies like the Red Sea over Rameses with as little effort as possible, no fighting, no bloodshed, one final annihilation of the Continental Army. General Howe believes that we Americans, loyalist and rebel, are all cowards who shoot from behind trees and refuse to fight as a battle should be fought...that we will scatter like sheep at the sight of a red coat and that he has only to make himself as noticeable as possible until he can declare total victory and return to England a rich man, to be knighted."

Audrey's wheezing diminished and there was silence. She roused suddenly, "The Continental Army is not a regular army, Rob. It comes and goes."

"Ice melts and water turns to steam on a hot day, Audrey, but it is still there to freeze or flood when the weather changes." A cat rubbed against Robert's leg, purring steadily. Robert picked it up and stroked the smooth silken fur. "We are the mice. Howe is the haughty, pampered cat who lazes on his cushion by the fire."

Sally Townsend struggled with all the dreadful implications of Robert's news, "General Howe has very poor regard for colonials."

"He has no regard. Howe and King George and Parliament and all of England have no regard, Sally, for anyone on this side of the ocean. We are lesser mortals, some cowardly species of human who cannot fight his own battles. They hire Hangar and his Hessians because they do not trust us." There was an acid bitterness in his voice. "King George has more faith in his Hanoverian cousins than in his loyal colonial subjects! The occupying troops will have little patience with any of us, and the Hessians will be especially heartless."

Beulah cringed at these words and Robert motioned to the children, "Better to keep them within the fenced yard."

Sally understood. "What else, Rob, what can we do for father?"

Robert squared his shoulders and pushed out his chair. "Money! Cunningham will have to be paid handsomely. I sent word to Uncle Peter up the Hudson... The Perseus, that Captain Stephenson commands, has just docked at Murray's wharf. Colonel Cunningham's brother and Richard Wardrop have opened an auction house. Maybe you've heard of it, Cunningham and Wardrop?" They looked back at him blankly. "Buchanan has approached Wardrop. I will offer Wardrop the proceeds of the Perseus' inventory to be sold at auction in exchange for father's release, if that is agreeable to you both and mother."

"Of course, Rob."

Robert stood to his full height and raised his voice like a preacher in a pulpit. "So be it!" He gazed at each sister in turn. "Now speak of General Howe with respect, and of Loring and his wife with discretion, no matter what you may think in private. No more references to bosoms and bellies. The English pay enormous heed to appearance and title. Howe is Commander-in-Chief of his Majesty's Forces in North America, a very important man."

"He is a womanizer, Rob, for all his grand worth." Audrey could not resist the last snipe.

Robert's anger surfaced suddenly. "Woman! Confine your remarks to within the walls of this house!" The interview was at an end.

Sarah appeared in the doorway and proceeded to her chair. "There is no need to shout, Robert." She flounced her skirts and leaned forward, two hands on her cane. Robert stood by the hearth, one hand on the mantel and one reaching to trace the vague silhouette of his grandfather's sword. He pivoted to face his mother's frown and read aloud the violent news from Jack Rivington's Gazette: John Clarke, shot and killed near Sterling Iron Works; Mrs. Thomas Newman captured by a Spanish Letter of Marque; Murray's stable fired by the Sons of Liberty before they fled across the Harlem River. All but one horse was saved. He did try to explain but bowed politely and left the room.

Sally and Audrey came in quietly and sat near the door. Audrey took up her stitchery.

Sarah picked up the Gazette and began to read the wild, speculative reports. Franklin had ceded Canada and Florida to the French; Congress would give New England to the Pretender and make the Pope Archbishop of North America. She mopped the sweat from her face and set the Gazette aside. The reports were not true but Sarah was nodding agreeably. "They will learn, the rebellious scum, and land themselves in hell for it...."

Robert returned after Sarah had gone to bed. "Will you close the shutters for the night, Sal, and bar the door.... Mother is of a mind...." He folded the gazette and placed it on the wide mantel. "I'll go back tonight, Sally, to summon Buchanan." and he muttered resentfully, "I'll face Buchanan more readily than I face my own mother!"

Sally protested, "It's almost dark, Rob and you've had no sleep."

"At night the sentries sleep. I'll sleep in the saddle. And I'll take the bay. He's stronger than the mare." The bay was Samuel Townsend's best hunting horse and he was a dark, almost black bay. He would blend into the night unseen. Robert leaned over and kissed his sister's cheek.

Sally grabbed his arm with a force that matched all the turmoil in her heart. "God go with you, Rob. Mother did not mean to offend you."

"Ignorance does not offend me, Sally. There are more important battles to fight..." He nodded and walked out into the night.

7

Firm as solid rock, that nobly braves
The raving fury of the lashing waves.

*R*obert Townsend set out on the south road through the Pine Hollow, over the hills to Jericho. This was a tiny settlement of devout Quakers on the north rim of the Hempstead Plains. The Quakers led quiet lives. They adhered strictly to the principles of their founder, George Fox, who had preached in years past from the hillside near the great rock above the mill. Like Samuel Townsend, the Quakers held to their beliefs: they would not take up arms; they would not strike back, if challenged; by their own suffering, they would promote the expansion of Christ's Kingdom on earth. They were a serious, frugal, hard-working people.

The bay horse was eager. Robert galloped over the hill to the Quaker village. A thin moon gleamed down on the darkened village and on milky white triangles of canvas. The pasture was covered with tents, soldiers encamped! Robert felt deep revulsion at these strangers with their instruments of war, laying among the peaceful Friends. It was a sacrilege, like the slap of a duelist or the rape of a virgin! Yellow flames of campfires speckled the blackness. Soldiers had trampled the fertile fields underfoot, slaughtered cattle and were cooking the meat. The smell of the roasting meat made his mouth water. Black forms stooped by the fires eating, drinking, laughing. Their voices rose eerily on the wind. They were singing a guttural, pounding, marching song.

At Underhill's farm, high on a knoll, Robert Townsend stopped his horse. He lifted his glass to his eye and scanned the scene: the square of an officer's tent with a handsome black thoroughbred tied outside; the butchered carcasses of five steers, trains of supply wagons; damaged fencing where soldiers had stolen rails for firewood; a string of cavalry horses. The horses stood on the edge of the camp, tied to heavy ropes, in two long lines munching piles of hay. He counted close to one hundred horses.

When he lowered his glass, his hand was trembling. His horse felt the tension and started forward toward the other animals. Robert reined him back. These were not British regulars, not a redcoat among them. They wore an assortment of clothing. It was a loyalist brigade, formed of recruits from the American side of the Atlantic. Loyalists would question a young man like him. Some were undoubtedly men he knew and they would accost him like the soldiers at Brooklyn Heights the day Long Island fell, but they would press him to fight for the British.

He looked again. A second unit wore white coats. Its members stood out oddly in size and silhouette - Cornishmen or perhaps Scotlanders? Robert lowered his glass, shook his head in puzzlement and looked again. They were shorter in stature, some with pale blond hair and red rosy cheeks and they nodded and gesticulated in an unfamiliar way. They were Hessians, foreigners, mercenaries. Jack Rivington's Gazette had reported their arrival. But Robert had not anticipated finding them here, away from the conflict, so very close to home. It was a large force for such a small village.

He moved slowly away. Darkness fell. He took his cloak from the back of his saddle. It was brown, like the horse, and he draped it over them both and pulled its hood over his head. Once he looked up for the dipper and the star in the northern sky and took his bearings. He turned his horse from the road, preferring the loneliness of the woods. His mouth was dry, his stomach heaved. He rode west, to Jamaica.

Thick saplings massed together, second growth after the huge primal trees had been cut. The grey stalks swallowed his solitary form. As the saplings bent to the firm thrust of the horse, he felt the brush of their branches, the tug of an ivy vine, the snap of a twig on his face and the ghostly swish of air as branches parted, then swept together again in his wake. His hands had stopped trembling when he rested them on the pommel of the saddle, but now he felt cold. The iciness ranged upward from the iron stirrups at his feet to a frigid dampness on the back of his neck. He longed to sleep.

Gradually, the wood gave way to forest and now the trees were more widely spaced - huge trunks, like pillars from some ancient forum, five feet in diameter, maple, oak, locust, tulip that the Indians used for their great dugout canoes. He threaded his way slowly. The horse's hooves thudded just above the threshold of sound, on leaf mold and moist shade-loving plants. Several times he returned to the road where he saw soldiers marching, oxen pulling heavy caissons, wagons stacked with tents and baggage. He turned his horse back into the woods. Toward midnight, he arrived at Manhasset. He rode quietly to the back of the Meeting House, dismounted and knocked. His legs trembled with fatigue. His head ached. The Meeting House was empty, the door locked. He dismounted warily, unbuckled the girth, slipped the bridle over the horse's ears. There was water in the cistern by the carriage shed and straw in the box. He drank, watered the horse and sank down into the soft straw. In moments, he was asleep.

When he awoke, the sun was rising bloody red in the east and casting a scarlet glow against the grey clapboards of the Meeting House. Its rays sliced like a knife across his eyes. He shook the sleep from his eyes and sloshed his mouth with bitter water. He mounted and urged the animal uphill to the Greater Neck and down into the marshes by the Little Neck. There were no soldiers here, only mud and insects and the foul smell of decaying shellfish. The smell made him nauseous because he had not eaten. He was thirsty yet he could not drink. At Alley Pond, he turned southwest across country to Jamaica and he fell asleep to the rhythmic sway of the horse.

The horse jerked to a sudden stop at the edge of the wood where the Jamaica Road snaked past. A coach and four trotted past. Robert recognized the matched bays of Judge Blackwell on his way to court. He would have to call on the Blackwells when he finished at the Presbyterian Church, to offer condolences. The Blackwell's only son had died of the pox.

He hailed the coach but it drove on. He rode after it, sleeping in fitful snatches, trusting to the instincts of the horse. His mind wandered. He imagined the British like some great hovering cloud that blocked the life-giving rays of the sun. The Sons of Liberty weren't much better, thugs who called themselves patriots, who tarred and feathered and burned. They had set fire to Jack Rivington's presses. Rivington was lucky to have escaped alive. But Rivington was young and active and could defend himself.

One thought recurred at the base of his imaginings. It was the treatment of his father and it triggered outrage and loathing. That the British and their Hessian and loyalist allies would take an old man who had surrendered willingly and treat him cruelly, was not tolerable. British efforts were organized, under the direction of army and government officials. They issued directly from England and from arrogant, ignorant and careless politicians. He questioned his own allegiance. As a Quaker? As a man? He rode forward toward Jamaica, tired, hungry, his mind nettled by a thousand prickly troubles. Resentment was piling within him layer upon layer, like silt on a growing delta, diverting the flow of the river, redefining the course of his life. Rebel threats receded and the crimes of Britain stood out in stark silhouette. Thoughts of King George, Parliament, promiscuous General Howe and his rapacious horde of foreigners, bombarded his brain.

A crude boxlike structure stood in the middle of the road and the Blackwell coach had come to a halt. Robert was so engulfed in his thoughts, he had not noticed. His horse came to a stop behind the coach. A soldier emerged, examined some papers, signalled the coach to proceed. Robert Townsend had no papers and urged the bay forward with the coach. He knew no password no sign and countersign? Would they question his right to be on the road at this early hour? Would they steal his mount? Worse would they impress him into their service?

"Halt! You on de horse!" It was loud and guttural and foreign. The coach rolled on. Robert stopped the bay. The soldier motioned him to dismount. He obeyed warily. Another sentry rode up on a bandy-legged cart horse, took one look at Robert's sleek thoroughbred and broke into a gloating smile. He wore the insignia of a sergeant, walked up to Robert Townsend with a bovine grin and lay a hand on the rein. "A fine animal you have to ride sir." Slowly, he ran his hand across the horse's shoulder and down its front leg.

Robert waited stoically and finally questioned, "May I proceed?"

"Proceed? What is that, sir?"

The Hessian was stalling deliberately, Robert knew. "I wish to pass. I go to the courthouse at Jamaica." He started to mount but the Hessian took him by the arm.

"And what may be your work, sir?"

Robert did not immediately answer. He chose not to reveal his mission.

He shrugged off the Hessian's grip. There was a pause. "Shipping, trading the goods my ships transport. I am a merchant."

"The ships bring you many fine horses like this?"

Robert stiffened. He did not like the oily presumption in the man's voice.

When he did not answer, the soldier continued, "Or do you ride your horse to run fast to escape the requisition?...Where are you papers, sir?"

Robert seethed inwardly. He had no papers.

The Hessian placed two thumbs in the rings of the bit, forcing the horse's mouth open, exposing the teeth to check its age. The animal lurched backward. The sergeant turned to the sentry with a flurry of gestures and nods and the sentry snatched at the reins to pull the horse away. Robert yanked the reins from his hand and slapped the horse across the chest. The startled animal reeled back and galloped away down the road. The sentry ran after.

Furious, the sergeant came at Robert with fists flailing. Instantly, Robert's arm went up. He struck out with the other, a solid blow to the jaw. It sent the sentry choking into the dust. Robert Townsend was a strong man, made stronger by the outdoor games of youth, but he had never fought. Now he quivered in every muscle from the shock of physical contact. The sentry stayed down, licking blood from where his tooth had stabbed his lip. Suddenly he leaped to challenge again but stopped at the sharp rebuke of his sergeant. He turned aside angrily and shouted at the sentry. The chasing, shouting, waving, only made the big horse run faster. The sentry came back empty-handed. The sergeant's sour look centered on approaching riders.

At the sound of hooves, Robert turned. Two horses trotted up. Jack Rivington, the publisher of New York's Loyalist Gazette and shopkeeper at Queen and Wall Streets, took off his hat and waved. He was a slim, urbane man in white stock and curled wig, whose long stirrups brushed his fat horse's knees. He was older than Robert. Rivington would have been a successful man, now that the British were in charge but he was too fond of a bottle of port, a good cock fight and horse race. He was an avid Tory because the affiliation promised greater personal gain. He was also a sometime employer and friend of Robert Townsend who contributed occasional items to the Gazette. He shouted now, "Townsend! Rob! Was that your horse? You'll lose a good horse letting him run free!" The narrow lips were smiling and the melodious baritone carried far in the still morning air.

Robert did not hesitate. "Jack Rivington! Free is a horse's natural state, better by far than a Hessian master! What brings you here?"

"The doings of the court make spicy reading! Triumph of British justice and all that! You can write it, Rob, if you choose. The paper will print it."

"Not today, Jack. My father's arrested! He's at the Presbyterian Church awaiting trial." The alarm in Robert's voice sobered his friend.

Rivington dismounted. "No doubt Samuel will be released!... Now tell me why your racer is galloping down the Jamaica road!" When he came closer, he grew serious...."Forgive me, Rob, I must introduce Cornelius VanRandt. Cornelius, this is Robert Townsend, my Quaker friend." VanRandt nodded. A third very large man with the stripes of a loyalist colonel on his sleeve, reined to a halt. "And here's Oliver. You already know Oliver."

"DeLancey! That old mare dump you yet?" Robert's voice lifted.

Oliver DeLancey dressed in cut velvet with silver buttons and could afford a good horse, but he lacked the seat and hands to ride well. He was too fat.

"She did dump me twice, but I landed on my feet!" Oliver DeLancey laughed. There was dust on his coat where he had rolled off this morning. "One day, Townsend, when I'm two stone lighter, svelte and trim, I will buy a Yorkshire racer and beat your American thoroughbred to ground. I may even catch your beautiful sister in my net.... How is Sally, Rob?" He rode up closer and saw the lined brow and balled fists of his friend.

Robert explained dolefully, "Father's arrested. Major Fanning came for him day before yesterday. Sally worries. We all worry!"

Jack Rivington spoke, "Fanning, eh? The toady braggart!... On Cunningham's orders, no doubt. We'll see about that. But first your horse." Rivington reined his horse around and trotted after the bay. He whipped the two soldiers back, slowed his own mount, walked quietly up alongside the bay thoroughbred and took the rein. The bay followed willingly. He winked when he handed the horse back to Robert. "Miserable horsemen, Hessians. Hands like iron and fat little legs like sausages. They don't sit a horse; they perch." He chuckled and cast an admiring glance at the horse. "When will you run her again, Rob? She looks a sure winner!"

Oliver DeLancey's heavy lips grimaced. "So Samuel Townsend's been taken? They can't be serious. Come, we'll ride with you."

Robert led off in a swift pounding trot. Impatience goaded him. DeLancey called him back. "Court opens at ten Rob, slow down! We've two hours to spare, two hours for a hearty breakfast."

Rob closed his eyes and breathed deeply. "I am starved for food, more for sleep but I can't eat, Oliver. Not now."

Rivington shook his head, "Nor could I, were any of my family in the gaol. We'll get your father out....Patience, Rob, and prudence and a bit of feigned humility are necessary to the management of an Englishman."

"Management? You mean payment, don't you Jack?"

"Management, Rob, was my choice of word. Englishmen are vain birds who prize their pecking order, their fluff and feather and squawk. You manage them like cocks in a cage. They have talons that are equally cruel but well-fattened and blind-folded, they are a just and friendly sort."

They rode on, silently at first, Rob, DeLancey and Rivington, three abreast, VanRandt behind.

DeLancey's horse had to jog to keep up. "Surely Blackwell will release him, Rob." His words were breathless as his round rump slapped the saddle.

Robert remained silent and Rivington responded. "Samuel Townsend will not come before Blackwell, Oliver. Blackwell is a civil magistrate. He will more than likely see Harborough or Ferguson, or maybe Cunningham himself or some other member of the military. It is the military courts which deal with treason and rebellion. We should pray it's Harborough." Harborough was Lord

Harborough, newly arrived from England with little notion of colonial affairs and an exalted opinion of his own importance, but otherwise a just man. Ferguson was American but a hot-headed loyalist, excitable and impetuous, and William Cunningham was the friend of Joshua and Mrs. Elizabeth Lloyd Loring, General Howe's newly appointed Keeper of the Provost, a man of careless integrity and active greed.

DeLancey spoke, "Samuel is no traitor and he has never lifted one finger in rebellion against the King, Jack. Regretfully he has signed some unpopular documents."

Unruffled, Rivington nodded and shrugged. "Nothing that guineas can't repair."

Robert who seemed lost in his own thoughts, had followed Rivington's meaning and reacted suddenly. "How many guineas, Jack?"

DeLancey responded, "As many as will buy estates and title and honor in England....I don't know. This is the first time that anyone of my acquaintance has needed a ransom."

"And if I do not have enough guineas?"

"We will vouch for your credit and your Quaker good name." Rivington was used to living on name, not fortune. He had amassed fortunes and lost them to huge gambling debts. He struggled constantly to juggle his exorbitant finances. His sly blue eyes were not encouraging.

They dismounted at the Sign of the Hart, a tavern next to the courthouse. DeLancey insisted Robert join them for breakfast. They ordered coffee, eggs, fresh steamed snapper and ale and conversed amiably and paid the bill in gold. Robert forced his throat to swallow and sat in gloomy silence.

The British held court in the Anglican church, a white clapboard building, surrounded by grey slabs of gravestones, on a dusty little knoll above the tavern, overlooking the flatlands. Robert thought cynically how these British positioned themselves in the place of God. The doors were locked. At ten precisely, the sextant unlocked the doors.

The took their seats in the front pew. The clerk announced the agenda and the judge entered. Rivington elbowed Rob, "It's Harborough, luck is with us!"

Rob saw little that was lucky in the stubby little man who entered in the square collar, curled powdered wig and drab black robes of a magistrate. His wig was askew, his collar grimy and the flour which whitened his wig had spilled over the shoulders of his gown. Yesterday's yellow soup or some more potent liquid stained his white judge's bib. He wheezed when he climbed the stair to his bench. But Jack Rivington's bony face had broken into a broad grin.

Samuel stumbled into the courtroom handcuffed and pale. His stockings showed the black marks of leg irons and huge dark circles enveloped his eyes. His wig had disappeared. His hair was whiter than Harborough's powdered wig and enveloped his head like a wispy halo. The skin on his face hung in translucent wrinkles over the bones of his face like wet sails on a broken mast. He had been imprisoned for three days. He sat on a hard wood chair set out for the accused, with head bowed, legs drawn up tightly under him. He smiled when he saw Rob and nodded calmly to DeLancey and Rivington.

The clerk read the charges. Robert stood up brazenly and Rivington pulled him down by his coattails. "The rules of order Rob! The British look gravely on those who interrupt. You must heed their rituals, like the Papists heed their liturgy!"

Lord Harborough scratched under his wig, wiped his hands on his bib and addressed the clerk. "You have a proclamation, have you not, from the Commander-in-Chief of His Majesty's forces?"

The clerk bowed and Harborough nodded.

The clerk cleared his throat and unfurled a long scroll with the flourish of a medieval herald. He read the whole in a high-pitched screech, without stopping to breathe, "By order of Sir William Howe, Commanding General of His Majesty's forces etc. etc., this twelfth day of September, in the year seventeen hundred seventy-six, I do hereby pardon all inhabitants of Long Island, previously deemed in rebellion, who shall submit to and obey the rule of His Majesty, George III, Sovereign of Great Britain and of his North American colonies, and of his representatives in North America, and who will swear allegiance thereto. God save the King."

The shrieking stopped. DeLancey wiggled his pinky in his left ear. Harborough directed the clerk to post the bill outside and to distribute handbills to all who requested them. Rivington grabbed one of the first. He would publish it in Saturday's Gazette.

Harborough shuffled some documents and spoke offhandedly to Samuel. "Townsend, a lordly name that one. I went to school with Charlie Townsend, Sir Charles, Champagne Charlie, we called him. Are you related by any chance, sir?"

"We are cousins, milord." Samuel answered softly.

"How come you to be denounced, then Mr. Townsend?... And have you no advocate?" Harborough placed his spectacles on the tip of his bulbous nose and arched his eyebrows to look over the rims.

"I speak for myself, your honor, as an honest man."

Robert jumped up before DeLancey could catch him and advanced upon the bench, "I shall speak for him your lordship." And he added with a bow, "I am Robert Townsend, milord."

"Sit down young man!" It was a harsh rebuke and Rivington pulled Rob back to his chair. "The accused has precluded advocacy." Harborough shuffled some papers and broke into a self-satisfied chuckle. "You have friends in high places, Mr. Townsend, and I see here that Mr. Buchanan records that you have contributed a considerable sum to the success of His Majesty's efforts in the Americas. He states you are a non-combattant, a Quacker?... What is that?"

Samuel corrected him softly. "Quaker, milord. It's my religion."

Harborough snorted and wrinkled his large nose. "And you have sworn allegiance to His Majesty the King?"

"No, milord."

"No?" Harborough's florid face turned sour.

"With your forbearance, milord, there is no need to invoke the Almighty to attest to the actions of a just and honest man. Such is the creed of my religion."

Harborough's head rolled sideways like a round red ball. "You proclaim yourself a just and honest man?"

"I would make no such presumption sir. God is my judge. I am his humble servant and I have confidence that you, milord, will act honorably in his stead."

Harborough broke into a self-satisfied grin. "We shall do our best to serve the cause of justice and the honor of His Imperial Majesty, King George." The room fell silent while he lowered his eyes to the reams of papers before him. He shuffled through them. His nose twitched continuously as his smile faded to frown.

Finally, he lifted his eyes, "Mr. Townsend, I am commissioned to find winter quarters for a number of British officers. Would you consent to quartering His Majesty's officers in your home, officers of merit and distinction." And he added with distaste, "in anticipation of your renewed freedom, of course."

Samuel stammered unintelligibly but Robert stood again. His voice echoed clearly. "We are honored by your lordship's generosity. My mother and sisters would make them most welcome." He swept into a deep bow and fell back on the pew. Rivington whispered into his ear. "Good, Robert, up and bow again! Fall down on your knees - we are in church!"

Harborough glared down while the minutes ticked by. "Then it is settled." He wrinkled his nose and brought the gavel down. "You are free to go Mr. Townsend... and I shall tell your cousin, Sir Charles, he owes me a favor."

It was too abrupt. Samuel sat for a moment open-mouthed. When he tried to stand, his legs would not hold his weight. They crumpled under him. He stumbled backward and fell into Rivington's arms. Samuel Townsend had used his last reserves of strength and now he folded like a dry reed before the flood. In three days, he had aged greatly. Leg irons had slowed the circulation in his feet. He could not walk away. Rob and Oliver DeLancey had to carry him out.

Samuel had not eaten or slept. They carried him back to the Hart for a meal of wholesome food and a fortifying bottle of madeira. Jack Rivington found a farm wagon to transport the old man home. They cushioned him carefully upon sheepskins against the jarring motions of the wagon, removed his stockings and massaged his legs. He was already asleep when the horses jerked the wagon into the road.

The journey home was arduous. DeLancey drove with his own and Robert's horses trotting behind. Some pink returned to Samuel's pallid cheeks and he slept. Exhausted, Robert slept too. His weary head bobbed against his chest as the wagon lurched over the bumpy road. He did not waken until the wagon turned north through the hollow and he smelled the giant white pines on the road to Oyster Bay.

8

What bard will not his skill employ?
What heart will not expand with joy?

*T*hey arrived late in the day under the shade of the giant locust tree. A warm summer breeze blew in from the sea and the sun splashed orange over the dark waters of the bay. The long shadow of the tree stretched eastward over the lane. Robert and DeLancey hoisted the old man out into its soothing, refreshing shade.

Samuel Townsend's welcome was warm and spontaneous. Sally and Audrey rushed to the door with the slave children as soon as they heard the wagon. Sarah and Beulah thumped behind. Samuel Townsend stumbled to meet them, bolstered on each side by Robert and Oliver DeLancey.

They propped him on cushions on the settle by the hearth and bathed his feet in warm water scented with cool mint. Beulah rubbed them with lard and wrapped them in clean linens and stretched them out on a stool. Then all assembled before him to hear his story, slave children on the floor, adults seated or standing in an semicircle behind. Samuel did not dwell on his captivity but thanked God for his deliverance. He did not mention justice. Life, friends, family had become more precious to him than a distant ideal.

"Cob, slaughter a fat calf. Invite our friends, Captain Youngs and his family and the good Captains Farley and Markham! Oliver, you'll stay of course and where is Jack Rivington?"

"He has his business to attend to, but I wager he stayed at Jamaica, for the races."

"Remember to thank him for his trouble." He winked at Sarah. "Beulah, prepare a table...."

"Rob run to the shore and hail the Katherine. Captain Farley can weigh anchor tomorrow instead of today."

Sally interrupted, "Father, the Katherine cannot sail tomorrow or for many days to come." Samuel stared back blankly and she stammered on, "They stripped her masts and impressed her crew, what was left of them, yesterday."

Samuel face blanched. His lips parted in suspended speech. "Is the Promise in port?" They nodded. "Then Farley will take you in the Promise. Surely they've not stripped her too." His voice floated over them melodiously and their difficulties receded like clouds after rain. "We shall have a celebration and I shall have my first good night's sleep in three days." He stood, staggered, reached for the mantle to steady himself and fell back again, "Pull on my boots! A man cannot walk in bandages and bare feet!"

When finally Rob lifted him unsteadily to his feet, he turned to Sarah, "I almost forgot, my dear, we must ready a room for the officers that are to be quartered here. The back room should serve admirably."

Sally protested, "That's your room, Rob!"

"I can live at Peck's Slip while the officers are here."

Sarah's cane clattered to the floor. With the help of her two hands pushing from the back of a sturdy chair, she straightened from the hip. She repeated Samuel's last words with indignation, "Officers quartered here? Under this roof?"

Rob spoke up, "Mother, it was a condition of father's release. Coe and Weekes are still in prison!"

"I have never allowed uninvited strangers into my home." Sarah's voice crackled with outrage. The memory of abrasive Major Fanning was raw.

"Mother, Lord Harborough promised they would be British officers, educated gentlemen...." Robert's voice trailed off. He had only the verbal commitment of a civilian magistrate. No army commander had promised anything.

"An officer of better breeding and manners than that blackguard, Fanning, or God help us, a Hessian!" Sarah's eyes closed suddenly. She bit down hard as her face suddenly exploded in pain. Sally and Beulah rushed to her side. But she had grabbed a chair and remained defiantly frozen until the pain subsided and her face relaxed.

During the lull that followed, Audrey burst out, "I do hope he is tall and rich and red-coated. Red coats make even a plain man handsome!" Audrey's flippant remark brought an uneasy relief.

Sarah corrected the thoughtless girl, "Audrey, silence!" The four syllables cracked like splitting wood. The meeting was ended.

In the morning, Robert packed his belongings and vacated his room. Cob slit a calf's throat and butchered the meat. The slave children dug carrots, potatoes and onions from the garden and harvested apples from the orchard. Beulah baked while Sally tended the roast on an open spit in the yard. The mahogany table was spread the length of the front room with the cherry gateleg extending in an ell through the door to the hall.

For the first time, Sarah Townsend noticed the absence of her silver and turned on the dark face of the slave. "Did you think you'd buy your freedom with Stoddard forks and knives!" She lashed out at Beulah with her cane, but her hip collapsed under her and she clattered to the floor.

Beulah stood silently as a pillar and let her mistress lay. Sarah writhed and grabbed for her cane. Robert reached mechanically for his mother to lift her heavy body. "The silver is safe, mother. Sally and I buried it with grandfather's tankard and sword. There are evil men abroad who've no care for Stoddard property or anyone else's. They set upon enriching themselves, like the scoundrels who burned Jack Rivington's presses and robbed the Hulet home in Cedar Swamp.... Beulah is innocent."

Sarah's purple face paled to candle white. She forgot Beulah. "Are you saying they'll come here?"

"They'll not dare, mother... with officers in residence."

Sarah Townsend gaped at him open mouthed. It was a rare moment when Sarah Townsend was distracted enough to forget her physical pain. They guided her heavy bulk to a chair and the old woman sat wringing a handkerchief in her hands and shaking her head.

DeLancey reinforced Rob's assertions. "Officers in residence will be good protection, Madame. Too many men seek their own advantage, like scavengers, and espouse no cause and enrich themselves on whatever side of conflict will gain them most..." The corners of his eyes crinkled upward under shaggy brows. "And we will eat Beulah's fine cooking just as well with wooden spoons and nimble fingers!"

Early in the afternoon, a wagon pulled up to the gate. The Youngs family, Captain Daniel, Mother, Peggy and Billy, came to join in the feast with Captain Markham of the Weymouth and his friend Captain Farley, newly assigned to the Promise. Captain Farley, a tall, serious man, pushed his way to the chair beside Audrey who goaded him all evening with requests to pass butter, salt, sugar, molasses. Sally smiled inwardly at her sister's flirtations and talked freely with Peggy Youngs, across the table.

A clatter of hooves and stamp of feet interrupted the steamed lemon pudding that was dessert. The conversation suspended itself in nervous apprehension as Rob pushed his chair back and went to answer the door.

The voice in the hall was respectful, but firm. "Mr. Samuel Townsend?"

"My father is at table."

A broad-shouldered, red-coated officer entered, hat under his arm, written orders in his hand. His face was sunburned healthy tan and his dark liquid eyes were kind. He wore the epaulets and insignia of an officer of rank, a Captain, and the gold braid sparkled against the brilliant red of his coat. He looked doubtfully from Daniel Youngs to Captain Markham and Captain Farley, then to Samuel Townsend and addressed Samuel as the oldest person present, with a deference that earned Sarah Townsend's nod of approval and Audrey's eager grin. Even Sally was intrigued.

Samuel spoke up. "I am Samuel Townsend." His voice was still weak but his face blushed red from the wine.

"John Graves Simcoe, 40th Regiment of Foot, at your service, sir,...I am to be quartered here." He bowed deeply, his voice quavering with the clipped syllables of proper British speech. "I trust I shall cause no inconvenience." The two halves of the Dutch door banged one at a time and a second soldier poked his bushy head around the jamb. He was shorter than Simcoe by a head, with a round, comical face, goose neck and pink nose that wrinkled and sniffed like a rabbit. He had ears like a rabbit too. They were so large they seemed to fold over at the top where the brim of his hat pressed them down.

Simcoe added awkwardly, by way of introduction, "My orderly, Sergeant Kelly." He smiled and his eyes glowed with a quiet amiability. He was a very attractive man when he smiled.

Robert rose and held out a hand. "Welcome, Captain...and Sergeant. Beulah, make space for the Captain. You are in time for the pudding or perhaps some wine to quench your thirst after a dusty journey."

Simcoe nodded appreciatively. "I should be most grateful." Robert led him around the table making introductions. Simcoe shook hands with the men and bowed gracefully to the ladies. His eyes lingered for a moment on Sally's shining hair. He sat at the space cleared for him at Samuel Townsend's right hand. Beulah set a plate of pudding in front of him and a decanter of wine and began to set a place for the Sergeant at the foot of the table.

"Sit down, Sergeant." Samuel gestured to the little man to be seated. It was obvious that Kelly's nose would not stop twitching until his stomach was filled.

But Kelly protested. "It would not be proper, sir. I take me rations in the larder as befits me station." He turned to Simcoe, "Shall I bring in your cases, sir, and put up the horses?" He turned to Robert, "Have ye empty stalls for the Captain's horses and space enough for the Captain's phaeton?"

Horses - the Captain had more than one and a carriage, a phaeton! They would have to make room in the barn. Robert nodded to Cob who left to turn out the mare. Simcoe sat down but he refused the food that was offered. Not so Sergeant Kelly. Sally passed him a plateful which he took to the kitchen all the while protesting that a sergeant could never consume his proper fill in the same company as his captain.

Conversation did not resume easily. Everyone stared in painful silence at the handsome newcomer. Samuel was obviously tiring and he spilled his wine. Sarah glared like a hawk, her resentment simmering just below the surface. Sally cleared the dishes with trembling hands. Robert uttered a few mild platitudes about the weather. Only Audrey spoke spontaneously and her careless words embarrassed Simcoe and DeLancey alike. "What a lovely red coat Captain. You must have paid a pretty sum to a London tailor!"

Sarah's jaw dropped. She could not correct her daughter without making matters worse. Simcoe forced a polite smile, sipped his wine and answered patiently. "In fact, Miss, a Boston tailor sewed the coat and did it masterfully." Sally watched his intelligent brown eyes. In only a few minutes, he had grasped Audrey's peculiar innocence.

Sergeant Kelly bustled in with a heavy case in his arms. "And where shall I store your books, sir?"

Simcoe flashed a questioning glance at Sally who answered, "In the corner by the window in the parlor. There they will stay dry and there is ample light by day to read and a whale oil lamp at night."

Robert, the journalist, perked at the mention of books, "And what is it you read, Captain?"

"The wars mostly... Xenophon, Caesar. Homer and Virgil made a great art of war. And I love Sir Thomas Mallory. I am a student of military history, as befits a professional soldier. And you, Mr. Townsend, have you read the wars?"

"I am Quaker, Captain. I do not find wars amusing or worthy of study." Simcoe went rigid. Sarah Townsend gawked in horror.

Oliver DeLancey retrieved the conversation, "I have always marvelled at the complement of sea and land forces in ancient Greece, Captain."

The Youngs left shortly after, with Captain Markham behind them. Before he left, Captain Farley had appointed Oliver DeLancey and Rob to meet at the barge landing at six bells in the morning watch, when the Promise would sail with the tide for New York City.

John Simcoe lingered at table with Robert and Oliver DeLancey and Captain Farley. Sarah pulled Audrey away to bed lest she commit another indiscretion. Samuel followed. Simcoe deliberately addressed Robert. "I did not mean to offend, Mr. Townsend, but I am ignorant of the beliefs of the inhabitants of this continent, specifically the Quakers. Please accept my apologies." He smiled. Robert nodded and smiled back.

Sally lingered and moved to the spinning wheel in the corner. Her foot pumped steadily on the pedal and the wheel droned its monotonous song. She had never observed a British officer closely and this Simcoe was like no one she had encountered before. He was immaculate in dress, impeccable in manner and the red of his coat gleamed against the white of his collar and the brown, almost black of his hair. He seemed shy in demeanor, compared to Fanning, yet he was an officer of great responsibility - a captain in the regular British Army. He read books yet his profession demanded physical stamina and exercise. He was tolerant and patient as was evident in his reaction to her brother and sister. He was a man of polish and education. And the hilt of his sword was made of gold. It caught the slim candle's rays and intensified them like distant stars in a night sky.

Captain Simcoe questioned them carefully about the island, about the local forests and plains, about the height of headlands and depth of bays, about springs and rivers and roads. He asked about the residents, about their origins and religion, about their crops and crafts and businesses.

But it was to Sally that Simcoe addressed most of his queries. Robert still eyed him warily. Sally answered truthfully with only an occasional word from DeLancey and Farley. Her voice was soft and welcoming. "We are mostly farmers and seamen. We raise cattle on the plains, some sheep, pigs, and vegetables in our gardens. We fish and clam. Life is simple. Our most prosperous inhabitants are the merchants and traders who own their ships like my father. Robert and Oliver can tell you of the neighbors better than I. They are male and freer to ride out much more often than I. Rob tends father's lodging and warehouse at Peck's Slip near Pearl Street and writes the news of gossip and parties that Jack Rivington prints. Rivington is a popular journalist and knows everyone in the city."

She faltered. Captain Simcoe was staring directly at her. When he realized her discomfort, he dropped his eyes and prodded softly. "Please continue. I would rather hear my own epitaph from a beautiful and accomplished lady, than a eulogy from the most capable of men!" The compliment was offered politely, with grace, but it was public.

Robert broke in with alarm. "My sister is spoken for!"

John Simcoe did not take offense. He turned briefly to Robert. "And well spoken for such a beauty, I do not doubt." He smiled again with sad, kind eyes and turned the discussion to ships, "My father was a sea-captain, so I know ships, that they are important to your commerce. But perhaps you would inform me of the details of this island's prosperity?" Farley met his gaze and smiled.

Ships - they had struck a common thread.

Simcoe bantered with the sea captain and finally explained his own mission, "I have been dispatched to find forage. General Howe has disembarked with 15,000 men. They must be fed and housed and horsed. I have been sent to see what can be had from the countryside: beef, pork, wood, hay, beasts and wagons to transport the burden. The General believes there should be sufficient supply from the farms and homes of the rebellious citizens who have fled, and no need for costly appropriations from loyal citizens." He looked hesitantly toward Sally with his next request. "And I am to make note of the lay of the land. Perhaps you would accompany me in a tour of the area, Miss Sally, and you, Robert,...and Colonel DeLancey and Captain Farley. I have ordered a coach for tomorrow at sunrise. Sergeant Kelly will drive. I need the counsel and knowledge of reliable local residents."

DeLancey emptied his glass. "I'm sorry Captain, but Farley and I must sail tomorrow, but Rob will stay." Robert flashed him a withering frown and Oliver DeLancey took no notice. "Rob has a fine comprehension of the land and harbors and I'm sure Sally will be glad to introduce you to all the neighbors."

Simcoe raised his clipped, refined voice. "I should be most grateful, Robert." He turned to Sally. "You, milady, have not accepted my invitation."

Sally was watching her brother. She noted his displeasure. A pallor drained his normally rosy cheeks and creases formed between his eyes over his long nose. A lone nerve in his cheek twitched involuntarily. His left eyelid flicked. He had not contributed to the conversation. What he did say was irrelevant and bland, as if his mind was not actively engaged and had galloped ahead into some far-off void. He had only reacted when Captain Simcoe had shown interest in his sister.

Sally answered John Simcoe, "I would be delighted to come, Captain, now that father is safe." The evening was ending. The men retired to the parlor. Sally's foot pushed the pedal and the spinning wheel turned. The wool ran the length of her fingers and spun from coarse, matted hair, round and round, on and on, smoothing the knots and easing the tangles, into fine thread. But not as fine as that which composed Captain Simcoe's coat. That wool was smooth as fine silk. For Sally, this strange intruder from across the sea seemed suddenly to bring a delicacy and sanity into the hectic life of these last few days, like a quiet breeze that smooths over the ripples on the waters after the storm. His impeccable manners healed insults and salved wounds. He was a helper, a healer, a kind man. It was her brother, Robert's reaction which disturbed her.

9

We have a stomach both for beef and battle.
Honest Whigs, once more, feed well your cattle.

*T*he tall clock struck seven when a shining phaeton pulled under the shade of the locust tree. It was cool in the early morning, with the dew still glistening on the September air. The horses blew and the gate slammed as Sergeant Kelly bounded into the hall. He collected the basket that Beulah had prepared for lunch, deposited it under the high box and stood wiping the last bit of grime from the gleaming black coach. The horses were matched greys and looked much like the hackneys of William Lawrence. Sergeant Kelly was delighted with his position as coachman of such a fine vehicle. His pink rabbit's nose which spread wide like a plum across the lower half of his face, twitched nervously.

Sally ran to fetch a bonnet, gloves and light shawl. She would need her hat by noon when the sun would blaze down unmercifully and the southerly would blow in the warm tropical air.

The little sergeant let down the step and stood like a proper footman to help Sally mount the high carriage but the Captain himself stepped up to lift her in. Simcoe's gaze settled gently over her shoulders as she sank gracefully onto the cushioned seat. She smiled back at him as he took his seat opposite. Robert climbed in last. He sat next to Simcoe, but slumped back into the corner. Captain Simcoe sensed Robert's reluctance and did not press him.

Sergeant Kelly's pink nose sniffed derisively. He considered the presence of a young lady, very unsoldierly, and he let his disapproval be known by a constant, incomprehensible grumble. He made sure she sat alone with the two men facing her. Sergeant Kelly climbed up to the box, grumbling his litany of complaints, namely that the Captain should watch the horses, not the young miss. Simcoe ignored him but he could not ignore his driving which was fitful and uneven because he twisted his goose neck around at regular intervals to check that his Captain was well-seated and Mistress Sally had not fallen into his lap. Every time he turned, he jerked the reins so that the horses broke stride and the wagon lurched.

From the elevation of the phaeton, John Simcoe, Robert and Sally Townsend could scan the countryside with ease. Simcoe turned his gaze away from Sally, to the scenery outside. "If you will direct the Sergeant, Robert, I should like to see the shoreline where possible, Young's shipyard and the settlement at the Landing." He pulled out a sketch pad and charcoal from a knapsack at his feet, and began to take notes and draw.

"Turn left at the crossroad, Sergeant. Go straight ahead to the harbor.... The shipyard is east on the shore road, but west of Cove Hill, and the rope yard is at the base of the hill, on the eastern side.

At harborside, Sergeant Kelly halted and John Graves Simcoe called for his looking glass. He stepped out to where the road ended and toed a pebble with his boot, then walked to where the cool water licked the sand. It was low tide. A great blue heron and a flock of geese flew up in a great flapping of wings into a clear blue sky. John Simcoe stood like a Greek statue, in the brilliant red and gold of his military uniform, a broad-shouldered, straight, strong silhouette of a man. He held a looking glass glued to his eye and scanned the horizon.

He saw a beautiful harbor, more beautiful and more wild than his beloved home in England. He knew his mission - to stem the exodus of refugees, to quell the violence of rebellion and convince the Americans that the rule of England was just and good. He had no doubt that British victory would ensue - no insurgent rabble could possibly defeat the best-manned, best-equipped army and navy in the world. But he shook his head when he thought of the logistics of supplying the huge force at New York under General William Howe. He was assigned here to assess what could be procured to feed, clothe, fuel and horse that immense force, from the pristine lands of this island and to do it without causing waste and resentment. It was a difficult, perhaps impossible task. There could be destruction and plunder. He was here to prevent it. He determined to protect the property of His Majesty's loyal subjects, to seize only what had belonged to the insurgents who had fled.

A flock of geese set down on the black water, necks tucked back, grey wings beating the air, honking, snapping at each other, without order or discipline, ruffling the glasslike surface of the bay. To John Simcoe they resembled Washington's army, the noisy, disorganized, chattering gaggle of fowl who flew off at the smallest sign of danger. He could not comprehend how reasonable men, landed men, farmers, magistrates, churchmen and artisans believed they could defeat the might of Great Britain, how they would desert their lands and their homes, run off like so many quacking birds, thinking they could fight a war. These Americans were at most one or two generations removed from their cousins in England; some had just arrived on these shores. And yet they were distinct. What had inspired their foolishness? Had they no respect for background and tradition? Should they not have expressed some gratitude for protection against the French, the Indians, for the safety of their shipping, for law, for order, for all the benefits that mother England had bestowed upon them? And as for freedom, didn't they understand that England with her parliamentary system granted more freedom than any European monarchy, than any other government on earth?

They were a strange lot, these Americans, bred to a different sire. Uncouth, self-willed and erratic, they expected to be treated like competent, reliable Englishmen. They didn't act like Englishmen. John Simcoe thought of them as some half-tamed beast, untrained and unpredictable. Even the Loyalists, these Townsends who extended to him the hospitality of their home, were different. Kelly had brought it to his attention. Robert seemed surly, almost morose, and had a limited sense of hierarchy and place. Sally, with her fiery hair, her energy, her self-assurance, had little proper ladylike reserve. Still there was a brazen spontaneity to her that he found attractive and he had insisted she come along today. He liked her and he did not dislike Robert. He sensed in Robert a certain reserve that his sister lacked, more like a proper Englishman.

He shook his head to clear his brain and turned suddenly, shouting back at Sally and Robert in the coach. "Had I my fowling piece, we should have goose for dinner!"

Sally laughed and Robert yelled back, "Next time, Captain and I will bring my hounds."

Of a sudden, as if they had perceived a threat, the geese rose in a body. They filled the morning skies and the sound of their honking echoed like so many trumpets heralding a glorious day. They swooped out over the bay, filling the sky with an exuberance of life.

When the honking died away, Simcoe turned and wandered back to the coach. He swept his arm out across the bay. "And who lives there?" He pointed to Hog's Neck, a protrusion of land running east to west. It sheltered the bay from the Sound with a swath of thick forest.

Sally answered, "Thomas Barney and he is more fanatically loyal than most."

Simcoe's sensed an antagonism. "You do not like him, Miss Townsend?"

She shrugged, "He does not like me."

Robert interrupted with the explanation. "His daughters are not as becoming as my sister and they are jealous." He changed the subject. "There is father's ship, the Weymouth. You met her Captain Markham. And that is the Promise, Captain Farley."

"They are former warships, I see." Simcoe knew his ships.

"My father owns four former fighting ships of the Royal Navy. They are useful vessels for the West Indian trade, after the navy retires them."

The coach moved on. They visited the shipyard and Youngs' rope yard in the cove. There were two ships on the ways, one 120 foot hull nearly complete, another a carcass of ribs awaiting flesh. There were stacks of lumber in various stages of seasoning and a sail loft with yards of canvas draped in the sun. There were sawpits and wagons and tool sheds attended by gangs of laborers, sawyers, plankers, painters, sailmakers. The yard resounded with the thud of broad axe and adze and the sharp ring of the mallet against hawzing irons that drove oakum caulking deeper into the seams and sealed the planking tight. There was a stack of spars laying on the shore just above the high water mark, ready for refitting. Simcoe was an astute observer and scribbled his notes avidly between prolonged glances through his glass.

The rope yard was smaller but equally busy. Kegs of tar stood at odd angles and oozed in the hot summer sun. There were bolts of cordage, cable-laid twisted left-handed for elasticity, stays, halyards, lifts and braces. A barge laden with huge coils rocked at dockside.

The coach stopped at Youngs' Farm where Mother Youngs served fresh bread and ham with cider while the horses drank from the spring. Captain Daniel was away, overseeing a delivery of hemp.

"Is there a bluff that commands these waters?" John Simcoe's mind sought out defenses.

Sally answered, "Cooper's Bluff. We can drive there now. But I warn you, an old recluse lives there, Joseph Cooper, with two old slaves. He is a gloomy, irritable man. He has lost six children and a wife. My mother and the ladies of the Baptist Church visit him regularly to see that he has bread and fuel." She added as if more explanation were needed, "His wife was a Baptist as are my mother and Audrey." She climbed into the coach.

"Was?" Simcoe questioned.

"She is dead as are their six children." She stated it as fact, without any expectation of sympathy.

"I do not know the Baptists. They are admirable Christians I'm sure?" It was a question. John Simcoe looked her full in the face and risked a more personal question. "And you are a Baptist, Miss Townsend?"

Sally's face flushed under his gaze. She brushed a stray lock from her brow, "Rob and I are Quakers, but I too carry bread to Joseph Cooper every week." John Simcoe and Sally Townsend did not lower their eyes but continued to stare one at the other. Sergeant Kelly looked back once and whipped the horses into a brisk trot, which jerked his passengers sharply against the seat. Sally righted herself with a hand on John Simcoe's knee. Robert glared at her blackly.

The Cooper home was in disrepair. The door hung loosely off a lower hinge while the upper hinge had been replaced by a crude strip of rawhide. Shingles were missing from the roof and creeper and spurge blanketed the kitchen garden. An old swaybacked horse nibbled weeds near a broken fence. Cooper was a shriveled, white-haired gnome with watery red eyes and wispy grey hair. His two slaves dwarfed him. They were both close to six feet but arthritic and hunched like their master from the hard use of many years. There was no woman to care for the house.

Cooper stood off suspiciously. As Robert introduced Captain Simcoe, he noticed the unusual absence of horses and cows - Cooper had hidden his livestock. John Simcoe walked with Sally to the lip of the bluff and sat her comfortably on stump. He took up his sketch pad and began to draw. Robert sat himself deliberately between them.

The Bay stretched out before them in two wide swaths, one on their left running east-west, the other on their right running north-south. Cooper's Bluff on a rocky outcrop divided the two bodies of water. From the high bluff, the inlet stood out starkly a little east of north. Plum Point on its western edge was the round flat tip of Thomas Barney's lands. Lloyd's Neck on the eastern edge of the inlet rose abruptly from the water and hovered like a mountain cirque over the bay. Simcoe immediately spotted two ships that plied their way into the harbor. They hugged the opposite shore beneath Lloyd's distant cliff.

"The deep channel is there." Robert pointed to the dark velvety stripe of water. He swept his arm back to the rock-strewn beach immediately below them and to the greenish water just off Plum Point. "All this here is shallows."

Simcoe motioned toward the cliff. "Who lives there?"

Sally answered, "The land belongs to the Lloyd family by Royal Charter. They live at the Manor of Queens Village. There are four Lloyds, Mr. Joseph, Mr. Henry, Mr. John and Mr. James," she corrected herself, "Doctor James Lloyd.... Doctor Lloyd was educated in London and is a fine surgeon. He lives in Boston. They are all friendly with father. Becca Lloyd is my friend."
Simcoe withdrew the glass from his eye with a slow pensive nod and smiled.

Sergeant Kelly cleared his throat. "Pardon for interrupting, sir. 'Tis time we be going." He wagged his rabbit nose at Sally with a loud harumph.

It was a long drive from Cooper's Bluff to the manor house where the Joseph Lloyds lived. The road skirted the eastern bay, wound south to the Post Road, through the swamps at Bungtown and back north through the whaling village to Horse Neck, a distance of about 8 miles.

The day was hot, one of the steamy, humid days left over from mid-July. The sun beat down on the black leather upholstery of the coach and black flies and mosquitoes tortured horses and passengers alike. It was not yet noon.

Huge trees lined the road and wilted in the glare. Even in the moving coach the air was still. Robert removed his waistcoat and loosened his collar. Sally beat the air with her fan. John Graves Simcoe mopped his brow at intervals with handkerchiefs supplied by the vigilant Kelly. Kelly sneaked swigs from a flask that he kept under the box and his vigilance waned. He drove more erratically than ever. When he started to sing, Simcoe ordered him into the boot and took the reins himself.

They stopped at Jennings' farm to drink and left refreshed by the cool water of the spring. When Mrs. Jennings offered Kelly another gill of sailor's rum, John Simcoe intervened.

Simcoe drove up the winding road to Huntington and over the narrow strip of sand that connected Horse Neck to the mainland. The lands of the Lloyd family fanned out into an expanse of 3000 acres and created an excellent harbor between Horse Neck and the mainland. There were several whaleboats and a barge moored there now. The sand was deep and the horses labored. Simcoe pulled to a halt to rest them. An osprey circled overhead. Ahead, a gang of black slaves was hammering the surface of the road. John Simcoe questioned and Sally explained. "We pack the road surface with oyster and clam shells. They form a durable surface that drains easily if flooded. Over there, the slaves gather the shells from the surf." She pointed to stooped forms carrying baskets from the shore. Others spread the contents flat and tamped them down with mallets. Simcoe whipped up the horses and the coach moved on. "How much farther?"

"A mile more to the Manor." Sally's eyes lingered on the red uniform that rippled over his shoulders and the soft flow of dark hair that folded over his ears. Robert was silent.

They arrived at the manor house as slaves set out a picnic lunch under a wide oak.

Mrs. Lloyd embraced Sally coldly, "Who's this you bring, Sally and Rob Townsend?" She walked forward with one outstretched palm to Robert and the other to the handsome officer in the red coat. Robert made formal introductions. "Mrs. Lloyd, may I present Captain John Graves Simcoe of His Majesty's 40th Regiment of Foot."

Her answer was cool but cordial, "A pleasure, Captain, to entertain His

Majesty's representative in my humble home or should I say, under my unworthy tree." Simcoe bowed. Mrs. Lloyd called suddenly, "Becca, Sally's here!" She curtsied politely to Simcoe.

Robert asked gently, "Is John Jr. at home? I was hoping to see him?" Mrs. Lloyd rallied. "He is away but Theo is inside. It is lonely for her without John Jr. Visitors are so rare." Theo was John Jr.'s wife and she was with child. She had been confined for over a month, hemorrhaging, but one did not talk of such things. One never spoke of neighbors who were "away" in the presence of an English officer. The war had lent new meaning to the word and John Jr. had fled to Connecticut to join the rebellion.

Robert inquired after Mr. Joseph and Dr. James Lloyd and Mr. Henry.

Mrs. Lloyd spoke carefully, weighing every word, "Mr. Henry is out riding."

Captain Simcoe stepped forward. His eyes drifted over the superb trees, the fine pastures, the rich expanses of salt hay in the marshes. The Lloyds were wealthy. Their men were absent; their women, reticent.

Suddenly, Becca, a tall girl of about eighteen years came running from the house. "Sally, I'm so glad you came! I've a letter from Aaron! He's with Micah." She stopped in mid-stride when she saw the British uniform. "Perhaps tomorrow..." Aaron Richbell and Rebecca Lloyd were to be married. Like Micah Strong, Aaron Richbell had joined Putnam's militia and was now somewhere in Westchester or Dutchess County, on the mainland with the rebellion.

Sally made the introductions. "Rebecca Lloyd, may I present Captain John Simcoe of the 40th Regiment of Foot."

John Simcoe bowed elegantly, "I am honored, Miss." His intelligent eyes observed every awkward detail.

Lunch was a silent affair and when they had climbed back into the coach, a sobered and humiliated Kelly resumed driving.

John Simcoe addressed Robert. "Colonel Cunningham had decreed that Joseph and John Lloyd's lands are to be forfeit. But I met Dr. James in Boston, an excellent fellow and physician, and quite loyal. I told him that by residing in Boston he is in grave danger from the rebellious rabble and he may yet loose his lands if he does not return to claim them."

Robert tried to explain. "He is a talented physician... Boston is his home." Simcoe could not understand why anyone would prefer a hotbed of radicalism like Boston to civilized, British New York.

Sergeant Kelly drove on and they did not speak further. Robert studied Simcoe. He held paper and pen and recorded figures and Robert Townsend realized that he was writing the inventory of what he had seen. These tall trees, the cattle, sheep, hay and cornfields, the entire wealth of Joseph and John Lloyd, and possibly James too, would fall to a British axe in the name of the King of England. The fields and forests contained the richest forage for the troops of His Majesty, Georgius Rex. The Latin seemed to depersonalize the monarch in Robert's mind, to remove him in time and in place from common humanity, to position him like some classical emperor hovering over Persia or Gaul. "Georgius Rex" the words punctuated a despondency that overcame Robert like the fetid air in an empty attic. He trembled slightly. He felt as if he were looking at something very precious about to crumble in his hand.

John Simcoe sensed his unease. "You are quiet, Robert. You do not espouse our efforts to protect you?"

Simcoe's own enthusiasm was building and Robert had to struggle to disguise his despair. He answered vaguely, "I dislike seeing what is dear to me disappear. I suppose I regret the changes that are inevitable."

"In the name of peace and order, Robert, you cannot object."

"In the name of peace....no." Robert's voice trailed off.

They drove on through thick primal forest, trunks that branched out fifty feet in the air, tall, straight, monster trees, smooth grey maple, stately oak, shaggy-barked locust whose tallest limbs begged the lightning's first blast, walnut and hickory, tulip and chestnut, the verdant first growth of the ancient newworld forest. Red fox, white-tail deer, pheasant, wild turkey, ubiquitous grey squirrels peopled the forest. John Simcoe marvelled at the trees and exclaimed, "What ships these would build!" He saw the glory of England in the bounty and beauty of the land. That there was life here, life that would end, sacrificed to the appetites of war, Simcoe did not conceive.

Robert's heart ached. So many soldiers, so many ships, so many who cared so little. They would rape the land, his land.

The coach climbed the high rim of the cliff. John Simcoe's excitement increased like a boy who had just hooked his first fish and dropped his second line. When the road ended in a lonely grove near a spring-fed pond, he jumped out even before the coach had come to a halt and called back to Rob. "I must see it from the height."

Sally put a hand on her brother's arm. "What is he doing, Rob?"

"Reconnoitering, Sally....He will report to his superiors and the British will send wood-cutters and harvesters and butchers. They have 15,000 men to feed, clothe and shelter." His voice shook, "Sally, those are material things. Don't let him take your heart!"

Sally laughed, "What a brother you are!" Then grew more serious, "How many troops Rob? How do you know?"

Robert did not answer. Dragging his feet like a tired horse, he walked off after Simcoe. He no longer laughed with her or at her. An intensity lingered around the circles of his eyes like a halo around the moon.

Robert joined Simcoe and they tramped through the forest to the edge of the precipice. The view was breathtaking. From the cliff, they looked straight down the harbor. It was a wide avenue of deep blue protected water. It stretched out before them for a good mile to where the Weymouth and the Promise rocked at their moorings, and the tiny village of Oyster Bay slept calmly in the sun. The houses were mere specks from the distant height. Barges, whaleboats, oystermen and fishing craft speckled the water, like insects on a pond. To their right, lay the inlet, leading to Long Island Sound. To their left lay the smaller south fork of the harbor, at Cold Spring and Bungtown. Directly beneath their feet, hugging the base of the cliff was the dark black depth of water where warships entered and set out to sea.

John Simcoe's handsome face came alive and he rubbed his hands together in satisfaction. He took Sally by the hand and led her out to admire the view. "This, Miss Sally! This is where we shall build our fort!"

Robert Townsend turned his back and walked away. The next day, he sailed with Farley for New York.

10

Work on, work on, ye jolly pioneers,
The town shall soon be knock'd about their ears.

Construction of the fort began almost immediately. Slaves cleared a road through the forest to the face of the cliff and tamped it down with crushed shell. They moved rocks and removed stumps and trees. They burned the scrub and razed the giant trees and stacked and sorted the hardwood for shipment to collection points on the shoreline.

First, the tallest trees came crashing down. Oxen hauled the immense lengths to the cliff top, where augurs had drilled cores vertically into the bowels of the cliff. They hoisted the trunks on end like ships' masts and pounded them vertically, straight down into the side of the cliff to support the weight of their massive guns. They built thick earthen walls of redoubts to withstand bombardment. They placed artillery, 24 and 32-pounders, on the battlements and trained them on the entrance to the harbor.

Back away from the cliff-face, adjacent to a spring-fed pond, they constructed barracks. They were drafty, cold quarters warmed by crude stone hearths which burned the trees they cut for fuel. Three hundred marines arrived for the winter. They fired the guns daily at markers in the bay and the gunners' aim improved steadily. The H.M.S. Halifax, a powerful frigate, lay at anchor on the opposite side of the channel, ready to rake an intruder with deadly broadsides. No enemy ship dared run the gauntlet into Oyster Bay Harbor.

Weeks passed. The maples yellowed and the oaks and walnuts reddened, then browned. The air cooled. The damp smell of rain penetrated the air and frost speckled the fields with its silvery hint of snow. A northeaster swept in from the ocean just after Rebecca Lloyd came to visit at Townsend's. Becca had heard the rasp of the sawpits, the crack and heave of the great trees falling. She had felt the earth tremble when the guns recoiled. Now she sat with Sally in the parlor sipping tea, while the driving rain rapped the windowpanes and turned the earth to a thickening glue. Her hand shook as she held her cup. "I wish they would be silent. I stuff cotton in my ears and still the explosions echo. I cannot walk in the woods. They follow me. I squirm at their ugly looks. We cannot sleep for fear.... And I have no company, Sally, no one with whom I can talk openly. Poor Theo spends most of her time in tears. The Hessian brutes seize our slaves. They shoot our cattle. I can still hear the poor beasts bawling. The milk cows have all disappeared. No cheese, no sweet cream, no milk, and Theo's baby on the way. I despair, Sally, that we will ever live happily again. There are times when I think I shall go mad!"

"Your Uncle James is in Boston." Sally offered a hope. James Lloyd had trained in childbirth in London at Guy's Hospital. He was respected by Tory and rebel alike as a fine surgeon and generous man. "Surely he would take you and Theo in."

"He would and Theo needs his help. But how can we find passage to Boston in these troubled times. Uncle Joseph took all our ships to Connecticut.... Do Townsend ships still sail?"

"Yes but the port of Boston is forbidden."

"I feel like a prisoner with the filthy Hessians for jailers."

Sally straightened suddenly. Points of flame reflected in her eyes. "We will ask John Simcoe. We will ask him to convey you to Boston."

"I could not go without Theo."

"For both of you, it may be your only salvation and that of the babe....I will speak to Captain Simcoe myself. If he has a heart beneath his golden braid, and I believe he does, he cannot refuse."

Captain Simcoe rode up at this moment and handed a handsome grey horse to Cob. He entered quietly and shook the rain from his hood. As he reached to hang his wet cloak, Sally called him into the parlor.

"Tea, Captain? It's still warm."

"Thank you, Miss, but I will be better company in dry clothing."

Rebecca's eyes widened and she whispered to her friend. "He's handsome, Sally! My days would pass more easily, if I had a handsome Englishman and not a horde of stubby Hessians for company.... Do you like him, Sally?"

Sally mumbled just above the threshold of sound, "Yes, I like him, but he is too duty-bound to notice."

"You are vulnerable Sally. I would be too."

Sally paused at her friend's remark. She questioned her own feelings for the first time. How vulnerable was she? She and Simcoe had very little opportunity for companionship, much less courtship. Simcoe's days were full, supervising the myriad activities of foraging parties. And she was always occupied. But she did enjoy watching the way he moved and she loved the deep melody of his cultured voice.

She said no more. The rain stopped and the wind subsided and Becca Lloyd departed next morning. John Simcoe agreed to secure passage to Connecticut for Theo and Becca. Only Sergeant Kelly complained that his esteemed Captain preoccupied himself with the disposition of "ladies". The little Sergeant never referred to a female by name and always in the third person. To him, "ladies" were a base, alien caste, far below the exalted military, far below the eminently important concerns of his master, John Graves Simcoe. But John Graves Simcoe found a transport for Theo and Becca because Sally Townsend had requested it of him. Theo and Becca accompanied prisoners for exchange and arrived safely in that hotbed of rebellion, Boston, at the home of their uncle, Doctor James Lloyd.

One evening, when dinner was complete and Samuel and Sarah and had retired, John Simcoe sat with Sally and Audrey near the hearth, reading. He looked up to find Sally watching him. He brightened, offered her a book and went on to describe the complexities of the great battles, Marathon, Thermopylae, Salamis, the Rubicon. His enthusiasm was infectious. Sally hung on every word.

They talked far into the night, long after Audrey had gone to bed. Their thoughts meshed like finely woven cloth as they poured over the accounts of conquerors and heroes. When the embers on the hearth had grown cold, Sally began to shiver. He drew off his coat and placed it around her shoulders. His hand gently brushed away her hair. Their shoulders touched. Their eyes met. His cheek was only inches from hers but he made no move. She was the first to speak. Her words fluttered like feathers on an updraft. "I thank you for my friends' safety, Captain, for delivering Theo and Becca to Boston."

There was a stiff silence before he smiled and answered teasingly. "I have created another infant rebel. I shall have to make it up to His Majesty, good King George!"

"Captain. I am very grateful." She hugged the coat around her.

He backed away and cast his eyes away from her at a dark corner crevice and murmured, "Wars create strange and wrenching loyalties, Miss Sally."

Sally thought he referred to the ancient histories recorded in the books, but he was talking of the present, of himself, of his inability to act upon his feelings and of the conflicts deep within his own heart. He said, "I am a mere captain. I must adhere to a soldier's discipline and to my duty to my king." He trained large sad eyes upon her face. They burned like brands into her soul.

Sally Townsend and John Graves Simcoe passed many evenings pouring over his books, while Audrey dozed or retired early to bed. Never once did he abandon his British decorum, nor Sally her reserve. They were companionable evenings, distraction from responsibility, relief from drudgery. There was no revelation of deeper commitment. He repeated the outings in the coach, more out of pity for the seclusion of the vivacious girl than from any ostensible prodding of his heart - and always under the judgmental eyes of Sarah Townsend or Sergeant Kelly.

Gradually, Captain Simcoe sought out the company of the beautiful girl more frequently, at noon by the well, in the orchard at dusk, late in the evening by the fireside. Sally did not discourage him. Sometimes he would arrive late in the night and Sally would lay awake in her bed in the room above, listening for the clatter of his sword and the thump of his heavy boots on the wide oak boards of the floor.

Warships arrived in Oyster Bay. They dwarfed the merchantmen of the West Indian trade. Frigates of 32 guns, ships of the line of 60 guns, all found safe moorings in the quiet bays of the North Shore. Oyster Bay was one of the largest of these. First the Halifax, 32 guns, dropped anchor in the channel under the Lloyd's cliff. Then the Rose and the Defiant and the H.M.S. Panther. More ships arrived. Their paintwork shone like black mirrors; their fittings sparkled in the sun; their portholes glistened with the brass of massive guns. Amid them, stood the Katherine, newly painted and refitted by Youngs and Townsend, for the foraging service of the British Navy.

Captain Markham of the Weymouth arrived one morning and asked to speak with Sally and Samuel. He had come on several other occasions to ride out with Robert but this visit was unexpected. His brows knit together over the bridge of his nose and his swarthy cheeks were hollow. He sat in the parlor with Sally awaiting Samuel. "I've brought you a packet Sally...from Micah."

Sally was surprised - Micah, her betrothed, had never written before. The match had been arranged long ago by Sally's mother and Micah Strong's maiden aunt. Sally Townsend did not blame Micah for a lack of ardor.

"Open it now, before your father comes."

She broke the seal and sat by the window where the sun gleamed on the brilliance of her hair and illumined the ink-stained paper. Her eyes widened as she read. When she finished, her voice was pensive, "Micah has released me from my troth." She glanced forlornly at Markham. "He has found another." She swallowed hard and smiled weakly and refolded the message. Robert would be glad. He had predicted the split. Now the casual announcement that she had been so easily replaced in Micah Strong's affections should have been humiliating but she breathed a long sigh of relief.

Markham fidgeted nervously. "I'm sorry, Miss."

His words refocussed the wanderings of her mind. She arched her proud neck and flung her head backward. "No, Captain, I did not love him. He did not love me. It's been so long since I've seen him, the memory of our courtship is dim." When she faced him again, the flush had returned to her face and the gleam to her blue eyes. "I wish him well. Did you speak with him? Is he happy?"

Markham was visibly shaken by her directness. He dropped his eyes and wrenched the brim of his hat. "I did not see him. The letter was given me by Caleb Brewster in Darien. Brewster said I should tell you he would have liked to deliver it himself."

"Brewster again! I thought I smelled Brewster in this!" Sally laughed. "How did you come to be in Darien?"

Samuel Townsend entered before Markham could answer. "Markham my man, you had an easy passage. You've brought us treasures from the Indies, I see."

Markham did not meet his gaze. Hat in hand, head bowed, he launched into an agitated torrent of words. "Sir, I have labored diligently in your employ these last ten years, and I have benefited from your patronage as you, I hope have profited from my service...." He turned a tortured face to Samuel Townsend. "I must resign my position."

The old man was standing by the doorway and now he steadied himself on the jamb. Sally moved to sustain him and helped him slowly into his chair. He slumped down, "Markham, I did not suspect...."

"I can only be honest with you sir as you have always been honest with me. I am joining the Whigs, the insurgents, General Washington." He threw his head back and Sally could see the knob of his throat bob when he swallowed. "Sir, I would beg you to hear my reasons."

The old man waved a weak hand to continue.

Markham's words lapped like waves upon a beach. They began in an even monotone which rose higher in pitch like a gathering storm wave. "The cause is just. I cannot stand by while the Royal Naval Captains seize my seamen and impress them into their service. And it is usually the ships of the very worst commanders who need men, whose crews sicken and desert. They kidnap our best men, some of them under my tutelage from a very young age, some of them mere boys, and they treat them rudely, brutally, give them the most menial of duties and seize them up before the mast for trivial infringements because they were born on this side of the Atlantic." He paused to catch his breath and gained volume and speed until his words ran together like water in a millrace. "Surely the cat o' nine tails is a vicious master. Yesterday, I heard that young Reed was seized before the mast, 180 lashes, skin shredded from his back to the bone sir, blood puddling in his shoes, no medical aid, sir, and he is dead." Here Markham's voice rent the air like a knife ripping canvas. He repeated the word with white horror in his eyes, "Dead, sir!" His hand reached for a sharp dirk which he wrenched from his belt and stabbed into the surface of the mantle. He calmed at the sight of his own violence. "I'm sorry sir." He twisted the dirk from its hole and rubbed his palm over the splinters of wood. He had more to say but his eyes had filled. He refused to cry in front of Sally but he could not speak further. He turned his watery eyes toward the window and some yellow leaves twirling on an updraft in the garden. A tear finally slid silently down his whiskered cheeks. "An ill wind tosses us like leaves on the gusts where and when it will, sir." He fell into a chair. "Forgive my weakness, sir. I am afraid."

Samuel placed a hand on his shoulder, "You are forgiven, Captain, for your strength not your weakness. We shall all mourn young Reed. I knew him. Will you carry the news to his family? They are in Milford, in Connecticut. I had no notion that the naval impressment had become so widespread."

Markham straightened to an imposing six feet. "I shall be glad to visit the Reeds, sir." He reached into the pocket of his waistcoat, pulled out an envelope and with trembling hands, passed it to Samuel Townsend. "These are the Weymouth's papers, sir. You will find them in order. I trust you will find a suitable replacement."

"And the rest of her crew?"

"I sailed here with only ten. The others were taken yesterday from their shore leave, and now sail aboard His Majesty's Ship Panther, of 64 guns, Captain Cornwell Royal Navy, in command. He is a merciful captain. They will not suffer abuse."

Samuel Townsend took the papers. His face was white as his hair. "The Weymouth cannot go to sea?"

"Not with her present complement, sir."

"At least allow me to pen a recommendation. My brother, Peter, lives in Orange County, on the Hudson. He owns an ironworks and could give you employment."

"Thank you sir. But I shall look to more warlike employment."

"They have no ships, no navy."

"They are building, sir, smaller craft in the Chesapeake and in New England, swift privateers with sharp hulls and angled ribs. They will be very swift with less displacement and great display of canvas. They shall depend on small bore cannon and rely on seamanship and speed. I should rather captain a tiny sloop such as these and depend on the allegiance of my men, than an expensive brigantine where I have to scramble for convicts and beggars to man my ship and everyone works with an eye behind his back to look out for the impressment gangs."

Samuel walked painfully to his desk and dipped the quill in the well.

In the interval, Markham addressed Sally. "I wish you health, luck and whatever happiness can be scraped from these troubled times, Miss."

"Thank you Captain." Sally flashed her glorious smile but her heart fell. She felt the separation, an emptiness of soul like a well draining slowly, its fresh water pouring out little by little across an expanse of sand into a threatening sea. That sea was widening perceptibly and life as she knew it was marooned on the opposite shore.

Samuel handed Markham the letter of recommendation.

"Thank you and good-bye, sir." Markham folded the letter. "Good-bye, Miss." He bowed to Sally, nodded to Samuel, and walked out. The door opened. It spread a triangle of light across the floorboards, and closed again in blackness upon his back.

Samuel stood by his desk leaning on his hands, trembling. His wrinkled face reflected the loss, the shrinking of trade and civilian shipping that was his livelihood and his life. He spoke feebly. "Send for Robert. I need Robert...and his friend Rivington, if he will come. Tell Youngs to fetch them or Roe if you can find him." He sank back into his chair and closed his eyes. "The situation is serious, Sally. Without crews, our ships cannot sail. Our existence depends on the prompt delivery of goods. We will need passes and permits for safe passage, and I fear I have already alienated those to whom I need apply."

Sally's bright blue eyes burned with compassion. "Father ask Captain Simcoe to help. He is a gentleman and he is British and will know the proper channels."

"He is only a captain."

"He will try....I know."

Samuel did not open his eyes. He straightened as if he meant to rise. The effort was too great and he slumped back, diminishing, retracting his arms and legs. The muscles of his face folded one upon the other, as if some apoplexy had struck him down.

Sally rushed to his side. "Father, did you hear me? It is not sinful to ask for help. John Simcoe has helped Theo and Becca. He will help us."

"It is not sinful, but neither is it prideful. Bring me brandy, child, the French brandy to warm my innards and fortify my blood. I am old." His hands tightened like claws on the smooth arms of the chair, and he straightened visibly. "I cannot *ask* John Simcoe, child. I will beg him." With a grimace, he squared his thin shoulders and thrust his head back with haughty, aristocratic resolve.

"Father come, you must lie down." Samuel Townsend hardly heard the gentle voice of his daughter. He had gritted his teeth and closed his eyes against the pain.

Sally rubbed his cheeks and hugged him to her.

Finally, he moved woodenly to her touch. "Send for Robert. Send for him soon!"

11

If fear prevails not, still let wisdom plead,
If both are slighted, treason must succeed.

Samuel Townsend's health improved. October came and went and Robert with it. He obtained an exemption from the naval impressment for the Katherine, the Weymouth and the Promise. The landscape browned. Maples yellowed and oaks turned to scarlet. Their green leaves dried, blew up like snowflakes in the wind and collected against fences and walls that lined the borders of roads. Rain wet them down to a slippery pulp and a rime of frost polished them to the slickness of smooth ice.

Roads were treacherous. Shipping too was difficult. Late autumn brought a season of storms from out of the southern seas. They were cold coastal storms and lashed the island with fifteen foot tides and monstrous breaking waves. On good days, a ribbon of ice lined the shore. On bad days, the northeast winds from off the shores of Labrador whipped the black water of the harbor into a maelstrom.

Cattle and horses grew thick coats of hair. Huge flocks of geese flapped and honked their way south. Hordes of grey squirrels scurried to bury their nuts; chipmunks and shrews burrowed deeper in their nests to sleep. In the deep forest, wolves howled. Like animals, soldiers dug in for the winter and British frigates sailed into the protected waters of Oyster Bay.

General Howe's minions spread over Long Island as rapidly as the winter cold. The initial force under Major Fanning, had moved on to Huntington, but three times their number of Hessians and Loyalists had replaced them in Oyster Bay.

The Yager Corps, under Captain George Hangar arrived in October. They were ill-fed, dirty and undisciplined Hessians and descended upon the village like locusts, buzzing, crawling, flapping their hideous wings and devouring everything in their path. They ripped the siding from barns and churches, stole rails from fences and leveled stands of timber to build winter barracks. They broke windows, robbed stores, appropriated sheep and cattle and burned houses to extort money from those they suspected had valuables hidden. Many could not speak English. Many more pretended not to comprehend the vehement objections of the population. They set up sentry posts at each crossroads and a whipping tree for anyone who protested. The whipping tree in Oyster Bay was the stately locust in front of the Townsend home.

But the home of Samuel Townsend, residence of Captain John Graves Simcoe, remained untouched. Simcoe protested the Hessian barbarity to Major Ferguson and Ferguson relayed the complaint to Colonel Cunningham. The rumor spread that Cunningham had laughed.

The Bucks County Dragoons, Loyalist troops, Captain Thomas Sandford in command, came in November after the Yagers. These were responsible soldiers. The contrast with the Yagers was obvious. Good colonial troops from the Pennsylvania county whose name they bore, the dragoons were mounted on fine horses and the Yagers eyed them with envy and greed.

Captain Sandford of the dragoons, was an old friend of John Simcoe from Merton College. He was taller than Simcoe by a hand and older by two years. His bony face framed huge dark gleeful eyes that peered out from high arched brows and gave him a perennial look of surprise. His shoulders were narrow, his chest concave, so that his red uniform coat hung upon his bones like a drapery. To Audrey who had only known country people and unschooled colonials, whose idea of good conversation was last week's sermon and who possessed the same long gangly frame in the female version, he was eminently attractive. Even Sarah Townsend liked him and at Audrey's insistence, invited him to Sunday dinner.

Captain George Hangar of the Yagers was another kind of soldier. He was Colonel Cunningham's man. Cunningham's family had made their money in human cargo - slaves. A stocky, robust man with full rosy cheeks, blue eyes and thinning hair, Hangar had the darting, beady eyes of a veteran mercenary. He noted everything of possible value and stored the estimates in a rapacious memory. His nose filled the center of his face pushing his eyes wide apart. It was flat and bulbous with open hairy nostrils that assigned him the look of a sniffing, hungry mastiff. His chin overhung his collar and his stomach overhung his belt. His uniform was white and usually stained with the remains of his last meal or the yellow splash of beer. He drank it by the gallon and acquired it in quantity from the navy stores. He did his drinking at Wright's Tavern and began promptly at two every afternoon. But on occasion, he drank rum in the same quantities and the rum made him violent.

As an officer, Hangar enforced discipline with the stocks and whipping post. Drink dulled sensitivity to his victim's pain. In the end, he became the pawn of sycophants who used his violent outbursts to their own advantage, and of Colonel Cunningham whose cruel commands he never questioned, and hastened to obey.

His troops reflected his shortcomings. He paid from his own pocket for beer for his men. They drank without inhibition. Arguments were frequent; fist fights and swordplay, common. The village inhabitants feared the drunken rampages, closed their doors and shuttered their windows when the Yagers came to town. The British and loyalist soldiers avoided the Yagers too. The more civilized British disapproved of Hangar's offhand acceptance of plunder. They treated him with thinly veiled snobbery, like a dirty, ill-mannered servant, tolerated only for the rare occasions when they could order him to perform base duties for which they need not soil their hands.

Hangar seethed at this treatment. His resentment grew like fungus in a bog. He directed it not at the officers who could strip his commission, but at the lesser inhabitants, the farmers, the seamen and at all those from whom booty could be extracted without consequence, especially slaves.

Hangar was at the Wright's Tavern - most people called it the Ordinary - at the crossroads of South and Main Streets, when Robert Townsend rode in with Austin Roe. They were dusty and cold, and stopped for hot cider and rum before going home. They tied their horses at the hitchrail outside and sat at a prominent table near the fire. Robert placed a guinea on the table and ordered two tankards.

With a nervous glance over his shoulder, Wright swept the shiny guinea into the pocket of his apron. He had only a grunt for Robert whom he had known all his life.

Robert noticed the coldness and teased, "Where's my welcome Jeremiah Wright? Or are you withholding it for payment? And where are you hiding Mistress Betty and Mrs. Wright?" The rooms above the tavern were the Wright family's home. The hospitality of Mrs. Wright and the welcoming smiles of her daughter had always accompanied the food and drink.

"Gone." Wright's lips shut like a snapping turtle's. He didn't say where. He had sent his wife and daughter away and hired a boy to replace them. The absence of the women was obvious to all the villagers. The tables had acquired a layer of grime, the floor was unswept and Wright stumbled about spilling precious drops with the erratic motions of a hunted animal.

He signaled to the boy with the snap of his fingers, "Serve Mr. Townsend and Mr. Roe while I see to the Captain."

Robert's shiny guinea did not escape the sharp eye of Captain Hangar. He sat across the room, in his customary chair, tilted back, legs stretched and crossed in front of him, arms folded across his chest, like an insolent pupil. His chin folded double against his chest and he looked out from beneath half-closed lids. He addressed Wright in a guttural jargon that rumbled like a kettle drum, "Who are the young gentlemen dat dey are not soldiers and can pay mit gold for cider and rum?"

Wright twisted his apron into a tight coil. "Mr. Robert Townsend, son of Mr. Samuel of this village, and his friend Mr. Roe of Setauket."

"Setauket? Where is dat?

"East, sir, and north on the Sound."

"A barbarian name.... Roe? Roe is the children of the fish, no? Or did you say crow like the squawking bird? I do not know the family." Hangar lifted a shaggy eyebrow, looked at the diminutive form of Roe, wrinkled his nose and motioned an aide to go outside where the horses were tied. When he hauled his bulk out of his chair, he walked brazenly up behind Robert, ignoring Roe.

"You play dice, Mr. Townsend?" Hangar's eyes narrowed. Robert could smell his hot breath on his neck. "You play dice or Captain Hangar will mark the place where your town will end."

Robert Townsend chose to ignore the threat. "I'm sorry Captain. You are newly arrived?" He held out a hand. "We've not met."

Hangar held his tankard in his right hand; his left rested on the hilt of his sword. He made no effort to shake Robert's hand. "George Hangar, Captain, Yager Corps." His face broadened into a self-satisfied grin. "I am in charge here for de winter." He waited, staring, while Robert withdrew his outstretched palm. "You have papers, Mr. Townsend?"

Robert rummaged in the pocket of his coat. Suddenly Hangar remembered Roe, "Und you too, Mr. Crow."

"Roe, sir, Austin Roe...." Roe rolled his tongue over the syllable and removed a leather packet from his breast pocket.

Hangar examined the papers and lifted a bushy eyebrow. When he spoke, the sibilants hissed venomously from between his teeth. "I see the name of General Howe. He is an important man. You are important men, too?" The question implied explicit doubt. Hangar meant to provoke.

Robert felt his blood boil. Wright stumbled against him sloshing beer on his boots. When Robert turned to avoid him, Wright caught his arm. "Filthy beast" was all Robert could decipher from Wright's everlasting grumblings but he could not mistake the warning in his eyes.

Austin Roe moved up to Robert's side. Hangar was examining their papers. He finished, refolded them and handed them back. "Important men, you drink beer mitt Captain Hangar?" He motioned them to sit. They could not refuse.

They sat erect while Hangar tilted his chair back, resuming his almost prone position. Wright filled the tankards and the Hessian gulped his beer. Robert and Austin Roe barely sipped. The liquid soured Robert's already angry stomach.

Robert's Quaker creed flashed before him: "Whosoever shall smite thee on thy right cheek, turn to him the other also." Matthew, fifth chapter, he knew it by heart. But he could not apply the verse to Hangar. There was a brutality in the presumption of the man, in the smug assurance that his most capricious command would be instantly obeyed. Here was a man who would watch another die, and gloat. Robert's Quaker upbringing had not prepared him for a scoundrel like Hangar. He could not quench the anger in his blood. He knew in his soul that despite the Gospel of Matthew, despite all the Friends' teaching, he would resist Hangar with force if he must. For evil, he would return evil, for deceit, deceit, an eye for an eye.

"Ve have a friendly game." Hangar licked his lips. Robert muscles tensed. Hangar drew a pair of dice from his pocket. "You have guineas I see. Ve play for guineas." He set the dice in the center of the table, removed a heavy leather pouch from a breast pocket, lay it on the rough surface of the table and squeezed and released it with grimy fingers. The coins jangled noisily. "Mr. Crow, you first." He passed the dice to Austin Roe.

Austin winced. Austin Roe was not a wealthy man. He had a few paper bills and five guineas that he could not afford to lose. He looked first to Wright, then to Robert in desperation and back to Hangar. His voice pitched higher, "I am not a rich man, Captain, and my name is Roe, not Crow."

"Not rich? I see your countrymen burying silver and jewels! You are richer than George Hangar!" He hauled his bulk upright, placed his elbows on the table and fleshy palms flat over the dice. "You have fine clothes, Herr Crow, and a very fine animal." He motioned to the horse tied outside and called to his orderly. "How much for the horse, Sergeant Bayer?"

"Twenty guineas, mein captain!"

"Twenty guineas is goot price for a horse." He counted twenty guineas from his pouch and pushed them across the table to Roe. "Now you have guineas, Herr Crow." Austin Roe's face blanched. He looked about desperately. Robert gripped his arm.

The horse was worth at least fifty guineas. Austin Roe had raised the horse from a colt, weaned and trained it. It was his most valuable possession and he loved it like a brother. His voice rose shrill and strident, "Please Captain, I cannot take your guineas. The horse is not for sale."

Hangar elected not to hear. He was already addressing Robert Townsend.

"And you Herr Townsend, do you too have need of guineas?"

Robert stalled only for an instant. He choked back the outrage that flooded his breast. He reached deep into the pocket of his cloak. "No thank you, Captain. I have a supply." Slowly, he pulled out his own leather pouch, set it on the table, loosened the thong and emptied it. Guineas tumbled out in a glittering, clinking mass. Hangar's eyes bulged like a toad's. He smiled with one corner of his lip. Robert Townsend watched as open-faced greed purpled the vessels of Hangar's cheeks and his bulbous nose twitched like a hound sniffing a bitch in heat. The sound of his breathing increased to a rapid pant.

Robert pushed Hangar's twenty guineas back, away from Roe and replaced them with his own. "You will permit me, Captain, if I lend Mr. Roe fifty guineas against his horse!" The ploy was unexpected. Hangar frowned but then his grin widened - there was much more to be won than a twenty or fifty guinea horse. A covetous leer filled the bottom half of his face. He wiped his mouth on the sleeve of his coat. For an instant, he squinted at the shining gold, then opened his gaze on Robert Townsend with unmitigated loathing. Robert Townsend stared back with a face impassive as a statue. He had made an enemy.

The play commenced. Townsend and Roe lost to Hangar over and over again. With each loss, Robert felt his empty stomach heave and hatred flare higher. The dice were weighted, he was sure. He lost more than one hundred guineas. When his money ran out, there were no horses tied in front of the Wright's Ordinary. Wright had spirited them away while Hangar counted his winnings. Hangar finally fell forward over his pile, like a serpent coiled over his nest, snoring loudly in a drunken stupor. Wright motioned the two men to the back door and they fled through a field high with dry cornstalks, then threaded their way to the rear of Raynham Hall.

Austin Roe finally spoke. "I am forever in your debt, Rob. I love that mare."

Robert whispered angrily, "We cannot live like this, Austin!" His hands trembled, his voice rattled like a loose wheel, but he continued. "We are Englishmen, not pawns in the games the Hessians play! They treat us worse than beasts or slaves! This is my father's orchard and I hide here like a thief!" He slammed a fist into the tree trunk and did not wince at the pain. Gradually, he sank to a sitting position, his back against the smooth bark. His brown hair fell forward over the creases of his face and a cold sweat poured over his shoulders. When he spoke, it was to question. "You work for Benjamin Tallmadge, don't you, Austin?"

"Who told you that?"

"I watch....I remember Brewster.... I watch Cob scrape the lather from your horse. You don't let the redcoats catch you on the road...."

Austin Roe nodded. "I admit it to you Rob, but you must swear to keep my secret! Swear it by your Quaker God, Rob!"

"I do not swear, Austin."

"And I never keep secrets from those I call friend...."

After a long pause, Robert answered, "The conflicts in this war cannot match the turmoil in my soul." His black stare centered on his feet. He could not look Austin Roe in the eye. "I will swear it, Austin, but only to you whom I count as brother!... I will not swear before God." Another long pause and Austin Roe counted the seconds by the sound of Robert Townsend's breathing.

"I want to join you, Austin. Tell me what am I to do."

"We meet as infrequently as possible and I do not know the names of all who are with us. That is for Tallmadge to know. For now, be one with the British, our invaders. Learn their names and units, the range of their guns and the number of their ships. You know Caleb Brewster. He will come. He will tell you... He has safe harbors the whole length of this coast and sails secretly back and forth. He will come here because the British are fortifying the west and he is looking for havens farther east to escape their blockade. You must give your word. There is no turning back."

"Brewster again, that lecher!" Robert laughed lightly. "You have my Quaker word." He grasped his friend by the shoulders, then closed his eyes and pinched the bridge of his nose where the creases marred the youthful smoothness of his face. His heart pounded and his frustration erupted. "Damn the insolent Hessian! Damn this invisible Cunningham who sends his henchman to do his cowardly work!"

"You have sworn, Robert. You needn't curse."

"Does Washington know our difficulties?"

"He knows. He relies on the news we send him - when it is able to reach him. He has difficulties of his own." He spoke softly, reverently.

Austin stood up. "Brewster will be here tomorrow or the day after. He will sail across the shallows and hide his skiff on the east bank of the cove under the hill, near Youngs' Farm. Be there!"

"Good." The single word thudded an end to conversation. Together they waited in silence for the night.

They crossed the field to the Townsend home after darkness fell. There was cold ham and cheese that Sally put out for them. They devoured it and fell fast asleep in their seats over the kitchen table.

They were still dozing when John Simcoe entered an hour later. His broad shoulders sagged and dark circles engulfed his eyes. Robert heard the clump of his boots. He was polite but distant. "Here is ham and cheese and a good madeira, Captain. You must be tired."

Simcoe sensed his reserve and answered pleasantly, "Thank you Rob, but a smile from your sister will relieve me as much. I am tired, but not very hungry."

Sally had come down to greet John Simcoe and stood directly behind her brother in the shadow of the door. She had overheard the compliment. Simcoe sensed her presence and blushed.

Robert interrupted, "Captain Simcoe, have you met my friend, Austin Roe, from Setauket?"

"A pleasure sir. Setauket, I have not visited the place. Forgive me if I seem inattentive. It has been a harrowing day." Simcoe sank into a chair and rubbed his eyes. "Hangar's men have raided the sheep meadow. They have cut the ears from the animals to eradicate the earmarks so that the owners cannot identify their own." He lowered his hands. Deep creases lined his forehead. Red tinged the whites of his eyes. "It should not have happened. The farmers are in a frenzy. My orders are to cultivate good will, to rally the loyal people to defend their lands. How can I succeed when savages like Hangar and his henchmen thieve and burn! Colonel Cunningham will not restrain them. He is no honorable Englishman! He makes enemies of our friends..." Simcoe hid his anger well. Only his tight fists and a stiffening of the jaw betrayed any emotion.

Robert looked away. Roe smiled sympathetically. But only Sally met his gaze and she could not reply. John Simcoe continued uncertainly, "Forgive me, I did not mean to burden you with my difficulties." Rising, he squared his shoulders and addressed Sally. "My difficulties are yours too. Do you understand, Miss? I did not come to cause you pain. I... We have come to bring the colonies relief... to end the violence." His voice trailed off. Sally nodded hesitantly. Robert Townsend and Austin Roe stared in stony silence. Hessians like Hangar received British pay.

Simcoe nodded to each person in turn, "I did not mean to intrude. Good night." He bowed formally, dropped his gaze and left before his frustration could pierce his iron restraint.

Robert and Austin Roe remained alone with Sally. Robert cocked his head clownishly and hissed out Simcoe's words with the same clipped consonants, the same prolonged vowels of a London habitué. It was a brutal mockery. "You must understand... Forgive me if I intrude!" His voice rose in pitch. "He brings an army of intruders! Relief will come when they leave us be and take their insatiable armies back to England!"

Sally Townsend faced her brother. "Quiet, Rob, he'll hear you! He is a guest in this house!"

"Guest? He is a spy in our home! They have sentries in our shops, in Wright's Ordinary! Let him hear! Let them all hear! They can't help but hear! This is how Britain treats her own citizens!"

He turned to face her and she struck him hard across the mouth. The blow split his lip. It bled and Sally countered, "John Simcoe asked only for our hospitality and forgiveness. It was you who treated him rudely." She turned on her heel before he could describe the insults he had suffered that night.

Austin Roe held him fast in his seat. His soft voice was steady. "Our mistreatment must not cause us to mistreat others, be they a Britisher or your own sister, Rob. We must live with them if we are to perform our calling."

"It will be a great effort, Austin. There's a blackness in my heart." He breathed deeply and Austin released his grip. Robert quieted enough to admit, "I will apologize to Simcoe in the morning."

12

Such noble death what right had he to hope
Whose odious treason merited a rope!

*R*obert Townsend did not see John Simcoe the following morning. Simcoe had already ridden off to drill his troops when Robert arose. Austin Roe roused him from a deep sleep. "Brewster is here. Dress quickly and come."

Robert jumped into his clothes and followed Roe to Quaker Rock where George Fox had preached so many years ago. It was a sacred place, a great grey presence at the edge of the mill pond, solid as the faith of Townsend ancestors. Steamy fog rose where the cool air of winter condensed over the warm surface of the water. Brewster was waiting, blowing warm breath into cupped hands. Robert Townsend almost did not recognize him. He had shaved his beard. His sharp eyes and hawk nose gave him the appearance of a bird of prey and like a bird his head rotated almost in a complete circle one way and then the other, alert, watchful. He wore a pointed dirk sheathed to the sash at his waist. The hilt of a second blade protruded from the top of his boot.

Robert greeted him eagerly. "I thought you'd left us Caleb!"

"I always come back like a fish to the home stream to spawn, to stir up the mud for our unwelcome guests. Did Austin tell you why?" Robert nodded. Brewster's voice rumbled ominously on. "There's snow in the air. The entrance to the bay is closely guarded. I came in over the spit, on the flood." The spit connecting Hog's Neck with the mainland would be dry at low tide. "I'll leave tonight on the ebb." He rolled his tongue over his lips greedily. "We need you Rob Townsend! We need your eyes and your ears! We need an observer here within the harbor of Oyster Bay and in the city. They've moored the Halifax, a frigate, 32-guns, Captain Pembroke, in the deep channel opposite Plum Point. You can't see 'er from here - the brass of 'er guns and sheen of 'er paintwork shine like jewels in the sun. No ship enters or embarks without her knowledge."

Robert glared back. "You came."

"It was not easy."

There was a pause. Brewster snuffled loudly through his beak of nose and wiped the back of his hand across his mouth. He held out his hand to Robert. "I welcome you aboard, Robert Townsend, because you are a civilian, because you can come and go without suspicion, because you are a writer and will describe accurately what you see and hear and because you have Tory friends who trust you. There are many reasons, Rob Townsend, why I am glad you are with us." The whaler's black eyes hooded over then flashed open knowingly. "The British command headquarters is here in Queen's County and in the city. Abe Woodhull watches the east. You will watch the west. Austin will relay what you observe to me at a point along the shore that he and I alone will know." He stopped to impress the two young men with the gravity of his words and stared at each in turn.

Robert glared back. He answered as he had been taught. "Townsends do not take up arms. We are neutral."

Austin Roe laughed testily. His words seemed to enhance his stature. He challenged Robert. "Were you neutral when your father went to prison? Were you neutral when Hangar cheated and lied, when the Hessians cut the ears from our sheep. I saw your temper burn when John Simcoe complimented your sister?... You are one of us, Rob Townsend! I know it! You know it! Caleb here will know it soon enough!"

Brewster asked again, "Are you with us Rob?"

Robert Townsend felt his chest fill and the blood rush to his head. He reacted instinctively. "Yes, but it is a fearful decision I make!"

"That we have all made." Austin Roe clapped him on the shoulder and turned to Brewster. "Brewster, you know Setauket Harbor, Strong's Neck, Conscience Bay?"

"I know it." He hid his expression beneath thick hooded eyelids.

Roe was insistent. "I can assure you safe harbor there. The Strongs and the Woodhulls are my cousins. They would cooperate with enthusiasm."

Robert finally spoke up, "Abraham Woodhull is my friend."

Caleb Brewster lifted an eyebrow. A thin smile barely disturbed the narrow lips. He unsheathed the dirk and stroked its blade. "Abraham Woodhull is with us because of what happened to his father. Like him, you are with us because of what you have seen and heard and felt. You will risk your lives. Nathaniel Woodhull is dead. He was struck down in the act of surrendering his sword."

Silence. Brewster fingered the point of his knife, flipped it to grasp the handle and tossed it with a thud into the earth. The action was decisive, as were his words. "This hand shall gut the Brit that killed him."

Dapper little Roe protested. "With your permission sir, I will avenge the death of my uncle."

Brewster said nothing. His eyes flashed open for a brief second to take the measure of his two companions. He bent to retrieve his knife. "You're sure you're with us, Robert Townsend?"

"Yes."

Brewster ran his blade over his bare palm and turned to Austin Roe. "How well do you know Setauket Harbor?"

"I grew up on its shores." Austin Roe pushed aside some moldy leaves where the ground was soft beneath. With a stick, he outlined the shape of a mushroom in the dirt. It pictured the prominent headland of Strong's Neck. The headland was connected to the mainland by a thin causeway which carved out twin bays east and west. Both were too shallow for ocean-going ships but they were easily navigable with oared, shallow-drafted boats like whaling craft. Backwaters and swamps lined their coastlines, perfect cover for small boats and raiding parties.

Brewster grumbled impatiently. "Will you sail there with me now?"

A greenish tinge came over the face of Austin Roe, "No sir, I do not sail....I ride a horse....I sicken at sea."

The black beard quivered. Caleb Brewster valued a man for his ability to master the sea and little else. He looked away in disgust and spoke with sarcasm. "And you propose to watch the fleet in Peconic Bay...from Setauket? From the back of your horse? Better from the masthead of a stout ship! Arbuthnot is there." His tone was patronizing. "You do know who that is?"

"I do not, sir." Roe weathered the insult stoically.

Brewster wasn't finished. His superior glance withered Austin Roe. "Marriot Arbuthnot Esquire, Vice Admiral of the Blue and Commander-in-Chief of His Majesty's ships and vessels in North America. He has an impressive title and he uses it like the lash!"

"Enough, Caleb!" Robert's rebuke was sharp. "Austin and I, we are not your common brand of whaler! We know insult and injury. We have endured them continuously from the Brits and Hessians. We need not endure them from you!" He added with a conciliatory shake of his head. "I have not heard of Arbuthnot either."

Brewster writhed at the reproof and turned to Roe's drawing in the sand. "We need help from the good people who live near the shore!" He stopped to qualify his statement, "... seamen or farmers who know how to beach and hide a boat."

"Selah Strong on the neck is my uncle. He has sailed those waters all his life."

The whiskers around Brewster's mouth parted in a vague suggestion of a smile. "So, my boy Roe, you do have salt water in your veins after all! I know Selah!"

"One thing more." Roe lifted his voice. "I'll need fast horses. The 17th Light Dragoons are in Hempstead and I must outride them." The 17th was a crack reconnaissance corps, well-horsed, precision trained and fast-moving.

"You may have my bay." Good horses were scarce. The British requisitions had appropriated most of them. Those that were left, were kept in hiding.

"Your bay is too flashy, Rob. I will find a darker one, brown or black, but Brewster, here, must first find boats."

Brewster's eyes twinkled. "Then we are agreed?" He held out a callused hand to Roe. They nodded, pledged their good faith, and Austin Roe went in search of his horse.

Caleb Brewster and Robert Townsend stayed behind. "It's a hard decision for you, Rob. The Quaker creed is a light doctrine but it places heavy responsibility on a man and allows him wide latitude of freedom. For that free-dom and for the responsibilities I have always shouldered, for my boat, for the safety of my crew, I can no longer live subject to Mother England who tells me how I must conduct myself, and taxes me for her efforts to make me abide by her rules! I cut my cables and man my own rudder!"

Robert Townsend's cheek ticked nervously. He answered with a hiss. "Yes." There was a guilty excitement building in his blood and a defiance in the lift of his chin. Gradually, his lips curved upward until he grinned from ear to ear. Overhead, a jaybird screeched approval from a chestnut tree and wings smacked the frosty air as a flock of ducks flew up from the still waters of the mill pond.

Brewster placed an arm around Robert's shoulder. "We'll sing freely like that bird and flap our wings, Rob, and maybe the Brits will shoot us down, but damned if we won't come and go when we please!" His tone was infectious. "No telling your family, your lover or your handsome sister, even if she blinks her big blue eyes...." Brewster had broken into a lusty laugh. "Do I get to see Sally this trip?"

"Only from a distance, Caleb." Robert pursed his lips unconsciously in imitation of Brewster's thin smile. He liked Caleb Brewster and all his rough-ness. He knew Brewster admired Sally, idealized her in his own crude way. The big whaler was a lonely man, more afraid of his own base temptations than of any visible enemy.

Brewster leaned back and filled his chest with the cold salt spray from off the marshes. He winked suddenly, "Mainsail full and running before the wind, a ship's full sails are surer consolation that any woman's billowing skirts!"

Robert laughed out of the corner of his mouth. "With that, Caleb Brewster, I cannot agree!"

He led Brewster to the house and entered by the kitchen door. Beulah was there. "Is our English Captain home, Beulah? Brewster's here. He does not want to meet him."

Beulah did not like Brewster. He wore fisherman's boots and tracked sand and salt into her kitchen. "And the Captain don't want to keep company with a mud licker like him! But he's out, drilling his cavalry so's they can flutter like the redbirds all over the island." She laid out bread and cheese. Sally did not appear. She had gone to take bread to Joseph Cooper out on the Neck and would spend the night at Youngs' Farm visiting her friend, Peg Youngs.

Brewster perked at the mention of Sally. "Tell Sally I missed trading compliments with her!"

Beulah fired back. "Compliments! The kind of compliments I'd give a dead fish! I don't tell tales, Mr. Caleb Brewster!"

"And I do not lie, Beulah. I sorely miss the sight of a woman!" He shook his shaggy head with pretended sadness. "But none misses me except the cold wooden vixen carved on my bowsprit."

"You right there, Mr. Brewster. You'd treat your buxom bowsprit better than you'd treat a flesh-and-blood lady! I seen you carry on! Miss Sally don't want no part of you!"

"Enough!" Robert appeared in the doorway with a scroll of papers. "Clear us a place on the table, Beulah. I've a proposition for Caleb." He unscrolled a long sheaf. It was a chart of Oyster Bay harbor. He laid his index finger on a blank space between the village and the nook. "This is the shipyard, Caleb. The British are collecting huge stores of raw timber, cutting all our best trees, walnut, oak... storing canvas and rope and oakum and pitch...." He paused to see if Brewster followed. "They are vulnerable, Caleb, to any party who would sail across the shallows, like you did today....The wood is dry. So is the sawdust in the pits, and the pitch for the riggings will burn like Saint Elmo's fire.

Brewster's face lightened with pure glee. "Townsend, for a Quaker, you smell a fight like a shark smells blood!" He slapped Robert hard on the back, pulled a flask of rum from his vest, poured a capful and downed it. He offered some to Robert who accepted. The hot liquor dripped fire into his gut and stanched a budding fear. He liked Caleb Brewster and his shrewd intelligence. He admired the whaler's daring. He liked the mental exertion of cunning and the exhilaration of risk. The thought of avenging the insults that Fanning, Hangar and Cunningham had imposed upon his family and friends inspired him. And he liked to walk and ride where and when he pleased, to trade with whom he chose, to fly as free as the migrating geese.

Caleb Brewster ate his bread and cheese, drank his cider and lay his head on the table and fell fast asleep. Robert Townsend watched a dry log burn on the kitchen hearth. The fire wrapped orange tongues around the logs. Red coals crackled. Sparks jumped. He imagined the shipyard engulfed in flames, the tarred rigging raining down clumps of flaming pitch, the burning masts lighting the sky like a witch's bonfire, then come crashing down. His mind advanced from the dry lifeless wood to screams and cries for water. Would men die? He sipped his cider, settled his gaze on the sleeping whaler draped over the rough boards of the kitchen table and swallowed hard.

Beulah interrupted his thoughts. "You gonna leave him here all day?" Brewster was snoring loudly.

Robert answered gently, "Until the tide changes, Beulah. Keep him safe and warm....Please!"

Beulah shook her head and rolled her eyes. "Only for you, Mr. Robert!"

Robert Townsend anchored his fears like a leadweight, somewhere down in the bottom of his gut, but they kept popping up again like persistent corks.

When it was time to leave, Brewster rose and stretched. Sentries were out. Together, they walked the mile to the cove, away from the road through the brush. They came to a halt at the edge of a clearing, halfway up the side of the hill that rimmed the eastern shore. Robert swung his arm in a wide arc. "Take your bearings by the light in Youngs' window, there." He pointed south. "Run the boat into the shore just below us where the salt hay grows thickest."

Brewster took offense. "Don't tell me where to moor a boat and I won't tell you how to sit a horse, Rob Townsend!"

Robert glowered. "Did I tell you that they are building a fort atop the cliffs of Joseph Lloyd? There will be guns emplaced."

Brewster's expression deepened. "What range guns?"

"Eighteen pounders. They can shoot one mile."

"Only sober gunners find their mark." A wry smile molded Brewster's mouth. "It takes handspikes, crowbars and bloody human muscle to man an eighteen pounder, and a steady eye to aim one. They drink and sing until they are blind.... On the flood tide in a good mist, we will run over the shallows before they sight their guns, before they open their rum-soaked eyes." He laughed.

Robert laughed too. Caleb Brewster was one of those rare men, a natural leader, who came alive under fire. His confidence was contagious. "I've never known the gun that made you cower, Caleb, or the saber or the knife!"

Brewster's black eyes crinkled at the compliment. "You never shall."

Robert continued. "When you land, take the path beneath trees. It eases off gently downhill. Follow it west to the shipyard. Captain Youngs will supply pitch. He'll cache it here where we stand and there are more casks by the dozen in the yard.... Return by the same path or if there is diversion enough, cut out one of the enemy craft and sail away like a bloody pirate!"

Brewster's eyes danced and his white teeth gleamed through his beard. "An enemy ship! The Halifax would surely engage!" His whole body seemed to expand. He could smell the smoke, feel the heat of battle.

Robert's mind raced with him. "You would hoist British colors. The fire will provide diversion. It will be dark. They will not note your lack of proper uniforms."

Brewster was chuckling to himself. "For a lubber, you are not stupid, Mr. Townsend." From Brewster, that was high praise.

Robert continued, "Sail in downwind on an easterly, and out again on a fair reach. I know my winds and my currents, Caleb Brewster! I have sailed a boat!"

The black-eyed whaler moved his jaw from side to side and rubbed the stubble with his hand. "I could do it with fifteen men!" He gazed with new respect on Robert Townsend. "How shall I know which day to watch for Youngs?"

"I'll send word by Austin via Setauket. Carry dark lanterns and an ember. The Hessians will not awaken until the flames lick their drunken toes....and Caleb, when you see him, have a kind word for Roe. The little man takes as many risks as you."

"His size is such that it draws my fire. I was too hard on him. I will apologize." He shook his head. "Tallmadge will bless you for this!" He turned his full gaze on Robert Townsend. Sharp points of light shone from the back of his eyes.

Robert questioned. "Tallmadge?"

"Benjamin Tallmadge is Washington's chief of intelligence. You know him." Brewster's eyes narrowed suddenly. He pulled a glass from his pocket, lifted it to his eye and studied the shoreline inch by inch. Robert Townsend followed his line of sight. He sensed somehow that Caleb Brewster had jumped ahead to imagine the smoke and blast of battle.

Robert pointed. "That's Cooper's house, there on the bluff where Sally goes to feed the old recluse."

"I'll anchor east of the bluff. I know the paths."

"I'll not tell my father." Robert added, "He has aged...." He frowned when he thought of Sally. "As for my sister, she is sweet on the British Captain."

"You mean Simcoe? Surely not Sandford?"

"Yes, Simcoe. I have more than a suspicion."

"Tell her there's not a Brit alive can match the prowess of a good colonial sailor? Tell her that no lace and wig and gold braid can replace a man's courage....that 'tis the custom for the Brits to keep a wench in every port and change his heart's allegiance as oft as he changes his post! Tell her that, Robert Townsend, if she does not believe it!" It was said boldly, with passion, and Brewster threw up his hands in defense.

Robert Townsend reacted like a brother. "It's too late, Caleb. We cannot compete with laces and wigs and phaeton coaches. But if he lays a hand on her, Caleb, I'll throw his body to the sharks! For that, Caleb Brewster, you have my Quaker word." Worry lines creased Robert's brow and contorted his face like a veil of smoke over wet logs. He added wistfully, "This Simcoe is not a bad man. But for this bloody war I might even have counted him a friend."

They skidded down the steep bank to the shore of the cove. The place where Brewster had left his skiff was a quiet backwater, deep enough for boats at high tide, choked with marsh weeds and mud at low. Brewster turned to say good-bye. "I'll come again, Rob, tomorrow, to New York at Peck's Slip. I'll bring Major Tallmadge. He'll want to meet you. Good luck until then."

Robert Townsend responded softly, "God go with you, Caleb."

The whaler had the last word. "And may he go with you. I pray in all his righteous wrath, that he sinks Arbuthnot and his bloody fleet and changes the heart of your sister!"

Robert helped him push off through a thick mass of sawgrass. Brewster rowed away so quietly that Robert heard no more than the distant ripple of a fish breaking the surface of the water.

He walked back along the empty path, alert, silent, like a nocturnal denizen of the forest, ready to dash to ground at the first sound of predator. He reached the edge of the wood. A white uniformed Hessian blocked the lane. It was past curfew. Robert Townsend was a fugitive for the first time in his life. Like a cunning wolf, he skirted the hill opposite Raynham Hall and came to the kitchen door from the shelter of the orchard.

13

When he approach'd the charming Fair
A modest look, a serious air,
Concealed his sentiment.

*I*t was nearly dark. Robert crept into the house like a hunted animal. Sally and Simcoe sat at the kitchen table facing the fire that flared brightly. A candelabra illuminated the whitened walls of the room. Robert saw only two dark silhouettes, of man and woman. Sally's red hair had escaped its linen cap and hung loosely forward. The room was warm. Her shawl had slipped exposing a bare patch of arm.

Simcoe sat next to her, shoulder to shoulder. He had removed his red officer's coat and folded it neatly over a chair. His sword and belt hung uselessly over the same chair. His shirtsleeves were rolled up. He reached across to hold a book open for Sally.

Robert stopped in the doorway, hands shoved deep in the folds of his cloak, blinking as his eyes adjusted to the light. Only his face was visible where the firelight shed a eerie glow across his brow. He let his heel fall heavily on the hardwood floor.

Sally turned abruptly pulling her shawl tightly over the pale skin of her arms. "Father came home from the dock two hours ago. He sent for you, Rob... Where were you? Mother is asleep." Her voice was cold and distant.

Robert did not answer promptly, but glared at his sister with cold, appraising eyes. "John Weekes offered me a ride home in his wagon. The axle broke. We were delayed." He lied. His pupils narrowed and his nostrils flared like an executioner carrying out a sentence.

Simcoe jumped up with alarm, but it was Sally who broke the pregnant silence. She stood deliberately between them. "We are reading, Rob... Shakespeare... He portrays battles so vividly."

Robert spat his reply with a voice brittle as thin ice. "A good Quaker does not read of bloody combat nor does a lady sit with an unrelated gentleman unchaperoned!"

Sally fired back indignantly. The arch of her proud neck spelled out her resentment. "Captain Simcoe is a thorough gentleman! More than that, he is a friend, and he does not think me less a lady for wanting to better the powers of reason that the good God gave me!" She placed her hand firmly on Simcoe's arm and let it rest there. "Mother has favored Captain Simcoe with kindness and approval. You, Robert Townsend, can do as much!"

Her aggressiveness raked her brother like the tails of a whip. His usually mild blue eyes shot red. Sweat trickled down his cheeks and beaded on the rough stubble of his beard. The drops of moisture glistened in the faint light with an eerie, threatening glow.

Sally continued, "Are you sick, Rob, that you make yourself so disagreeable?... You sweat. Have you a fever?"

Robert sucked in his cheeks for control. "You are compromising your good name, Sally!" He turned his wrath on Simcoe, "And you sir, are a guest in this house! Do not betray our hospitality by seducing my sister!" A thin straight white line defined the space between his trembling lips.

John Graves Simcoe stepped elegantly around the table. With the firelight behind him, his face was dark, but there was no mistaking the indignation in his voice. "I resent your implications, sir, and I am well aware of my status in your father's house! Other members of your family and Mistress Sally have treated me with a graciousness rare in these troubled times, on these uncivilized, primitive shores." His voice slowed menacingly. "A graciousness evidently unknown to you." He paused to swallow back his anger and draw his sword from its scabbard. "I have not, will not, betray the trust that Miss Sally, Mr. Samuel and Madame Sarah have conferred upon me. It would be appropriate, sir, for us to discuss any further accusations beyond the hearing of this fair lady, if she will kindly step aside!"

Sally did not move. She pushed down on Simcoe's arm that held the sword, but she spoke to Robert. "You accuse him falsely, Rob!" And to Simcoe, "John, lay down the weapon!"

Robert glowered. His lower lip quivered on the verge of speech. Suddenly he seemed to retreat, pushing his head forward, sucking it between hunched shoulders, then drawing it down into the crevice like a tortoise. He said darkly, "I am not armed, Captain. I do not believe in armed combat."

Sally spoke with sympathy then, "Please, Rob, you are tired. You are ill." She continued trying to fill the deathly void with the sounds of her own speech. "Captain Simcoe is guest and protector or have you forgotten the conditions of father's release.... John Simcoe is the soul of discretion, a friend and a brother, like you, Rob. You have been away too long."

Her words stung Robert Townsend like the swipe of a sword against his cheek. He had not blinked an eye. Her three words "like you Rob" echoed. In his heart he screamed, "Not like me!" John Graves Simcoe was born on a different continent, bred to a different order, English-trained, English-bred and honed to a very English code of honor. But Robert suddenly realized that his sister did not need nor want the protection of a brother, that he could not provoke a duel with Simcoe without endangering his father and all the preparations he had made with Brewster and Roe. He would act with discretion and reason and great restraint, but he knew he was being replaced in his family's graces, replaced in the faith of his favorite sister, by his avowed enemy.

Gradually, his facial muscles relaxed. He wiped his mouth on the back of his hand and rubbed his hand across the front of his shirt. It was not a proper English gesture. It was crude, almost barbaric. Slowly, he straightened then bowed deeply to John Simcoe. "Forgive me, Captain. I am tired...and I am too anxious a brother."

Simcoe straightened, hesitated as if judging his sincerity and replaced his sword. He nodded regally. "Forgiven and forgotten, Robert Townsend."

Robert Townsend could not muster words to answer. Bowing again to Sally, he stammered, "Tell Beulah to bring a plate to my room." When he straightened, the two men's stares locked together. Silence defined the distance between them. Robert muttered, "Good night, Captain." and clomped up the stairs to his chamber.

Sally and John Simcoe stared after him. Never before had Robert Townsend attacked her so. Her hand rested on Simcoe's arm and she did not withdraw it. She felt a peculiar strength emanate from his taut muscles. It was strong and warm and restrained and it dispelled her fear, a fear that her own brother had instilled. She heard Simcoe's voice speaking calmly like music in the prickly air, something about trouble and suffering, but she hardly heard. He had brought comfort and order and insulation from fear. The assault had come from a member of her own family!

Gently, John Simcoe removed her hand from his sleeve but he did not release it. He held it possessively. He had turned to face her so that the firelight threw rosy streaks across the fine bones of his face. "Sally, I did not think how suggestive our conversations must appear. It is wartime and I was thinking only of some small respite for myself from the boredom and the loneliness... and of the exquisite pleasure of your company. You must forgive me."

Their eyes met and held. "John Simcoe, there is nothing to forgive. You have not offended me. Let's both forgive Rob."

Simcoe raised her hand to his lips and kissed it. "You do me great honor, Miss Sally."

Sally Townsend let her hand linger there. He brought it down slowly then released it. His head came up to meet her gaze. She covered the spot where his lips had touched, reverently, with her other hand and diverted her eyes to a shadowy corner, somewhere lower and to her right.

John Graves Simcoe took up his coat. "I will not compromise you further, miss." Retrieving his sword and his book, he turned on his heel and left the room.

The hearth fire dwindled to embers. The candles burned to pools of soft wax. Sally Townsend stood for a long while alone, her feet anchored to the spot. When Beulah came to fetch Robert's plate, Sally crept to the parlor where John Simcoe had left another volume of Shakespeare's works. She opened the book. Her fingers smoothed the yellowed pages where John Simcoe had touched. Her lips mouthed the words that he held inviolable in his heart.

Alone in his room, Robert watched a mouse nibble at his plate. Cold tears chilled his cheeks. His weakness galled him. Embarrassed, he slopped water into a bowl to wash the sweat and tears from his face. He stripped off his clothes and stood for a moment naked in cold air which seeped into every pore and deep into the marrow of his bones. Gooseflesh speckled his bare skin and he shivered. He stiffened his joints against the cold as he would steel his neck against an executioner's blade. It came to him suddenly that he was a spy in his own house, in this village. He was the unwelcome one. With each breath and motion, he lay his head upon the block. Only by deceit and cunning and constant vigilance, could he escape the executioner.

His meal congealed on its plate, an apple, thick chowder and cider, and a hard-boiled egg sliced so that the yolks glared up at him like round, suspicious eyes. He mashed them between his teeth and washed them down with the cider. He left the chowder and fruit for the mice. He lay down and slept fitfully, under a scratchy blanket, like a monk in a hair shirt doing penance for some dreadful, irrevocable wrong. Thoughts of the future rattled his every bone and fiber.

14

The lands of some great rebel he shall get,
And strut a famous Col'nel en brevet.

*I*t was late morning when Robert Townsend awoke to the scurrying of the mouse. He threw a boot at it and cursed the lazy house cats. The chowder had turned to paste and the apple had been gnawed but he ate it, dressed and descended the stairs. Beulah poured him a cup of black India tea. Voices from the parlor echoed through the walls. Sarah's voice rose peevishly over the sounds of maple logs crackling in the hearth. His mother was talking about him. "Never home, never here when he is needed, flitting around New York, dancing, cavorting with dissipated officers, common seaman and barmaids!" She did not like Caleb Brewster or Oliver DeLancey.

Samuel's voice contended softly, "Sarah, Robert is tending my accounts in the city. He minds our inventories. He oversees the routing of our ships, the maintenance of our warehouse, the meager sales in our shop. Most of all he cultivates clients and contacts and corresponds with our agents abroad. Without him our prospects would be far more grim."

"He has lost the value of two ships! He stopped at the ordinary on his way home! Sergeant Kelly saw him! And he sleeps all day when a righteous man would be hard at work! He would do well to appreciate and respect his family!" Her voice crackled with indignation.

The old man's voice rose. "He has negotiated wood and beef contracts with His Majesty's Army that may well save me from a debtor's prison....The ride from the city is long. He was thirsty. Sarah be forgiving. He is your son!"

Sarah Townsend did not take correction lightly, "Forgiving? You are no help to me, Samuel! You foment his slovenly behavior! You allow him to ignore his mother and sisters. It is as if we embarrass him in front of his snooty British friends."

Robert froze with his hand on the doorknob. He knew his mother would have liked nothing better than to acquire those same contacts and friends. Her derision stemmed from envy. Nothing his father, Sally or anyone could say would reverse her displeasure. He waited for Sally to defend him. Silence. He pushed the door open.

Samuel sat like a shriveled leaf in his armchair, stroking the silky grey cat which lay like a lap rug across his knees. Sarah did not even look in his direction. She sat patting her skirts and shifting her hefty weight in her seat. Audrey sat on her right, knitting. She smiled when she saw him. Sally was not there.

"Mother, father, Audrey...." He nodded good morning.

"It is almost noon!" Sarah barked.

Robert stood in the doorway. "Jack Rivington and Oliver DeLancey bid you regards, mother, father. And you too Audrey. Where's Sally?"

Audrey answered mildly, "It's market day... Sergeant Kelly, Captain Simcoe's orderly, is escorting her."

Robert turned to Samuel, "Father may I speak with you in private?"

Samuel motioned to Audrey who pricked her needle into her stitchery and rose agreeably. Sarah exited imperiously, exaggerating her limp and rapping her cane noisily with every scuff of foot.

Robert shuffled nervously across the room. "Tell Sally that I did not mean to insult her last night." He gripped his fingers around the leather of his belt to still their trembling.

Samuel Townsend waited. He sensed that Robert was struggling with some deep revelation, like a man overboard, groping for a float that would prevent his sinking. "Sally will be back soon. You can make your own apologies."

Robert pulled Sarah's empty armchair close and sat down. When he lifted his head, the soulful eyes wrenched his father's heart. "I must leave, father. I am not wanted here."

Samuel's sharp blue eyes returned his sad stare. "What is it, Robert?"

Robert's lips parted but no sound came. He rubbed his hands together. When he finally spoke, it was slowly, judging the configuration of each syllable, feeling its cracks and weighing its density, "I have saved us three ships, the Katherine, the Promise and the Weymouth, Captains Farley, Becket and Shaw. The others are disabled because they lack crews to sail them."

Samuel frowned. "That will cut our profits in half. What happened?"

"Some joined the rebellion. Some returned to their homes to protect their property from the invaders....The Royal Navy has impressed others...."

The old man reached for a cloth to blow his nose. "Three ships can reap an ample profit if we choose our cargoes with care. Have we His Majesty's leave to sail?"

"In writing, signed by General Howe and Joshua Loring." Suddenly Robert's eyes flashed upward to meet his father's with a searing intensity that made the older man blink. "But to sail only for the collection of forage for the British and Hessian forces, not for the West Indian trade or for London. To sail the ocean we must await a convoy to assemble, because of rebel privateers. The delay triples our time in port and reduces our profits by half. We make one voyage when we used to make three. Our profits may not cover what we need to maintain fittings and canvas and pay our crews," He stopped to breathe.... "They do not allow us any suggestion of prosperity. They want us to pay their taxes but they refuse us the ability to earn the funds! We have cooperated in every way with the authorities and still they forbid us every colonial port except New York! These bloodsuckers will impoverish us all!"

"Then we must lade only the most profitable of cargoes. The soldiers are fond of their rum."

Robert's keen blue eyes flashed in understanding. There had been restrictions before like the tax on tea, but never had the freedom to sail wherever and whenever, been so curtailed. Still it meant that the three ships would be outfitted and manned and exempt from the naval impressment. Townsend shipping interests would survive, perhaps thrive, by supplying the British army with its favored rum.

Samuel heaved a sigh and questioned further, "Is there the option of increasing trade in the future?"

"When the war is won we will be free to sail wherever." The words spat sarcastically from the side of Robert's mouth.

"Won?" The old man's eyes twinkled slightly. He observed his son intently.

Robert replied, "As the British sway increases, we will have access to all the ports which they control at a price which they will exact. If the colonials win, there will be no restrictions...." Robert recited these last words in a dull monotone which contrasted with the smoldering zeal in his eyes.

The old man searched his son's face. "What are you not telling me, my son? Are you trying to sweeten the pill for an old man? Tell me without reservation what is in your heart."

Robert wiped away beads of sweat from his face and grimaced. "It is my humble opinion, father, that our trade will profit more if the rebellion succeeds."

The old man's blue eyes twinkled. His voice burst forth like a trumpet. "Well-spoken, son! I've thought likewise for a good while!" The joy of the older man was plain.

Robert blinked from emotion and fell to his knees in front of his father who tousled his hair as he had done when he was a small boy.

Samuel's voice did not waver, "Do not reveal what I've said or what your feelings are to your mother, or Audrey or Sally and whatever else you accomplish, tell no one, trust no one. You are my son. Know that I will always trust you."

Robert Townsend no longer disguised his emotion. His voice cracked; his chest heaved, but he did not permit himself to cry. "I try, father. To trust is difficult when a man's allegiance is in doubt.... Will you give me your blessing?"

Samuel sensed the unspoken and stroked the tangled brown hair. "Is it such a dangerous thing you do, son?"

Robert's voice fell to a whisper. "Yes, sir, it is."

"You were a good and obedient lad... brave, impetuous. I trust that you are an honorable and just man. Go! Do what you must! I will talk with your sister, but I cannot appease your mother.... There is a stubbornness comes with age." Finally he added with gravity, "My blessing and God go with you, Robert."

Robert rose but did not go. "One more favor, sir, I need your horse, the big bay."

"My legs are too stiff to ride. Take him.... Care for him well. Better you than some Hessian blackguard."

Robert left before Sally returned. He rode his own dark chestnut and led the bay in tow. It was a leisurely ride along the great road to Jamaica and on up the Flatbush Road to the ferry at Brooklyn Heights. He knew the sign and counter sign and bore a letter of recommendation from General Howe in his pocket. But as he neared Jamaica and the Beaver Pond, the sky turned from blue to iron grey and thick clouds rolled in out of the north, like the smoke of battle. He wore only a light coat. From the heights over the river, in a cold wind that blew the first flakes of snow in his face, he looked back once across the devastation of Brooklyn, then across the river to the wharfs and warehouses and crude wooden buildings that formed the ugly blot of the City of New York. Fields and forests surrounded it on three sides, the river on the fourth. River and harbor were crowded with ships, forty-nine ships of the line, plus frigates, fireships, sloops, snows and brigantines. They formed a second, larger, floating city which housed enough men to triple the population of New York.

He boarded the ferry. His stomach heaved. He vomited over the side. Bareheaded, with his coat hanging wet upon his shoulders, his stomach sucking the frigid air, he shook convulsively. Fear gnawed at his heart like a hungry rat. How could Washington and Tallmadge and Brewster and Roe claim victory over so many, so powerful? How could he have been so reckless as to imagine it?

The ferry came to rest at Murray's wharf. He led the two horses down the gangplank. A Townsend ship, the Promise, 230 tons, 16 carriage guns, a dwarf among the British Navy's giants, lay to, awaiting her cargo. Farther on, the captured rebel sloop, Sutherland, in Burling's Slip rocked against the pilings. A notice posted on the bulkhead and at Grace's Tavern, announced the auctioning of the Sutherland with all cargo tomorrow, Friday, at noon, or Saturday in the event of rain. The Sutherland would bring a tidy sum to the Royal Navy coffers, part of the theft of war. Robert would be there to place his bid, if he had funds enough. He would tally the accounts tonight.

Wet snow slapped at his face like raw spit from the sky. The emptiness in his stomach cried out for food. His shaking limbs craved warmth. He mounted the brown horse and, leading the bay, proceeded down the cobbled street. He was suddenly conscious of the stares of jealous pedestrians, hurried, slant-eyed, envious glances from under shaggy brows and wide brims pulled down. He shrank from their eyes and headed quickly for the safety of DeLancey's stable.

When he returned to the darkening street, the snow began to stick and fill the cracks between the cobbles, sheeting their exposed tops with ice. Darkness was falling. A lamplighter was busy with his wick. The flame sputtered and went out. Shadows hovered in the alleys and cast the larger buildings into deep blackness. Snowflakes clung to his hair and tiny ice pellets pricked his bare cheeks. He walked toward Peck's Slip and the small house across from the warehouse. He had almost forgotten. Brewster had said he would bring Tallmadge. Brewster was not due in the city until well after dark. Robert Townsend was early.

The familiar sign of a tankard rattled in the wind over Grace's Tavern and the smell of hot chowder and the comfort of human contact lured him like a moth to a flame. He leaned his weight against the door at the same time that the keeper within pulled. He tumbled forward into the room, squinting into the brightness. A huge four foot log burned red in the wide hearth. Chandeliers, five candles each, blazed with a profusion of light in the center of each table. British soldiers were everywhere, singing, drinking, raising their mugs high in cheerful toasts to their General. A gruff voice rumbled over them, "Catch the cough and fever, Mr. Townsend! Fools go out without cloaks on a stormy day like this when a body be needing oilskins and woolens! Come in and dry out." Angus MacRae, the innkeeper, fussed over him like a mother. "Give me the wet waistcoat to dry by the fire."

Robert stamped his cold feet and handed his coat to the officious little man. "And no gloves nor hat! Hair froze to the bones of your skull, cheeks redder than a rooster's cock! Like some crazed whaler who would man a crow's nest in a gale! Shake off the snow and sit down.... DeLancey's there by the fire." He pushed Robert toward a corner table. "I've a good black ale, leg of mutton and hot steamed pudding... and I'll put the coat to dry before the fire!"

Robert stiffened at the sight of so many red-coated officers but MacRae poked him forward.

DeLancey's round face crinkled in a wide grin, "Rob, come, we're raising a glass to Washington's latest rout!" He had seen Robert enter and elbowed away the officer at his side then downed his ale and moved to make space between himself and the ocean of redcoats beside him. "How's your father? How are you? You look worse than a flea-bitten militiaman!" Peels of laughter followed the remark.

Robert felt every muscle of his face tighten. "Father's better, Oliver, thank you. I sent you a brace of partridge in appreciation for your help. I trust they arrived. And I've left two horses in your stable."

DeLancey burst into another peel of laughter, "The partridges arrived and the smell was worse than the sulphurs of Hades, but come, celebrate. Our brave general has received the Order of the Bath for his resounding victory on Brooklyn Heights! The good frigate, Rose, brought the news from London only today! She docked at noon." He signalled for ale for Robert. "My man, Tom, will treat your mounts well, have no fear." DeLancey rose, placed his massive arm around Robert's shoulders and leaned forward toward a sullen officer across the table. "Forgive me, William. I want you to meet my friend, Robert Townsend, of this city and Oyster Bay, Queens County, Long Island. Robert Townsend, may I present Provost Marshal William Cunningham.... You already know Cornelius and Jack." VanRandt and Rivington nodded pleasantly.

Robert held his face immobile. With stiff formality, he masked his fear. "Marshal, my congratulations on the success of your commander." Cunningham took his offered hand weakly and discarded it like a soiled towel. His face was flushed with the glassy good humor and red stare of a man who enjoyed strong drink.

"Cunningham!" The name suddenly struck a chord. Robert's hand tingled where the man had touched. He rubbed it unconsciously against his shirt as his recognition surfaced. Cunningham was Fanning's and Hangar's cohort and the pawn of Joshua Loring! A man of low origins, despised by the army officers, he was employed by the Ministry as Keeper of the Provost, the King's prisons, in New York. Cunningham was the man who had jailed Samuel Townsend. He was the collector of bribes and extortion. Robert Townsend sucked in his cheeks to disguise his revulsion.

DeLancey was speaking. Robert hardly heard. He sat sandwiched like a sheep between wolves, studying Cunningham. The man writhed like a snake under his stare. Cunningham was an ugly man. He was carelessly dressed in wrinkled black broadcloth coat, white shirt, and unpolished buttons. His hair was red and stringy. An ugly scar pitted the left side of his face from cheek to hairline. He was broad-shouldered, well-muscled, and squarely built, not unlike John Simcoe. But the likeness to Simcoe stopped there. Where Simcoe was healthy and tanned, Cunningham's complexion was plaster white with the rosy tinge of the heavy drinker. A puffiness swelled his nose. Wide nostrils twitched constantly like a dog smelling out his territory. The two nasal cavities filled the center of his face. His narrow chin protruded almost like a beak beneath a lipless, pincer-like mouth. But his eyes were his most frightening feature. Cunningham had angular, almost oriental, eyes, and they were blue. If they had been brown, they would have been eminently attractive in someone of darker complexion. But only the tiny dots of his pupils were dark. The liquid blue irises against the whites of his eyeballs and the pallor of his skin looked unhealthy and menacing. A young muscular mulatto, slave and bodyguard, accompanied him everywhere he went and stood behind him now.

Angus MacRae brought stewed mutton and ale. Robert cut into his slab of mutton with energy.

Cunningham eyed him coldly. "Townsend, I know your name." He snuffled as if repelled by a rotten smell, pinched snuff from a silver case and inserted it into his nose.

"It's a common name in England and in the colonies, sir."

Cunningham sneezed. "'Tis the name of peers and prime ministers." This was a referral to Charles Townsend for whom the notorious Townsend Acts were named. But the remark was barbed. Cunningham was a snob. He deliberately exalted the British Townsends at the expense of Robert and the American branch of the family. Cunningham sniffed and exploded in another sneeze. Drops of moisture escaped his handkerchief and landed on the table. Angus MacRae wiped it up.

Robert swallowed his mutton and felt his appetite diminishing. He answered flatly. "The Townsends of England are distant cousins, sir. I have spent all my life here, in the colonies. I was born here."

"You are the owner of merchant ships, are you not?"

"Samuel, my father, is." Robert smelled a threat.

"And you have not enlisted in DeLancey's Brigade like VanRandt here? Are you afraid to fight, Mr. Townsend or is it that your loyalties waver?" The question was baited and Cunningham had posed his question loudly for the whole tavern to hear. Robert could not answer without incriminating himself.

DeLancey leaned forward to defend his friend. "Rob has not joined up, William, because Rob is a Quaker. Quakers frown on killing. Rob serves in other ways, by keeping his family's ships afloat to supply our every effort.... Sir Guy Carleton made him sentinel on Lower Broadway."

"A difficult and dangerous service, I'm sure." Cunningham's tongue slid derisively over the words. The mention of Sir Guy seemed to subdue him. He dismissed further defense with a haughty sniff and another pinch of snuff.

DeLancey deflected the conversation with a compliment. "I hear, Colonel Cunningham, that you are an excellent shot, both with fowling piece and musket."

Cunningham sneezed again and twitched his nose irritably. He addressed Oliver DeLancey without reference to his rank. "Mr. DeLancey, I do hit a pigeon at twenty paces. I would demonstrate but 'tis a pity to waste good powder on pigeons or for that matter even good corn." He laughed unexpectedly and DeLancey and Van Randt laughed with him in an effort to defuse the tension. "Corn is for the chickens that we eat. Pigeons await their bullets. Stupid birds, hanging would better suit them....Easier and less costly to let them sit and starve." Cunningham touched his napkin daintily to his lips. His face pinched together as he picked a bone from his teeth. "Don't you hate pigeons, Mr. DeLancey? They are much like these ignorant colonials. Something in the air or the soil of the continent must dement them. They soil our fair cities with their droppings and squawk if they are penned... so like their human counterparts. 'Tis a disagreeable job, imprisoning them, but so greatly necessary."

Oliver DeLancey blanched. Cunningham had not distinguished between loyalist and rebellious Americans. Many of the soldiers present were loyalist Americans. No one dared challenge him and Cunningham did not retract. He tucked his napkin into the collar of his shirt, stabbed his mutton hard with his fork, sneezed and sliced more meat.

Jack Rivington, the journalist, tried to retrieve a shred of dignity. "We are not all sots, Marshal, nor are we all like the pigeons you so aptly describe. We have our hawks and eagles...." He clapped for MacRae to bring another round of ale.

Cunningham took another pinch of snuff and turned haughtily to Rivington. "And turkeys and gaggles of cackling geese.... 'Tis a strange and uncivilized place, this America, Mr. Rivington. But the hunt is always amusing and the fairer sex seems willing enough!"

Robert's blue eyes shot cold flame. "With all due respect, sir, I do not consider *willing* a fair description of our ladies." Cunningham did not flinch. His lips curled upward. "Ladies? On these wild shores? I have yet to meet one."

Robert jerked as if to lunge at Cunningham, but DeLancey's powerful palm pinned him to the bench. Rivington held his other arm. DeLancey's voice bellowed, "You'll come to my ball, won't you, Rob, and bring your handsome sister? Perhaps Marshal Cunningham has been traveling in baser circles that he has not met any proper ladies such as your sisters, here in the colonies!"

"Ball" the word rang out irrelevantly in Robert's brain. He struggled vainly against the two powerful grips holding him down, then let his muscles slacken. Rivington whispered in his ear, "Calmly Robert, he is a powerful man!"

Robert said nothing. Finally, with a grimace, he answered DeLancey, "A ball? What ball?"

"We are planning a Yuletide ball to congratulate Lord Howe on his elevation to the Order of the Bath."

Of course I'll come, Oliver.... We must show our British comrades the hospitality and deference they so humbly demand...." He spat the words with venom. Then his tone softened. "And we must demonstrate the virtue of our members of the fairer sex." He stopped, took the measure of Cunningham and added, "Sir William evidently does not have great appreciation of their virtues!"

Cunningham reacted vaguely with another fit of sneezes. "So you have sisters, Mr. Townsend, handsome sisters?"

"I have two sisters, sir. These other men are better judges of their respective beauty." He stabbed a slice of mutton with such force that the fork stuck in his wooden plate. He pulled it out, ripped off the bite and swallowed it without chewing.

Cunningham stood up abruptly, posed with his left hand on the head of a gold-tipped cane, his right over his heart, then reached for his glass. "Gentlemen, a toast, to Sir William, Lord Howe, and to the fairest flower of colonial womanhood, Mrs. Elizabeth Loring!" And now, gentlemen, if you'll excuse me...." He motioned to his slave, "Come Richmond." Richmond responded like a trained animal.

Cunningham nodded condescendingly at Robert, "Townsend, I shall have need of supply ships. I trust we may be of use, each to the other and I await with impatience the acquaintance of your eminent sisters."

The door banged once on William Cunningham's back and blew open again on a cold gust of wind.

Angus MacRae rushed to close it. "Cold as the block ice that chokes the rivers, that one, with his haughty insolence! Drinks so's it gives him courage, then goes off to the whores every night. It's no wonder he knows no ladies! Whores at night! Wars by day! His days and nights ring to the same tune! Bargains his immortal soul! Keep your sisters away from him, Robert!"

DeLancey quipped, "Not so loud, Angus!"

Angus glanced furtively at the redcoats still remaining and sniped back, "Let them hear drunk as they are! Let General Howe hear from out of the folds of his silken bedsheets! He's a bloody philanderer and Loring, our esteemed Commissary General, is a feckless cuckold! Cunningham and his ilk will lose us the war!" More soldiers got up to leave. MacRae stood by the door with his hand out, grumbling. "And they expect us to house and feed them! Never an ounce of gratitude like I was a slave in bondage! The good colonials at least leave me a farthing!" DeLancey handed him a guinea. The echoes of insult still prickled the air, and settled softly on the surfaces around them.

DeLancey broke the pall. "The 20th, four days before Christmas is the ball, Rob, at the Manor. Lord Howe, will be guest of honor. Bring both your sisters...and I apologize for Cunningham. I have written to Lord Germain to request his recall."

"Did you invite Cunningham to the ball?"

Jack Rivington corrected him. "Marshal Cunningham. He has a title. Oliver had to invite him...."

DeLancey lowered his voice. "I'd as soon seat him with the rats in the pantry but he will arrive with a train of fawning retainers to drink my wine and devour my beef and pinch the ladies, then leave promptly in a flurry of apologies to head for the bawdyhouse... He goes there every night. He has the discretion of an stag in rut." DeLancey had lowered his voice to a whisper. He did not often display open dislike. Now he glanced derisively at the few soldiers who remained in the tavern. Angus had brought them two more pitchers of ale and one by one, they had collapsed in a drunken stupor. "Those will not win any wars."

"How comes Cunningham to be a Marshal? What is his background? I would have thought the warrior caste above his station."

"It is above him." Rivington replied cynically, "He is a civilian, but he has a royal appointment. And they say he has a brand upon his arm. Kidnapped a shipload of indentured servants and arrived in Boston in '74. Liberty boys freed the poor wretches and set upon Cunningham, dragged him face down over the cobbles.... But he escaped and has been wreaking his vengeance ever since. He is an Irish rogue and friend to Loring."

"Why do the Howe brothers tolerate him?"

"The selling of men is lucrative enterprise, Rob. I'd wager that was not the first shipload he sold. He has bought his position, paid the price. The office attracts his kind of scavenger - Keeper of the Provost, of prisons and prisoners. It's a plum for men of ambition who lack means and title and have no conscience for the sufferings of their fellows. It is very lucrative."

Two soldiers suddenly got up from their table, lifted a drunken comrade up by the armpits and headed for the door. Angus MacRae blockaded their path. "Ye owe the price of eight bottles, gentlemen."

The first in line shook his head. "Eight bottles! Are you blind, man? I counted only four!" His fellow cheered in agreement.

"I cleared away eight bottles, sir!"

"Here my good man, the cost of four bottles to you. Let the other four be the price of His Majesty's and Marshal Cunningham's benevolent protection." He tossed the coins into the sawdust on the floor. Angus MacRae had to stoop to pick them up.

Robert sopped the last of his gravy with a crust of bread and licked his greasy fingers. The departure of Cunningham had left him with an insatiable hunger. DeLancey and his friends chattered on, soldier talk of the latest weapons issued to His Majesty's troops, new muskets and cannon and longer, sharper bayonets. Angus removed plate after plate.

Finally, Robert Townsend pushed his chair back from the table. "I have loosened my belt by two holes, Angus, and my head spins from too much ale!" He stood up.

"Your waistcoat is dry and here is the melton cape I promised to keep ye from the cold. Wear it faithfully...and take a lantern, gentlemen, 'tis slippery dangerous dark and snowing heavily." Angus hung his apron, followed them out and padlocked the door.

The four friends exited together. Snow poured out of the black sky. A fierce wind blew brutally down the narrow streets. They walked huddled together, heads bent into the wind, away from the tavern, past the sentry where DeLancey showed his pass. At the head of Peck's Slip, Robert bid his friends good-bye. He stood for a moment, watching them go, then turned and staggered his way over the cobbles to number forty-one. He had eaten too much and was mildly drunk.

It was a narrow, unpretentious house, aligned shoulder to shoulder with its neighbor, two rooms deep and two stories high. Five steps led up to a landing in front of the door. Robert mounted the steps and entered. He knew the house by heart. To his right a staircase led to the two rooms under the eaves. A curtained opening in the rear wall gave way to the kitchen. Voices echoed there now. He pulled back the curtain. On the broad kitchen hearth, a fire blazed and three men sat at a table, silhouetted in the fire's glow. A single candle burned between them. He flung off the cloak, and walked toward the light. He had expected two visitors, not three.

Caleb Brewster rose from the table. "Eleven o'clock, Rob Townsend, you're late! Stewart let us in." Stewart was shopkeeper and watchman at

Townsend's warehouse.

"You told me night, Caleb. You did not assign me an hour. I was at the tavern where I met the infamous Marshal William Cunningham! The Rose brought news from London - General Howe has been knighted!" He laughed lightly from out of one corner of his mouth. "Knighted for blundering over the Brooklyn heights and snoring away the nights and days with mistress Betsy." He snickered again. "He lets Washington escape because he is dawdling with his mistress or devouring sugar cakes with Mrs. Murray, and for this he is knighted! God has blessed us, gentlemen, with the benevolent General Howe, or by now Washington and his army would have drowned in the East River!" He laughed and with a casual wave said, "The British are issuing longer and sharper bayonets, have you heard?"

"Rob Townsend, you're drunk!" Brewster gave him a gentle shove and he fell into a chair. The dark whaler continued, "How did you like Cunningham, Rob? Drake here," he motioned to the second man, "would like to kill him."

Drake had a voice that whined like steel on a whetstone. "I would like to draw my blade across the cushion of his throat." His right hand was missing the thumb. He held his gloves between the second and the third fingers and twisted them in a stranglehold. The hatred in his voice shocked Robert Townsend more than the murderous action of his hands.

Brewster and Drake fell silent and the third man spoke up. "Cunningham has requisitioned the city's sugar warehouse for use as a prison. Drake has a brother there.... He attempted to escape. Yesterday, he was sent to the hulks. You are familiar with the hulks, Mr. Townsend?"

Robert sobered suddenly. "The old ships embedded in the mud of Wallabout Bay? Yes, sir."

The third man unfolded long arms which reached almost the length of the table. His face remained in the shadows. "Cunningham needs no executioners. He withholds food and medicine and blankets from his prisoners. He nails them in at night. Cold, damp, filth and disease do his gruesome work. They all die." He stopped to emphasize the horror of his words.

Robert Townsend's mind raced backward to envision Cunningham: the cold white slant eyes; the icy pallor of the skin; the pointed chin. He understood the absence of laughter, the brutal callousness and crass insensitivity. He thought of his own father who had barely escaped, and of his father's friend, George Weekes, who had not. Weekes was dead. These were Cunningham's pigeons, no more, no less, poor frightened birds that scatter when the guns discharge. His voice was brittle when he finally spoke. "I, too, have cause to murder William Cunningham."

Brewster muttered, "Murder is the killing of a god-fearing man. Cunningham is a fiend from hell."

The third man broke in with authority. "Enough, gentlemen!" He held out a hand to Robert, "I am Benjamin Tallmadge. We have met once years ago. I know your passions well enough, Robert Townsend. Listen well! Drake here will be your immediate contact in the city. You will work with Woodhull, Roe and Dan Youngs on the island. You must learn the position, manpower, weaponry, movements etc. of the various army regiments and the ships of the Royal Navy. You must note troop composition - Hessian, British, loyalist American, other nationalities who may or may not sympathize with our cause - and the location of army and navy barracks and provisioning sites. Also the residences and habits of prominent loyalists who could be seized for exchange or held for ransom. I trust to your intelligence and observant eye."

"I shall do my best, sir."

"Your contract to transport British supplies should permit you free access and egress. Have you a pass?"

"Yes, sir, signed by Lord Howe himself."

"Good." He paused, flashed a knowing glace at each man, then proceeded on. "Between Burling and Beekman Slips there is a coffee house, The Swan. Drake here is the keeper. You will order coffee and deposit your missives once a week within the pages of the Gazette. I repeat, - order coffee if you have news. If you have no news, order cider, tea or anything else....Do you have any questions?"

Robert Townsend had none. Coffee if news; cider if none. The knowledge burned like a smoking brand into his brain. His keen mind was already sweeping ahead to the deceptions which would insure success, perhaps preserve his life for the duration of the war.

"And you Drake? Any questions?"

Drake shook his head.

He reached into his waistcoat and held out a parchment. "Remember, we do nothing to imperil our efforts.... Drake, no violence, no murdering this fiend Cunningham whatever the reason. For all of Cunningham's faults, remember, he is a predictable evil." He turned to Robert. "Townsend, you are a popular journalist. Cultivate the British and loyalists alike, the Hessian commanders, even Cunningham. Acquaint yourself with Howe, if you can, and Henry Clinton and this John Simcoe who resides in your family's house. He has a solid reputation and is slated for promotion."

"Yes sir."

"If you need stronger, more violent action or protection, you call on Drake... or Brewster if you can find him. But I repeat, under no circumstances endanger your position." His voice slowed to enunciate. The emphasis was plain. "And we must assign you a code name. I think Culper suits you?... It is a common enough name, like Drake, not likely to incriminate an innocent person. And you are a young man. We'll make that Culper Junior."

Robert Townsend's temples pounded like hammers. The man's steady bass rang in his brain, like the peal of a bell, back and forth, over and over. He looked at Drake who sat like a spider with his legs and arms gathered under him, picking the grime from under his fingernails with his good thumb, a tight coil of suppressed passion. Robert Townsend would have to stifle his passions with the same rigid control. He did not flinch. Events had rolled over him like a tide in a marsh. He answered quietly, "I will perform my part with diligence and skill to the best of my ability."

Tallmadge stood up. He was a very tall man and looked down on Robert like Moses from Mount Sinai. This giant was Washington's chief of intelligence. They shook hands eagerly.

Drake started to unfold himself in an effort to rise, but Tallmadge motioned him to stay. He continued, "You will use your own separate contacts, known only to each alone, and know there is little I can do if you are arrested?"

They each knew what to expect. A beating to extract information, interrogation, a hangman's rope and a pauper's grave in a potter's field, or worse the

Cunningham's hulks, starvation, oblivion. They were spies. They would receive no sympathy, not even an acknowledgment from the mainland.

Still Tallmadge wasn't finished. "One more matter." He rose and drew back the curtain to the front room. "Come forward, Mary."

The small form of a woman emerged from out of the darkness. At first, Robert thought she was only a girl, but when she came into the soft candlelight he could not help but notice the exquisite shape of a grown woman. Her eyes shone a deep, almost violet blue. Black curls escaped her ruffled cap and framed a face perfect in its symmetry and complexion. She was very beautiful but tiny, minute, almost fragile in size. Robert Townsend stopped breathing.

Benjamin Tallmadge's words drifted over him from the hazy periphery. "This is Drake's sister-in-law, Mary. Her Tory neighbor denounced her husband and Cunningham has condemned him to the hulks. Brigands have burned her home and cast her out upon the streets."

Drake interrupted, "Not brigands, soldiers sure as the sun rises and sets, dressed in borrowed rags, to cover the bloody scarlet of their coats."

Tallmadge continued in an icy monotone, "With winter approaching, Mary would be robbed, raped, left for dead. She could not survive in this wartime city." Robert stood with lips parted slightly, hearing but not hearing, unsure of where Tallmadge was leading. "You live quietly here, conduct most of your business in the ordinaries and coffeehouses. No one will suspect she is living with a man. I would take her with me but not in such a storm.... Will you give her sanctuary?"

"Of course." Robert did not stop to think.

"Mary will be of some help to you. Gradually let it be known that you have acquired a mistress.... They seem to be in vogue with our redcoated guests." He signaled Drake and Brewster to go. "We will use the rear door." He wrapped his long fingers around Robert Townsend's shoulder and held him at arm's length. "Townsend, good luck."

The three men ducked out. A gust of white, cold sleet sailed into the room behind them. Wind rattled the hinges but Robert held the door open until they vanished from sight, then quickly closed and barred it.

15

To this fond Swain, she did avow,
Friendship was all she could bestow,
On this her mind was bent.

When he turned back to the warmth of the room, the woman was standing in the firelight. Her presence lent a humanity and sense of companionship to the little house.

Mary Drake broke the enveloping silence. "The sleet blew in... I'll wipe the floor..."

"It will dry overnight."

"The melt will freeze when the fire dies.

Robert went for a towel. With the fire blazing, the sleet was already freezing to the floorboards. He rubbed hard.

"I have a bottle of brandy. It will warm us both." There was a queenly grace and a quiet assurance about her. Robert gazed up at her vague outline in the gloom by the door.

"Thank you." He stood up awkwardly. The floor was dry.

A bottle appeared from out of the folds of her skirt. "I saved this bottle from the flames." She brought a tin cup out from under her apron. "I have only one cup."

"There is another in the kitchen but first bring your belongings this way. You can sleep in the loft above the kitchen. It is warmest." It was the requisite offer of a hospitable host, kind but thoughtless. He started for the staircase.

She did not follow. "Please sir. I am embarrassed that I have only a small bundle. The fire and the raiders took all. I am fortunate to be alive." There was no self-pity in her voice only a quiet, apologetic pride.

"How did you come by the brandy?"

"It was the closest thing at hand when I fled. One grasps for trifles... the little luxuries from a place and time that is disappearing. Share it with me." He placed a second cup on the table. She filled it to the brim.

He gulped the brandy and felt it singe his throat.

She sipped daintily. "If you have a blanket, I shall be happy sleeping here in the kitchen by the warmth of the fire where I will not cause you trouble."

No clothing, no effects, he did not even remember her name! Then it came to him, Mary, like the Papist's virgin, but without a child, turned out of her house, like the first Christmas. Nothing and everything flooded Robert Townsend's brain, his sister, his father, war, treachery, passionate love. He could not refuse this Mary. In his confusion, he blurted out. "Tomorrow we'll buy whatever items you need."

She corrected him immediately. "No sir, not tomorrow, I must not be seen on the streets. Not so soon, but in a week or two.... My stature is such that they are sure to recognize me!"

She was right. Men would not forget easily that perfect, diminutive shape. She spoke again with a voice so soft it fell on Robert like a snowflake on sod. "I will remain indoors but I am an excellent seamstress and I can cook, wash and read and write." She was proud of that and lifted her chin.

"Yes...." Robert's own thoughts tumbled against one another like pebbles on the shore. Only vaguely had he heard what she said. There were so many contradictions. She was so delicate yet he had the impression of zealous, unbending purpose. She walked like a patrician, yet she was a pauper. She was intelligent and educated, but female. She spoke clearly and correctly like an Englishman with no shadow of colonial accent and she was a proven rebel. She reminded him of his sister, Sally.

But this woman had endured much more than Sally in her young life. Watching her, with the fire of determination shining through every pore, he thought clearly that this woman could have been the flame that fueled the man, that pushed the husband to the ever more daring actions which finally condemned him to the hulks. Clearly she was a woman worth dying for. After a long silence, he mumbled, "I suppose I should say good-night."

She tilted her head sideways and he was struck again by the straight nose, the convex curve of her lips, the soft descent of the shoulder to breast, the tantalizing curling wisps that fell gracefully over her neck. He reached out and she spoke again. "Before you go, do you have a blanket?"

His heart was burning like fire in a forge, the heat walled in and growing. He could feel his will bending, like the strip of iron that softens and bends to the mallet. He stooped to retrieve a blanket from the chest in the front room and handed it to her with a shaking hand. She was still standing in front of the fire, arms locked together beneath small rounded breasts and tucked for warmth beneath a woolen shawl. It was an image whose beauty he did not want to disturb and it engraved itself on his mind more than the strictures of Tallmadge, more than the taunts of William Cunningham and George Hangar, more even than the sad, sagging image of his father before the magistrate. He could die for this woman.

She took the blanket, wrapped herself in it and rubbed the coarse hairs of the wool against her cheeks. She raised her head defiantly, "Sir, if you hear me cry tonight, I apologize. Know it is not because of your kindness."

"Cry? You mean weep?" The thought contrasted so with her self-assurance. Robert thought incongruously of newborn infants and whimpering pups.

But her eyes held a glint of liquid about to overflow, "I have born up bravely until now, but I cannot contain the anguish I bear forever...my husband, my home, my family's heirlooms, my wedding dress... I had a little dog...." Her voice barely cracked. "But I will not bore you with self-pity. Thank you for the blanket...and for allowing me sanctuary, Mr. Townsend."

Robert turned to go. The thought of weeping, the mention of another man, even in his confusion, sent a cold resistance down the length of his spine. He wanted suddenly to escape before his own wounded emotions opened and started to bleed. He took another candle, lit it in the flame of the first, turned and walked stiffly toward the stairway to the upper rooms.

He was asleep instantly but awoke early half-conscious in the greying dawn, and heard the sound of her weeping. It was haunting and painful, like the whimpering of an orphaned animal. It tortured him like the slow turn of a screw, twisting deeper and deeper into the flesh of his soul.

He lay immobile and rigid, watching the slanting rays of light expand across the floor of his loft, from black to hazy purple to deep blue to grey. Through the gable window, he could see the roofs opposite outlined in white-crusted snow against a gunmetal sky. Winter had arrived, the penetrating, dark-ening, dead time of year. No Christmas and New Year could lighten his dread.

He turned his thoughts to DeLancey's ball and gradually a new con-sciousness came over him. He felt it in the marrow of his bones. In less than one day, this strange little woman had wrought the change in him and he recognized the thump in his chest and the swelling of strong physical desire.

But Mary was married. He did not want to fall in love, not now, not with her. If he were caught spying, he would be snatched from his perch like one of Cunningham's pigeons, drawn, plucked, quartered, sent to the cruel hulks to die. He prayed fervently that he not be caught and that he would walk away alive and free and a happy man - "With Mary... Lord help me in my distress!" He spoke the words aloud and trembled.

The dawn was still grey when he heard rumblings downstairs. He rose, dressed, and lingered on the landing. When finally he descended the stairs, she had dressed, rekindled the fire and made tea. Its sweet steam perfumed the air. Cups and spoons rested on the table and two bowls for porridge. The blanket was folded neatly over the back of the tall settle where she sat with her feet not even touching the floor.

She spoke when she heard the scruff of his boot. "Good morning, sir. I did not want to wake you. I trust you slept well?" She was smiling. The happy lines at the edge of her eyes had banished any tears.

"Very well, thank you." He lied.

"If you will show me where you store the flour...I am a good cook. And sugar for the tea?"

He lifted a crock of sugar down from a high shelf and rummaged through an empty cupboard. Some ship's biscuit encrusted with mould was all he could find. He groped for an excuse. "The mice, weevils...I am a bachelor."

Mary simply nodded, no reproach, no complaint. "The tea is hot." She poured two cups.

He wasn't listening. He shoved his arms into the sleeves of his coat, "Stewart will have flour in the warehouse."

"Drink your tea before it cools."

Tea. He really preferred sweetened coffee but sat dutifully and drank. The bitter liquid scoured his mouth like a rinsing of soap.

"I'll be back shortly?" His departure was sudden. Mary followed him to the door. Robert bounded down the icy steps across the street to the warehouse. The cold air composed his mind. At his knock, a deep growl sounded from within and a heavy weight flung itself against the door. The raspy voice was unfriendly. "Laddie be quiet! Who be there? Always the rogues come calling when a good man wants to sleep!" The barking stopped.

"Stewart, it's Robert!"

The heavy door creaked on its rusty hinges. Stewart the keeper, stepped aside and held a shaggy collie by the collar. It was warmer inside. The warehouse smelled of spice and rum and coffee and tobacco. There were barrels of flour and sugar, casks of salted pork and beef, more hogsheads of rum, shingles and log-wood, even some silk that Solomon had purchased from a China trader. Robert assembled what he needed and begged two eggs from tightfisted Stewart. He shoved a dusty bottle of the wine and another bottle of good French brandy under his cloak. Stewart let him out grumbling his loss, especially the brandy.

Breakfast that morning was better than a banquet. Mary was an excellent cook. They ate heartily, eggs, stewed apples and salted beef, biscuits with churned butter. The hot tea with brandy washed it down. At the end Mary smiled up at him. His fears vanished. He was content. He pushed his chair away from the table, to a position by the fire and fell fast asleep.

16

Unarmed we appear in every part,
And least protected at the heart.

The weather did not improve. Tallmadge came for Mary, but Mary refused to leave New York before she had made every effort to free her husband or to assure that he had food and warm clothing. She spoke of her husband often and called him Tom. Robert felt a quiet aversion to the name. A bile would rise in his stomach as if he had tasted rancid meat, whenever she mentioned the name. But he stayed with her like an insect drawn to light and did not return to Oyster Bay.

Mary questioned Robert hesitantly at first but more aggressively as the days passed, about the possibilities of sending her husband relief and effecting his escape. Robert explained patiently the hazards of approaching the hulks for any reason at all. Time had wedged the scuttled ships tightly into the slow decay of the tidal flats. At low tide, the hulls listed wildly on their keels, like jumbled markers in an old graveyard. At low tide, they could be approached only through sinkholes thick with sticky mud. At high tide, boats could sail across with the suck of the ebb and return with the next flood, but they feared the swift eddies which could wash them out to the deep Atlantic. Robert doubted that a boat-man could be found to attempt the crossing. Navy launches brought a new crop of the condemned and the meager provisions each week. The rotting food and moth-eaten blankets were lifted aboard by a giant hoist and claimed instantly by a scramble of ghostly bodies. The launches did not linger. No one lingered to console the condemned.

No free man entered there. They feared the filth, the horrendous smell of excrement and the thick miasma of the tidal flats. Worse they feared the proximity of pestilence and death. Men who supplied the hulks sickened. Few prisoners survived to fill out their sentences. A few were exchanged. Fewer still escaped. The hulks became the object of superstition and dread, a place of evil vapors, spirits and devils, a gaping mouth of the Netherworld. Prisoners were left to die, their names erased from men's lips, from all annals of the living, their fate so horrible that no one dared acknowledge their existence.

For Mary's sake, Robert Townsend made inquiries. When the ice had melted and the sky had cleared, Robert went for his horse. Ben, DeLancey's slave, frowned when he saw him. "Your horse, the one you rode in on, Mr. Townsend, can't go. The other one, the bay, kicked 'er yesterday, in the cannon bone. She'll be laid up for a month certain."

"Then saddle the bay, Ben." Austin would have to find another.

Robert's first contact was Thomas Buchanan, the wealthy New York merchant and owner of the 300-ton ship, Glasgow, who had helped to free his father. Buchanan had willingly aided Samuel who had not yet come to trial at the time. But interceding before a court on behalf of a defendant was far different from liberating a condemned prisoner of the hulks. Robert was not at all sure of his reception at Buchanan's now.

He was early for his appointment with Buchanan who sat like a Scottish laird at his desk in a small parlor with a blanket over his knees and feet resting upon an iron foot-warmer. A strapping young slave attended him and a strikingly handsome officer, unknown to Robert, sat opposite. The misses Buchanan sat demurely to one side.

"Rob Townsend, you look like you've just come from the hunt or a hot and bloody cockfight!"

Robert calmed his nerves. "Too warm today, sir, even for the cocks!" It was a lame excuse. The weather was cool.

Buchanan made introductions, "Robert Townsend, I would like to present Captain John Andre and of course you know Prudence and Felicity, my daughters....How's your father?"

Robert bowed to the ladies. "Father's well, thank you, sir, and sends you thanks and appreciation for his freedom." He bowed to the officer. "Captain Andre, I'm honored."

Andre spoke up in a deep melodious baritone. "I believe we have a mutual acquaintance, Mr. Townsend... John Graves Simcoe. He has spoken highly of you." Andre's blue eyes were lively, his handshake hearty, his manners impeccable, but Robert sensed a surfeit of friendliness. Andre was like a pup with a wagging tail, too eager to please.

Robert smiled back with deliberate openness, "Captain Simcoe is quartered at my father's home, a very amiable and personable officer and a learned man. We are proud to have him with us." That much was true. Robert turned to address the Buchanan daughters, but Andre was spouting poetry in French, by a dramatist named Corneille. The girls did not understand a word but they clearly loved the sound of Andre's voice. Andre also sketched and sang. Robert sang too, but hoarsely. He spoke fair French but could not quote poetry. Finally, Andre got up to go and the starry-eyed girls followed him from the room. They did not return. Buchanan dismissed his slave and he and Robert were left alone.

Robert began discreetly. "I am grateful, sir, as is my father, for your generous intercession with His Lordship."

Buchanan nodded. "Lord Harborough is an old friend. We were at university together."

Buchanan continued to fill the lull, "Andre is newly arrived from London, a most likeable and intelligent chap. He has the favor of the Howes, both William, our Commander-in chief, and Admiral Sir Richard." He glanced sideways at Robert. "He has spent time on the continent like yourself, Rob, and is very popular with the ladies as you can see." Buchanan plastered a pleasant grin on his face and motioned him to pull his chair closer. "You didn't come to cultivate Andre or lament his flirtations, my boy. Andre is gone now. You can talk freely."

Robert Townsend's face turned grave, "A private matter, sir, for a friend and kind lady." Buchanan lifted an eyebrow and Robert finished the sentence, "whose husband has been condemned to the hulks."

Buchanan went rigid. His breathing accelerated loudly and his voice jumped an octave. "What are you asking me, my boy?...If it is for a release or even relief of one of the condemned, you must apply to Provost Marshal Cunningham. I can do nothing. Say no more."

Robert blinked, stammered and scrambled for words but Buchanan hadn't finished. He spoke in a nervous falsetto, with trembling lips that struggled to mould themselves around the awful syllables. "Robert, my boy, I tell you this in strictest confidence. They are there to die, to rot into oblivion, the just with the unjust....I am powerless. Andre is powerless. You would have to see Cunningham or Loring at your peril." The old man began to shake uncontrollably. That he had seen the horrors, Robert had no doubt. He ended with a warning. "Do not even tell me the name!" Robert listened intently and Thomas Buchanan babbled on. "I am an old man like your father and I am devoted to my king and mother England, but I know all is not well in the motherland."

Robert Townsend felt his chest contract. Buchanan coughed and almost choked. His face turned white as snow. Robert clapped for the slave, poured a glass of brandy and held it to his lips. In a few minutes, when his breathing eased, Buchanan offered what solution he could. "There are fugitives in the swamps. You will endanger yourself. But you are a braver and younger man than I." Buchanan's voice trailed off, his eyes closed. He held up a hand and spoke weakly. "Your lady must be very beautiful....Let the husband die....Marry her yourself if you love her... and if you go to the swamps, guard yourself well. Brigands and murderers reside at every turn in the trail. Go now! Leave me be!"

Robert did not leave immediately. The old man suddenly gripped his chest in obvious pain. Robert called for Andre and the daughters but they had disappeared. The slave entered with a pitcher of water. Robert would have stayed but Buchanan screeched at him with bulging eyes, "Go on with you! Get away from here!"

Robert Townsend backed away from Buchanan, ran to his horse and trotted away through the dusty streets to the ferry across the East River. He climbed the steep cliffside where Putnam's men had fled from the British only months before. The bay horse was heaving hard at the top where Robert stopped for the first time, not so much from fatigue as from foreboding. But the sun shone brightly and the view of the harbor spanned miles. The ships of His Majesty's Navy, a vast forest of masts, crowded the waters from the tip of Manhattan to Staten Island. A despondency seized his heart as he turned from the bay toward the Flatbush Road. It led over the rolling hills where the colonial militia had fled in chaos and led to the southern inlet where the prison ships lay imbedded in the mud. They called it Wallabout Bay.

A morbid curiosity taunted Robert Townsend as he climbed the gentle hills. He eased the horse away from the road to the crest of the hills for a better look. The dense forest on the hilltop blocked his view but he was conscious of a nauseating smell, like that of masses of rotting fish. He had heard tell of fish kills when the tide turned red or brown, but they were rare and he had never seen or smelled one.

He urged the horse forward down the treacherous slope, skidding and sliding on the soft decaying leaves. A mist emanated from the earth like steam rising from a cauldron. The stench made his stomach heave. When he reached the flatland, he stopped to tie his handkerchief over his nose. The realization seized him suddenly by the throat. The smell was not of animals or their excrement. It was of the decay of human flesh.

The horse too recognized the stench and quivered nervously. The ground softened suddenly. The big animal plunged deep in mud up to his knees and lurched backward onto firmer ground where he stood with nostrils flared, ready to bolt at any provocation. Robert murmured to the horse and stroked its neck and the sound of his own voice pierced the stillness like a knife. He dismounted and led the horse back up the trail and tied it to a tree, took his glass and climbed into the branches. His hand shook violently and he almost dropped the glass but he steadied it against a limb before raising it to his eye.

Three ships lay scuttled in the tidal mud about two miles out from shore. With the glass, he could read the names, the Scorpion, the Jersey and the Good Hope. The Jersey had been a magnificent ship of the line, painted bright blue with white clouds of canvas hovering aloft, armed with two rows of gun ports and 64 guns. Robert had seen her sail down the harbor several years ago. But she had seen defeat and suffered dreadfully from shipworm and rot. There she lay, her deck tilted crazily at a 30-degree angle over the sea floor, fouled with barnacles and weed, stripped of her lines, of her canvas and of her noble mast, naked as a slave upon the block. Even her gun ports had been boarded over leaving only two tiers of holes less than a foot square and ten feet apart, the only openings to air the entire human cargo in the lower decks.

At the break of the quarterdeck, soldiers stood behind a thick barricade, their muskets set in peepholes, sights trained on the hapless prisoners in the waist. It was dinnertime. The ragged prisoners moved like so many insects swarming up and out from the hold. Some could not walk. Some, exhausted by the climb, collapsed on the lip. Others lifted or prodded these to crawl or shoved them to the side and stumbled over them. A huge copper cauldron stood over a meager fire and men were hauling containers of stagnant, salty water from out of the bay to fill the cauldron. Other prisoners were skinning rats. A jailer walked up and tossed the skins too, into the cauldron.

Robert retched, almost let go his branch and caught himself. What monster had done this? His whole being revolted at the scene yet he held on and watched, fascinated, an onlooker at an execution. He could not move. He could not find words to speak, to scream in protest. There was no one except the horse to see, to hear, to smell. A half hour later, he was still watching when guards beat back the prisoners into the filthy sewer of the hull and nailed down the iron grate as you would pen a herd of savage beasts.

When Robert Townsend climbed down, his whole body shook uncontrollably. He patted his arms and legs and ran his palms over his chest to steady himself and to prove that he was alive and what he saw was not a Satanic dream. A weakness overcame him. He stood for a moment leaning on the horse's shoulder for support, listening to it breathe, feeling the warmth and comfort of another living creature. The animal pulled away and he moved with it. He hoisted himself up onto its back and pressed his legs into its sides and moved swiftly back up through the trees. Suddenly, the animal stopped, nearly spilling Robert forward. Water had invaded good ground like so many insidious pinpricks, puddling and eddying in tiny pools. The horse refused to go on. The water was pure and Robert let the horse drink. He rinsed his own dry mouth. They slogged farther into the brush until they reached solid ground and fled as fast as their tired muscles would permit.

It was late evening when he reached the settlement at Flatbush and he decided to remain for the night. At the Inn, they knew him. Everybody knew his horse. They had bet on him and won. The big bay was among the fastest on the Jamaica track. He handed the horse to the hostler, entered and ordered a mug of ale and plate of stew. But he did not digest his food and lay awake far into the night, under a thin blanket on the hard floor. The scurvied prisoners of the hulks welled up in his dreams, pricking and prodding him into wakefulness.

As soon as dawn broke, he saddled and rode away east to the Jamaica Pike, then south again skirting the brown stubble of the plain. His head ached; his mouth was dry; his feet were numb in the cold iron stirrups. He pulled up the hood of his cloak and rode hunched over the pommel like a fugitive. Hunger gnawed at his stomach. At mid-morning, he halted and with the Jamaica swamps near on his right hand, he stopped at a gurgling spring to drink and bite into a crust of stale bread. It desiccated his mouth and lay like a log in a jam somewhere deep in his throat.

He turned south into the swamps where the road narrowed to a single muddy trace. It followed a sharp rib of land bounded on both sides by thick scrub oak, thorny locust, beach pine, and the heavy, poisoned ivy. Stems the width of a man's fist draped over the trail like snares. The horse marched bravely on, pushing aside the thick, thorny branches which closed quickly behind like an impenetrable curtain.

Robert looked for the sun above the naked branches but no sun was visible. Iron clouds wiped grey light evenly across the sky. Minutes, hours melted into oblivion. He lost all recognition of where he was going or from where he had come. Thorns tore at the animal's chest and forelegs, grabbed his own clothing and gouged deep gashes his boots. He reached up to wipe his neck, took his hand away and smelled fresh blood on his fingers.

A voice in the accent of the sea sounded suddenly from out of the denseness. "Who goes, mate?"

He hauled back on the reins. The voice was human but it baited his fear and he answered impetuously with his true name. "Robert Townsend of Oyster Bay." He bit back his words and corrected himself, "Culper...Culper Junior, tell your captain!"

"I 'ave no captain! We've no ranks - all are equals 'ere!"

Robert was about to spur the horse forward into the tangled brush when the voice spoke again. "Do ye come for pudding, mate or for an able seaman's grog?"

It made no sense. Robert did not answer and shook his head to clear his addled brain.

The voice crashed again impatiently in the silence, "I said mate, do ye crave pudding or grog?... Taste the pudding, drink the grog or deliver your wealth." Three men crawled out from the undergrowth. They were bearded and dirty. Their clothes were ragged and spotted with the oily black muck of the swamp. They had sabers sheathed in their belts and held duelling pistols pointed at the center of Robert's chest.

Robert Townsend took a guinea from his pocket and flung it to the ground. "There you see my wealth!"

The speaker did not flinch, "What use be wealth to a man who cannot show 'is face again in the blaze of sun on the deck of a square-rigged ship and feel the sting of the salt in 'is face?... Your horse is worth more than your wealth, mate and your clothes!" His henchman picked up the shining gold.

Robert's patience snapped. "That's daring speech for a grubbing thief!"

A faint light shone from the narrow eyes beneath the broad brim of a sailor's hat. The man stepped forward and seized the horse's bridle. "Aye, and too elegant a horse to risk in these wild places. He'd fill a poor man's plate or bring the price of a 32-pounder! We'd fill some hefty British graves with a 32-pounder!"

"Or leave 'em to rot in the stinking swamp!"

"Quiet, Hurley!"

Robert interrupted, "I come to seek an escape from the hulks!" He blurted the words in a high-pitched voice that peeled like a bell. He caught the reaction. It was very slight, a faint tightening of the jaw and tip of the hat's brim. Robert sat still and vulnerable, shivering with cold.

They ignored him. "That horse would pull a 32-pounder!"

Robert shouted again. "Culper Junior is my name! I come to seek the deliverance of Thomas Drake!"

The broad nose twitched and the hat's brim steadied. "Drake? He knows no Townsend or Culper."

"I come at the bequest of his wife."

They burst out laughing at that. "Tom Drake 'as a wife mates! He 'as a woman to blame for the stripes on his back and 'is days in that hellhole!" He turned back to Robert. "And do ye know the witch's name, mate?"

Robert answered, "She is a finer lady than you pirates would know! Mary, her name is Mary!"

The man grunted. The hat brim lifted. His narrow eyes met Robert's and held in challenge. "Ye waste your time on Thomas Drake. He'll not survive the week!"

Robert's thoughts raced. Mary was a widow, free to love, free to marry! The reality raced down upon him like squall clouds on a gale. Drake, dead in the hulks, dirty, starved, sick, naked, cold, his lifeless body thrown to the sharks. He could not wish that fate on any man, certainly not the husband of Mary. His lips wrapped fearsomely around the words. "How do you know?"

"Get down from the horse and come wi' me." He led off down the narrow track.

"I'll not leave my horse!"

"Then tug 'im after you mate!"

Robert Townsend pulled the bay through the thick growth. The animal inched forward, ears pricked, nostrils flared, holding each hoof above the ground tentatively, before letting it fall onto the soft decay, terrified that the spongy earth would not bear his weight. The other two men closed in behind the horse. The track became puddled and more overgrown. Finally, they turned from it completely and Robert lost all sense of direction and of time.

It grew dark. Robert smelled smoke on the damp mist before he spied dark silhouettes lurking for warmth around the fires. It was a scene out of Hades or the hell of Christian believers. Crude wooden hovels circled struggling fires. It took a moment before Robert recognized the moving shapes as human. They were distorted and thin. Their clothing hung in tatters. As he moved closer, he distinguished faces. Some were covered with blisters and sores and gazed out from the bleak grey mask of scurvy. They stared up at him from sunken, hollow eyes. Some moved unevenly, limping, with the aid of crutches, but without shoes. Some lay prone, unmoving. Others sat hovering over the fires or over the forms of their neighbors. They looked with longing at the horse. "What have you brought us, Freeman?" A tall man stepped out from what looked like a discarded officer's tent.

"Says he knows Drake, Doctor. Says he wants to deliver Thomas Drake." The two companions laughed.

"See to his horse and tell him to come in."

"Aye aye, sir." The man fingered a sharp dirk.

"Feed and water the horse, Hurley! He is a nobler creature than you! We are not thieves here!" Hurley reached for the rein, but Robert pulled it back.

"Your horse is safe, sir. Have no fear." The doctor ushered Robert into his tent.

The interior of the tent was surprisingly warm. Red coals shone in a brazier and a pot of hot liquid bubbled over them. A candle shed uncertain light across the surface of a crude table. The doctor motioned to a stool near the brazier. "Sit there, it will not rest your back but it will warm your feet." He smiled.

Gratefully, Robert Townsend sat. "I am Townsend, Culper Junior."

The doctor did not react. "Soup?... We make it with the mollusks that line the shore. It is a comfort because it is hot and nourishing. We have no spirits, no rum or stout ale." He ladled the steaming liquid into a tin cup and handed it to Robert.

"Thank you." Robert remembered he had not eaten since the stale bread early that morning. He sipped eagerly.

"Now Mr. Culper Junior, about Drake, his case is hopeless." He laughed a quiet nicker like a horse.

Robert objected. "The condition of prisoners in the hulks, sir, is not a subject for frivolity!

The doctor lifted his eyebrows. After a pause, he stated coldly, "You are not accustomed to cruelty, Mr. Culper. We are not laughing at you or at the prisoners in the hulks. We laugh at the irony of our fate. We were honorable men once. We preserve the core of that honor even now." He paused gravely and sighed. "What you ask is not possible. Thomas Drake cannot be saved, delivered, rescued or whatever miracle you want God or man to perform." He stopped to pinch the bridge of his nose and closed his eyes. When he opened them again, red blood lines flecked the whites. He continued fitfully. "We tried to rescue the man you seek last Sunday, the Lord's Day, when you would think the bloody English would permit a mission of mercy. He was to be exchanged for Murray. They gave us a whimpering idiot instead." He met Robert's gaze and then slowly anchored his eyes on the flame of the candle. "The man will be a burden to his family. He is quite mad, driven so by their beastliness. I know of no medicine to relieve the torture of his soul." He licked his thumb and index finger and pinched out the lighted wick. "Our lives are fragile, Culper, like this flame...Drake is sick." He took a brand from the brazier and relit the candle. "Drake cannot walk. If we had liberated him, he may not have endured the journey to this camp. He could in no way have endured the existence here. He will die in prison. He is most probably dead already...."

Robert stood in shocked silence, sucking his cheeks between the ivory of his teeth and staring blankly at his own hands gripped together tightly around the empty cup. The doctor elaborated further. "The laughter that you hear, my own laughter and the others', is that of desperation. Some whom you see here, have been to the hulks and back. They laugh at the capricious God who sentenced them. They deplore the beastly men who jailed them. By their deaths they condemn the men who jailed them. While they live, laughter is the only defense that God permits them or they would go mad."

"Could I see Drake, talk to him." It was his last scrap of hope.

"Not without endangering everything we have established, your whole intelligence network and our humble encampment. The hulks are unapproachable....Drake cannot be rescued. You understand." He turned up the empty palms of his hands. "I cannot put what few healthy men I have at such risk."

Robert Townsend pushed his chair away from the table. He did understand. "I should not have come." He glared at the thin candle flame. A light puff would blow it out. They sat in silence a while. A bond of sympathy extended between them like the yoke that links two oxen together to lean into the harness to drag a great weight.

Robert broke the stillness. "You are a doctor? Can I bring you clothing, food, medicines...?"

"I am no doctor although I did have some little training long ago. The men have given me that title because I try to give them some solace in their troubles, some relief from physical pain. I wipe away sweat, bathe, feed, clothe as best I can. We have no medicines."

Robert repeated. "Tell me what you need. I have a warehouse of materials that will only go to feed the British."

"No, you must not. The fighting troops need it more than we. The whaler, Brewster, he supplies us when provisions can be had or we steal from the Tories. We fish, clam, snare the ducks. You must not compromise your position."

"I stated my true name."

"Freeman will not betray you nor will his mates. We do not use real names here. He has already forgotten...." Another silence while the doctor tilted the candlestick. Hot beeswax dripped onto the table. He scratched it up and rubbed it into a tight ball between his fingers and mused. "We are all soft like the wax, for God or fate or events to mold." Suddenly his face broke into a smile, "But I am forgetting my manners....You will stay the night? It is too late to return now and too dark." He clapped his hands and boy entered and placed a tray of bread and cheese on the table and a steaming hot bowl. "Cook loves to steam pudding every night so we use the word for sign and counter sign....I regret that we have no dishes."

He passed a large wooden ladle to Robert, who hesitated in spite of his hunger.

"Eat, God gives us the fishes in the sea. We will not starve."

Robert Townsend dipped into the communal pot and ate heartily. He had completed his mission without success. Something the doctor had said was slowly seeping to the surface of his consciousness. It was about the importance of his position. He was at one with this strange man tonight, at ease with all the unfortunates in the camp. But he was no longer at ease with some of his oldest connections, no longer at ease in his own family. He chewed his bread and cheese, slurped his soup, loosened his belt and relaxed. When he had finished, he remarked simply, "Doctor, I am in your debt. I have learned much."

The doctor rose, "I pray we will prevail, for you, for these." His arm swept in a wide circle and he broke into a smile. "Ours is a great human experiment, government by such as these.... If all our visitors ate like you, we would surely starve. It is night. There is a cot. I shall wake you in the morning."

Robert Townsend slept soundly.

17

Too late perceiving in confusion,
That what he sought was all illusion.

A hard jerk awakened him in the cold gray morning. "You'd best be going, Culper. Freeman will take you to the Kings Highway." The doctor loomed over him, smelling of sweat and smoke.

Robert sat up shivering and itching from the straw and insects in his bed, but rested. He shook his head groggily. The Kings Highway wove north to Flushing where he would turn east to Jericho. From Jericho, it was a short ride to Oyster Bay. He would make his apologies to Sally, review the balance sheets with his father and return to New York by boat.

The doctor offered him cider and a thick porridge. He ate uncomfortably under the glassy stare of the fugitives. The doctor reassured him. "We are ragged but we do not starve. Hunger makes for excellent scavengers and fine fishermen!"

Freeman was waiting with the big horse saddled and eager. "Best ye lead 'im for the first mile." With a surly smirk, he struck out through the maze of branches.

He reached the Kings Highway two hours after dawn. When Robert turned to thank his guide, he had already faded like a ghost into the brush. He mounted and turned the horse northeast. A soft southerly blew at his back and rustled what brown leaves were still connected to their branches. The sun warmed his face. It was a glorious day. He dozed in the saddle. His head jerked back when the big bay came to a sudden halt.

A deep voice shouted at him and a firm hand held the bridle. Robert cleared his head. "Present your pass, man!" He had arrived at Flushing where a sentry was posted at the junction of the roads.

The sentry was British, not Hessian. Robert fumbled in his pocket for the letter from General Howe. The sentry took one glance and snapped to attention with a brisk salute.

Robert pushed the bay steadily on. There were sentries at Whitestone and Manhasset. He skirted the Hempstead Plains and came to Jericho and another sentry who was asleep at his post. He had red hair, freckles and a face red as a ripe apple. He read Robert's letter and handed it back with a sneer. Robert decided he was Irish and Papist, and therefore lax in his duties to the English tyrant.

It was noon when he arrived home and handed the bay over to Cob to cool. He hesitated at the front gate and stood staring at the facade of the house, his home, a place engraved forever in his heart. The dogs came up to greet him. On the doorstep, he bent to scratch their ears and scrape the mud from his boots. The blood rushed to his head.

Sally heard him and opened the door. "You dare come here, Robert Townsend, after the embarrassment you've caused!" She whirled and slammed the door in his face.

But the door bounced back and he caught it on the backward swing. Without thinking, he shouted after her, "Sal, I'm sorry!" She turned on him, her face white with anger. "After what John Simcoe has done to help this family! *Sorry* is a pitifully small word."

"I'm your brother. I have my pride!"

"But you have forgotten your manners! Apologize to John, not to me!"

"John?" He stopped short at the name. It was Captain Simcoe she was talking about. "Captain is the man's title! Are you so familiar now?" He did not retreat for the sake of family harmony. "Do you really think he means to treat you as a gentleman would a lady? Look at Howe! Look at Clinton! Look at Hangar! They'll populate the colonies with good Tory bastards and win the war for noble England without a fight!"

"John Simcoe is refined and restrained and he is more courteous than you, Robert Townsend!... You look and stink like a mucker!" She stared him down and walked away in a huff.

Robert watched her go. To oppose his beautiful sister now would only further exacerbate her and jeopardize his position within his own family, the position Tallmadge thought so vital. She would calm. He would approach her again in the morning. He stood for a moment absorbing the hospitality of his home, the warm fire, clean water to drink, fresh food, a bed without vermin, sisters who complained and argued, a mother who nagged. It was a good home. He loved it deeply but the admission of that love stuck somewhere in his throat. He unfastened his mud-splattered cloak, hung it on the hook in the hall and stomped into the parlor to see his mother and Audrey and blurted the only news he knew would be welcome. "The DeLanceys will hold a Yuletide Ball on the 20th."

Audrey gave a little jump. "A grand ball!"

He grumbled an answer. "Oliver requested particularly that I bring you, Audrey! And Jack Rivington has asked to have the first dance."

Sally had overheard and poked her head in the door. "Jack Rivington is an old man....You want to even accounts with me, Robert Townsend, see that Oliver DeLancey invites John Simcoe!" She spoke civilly, but with a cold edge to her voice.

"He'll invite Simcoe without my saying, Sal. The ball will celebrate the knighthood of Sir William, Lord Howe. The whole British officer corps is sure to come."

Sally's voice lightened further. "John needs to laugh, to dance and sing.... Robert, you're not listening!"

His mother was staring at him. "You smell, Robert, of the stable and the docks! Go wash!"

Robert Townsend remained silent, unsure what outbursts he would provoke and from whom. Sally pulled him around to confront her, "Robert Townsend, there is no romantic attachment between me and John Simcoe!" Such vehement denial proved otherwise.

Sarah raised her voice peevishly, "To the kitchen, Robert! Beulah will heat water and show you how to use the soap!"

Robert held up his hands in exasperation. "I must speak with father. Where is he?"

"Here." Samuel had avoided the family squabbles and entered quietly from the hallway. He sank onto the settle in front of the fire. He had overheard everything and his voice hovered in the prickly air like balm on a wound. "Don't inflame your sister, my son, and do not prejudge John Simcoe!... Mother have patience." He waited while Robert's frustration ebbed and Sarah's annoyance cooled, then continued, "Come, sit. Tell me about the fire in the city. How much did we lose?"

Robert relaxed but he did not sit down, "We were fortunate, father. The fire did not touch us, but one third of the city is in ruins. For us, business is good and will improve. The fire has increased everyone's need for goods to replace what was destroyed. We had 54 visitors in the store so far this month, only 30 the month before. We shall do better than survive. I've a contract for supplying troops signed by General Howe himself and a pass to facilitate my travels to and from the city. We may even thrive...." He added as an afterthought. "And I've hired a housekeeper at Peck's Slip."

"Good!"

The single word was Robert's only praise. He stood stiffly silent, eyes locked on his father's, hands shoved deep into the pockets of his coat. When he spoke, his words were bloodless as the dry floorboards, "The Promise, Captain Farley, docked yesterday. He should have a shipment of Tobago rum and French silk from Martinique...."

Audrey spoke eagerly now, "A silk dress for a grand ball, how decadent!" She threw her arms around Robert's neck and hugged him. "Tell Mrs. Burke I shall come to Peck's Slip next week, Rob, to fit a new gown." Mrs. Burke was the seamstress.

Robert spoke up, "Audrey, I have allotted the housekeeper yours and Sally's room."

"Why can't she sleep in the garret?"

"She's too much a lady for the garret." Too late he snapped his lips shut.

Sarah's eyes sparked. She rapped her heavy cane on the floorboards like a gavel. "Robert, who is this woman, a housekeeper who must have the finest room in the house so that your sisters cannot sleep in their own beds?"

"A good woman mother, whom the events of war have disinherited."

"Robert, ladies do not accept housing from young and single gentlemen... What is her age? How does she look?"

"She is small." He could not admit more.

His mother prodded, "Short? Small-breasted? Uneducated? What do you mean by small?"

"Mother, I cannot properly conduct our business if I have to maintain a house!"

Samuel cut in. "Enough!"

Sarah Townsend was not to be silenced. "I would like to believe, Robert, that you will not disgrace this family by hiring a harlot!"

Samuel Townsend silenced his wife with a scathing glance.

But Audrey's innocent curiosity was tweaked. "Is she pretty, Rob?"

John Simcoe walked in unexpectedly. Conversation halted. The family regrouped, forcing their antagonisms underground and walling them from this stranger's perceptions. Simcoe was thinner and paler than Robert remembered. The leanness chiseled his jaw and outlined his cheekbones, delineating the blackness of his eyes and redness of his lips. He was shyly attractive, handsome and erect.

Simcoe nodded politely, "Robert, welcome home. It's good to see you."

Robert bowed politely, and John Simcoe bowed in turn. "Captain, if I've offended you in the past, please accept my apologies."

"If I'd a sister as lovely, I would surely defend her as ardently."

"Robert, pour us a glass to celebrate your coming.... There's good port in the decanter." Samuel was truly glad to see him.

Robert's wide face opened cheerfully. He squared his shoulders, and reached for a crystal ship's decanter that rested on the table. He poured three glasses for the men only. The liquor warmed and revived him, but he remained alert and watched Sally flush under John Simcoe's steady gaze.

Samuel spoke again. "Ladies, leave us men to discuss affairs." The three men spoke of ships and armies and politics and religion. Robert was surprised at the erudition of Captain Simcoe and the deference with which Simcoe treated old Samuel. He was surprised at himself. He genuinely liked Captain John Graves Simcoe.

Townsend family discord did not resurface that night in the presence of John Simcoe. Sally masked her anger and Sarah oozed courtesy. Robert retired early and slept well.

Sally was at the door when he descended the stair late the next morning. "I go to Joseph Cooper's with bread, Rob." No more was said. She stepped past him and walked briskly down the lane. Joseph Cooper was the old widower who lived with two ancient slaves, miles from the village on an isolated spit named Cove Neck.

Robert watched her disappear. He walked to the dock intending to sail back to the city but there was no launch dockside when he arrived and the Promise was already under full sail gliding down the center of the harbor like a giant swan. He had overslept and missed the tide. He could ride to the city but his bay was tired. He could wait until tomorrow for another tide and another ship, or saddle old Horace, the plow horse, whom Simcoe had rescued from a wood wagon. Horace would not be needed until spring. The thought of old Horace and his stiff-kneed gait was not something Robert contemplated for long. He went to saddle his bay.

He was eager to escape Oyster Bay and his mother's biting tongue. By sunset, her suspicion that Robert Townsend kept a woman in New York, would spread all over the village. The rumors would ignite and blaze. There would be finger-pointing and gossip. Then the knowledge would grow old and settle like pollen in the dust. He hoped Sally's infatuation with Simcoe would likewise diminish. It was time for him to leave. Robert decided to spend the night with his brother, William, who was encamped with his unit near Hempstead. He wondered if William kept a mistress. His mother would never accuse William of such an abominable transgression. William was her perfect son.

18

Teach thee to handle with peculiar grace
The snuff-box, toothpick, and the toothpick-case.

William was glad to see him. William was the Townsend brother closest to Robert in age. As a boy, Robert, the younger, had grown faster and earlier and stood even in height with William for six years. This was a source of stiff contention in their growing years. They competed for everything, from elbow wrestling, to taffy pulls, to apple-picking, to horse races, to rowing and sailing competitions on the bay. Robert usually won and William ran crying to his mother. William was his mother's child, always neat in appearance and careful in manner; Robert was his father's. Robert preferred comfort to looks, and stark honesty to sugary politeness. William hated to get his hands dirty. Robert reveled in digging out the crawly creatures of the tidal flats and running them down his sisters' and William's backs. Sally would throw sand back in his face. William would always squirm and run home squealing and Robert would go to bed hungry.

William loved the spit and polish of the army, precision and punctuality; Robert was more spontaneous and would have chosen the exhilaration and latitude of the cavalry. Their rivalry extended to politics and religion. Robert was Quaker, a tolerant and free-thinking sect; William, like his mother who exacted perfection by threat of punishment, was a rigid New Light Baptist and lip-serving Anglican. Robert espoused the colonial cause. William was a diehard Tory.

In his youth, Robert gravitated away from William to his sister, Sally, who like himself and like their father Samuel, preferred sand worms, fish hooks and horses to powdered wigs and polished boots. But William had finally surpassed Robert in height and breadth and the rivalry had cooled if not to friendship, to familiar acceptance.

William received his brother cheerfully at a camp table in front of a well-appointed officer's tent. He affected clipped British speech. "Capital surprise, Rob! You've arrived before the rain! Have you heard, the 17th is posted here in Hempstead and Arbuthnot will winter his ships in Peconic Bay." He clapped an arm over his brother's shoulder. "Come! We must drink to civilization and the motherland with good Tobago rum!" He poured out two glasses from a crystal decanter that matched the one in the Townsend parlor. William enjoyed all the privileges of the British Army, from his powdered wig to the white kidskin gloves on his lily-white hands, and a personal valet.

Robert greeted him flatly, "Hello, William." A liveried lackey led the bay away. He entered William's carpeted tent like a hound without a pedigree, in muddy boots and wrinkled coat. He shoved his woolen mittens into the sleeve of his coat and brushed his hair from his face. William wrinkled his nose in silent disapproval which fell like a cold wet rag on the back of Robert's neck.

William closed the flap against coming rain. It was warm in the tent. A fire burned in a small brazier and William offered him more rum, a Stilton cheese, honied ham and fresh-baked bread. The bread was still warm. With large sad eyes, Robert observed his brother. William was growing fat. He could not have tolerated life in the swamps. He could not have understood why anyone would undergo danger and discomfort, probably would not ever admit that such horrors could exist under benevolent British rule. The two brothers ate heartily and drank to their mother's health, to sister Audrey's health and sister Sally's beauty, to General Howe, to Admiral Marriot Arbuthnot, to the King and Queen and the inexorable justice of British law. William was in high spirits.

Robert matched his brother glass for glass but the rum dulled and depressed him. He chose his words to flatter. "You live well, brother! Mother would be pleased."

"I have persuasive and influential friends, Rob." Robert was silent and William winked and rambled on, dropping names like pebbles in a pond. "Mrs.

Loring, that's Theo Lloyd's aunt, provided introductions. She'd speak for you too, Rob. You know that her husband is Commissary General."

Robert grimaced and choked on his drink.

"Too much rum, Rob?" William rose and pounded his brother between the shoulders. When Robert eyes stopped tearing, they resumed conversation but did not return to the subject of Loring. Soon William's eyelids began to droop and his speech slurred.

Robert's fine dinner welled up in his throat. He excused himself in time to exit the tent where he projected the whole meal of British delicacies into the colonial dirt. When he returned looking ghostly and sick and wet from the rain, William had rebounded with another glass and bellowed, "You civilians can never hold your whiskey!" His head bobbed and he held himself erect leaning on two wobbly arms propped like stiff columns against the surface of the table. His legs gave way suddenly. Robert hauled him onto his cot. An orderly led Robert to another tent and a sleeping pallet. Robert groaned his thanks, grateful to be left alone. He was cold and wet and very tired.

In the morning, he awoke before the first light. He lay in the stillness, under the warmth of a thick blanket, clear-headed, reviewing in his mind all the events of yesterday, from his own nausea, to the poverty of the people of the swamps, to the careless indulgence of the Loyalist troops and brother William, to the dangerous advent of the British fleet under Admiral Arbuthnot in Peconic Bay and the posting of the 17th Light Dragoons, a crack cavalry unit, in Hempstead. He had learned much that General Washington should know. Would the information do any good? The Continental Army was in full flight toward the Delaware. It had been retreating since the disastrous Battle of Long Island. He swallowed hard. He could never support the king after what he had seen and heard and smelled. He could never support the king because of what and who he was. At The Swan, he would order coffee and leave his news in his Gazette for Drake. Justice, and human sympathy propelled him.

A cock crowed. The encampment was stirring with the clink of pots and skillets, smoke of camp fires and the grey, undulating bodies of soldiers in the wet dawn. He sat up. He was hungry. William entered to announce the morning's breakfast. William had already shaved and dressed. His valet had powdered his wig and polished his boots. Only his red eyes and a shaking hand betrayed his intemperance of last night.

"Morning, Rob! Sun's out! A sparkling day!... A good bout of rum shake your brain and purge your gut?" His tone was so cheerful and the hour so early, Robert wanted to reach for the chamber pot and hurl it at him. Instead he groaned, "What's for breakfast?"

"Eggs, Rob, and you love them lightly fried with the yolks still runny." William liked his fried hard. "And kippers! Delicious! The Scots in the company smoke their own!"

Robert stood up and pulled on his breeches. The thought of kippers, fried in suet and heavily salted, disgusted him.

William was talking again, "I've a wash stand, warm water, mirror and razor, Rob. The razor's sharp." For William it would have to be.

Robert smirked at his brother but held his own thoughts to himself - William's cockiness did not make him right; his dandyism did not imply bravery nor did his over-confidence automatically confer victory. Robert sensed that the smugness that he perceived in his brother and in so many Britons, was a weakness. The British saw this war as a series of postures, not as a toe-to-toe fight. They wanted to protect property and maintain order and civilization. They tried to re-create England with wagonloads of trappings and retinues of servants. They sat by warm fires sipping port and rum and feasting on New York beef off silver platters stolen from the local houses. They expected their presence alone to insure victory. They ended only by exalting themselves.

Robert Townsend conceived all this in his mind while William talked endlessly on. It would be a long war. For the colonies, the longer the better. For this, he hoped fervently. He could not allow himself the luxury of doubt which could only lead to paralysing despair. He nodded occasionally to encourage William, munched his breakfast and stopped listening.

He refocussed when he realized that William was talking about himself. "Did I tell you that I have subscribed for transfer to the regular army? When we win the war, Rob, I shall be in the forefront of the colonial command - I am thinking of entering the political affray...." He paused to laugh. "I was there in Brooklyn. I saw the militia scatter! Ragged bunch of damn rascals with shovels for weapons, straw in their shoes, squawking, flapping, throwing down their muskets like a collection of tinkers and gypsies. Not a proper soldier in the lot!" He added unceremoniously, "Like you Rob - that's why you make a better journalist and I, the soldier." William thumped his chest and pushed it out like a rooster puffs his feathers.

The display sickened Robert and a knot of anger anchored in his throat. When he ate his kippers and eggs and drank his coffee, they sloshed like mud water in a sewer at the bottom of his stomach or like the foulness in the copper cauldron of the hulks. He managed to hold his breakfast down but he could not pretend his love for his brother much longer.

When he went for his horse, it was raining lightly. The groom was evasive. Finally, he explained that the horse was gone, requisitioned by a bold officer of the British Legion, one Banastre Tarleton. Tarleton had left one of his other mounts as a replacement.

William came out in the rain to explain. "You understand, Rob, the army has first priority.... The quotas... I've conveyed your bay to Captain Tarleton. Captain Tarleton is a talented officer, sure of promotion, deserves a good horse. Here is the receipt. That bay should fill father's quota for several years." William continued blithely. "You needn't worry. Tarleton is an excellent horsemen. His mounts are well cared for." He pointed to a ganted nag. "This one will carry you back and forth to New York as well as the next."

Robert seethed. He would have liked to smash his brother's teeth down his throat. He stared at the poor beast in mute rage. It was smaller than his bay by a hand and ewe-necked with only a matting of hair to hide the points of its hips and stripes of its ribs. The army had used it meanly and was discarding it. He lashed out at his brother. "You gave away my horse to curry favor for yourself!"

William answered with a careless wave of the hand. "I admit the gift will advance my opportunity for promotion."

Robert ground his teeth in fury and spat out a curse. "You are a thief, brother William! God damn you!" His own anger shocked him. William stalked off to his tent.

When he calmed, Robert examined the horse more closely. Its legs seemed clean and its hooves were trimmed. Perhaps with some oats, extra hay, a few months rest....The saddle and bridle were his own. They had left that at least. Robert mounted and left as soon as possible. He had one thought in his mind - how to get his horse back.

But he had learned much and the sky had cleared. He knew now that there was a new unit assigned to Hempstead, that Arbuthnot was in Peconic Bay, that the Loyalist cause was stupidly confident and self-serving, but also that the rebellion needed everything from optimism to fresh vegetables, to black powder, lead, horses and new shoes. Who would supply them? Who would pay? When would Washington's avalanche of retreat come to a halt? What would become of him, Robert Townsend, if the Tories won? He cursed that day. What would become of Mary? When he thought of her, his reason returned and he perceived what he would do. Like his ancestors before him, he would flee, into the anonymity of the unknown territories. He would take Mary with him and start over.

In his haste, he pushed the skinny horse fiercely through the muddy lanes and only slowed when the animal balked at Newtown Creek. He dismounted, watered the tired horse and walked it the rest of the way to the ferry. It started to rain midway across the river. He arrived wet and bedraggled at Peck's Slip at noon.

41 Peck's Slip was dismal grey in winter. Constructed of granite blocks, quarried at Rhinebeck up the Hudson, it squatted near the waterfront like a barnacle on a piling. The windows, two below and two above in front and back, were shuttered to keep out the cold. With shutters open in the clear light of summer, the house had an expansive, welcoming look, but now with shutters closed, the narrow house looked lonely and forbidding.

Robert first hailed Stewart at the warehouse which had a shed at the back. Stewart took the horse resentfully, "I run a warehouse, not a stable....Ye make a good man groom to a mute beast and an underfed mangy nag at that!" But he threw a tarp over the horse, measured out a beaker of oats and led the animal to a stall at the back filled with dry straw.

Robert bounded up the five short steps to the small square porch in front of number 41. It was locked. With shaking hands, he searched his knapsack for the key.

"Mr. Townsend, you're back so soon!"

Startled, Robert Townsend almost fell from the porch. Mary stood in the street a few yards away. Her violet-blue eyes pierced the grey dampness like the brilliance of a fine jewel. Her cheeks and nose were red from the cold. A voluminous cloak covered her from head to toe, its hood speckled lightly with glistening raindrops, its wet hem dragging across the slick cobbles. Beneath it, she carried an armload of firewood.

He avoided the one subject he knew she would ask and fell back on the comfortable codes of courtesy. "I am at your service, Mrs. Drake." He bowed. "I hope Stewart has provided everything you need."

Mary responded cheerfully, "Yes. He is a kind and generous man." She waited.

Their eyes locked momentarily and they stood in silence in the rain.

Mary was the first to look away, "Open the door, Mr. Townsend, or this wood will be too wet to burn."

Robert opened the door and stood aside to let her pass. His sleeve caught suddenly on the hinge. When he pulled it away, he bumped the logs which tumbled noisily to the floor.

Mary laughed nervously. "You've torn your sleeve."

He shut and barred the door. She threw back the hood and smiled up at him. He averted his eyes, lifted the weight of the wet wool from her diminutive shoulders, shook it and spread it over the back of a chair to dry. They gathered up the logs in silence.

"The fire needs tending." He stated the obvious.

"There is dry wood in the box."

But the box was nearly empty. Only two skinny logs and some thin bark remained, enough to rekindle the fire, but not enough to suck the moisture from wet logs. He added them to the fire anyway and stirred the hot coals. A faint flame sputtered. "I'll ask Stewart to split more wood."

"Mrs. Cockle, your neighbor, has extra. This wood I brought came from her."

"Tell her I will pay her gladly."

Her soft gaze settled upon him. "What news of my husband?"

Robert replaced the poker with a clang before answering. He blinked at the black chasm of the room behind her. His words, when they came, were dry and lifeless, like the bark in the kindling box, faint scrapings from a dead surface, not the thick, tough grain of the core. "There is no word. I think he is alive." His eyes met hers and his voice left him. He could not tell her of mad Baker, of the conditions aboard the death-ship, Jersey, but neither could he avoid her eyes.

"Is there no more. The breath of one sentence, is that all you can ascribe to him?"

He began, "I may not even be able to allow him that... He was to be exchanged but did not arrive with the other prisoners at the collection point."

"You did not speak with him?"

"No. How could I? No one can approach the ships." The syllables fell dully.

A pallor crept up from her neck to her brow. Her eyes widened visibly. Her chin rose up in defiance of grief.

He blinked to fight back moisture filling his own eyes. He placed a chair near the fire and a shawl around her, took her by the shoulders and eased her down. He stacked the wet wood in the woodbox and threw a wet log on the fire. It hissed and filled the room with a thin layer of eye-stinging smoke. "Enough smoke to disguise tears." She voiced the thought.

He took the poker, stooped low and tried to encourage the flames. Finally, he started to speak at the reluctant fire as if the wet wood would absorb his awful words like water from a sponge and fling them away up the flue with the ashes and smoke.

"Mary," He stopped at the sound of her name and stammered, Mary, no one will approach the hulks for all the guineas in the realm.... There is pestilence there.... It rages like a bonfire."

She rallied bravely, "I would steal payment if it meant his freedom." Her eyes were dry even with the sting of smoke. A thin orange flame crackled to life from the new wood.

Robert explained further, "Rumor has it that he is sick. Only God knows."

"Rumor? There is no certainty in rumor....How sick?"

He poked hard and a shower of sparks exploded up the chimney. "They say he is dying."

Her chin fell to her chest and tears welled up but she rallied again to ask, "They?"

"A partisan group, sympathizers who eke out a meager existence in the swamp...."

She closed her eyes and sat immovable as a statue. Time passed. The fire waned. Robert poked it again with trembling hands but no flame sparked. He longed to touch her, to comfort, to soothe, but he gripped the cold iron of the poker and stared at the steaming logs until his own eyes smarted. Finally, he rose to light another candle before the first went out.

When she spoke, her words drifted across the damp air like flakes of dead ash, "I knew. I think God planted the cold knowledge in my soul. Tom Drake has no air to breathe, only damp, smothering smoke. Like our fire, he is sputtering out."

A gust of wind drove the smoke back down the chimney and into the room. Robert threw open a window to scour the room of smoke. Mary shivered and gulped the fresh air avidly. "What is to become of us?

"Us?" The word echoed alarmingly in his ears. He tried to read the expression on her face but it was blurred at the edges in the soft candlelight. He repeated, "Mary, Thomas Drake will not survive."

"Yes, I understand." Her violet eyes widened with apprehension. "I am with child. I will bear the child of Thomas Drake."

Panic raced like a charger through Robert Townsend's brain. The thought was incomprehensible. He stopped to breathe, his chest heaving like a bellows. "Mary, Mrs. Drake, you know Benjamin Tallmadge. You know what he has suggested. I have let it be known that I keep a mistress.... I am a spy. If I am caught, they will hang me and bury me in a pauper's grave or condemn me too, to the hulks... like Tom Drake." He stopped suddenly. She was holding up her hand, laughing lightly at death!

"Mr. Townsend, I know who you are. You are Culper Junior. Tom Drake was one like you, conspirator, impersonator, or if you prefer, spy... I am not laughing at you. I am not rich like you, but I was brought up honorably in a good family and married to an honorable man.... Look at me now. I shall mother a bastard. I laugh at the irony of my fate. But you, Mr. Townsend, will be cock of the mark. They will think you virile and manly. You have conquered your woman!" Robert was about to protest but her sharp eyes stopped him. "Please, do not think I am accusing you. None of this is your doing. You are generous and kind and brave, Robert Townsend! But you must not expect me to grace your bed. I am not a paramour!" She glided perfectly over the French with a lilting mischief in her voice.

He stammered back in confusion, "Never! I would never demand such disgraceful service of you."

She tilted her head in silent agreement. Their eyes met. "Then we understand each other. And please, do not deny me my laughter and I shall not deny you yours." She cocked her head and added, "Mr. Townsend. You are every bit the gentleman I thought."

He shoved his hands deep into his pockets and hunched his shoulders pensively. His head came up suddenly in the wake of a new thought. "Mary Drake, have you ever acted in a play?"

Again she laughed. "I act continually, Mr. Townsend. And so do you. But I am more adept than you." She lifted her chin and paused to emphasize what she was about to say. "You see, I too am a spy. Thomas Drake has sacrificed himself for me."

"He must have loved you very much." The reply was spontaneous.

"And I loved him dearly." She said it not with sadness but with strength.

Robert fought for control while the sound of her voice reverberated in his ears. Even pregnant with another man's child, he knew he was sliding headlong into an attachment that he could not control. He sat down and gripped the rough edge of the table to steady himself.

"I want my child to bear your name, the very respectable name of Townsend. I will be proud." She lay her hand over his. Her touch rippled like a breaking wave over every nerve of his body. He nodded. He could not speak. He would dare; he would fight; he would douse the fires of hell for this woman! But could he suppress his own passion and play a lover without the spontaneity of a deep human connection? He wanted to be the very real father of this child, of more children born of Mary. He would bear the wrath of Sarah, the suspicion of Sally, the gentle admonition of his father. He would bear it all for Mary. He rose, closed the window and sat down again.

Staring at her across the table, he swallowed his words. They struggled like a animal caught in a trap, to claw their way out, but he slammed the cage shut. He could only spout denial of his true feelings. Finally, he listened to himself talk as if from a great distance, "It will be in name only, to impress the British and the neighbors that you are quite legitimately in this house. We shall have to create a story to hide your true identity...."

"You cannot conceal my identity. Look at me, Robert. Look at my size. There's not another woman who looks like me in all New York. Tell them the truth, but blame the Sons of Liberty. The brigands were dressed as such. Announce how glad I am to be delivered back into the happy British fold and I shall make a very excellent mistress." She squeezed his hand and smiled broadly. "It is a brilliant scheme that you have hatched, Mr. Townsend."

"Robert. Call me Robert... or Rob, like my sisters."

"And you must call me Mary."

19

'Twas his to comment, his to analyze,
And draw the cobweb curtain from our eyes.

*R*obert Townsend sipped his coffee slowly over a copy of Jack Rivington's Loyalist Gazette. It was mid-afternoon at the Swan. He had no word of Thomas Drake, no word of Banastre Tarleton, no word of the whereabouts of his horse. He scanned the front page of the Gazette, the lists of prisoner exchanges, the embarkations, promotions, the endless proclamations of lordly officials. He deduced troop strength and deployment and noted the inventories of captured colonial ships.

Today the Swan was quiet. Only a few patrons, a merchant and an officer or two sat around in small groups at rough circular tables. Robert Townsend sat alone, brooding over his beautiful horse. He looked at his watch suddenly, set the quarto pages of the Gazette down under his saucer and flicked a guinea carelessly onto the table. Drake bowed obsequiously. "I thank ye generous sir." Their eyes did not meet.

Weeks passed, dull weeks, impatient weeks. The British entrenched in New York City. Days, Robert Townsend began to escort Mary about the streets. Evenings, he frequented the ordinaries and coffeehouses which were the havens of the New York Tory contingent. At Grace's Tavern, he met Oliver DeLancey, who announced with a wink that Rob Townsend had hired a housekeeper. "She's more handsome than you, Angus!"

Angus MacRae, the tavern keeper, was not fooled. "You mean a softer breast where to lay his rakish head!" Angus looked down his long Scottish nose with an eyebrow raised and turned his back. But Oliver DeLancey bellowed louder, filled a tall bumper high with ale and raised it over his head. His voice echoed from the rafters. "To my esteemed friend, Rob Townsend, and to the lady of his house who commands his heart."

Marshal William Cunningham stumbled past to the door on the arm of his slave. He had overheard. His cheeks reddened in envy.

Good will heightened with the departure of Cunningham and DeLancey shouted, "Mistress Mary must come to my ball, Rob!" There were loud hoots and lusty good wishes. As the room grew warmer, they switched from ale to rum. Officers loosened their stiff collars and dribbled liquid down the fronts of their waistcoats. By midnight, Grace's was ringing with loud, lewd song and Angus was demanding payment for five gallons of rum. Robert promised Angus he would make it up from his warehouse stores. Rivington and DeLancey stumbled to rooms upstairs. Robert Townsend weaved his way home, the few blocks to Peck's Slip. Mary was already asleep but had left the door unbarred. The effect of the rum suddenly overcame him. He fell onto his bed fully clothed and slept far into the morning.

Robert Townsend met with rejection when he invited Mary to the ball. She answered, "No." with unequivocal sharpness.

Her reasoning baffled him. "I have nothing to wear. I do not want to shame you!"

Robert laughed but Mary's glance silenced him. He tried again. "My sisters have many gowns. I have silk in the warehouse to tailor one."

He met another refusal. "It is difficult enough to accept charity for necessities. I do not need it for frivolities."

December 20th, the date of DeLancey's ball, was near. All New York was talking. Wardrop's store had sold shiploads of silk brocade. Seamstresses could not keep up with orders. Marriageable daughters primped and polished. Elderly matrons discussed eligible suitors and local bachelors lamented the flamboyant competition of the British officers whose uniforms, manners and continental poise outshone even the best-looking and best-dressed colonial.

Sally arrived at Peck's Slip on a snowy afternoon, in a coach and four with John Simcoe on one arm and a selection of dresses on the other. She dismissed Mary's objections with a wave of her hand. "A loan is not charity. We will shorten the green and pinch in the waist and you shall look ravishing as a princess in a castle."

Robert left with John Graves Simcoe in the early afternoon to escape the female banter. They headed for the Swan and some strong, hot coffee. Robert deposited his missive for Drake under the very eyes of the Britisher and they trudged on together through a dusting of snow to Jack Rivington's. His print shop was a squatty building that dominated the corner of Queen and Wall Streets. It was a dark office with small windows front and rear and a plank floor that rose and fell with the contours of the earth beneath it. There was a small garden and pit behind where Rivington bred fighting cocks. A constant flow of customers, especially the cream of the officer corps, stopped by for news and company and to watch the cock fights or to announce their most recent feats of valor, hoping to advance their rank by mention in Jack Rivington's famous Gazette. For Robert Townsend, the print shop was the best opportunity in New York to collect rumors and news firsthand.

Jack Rivington worked very hard. Sometimes he toiled late into the night to produce a quarto edition every Wednesday and Saturday. Once the issue was complete, on Thursday, he conducted a cock fight. Then he left a slave in charge and settled himself at Grace's at the foot of Wall Street, to drink until his eyes started to close. He was always good company except when he drank himself into a stupor. Then his slave gathered him up to his bed where he slept until three o'clock the next afternoon. The cycle began again: fierce chaotic activity, drink, sleep.

Today was Monday. Jack was alert and there were few customers. Robert and John Simcoe watched while he set up his sticks of type, slopped the tompion in the ink and spread ink over the rows of type. Robert took up the huge iron arm of the press and swung it over the paper. Jack lowered it and retracted it again to produce the print. Robert lifted out the printed page. It was eye-straining, back-breaking, boring work and Jack Rivington tolerated it only for the constant flow of visitors.

Today's pages concerned the delivery of fodder and horses, requisitioned by quota from each village, and delivered to various points for collection. This was the responsibility of officers like John Simcoe.

Jack Rivington checked his facts with Simcoe. "The requisitions will fall hardest on the people you are sent to help, John. Fifteen thousand soldiers need wood, meat, grain, drink." Rivington's tired face was rutted and lined.

Robert interrupted, laughing derisively. "And horses. I've lost my bay. My feckless brother, Will, contributed him to one of your officers, Banastre Tarleton. Do you know him? They left me a wasted nag."

Jack Rivington shrugged. "Ask Will to get him back."

Robert Townsend laughed derisively.

Simcoe spoke up softly. "I know Tarleton. He is headstrong and ambitious. He loves a good horse but he is reasonable. If I leave now, I may even catch him at Merchants." Merchants Coffee House was only two blocks from the printshop at the foot of Wall Street. Titled officers, those with money, went there.

After Simcoe left, Rivington spoke up encouragingly, "He'll find the bay, Rob. He found old Horace."

"Old Horace is no use to them. The bay is in his prime and fast. I hear this Tarleton likes a race."

"Race horses don't win wars, Rob, too high spirited."

"They'll run him to death and break his wind or make an outlaw out of him. They've seized my property without my consent. They're proving the rebels' are right in their argument."

"Quiet Rob or you'll have us both in the gaol! The soldiers will take what they want and say they needed it and the officers will rake a tidy percentage off the top, corrupt as the Papist princes of France!" Rivington rubbed his red eyes. "Then they will shunt off the blame to the poor underpaid Hessians. I don't blame you for your resentment. But it's better than anarchy. As for your brother, William...."

"I'll never speak to him again." Robert's muscles twitched. He swung the heavy iron arm of the press violently. It slammed down under the strain.

Rivington inked his tompions. "I should have oiled the arm earlier this morning."

"I'll do it. Where's the oil?"

"On the shelf."

Robert reached for the oil but his resentment lingered. "Old Horace was rudely used. Lord Howe could at least collect enough forage to keep his animals fed."

"Replacements are too easy to obtain." Cynicism rang in Jack Rivington's voice, "They're a greedy bunch, these Brits, treat us like lackeys and expect us to cheer and wave flags and give of our livelihood until our pockets are empty and our blood runs dry. And the Sons of Liberty are no better." His lips quivered; his red eyes watered. "We will win the war and gain nothing except a quiet space to grow a little garden. We had more before it all began. In they end we will lose." Rivington turned his face away.

"Cunningham, what do you know of Cunningham?"

"Low-born, Irish, unmannerly, cruel, a snob. Insinuates himself into the good graces of the officer corps, hoping their company will bestow on him a smudge of respectability. But they hate him. They say there is a brand on the inside of his right arm. He wanted me to print a eulogy of his accomplishments as marshal. I refused. It would have been a catalogue of executions. Why?"

There was a silence. "A brand means he was imprisoned...."

Rivington shrugged. "Many men are."

"Where did our fine General unearth such a knave?"

"Our fine general has other concerns and mistrusts any officers who might overshadow him. No fear of competition from Cunningham. The king has sent us some fools for commanders." He flashed a slant-eyed glance at Robert and cautioned. "Don't repeat those last words, Rob. I will deny I ever uttered them and declare love for my king!" He reached behind the press for his flask, flung his head back and took a long swallow. The liquor made him bold. "Lord Howe should be strung from the gatepost by his dilly for all his efforts to win this war! Could stretch it long enough to wrap around his neck! Knighthood! Lord! The words connote chivalry and courage. He's no braver than a clown." Liquid dripped down Jack Rivington's chin. He rambled on, "Lord of what? Howe is Lord of another man's wife!" Rivington looked up suddenly, cognizant of his own words. "If I were to print what I feel in the marrow of my loyal bones, Cunningham would draw and quarter me!" He took the flask, emptied it down his throat and flung it hard against the iron arm of the press. It clanged to the floor. Drunk, Jack Rivington could not contain his words. His red eyes looked for sympathy. "Oh Rob, what a relief to tell the truth! Rumor says Howe is organizing an assault on Philadelphia.... If he is successful, displays some ability to command, controls his troops and his lust.... but I am despondent."

Robert Townsend's ears pricked. He dangled a bait and Rivington snapped it up. "Philadelphia is the seat of Congress, the rebellion's capital! A march on Philadelphia would produce a decisive victory!

Jack Rivington's head fell forward. His gaunt shoulders stooped. "What victory? The congress will run like a rabbit to another hole. Rob, you are a true friend and I know you would help me if ever I needed... Please." The supplication was not typical of urbane and polished Rivington. "Don't ever repeat what I am about to tell you! The capture of Philadelphia has no value. It is another extravagant and costly pose. The officer corps is corrupt and self-assured. They see no need to fight. This war is a means of enriching themselves, of advancing their position. They are all like your brother William." He corrected himself. "Maybe not Simcoe... but Cunningham dines at Grace's every night. He drinks. He talks. I listen and I want to vomit the good food I've just consumed." Rivington rose and walked mechanically into the dim rear of the cavernous room. He sank onto a crate. He muttered, "I print what flatters them. It keeps my family fed. I cannot print what I think. And I drink. The bottle is my only solace."

Suddenly, he smiled wanly and he walked back into the light. "DeLancey came here yesterday with the announcement of his ball. I will print the invitations. He knew about Philadelphia. Everyone knows. They are so smug that they are fools. Capture of Philadelphia will bring no strategic result." His mouth clamped shut. His shoulders collapsed. He reached for a second flask behind the joint of the great press.

Robert Townsend grasped his arm and pulled it away "No more, Jack." But he knew Jack Rivington would retrieve the bottle again and drink himself silly. He left the printer with a heavy heart, musing how darkly he himself despaired for Washington and Putnam and the Philadelphia Congress and thinking that the loyalists suffered a like fate. What the outcome would be, he dared not think.

Robert Townsend returned to Peck's Slip in the late afternoon to find a party going on. Mary, dressed in green silk, twirled around the parlor with Sally. The skirt spun wide in ripples that floated over the air and reflected whatever specks of sunlight still shone through the thick glass windows. The vibrant green reminded him of the great leafy canopy of summer. On Mary it contrasted brilliantly with the jet black of her curls and the violet-blue of her eyes. He forgot all about his hopelessness and his horse.

20

We'll smile, nay we'll laugh, we'll carouse and we'll sing
And cheerfully drink life and health to the King.

A few days before the ball, Robert ran to meet Captain Farley. He had just anchored at Beekman's Slip. Farley waved and shouted, "I've brought you a surprise, Rob!"

The gangplank slammed down and a tall, ungainly figure emerged. She waved frantically and walked gingerly down the gangplank on Farley's arm. It was his sister, Audrey. The presence of so many red-coated officers had improved her health. Her eyes were brighter, her cheeks fuller and pink. She would never be beautiful and would always exist in the shadow of her sister, but there was a new animation that held a quiet attraction. Audrey was shopping for a husband.

Winter arrived a few days later. A foot of snow fell overnight. It decked the trees with a frosting of white, and blanketed the lanes in an even layer filling the crevices, disguising the scum underfoot and wiping the grey-brown city clean. Where the salt spray had blown against the surfaces, a film of ice formed. It lathered the wharves, ships, and seaside buildings in a coat of glowing white. Even the river, with its mix of salt and fresh water froze quickly. When the tide rose, it washed up huge chunks of ice. When it ebbed, it left them piled haphazardly. At night, the chunks crashed violently against one another, cracking like blasts from a furnace. Ships at dockside stood immobile, wedged in aprons of ice, their hulls battered relentlessly. They would remain there for the winter, locked in an icy vise, until the spring thaw released them or until it punctured their planking and left them scuttled high up in the tidal mud, like the infamous hulks.

Sally and Robert had struck a tentative truce: John Simcoe came to visit without Robert's objection; Sally accepted Mary as part of the household. Sally and Mary eased into friendship. But neither Robert nor Sally delved the other's feelings nor criticized in any way.

Robert withdrew from all confrontation. There were moments when he stared at a speck of mud on the floor, an ember on the hearth or the vacant air, as if he had removed his soul from the company of men.

But 41 Peck's Slip was crowded. The ice locked everyone in the city. Neither Sally nor Audrey nor Robert could return home by boat. Robert devoted himself to the little household. He surprised himself by actually enjoying the sound of the chattering women. He would sit with them, by a blazing fire in the tiny front parlor and scribble the bills of lading and follow Mary with his eyes, but he spoke little.

John Simcoe visited frequently. He had seen Tarleton who, when he realized the horse belonged to a good merchant family like his own in Liverpool, and that the Townsends included a beautiful and eligible daughter, promised to restore the horse.

Tarleton brought the bay to DeLancey's stable on a cold afternoon in December. Robert was there to accept his horse and offer his thanks. Tarleton greeted him with a proud apology. "Forgive me, Mr. Townsend, but your brother, William, did not apprise me of the horse's ownership. I too should resent the loss of such a fine animal."

Robert was surprised at Tarleton's candor. "My brother William is not a horseman."

The implication that William did not know one horse from another, was damning. Tarleton understood perfectly. He nodded. "Quite." The single word came down like a curtain on any possibility of advancement for William. "I do not condone theft, Mr. Townsend, even by one's own brother."

Robert smiled. Their conversation turned to the slender difference between foraging and looting. Tarleton voiced the beliefs of his senior officer, John Graves Simcoe. But Robert sensed a cynicism. Without the intercession of John

Simcoe, Tarleton would not have returned the bay. His motives were selfish. The Tarletons of Liverpool trafficked in slaves. Tarleton would do whatever was needed to advance his career. He talked on. "Hessians loot and steal. They have no principles."

Robert sensed that he was talking about himself. And Tarleton's aversion to lesser civilians like Cunningham and Loring, was overstated like a convict whose loud protestations of innocence only served to prove his guilt.

Captain Tarleton insisted they share a mug of ale to celebrate the horse's return and pulled Robert into the nearest alehouse. When finally he left, Robert breathed relief and went to see the horse. Tarleton had taken good care of him.

DeLancey was there himself when he arrived. "Rob, I see you've found the bay! John Simcoe bring him in?"

"Ban Tarleton brought him back."

"I'm glad. Now you can celebrate Lord Howe's promotion without reservation! You're coming to the ball?"

"I shall be an enthusiastic guest!... Oliver, what do you know of John Graves Simcoe?"

The question surprised DeLancey and Robert explained further. "My sister and Simcoe...."

DeLancey bubbled at the thought. "A love match? I can see it in your eye. You should applaud her choice, my man!" He proceeded to eulogize John Simcoe. "One of the best officers in the army!" And Simcoe was the King's man to the core.

Robert had to admit that his family owed much to the man. He nodded agreeably as DeLancey sang Simcoe's praises but he thought of Sally. Sally was in love with the man. He could only stand aside and watch.

The morning of the ball dawned with a clear sapphire sky devoid of any smudge of cloud. The mercury had fallen to zero. Robert had wakened periodically to add fuel to the fire through the night. Audrey slept near him. He could hear the low rumble of her breathing.

Sally, Mary and Audrey dressed for the ball by the warmth of the kitchen fire. They banished Robert to the cold front room. He tried to read; he tried to write. He brushed and powdered his own wig with careless speed, spattering good flour across the front of his vest. In frustration, he threw the wig in a corner and queued his thick brown hair with a black silk ribbon. He was pulling on his best black coat when he heard the thump of hooves in the billowing snow.

Captain John Graves Simcoe jumped out of an elegant coach with a liveried driver and a footman whom Robert recognized as the fastidious Sergeant Kelly. Two fine horses, brushed to shining sleekness, pulled the coach.

Robert threw open the door. His voice was cordial. "Come in Captain. The ladies are nearly ready."

Simcoe entered dramatically in a wide black cape which he had flung open on the left side to expose his sword and brilliant red swath of uniform. His black knee boots shone like mirrors. He stood like a conqueror, straight and tall, with his hand draped gracefully over the hilt of his sword.

The girls emerged: Sally in pale blue silk; Audrey in Christmas red, high-necked and long-sleeved for warmth; Mary in full-skirted, emerald green. Robert's heart expanded to fill the ample cavity of his chest.

Captain Simcoe offered his arm, Sally on his right, Audrey on his left. Robert led Mary. Stewart held the door. He had shoveled and sanded the steps and now stood alert with broom at hand to scatter the last flakes of snow from their path. The horses, matched greys, snorted and their breath frosted the cold crisp air. Robert recognized the horses. They had belonged to James Lawrence who had escaped across the sound to Connecticut.

Audrey could not hide her excitement and wiggled into her seat like a distracted schoolgirl. She talked continuously to hide her tension. "Does our city compare to England, Captain, to London and the castles of Northamptonshire?"

Simcoe fielded her childish enthusiasm with discretion and sympathy. "New York is smaller, Miss Audrey. DeLancey's is just as grand and much less damp than our castles because it is constructed of wood, not stone."

The coach clattered noisily over the cobbles. Robert sat quietly in the corner. His sisters chatted and laughed as familiarly with this officer as they did with him. Clearly Simcoe was a favorite.

Audrey questioned constantly, "Is it as cold in England as in New York, Captain?"

"England is quite as warm as America."

"And France, Rob, did you know the Captain has been to France?"

"An Englishman is never warm in France." John Simcoe's eyes twinkled, "The French have only cold stares for anyone who mispronounces their language." Robert laughed. It was the same when he spoke French.

Audrey persisted. "Our brother Solomon is in Paris. He has visited, the palace at Versailles and King Louis and his beautiful Austrian queen! He sent us a bolt of French brocade and bottles of brandy for father and perfume that smells like roses even in winter!" Solomon was in France with Benjamin Franklin working on behalf of the rebellion.

Robert frowned at his sister.

But Audrey would not be silenced, "You speak French too, Rob! You could speak with the Captain."

"Like Captain Simcoe, my French is not faultless."

The coach turned into DeLancey's drive as if into a fairyland. The mansion resembled most colonial homes except in its dimensions. It was a white Georgian Manor, a rectangle of shingle and beams, a grand house, more kin to castle than to home.

A massive pillared porch anchored the front to an avenue of elms whose denuded branches drooped with the weight of snow to form a long arcade. Liveried slaves stood with torches lighting the way for the numerous guests. Heat from the torches had melted the top layer of snow which had turned to a mirror of ice and reflected the glittering light in shimmering prisms that sparkled like diamonds.

The coaches pulled up in a long line and disgorged passengers bedecked in jewels and silks and red uniforms of every regiment and rank. Oliver, his parents and sister stood in the central hall to welcome the guests. Holly and mistletoe, bayberry and juniper, festooned the doorways. More slaves with sconces illuminated the entry. The Prussian blue interior glowed like a clear summer sky. The downstairs rooms had been emptied of contents except for chairs that lined the walls. Yule logs burned brightly in four massive hearths and servants moved among the guests like drilled soldiers, with trays of sweetmeats and cakes. There were musicians, with lutes, violas and a harp.

Oliver greeted them heartily with a slap on the back for Robert and deep bow for Simcoe, but his eyes followed Sally and Audrey. The eyes of most men followed Sally.

Simcoe steered the girls toward the punch bowl where a sober Jack Rivington invited Audrey to dance. Simcoe led Sally to the floor and Robert was left with Mary.

A hush fell over the revelers when Lord Howe and Mrs. Loring arrived with a bevy of well-wishers. The music stopped and they entered like royalty at court, stiff and formal. Portly General Sir William Lord Howe, newly knighted, chest gleaming with colorful ribbons, escorted a tightly corsetted, brilliantly blonde and buxom, Betsy Loring. Robert smiled at the contrast. And Joshua Loring? Robert wondered silently who would accompany him. The notorious Marshal William Cunningham entered alone except for his slave.

When the music resumed, Mary tugged Robert's sleeve. "Rob, look!" John Graves Simcoe was dancing with Sally Townsend. Simcoe had a lightness of foot which, coupled with perfect rhythm and agility, made him stand out. As for Sally, she matched him step for step with supple graceful movements. They danced with abandon, smiled and talked, while the matrons of New York glared down their patrician noses. Gradually, the other dancers stepped aside. When Lord Howe and his paramour twirled to a stop, it was the signal for all to rest. But Sally and John Simcoe twirled on. The music stopped. The onlookers clapped. Simcoe stammered a bashful apology to His Lordship as Sally led him triumphantly to the punch bowl.

Mary tugged Robert's sleeve again. "He is in love with her, Rob, and she with him."

Robert did not answer. He knew. It had been happening ever since John Graves Simcoe had arrived in Oyster Bay. But it made his heart ache. It meant a loss of companionship, a loss of happiness and youth and lighthearted play.

Mary sensed his anguish. "She is a grown woman, Rob. You cannot choose where she will give her heart."

"He is a Britisher, Mary. He will break her heart like brittle glass."

"There is not a heart alive that cannot break, Rob." She whispered it so softly, he knew instinctively her heart had broken.

William Cunningham stalked abruptly into the room, alone and mildly drunk. The icy blue eyes scanned the room and settled on Sally's brilliant red hair, then Mary's lively curls. Effortlessly, John Simcoe handed Sally around the floor. Cunningham elbowed through the ranks of dancers to her side. Captain John Simcoe had no choice but to step aside.

Cunningham's lips drew back in a narrow smile. "You do not object, Captain." He dismissed John Simcoe with a flip of the hand and held it out to Sally. "Miss Townsend, I have wagered Major Grant that I would dance with the loveliest girl at the party. You will win me 50 pounds...."

Sally blanched. John Simcoe bowed stiffly. His right hand sought the hilt of his sword.

Sally stood in stunned silence. She left the Marshal's hand to dangle in mid-air and formulated her response. "I do not dance, Marshal Cunningham, for yours or my own personal gain and I do not dance on command like a trained puppy."

Cunningham's eyes narrowed. He nodded coolly. "No?... And what did Captain Simcoe offer to entice you? Has he lured you with promises of eternal fidelity, of sweets and perfume, or perhaps of the warmth of his bed?" ~~Sally blanched.~~ Cunningham laughed. The music played. He placed his hand firmly on Sally's waist and pulled her hard against him.

John Graves Simcoe froze. Not a muscle moved in the marble of his face but his knuckles were blue where his grip tightened on his weapon. He unsheathed the sword and ran a finger down the sharp edge of the blade.

Robert Townsend was quick to catch his arm. "She is a resourceful girl, Captain. Do not insinuate yourself. You will gain nothing."

"He has insulted her. He has insulted me. She will think me cowardly."

"She will think you intelligent and discreet. Your superiors would think you rash. Without you, her..." and he corrected himself, "our hardships would triple....It is but a dance."

John Simcoe's muscles tensed against Robert Townsend's hard grip. "It is just such brutes who ruin the good name of England."

"He is Irish. England has not yet civilized Ireland!"

The rhythm accelerated. Cunningham was a clumsy dancer. Sally outpaced him in every step. The music stopped but Cunningham did not release her. Suddenly, Rivington was there with Audrey, sweeping lightly into their path. Audrey stumbled and collapsed and Rivington lowered Audrey to the floor directly between the Marshal and his partner. It seemed an obvious ploy but it was not pretended. Sally bent to her sister's side and Cunningham moved away. He had already won his bet.

"Order the coach. We'll take her home." John Simcoe directed his words to Sally.

Audrey revived and protested vehemently. "No! Mother should never allow me to come dancing again."

Oliver DeLancey interrupted, "There is a room upstairs..."

They laid Audrey on a magnificent canopied bed. Audrey spoke breathlessly. "Go back to the ball. Jack will stay with me."

They left her reluctantly with bleary Jack Rivington and descended the great stair. The music had stopped to signal the departure of Lord Howe who made his exit with Colonel Cunningham trailing behind. The merriment diminished. The ball had been a dismal failure. The soldiers had come to impress their commander, to seek promotion. The colonials had come to ingratiate themselves with the British officer corps. No one had come to celebrate the season. The British presence in New York had altered the very basis of society. They introduced an emphasis on position and purchased rank, that the colonials, who judged a man for his talent and energy, had always rejected outright. The British controlled not only the conduct of trade, actions of government and strategy of war, but more subtly the basic relationships between men and women: who danced with whom; who befriended whom; who should be accepted or scorned. Women welcomed the etiquette, order and panache of the Englishmen. The colonial men, like Oliver DeLancey, Jack Rivington and Robert Townsend, found themselves outnumbered and eclipsed by the worldly English.

Lord Howe, now that he had been knighted, expected the homage due an absolute monarch, as did Governor Tryon of New York and William Franklin in New Jersey. They did not understand, the self-reliance and spontaneity of the inhabitants of the New World. Justification for British actions lay an ocean away. Only a few of the highly perceptive ones, like John Graves

Simcoe, penetrated the disturbing reality.

Jack Rivington appeared suddenly at Robert's side. "It's Audrey! She's coughing again."

John Simcoe ordered the coach immediately and they took Audrey home. Audrey shivered all the way. Robert placed his cloak around her but his eyes were on Sally, the set of her deep blue eyes and the fullness her lips, the tiny involuntary motions of muscle and nerve. Sally's ailment of the heart was more severe than any of Audrey's symptoms. Sally could not repress her emotions although she tried hard. The war spiced common movements with urgency and the apprehension that a man or woman's existence and all they held dear, could disintegrate in the flash of an instant. Sally loved with all the uncertainty that war engenders. Love tortured Sally as it did Robert.

The coach plowed through the thickening snow. A sudden coughing fit shook Audrey's thin frame. Mary held a handkerchief to her mouth. It came away stained red with blood.

They put Audrey immediately to bed. "She should be bled....I can summon a surgeon within the hour." Simcoe spoke knowingly.

"No!" Sally snapped back, "Audrey hates the fleam and so do I. Bleeding will only make her weaker."

Silenced, John Simcoe backed away. "Then I will look in tomorrow if I can be of service. The snow is worsening. I should be going." He bowed ceremoniously and left.

Mary, Sally and Robert divided the night hours between them to watch if Audrey awakened. When Robert went to relieve Mary, she lay slumped in her ball gown, an old shawl pulled about her shoulders. Audrey breathed evenly. He lit a new candle and on impulse reached to touch the tiny black curls that framed Mary's face. They flowed like pure satin across his callused fingers. He let the hand linger just above the whiteness of her skin. She did not waken. He removed his hand reluctantly and held it out, separate from himself, a trembling black silhouette in front of the orange flame. If he could possess Mary, if he could caress her with his body as he had with this hand, he would be a happy man.

21

Firmness and enterprise united wait,
The last command to ignite the stroke of fate.

*R*obert jerked his shaggy head alert. A dog was barking. Stewart was bellowing at the door, rattling the knocker and shaking the knob. "Wake up sir, there's a visitor, a tall bloke, with shaggy brows like cornices and legs the length of beanpoles, in the warehouse, by the hogsheads of rum." Stewart continued shouting above his own noise, "He's waited an hour already sir, in deference to your reveling of last night. I said I'd not dare to waken ye."

"He'll wait a moment longer Stewart." Robert Townsend pulled on his boots, wrapped himself in a cape and answered the door. Stewart's collie bounded into the room.

Stewart collared the dog but it continued to bark. He shouted louder. "Sir, this man will not wait. He's prancing like a racehorse at the gate. Watches me, watches the window, fairly paws the ground at every click on cobble in the street." Stewart lifted both eyebrows. "Eyes that flash in his head, like the eagles on the Palisades. He'll not wait much longer, sir, unless he fell asleep. Give 'im some of your best brandy to calm the nerves. And I said I would not disturb the house with poor Miss Audrey so sick."

Robert shouted back, "Lower your voice, Stewart, and quiet that dog, before you rouse every maven in every brothel in the port!" He added with annoyance, "How did you know Audrey is sick?"

Stewart lowered his pitch but not his volume, "I watch sir, and Laddie watches." The collie quieted under the soft stroke but Stewart babbled as Robert pulled on his clothing. "The tall gentleman told me I was to wake ye. 'Twas a fine ball, I'm told! Finer than the June fest at Josiah Martin's! And your friend Mr. DeLancey, danced with Mrs. Loring! I'd like to have seen it! Poor DeLancey!" He laughed. "The Loring rules the General like Lady Macbeth! When the curves of a woman confound a lord of the realm, 'tis a dreadful disgrace, sir!"

"Stewart, stop your meddling tongue!" Robert reached the excited Scotsman who diminished his volume but not his harangue.

"I meddle no more than she, sir, the Lady Loring Macbeth! Men died in Dulcinane on my good Scottish heath, as good men die in Westchester, because of the inducements of Eve! And The Loring living openly with the General at his quarters on Maiden Lane!" They had reached the warehouse door. "Come! I hope the beaked one is still there...in my quarter at the back... with the horse!"

The warehouse was cold. The north wind had blown snow between the cracks and underneath the door. But the small room that was Stewart's home, was snug as an earthen cottage on his native moors, and smelled heavily of tobacco and whiskey and horse manure. The nag Robert had brought from William's camp stood in an adjacent stall. Stewart waited with the horse.

Robert entered the room and locked the door behind him. Benjamin Tallmadge himself slouched in a chair with head resting on folded hands on a bare plank table. He was asleep. A dish of whale oil shed an eerie light on his high cheekbones and cast deep shadows in the crevices of his cheeks.

Robert touched his shoulder and Tallmadge jerked awake.

"Sir, I'm sorry you had to wait. Stewart just now called me."

Tallmadge kicked a chair out for Robert. "Wonderful peace, Rob, is sleep." He motioned Robert to sit down. "Tell me about the ball."

Robert collapsed into the chair. "Too many uniformed Englishmen, too few ladies. I left early. An obnoxious man, one William Cunningham, tried to force himself on my sister."

Tallmadge frowned. "Your sisters should stay in the country until this bloody business ends. Cunningham is the vilest butcher."

Robert wrung his hands together. "Sir, I have willful sisters. I cannot control them."

A silence ensued. "I received your news of Philadelphia. It was helpful."

Tallmadge folded his hands, straightened his back and eyed Robert narrowly. "I want you to burn the shipyard at Oyster Bay. It must be soon, very soon. If we wait, the harbor will freeze us out. Already Brewster must drag the boats across the shallows on the ice. Choose a night with a howling wind to dull the noise and fan the flames. And pray for a thaw."

Robert jerked alert. His dark brows knitted together over the long straight line of his nose. "Why so sudden? Why now?"

"We need a victory. We need to show our British counterparts that we can gut their soft bellies. It's why I came myself, to convince you." Benjamin Tallmadge stood up and stretched to his full height.

Robert turned his chair around, straddled it and shot his next words at the tall soldier. "Did you know that Mary Drake is pregnant?"

"I did not know. How far along?"

"Three, four months. Long enough to be sure but not long enough to swell. Is there any news of the father?"

Tallmadge's shoulders deflated. "Her husband, Thomas Drake, is presumed dead, washed out with the tide."

"She will not accept presumption in the place of fact."

Tallmadge nodded feebly and stared into the blackness, "If Tom Drake is alive... he may come here. Did he know she is with child?"

"No." The thought of Drake's possible arrival unnerved Robert. "There must be a record of Drake's death."

"Cunningham, keep records! Records assign guilt. Better records are kept of the pedigree of race horses and the cargo of slave ships than of prisoners in the hulks!" Tallmadge finally met his gaze. "And you must not go back to the swamps. It is too dangerous and you are too valuable here. I believe Drake is dead. It is probable that you and I and Mary shall never be certain.... But when will you burn the shipyard?"

"Can it wait for the New Year?"

"Yes, but no later."

Robert Townsend sucked in the soft tissue of his cheeks until he tasted the saltiness of blood on his tongue. "What shall I tell Mary? That the child is fatherless?"

Benjamin Tallmadge shrugged. "Tell her nothing. Let her enjoy the spirit of the season. If you tell her he is dead, she will mourn. But why the concern for Mary?"

Robert ignored the question. "I will not tell her a falsehood."

"You Quakers are a damnably honest lot!" Tallmadge snickered.

Robert protested. His eyes flashed. "This whole spy business is one great lie. I lie every day. I compromise my integrity and my safety and deny my religious faith!" He met Tallmadge's stare squarely and the full force of his frustration exploded. He clutched the back of the chair, pushed himself up and stalked off into the darkest corner of the room.

Tallmadge responded with sympathy. "Is it so difficult to pretend to be what you are not? Children do it every day."

"The effort wears!" That was bald truth. Robert Townsend did not hear Tallmadge's next words. Tallmadge prattled on, sterile words of encouragement, apologies for Washington's demoralizing retreat across Jersey, for the huge desertion rate of the continental soldiers.

Robert closed his ears. He locked his jaw and met Benjamin Tallmadge eye to eye. "I will burn the yard. On New Year's Day when they have drunk their fill, Captain Youngs and I will warm their beer-soaked beds!" He added with trembling lips, "If I can exit this city and go home over the ice." The vehemence in Robert's voice shocked Benjamin Tallmadge.

"The ferry will cross tomorrow." Tallmadge tossed a pouch of guineas on the table. It landed with a dull jangle. "You have a horse, a bay. Roe needs him. There is payment.... Escort your sisters home to Oyster Bay."

"I don't want payment, not from Austin. The horse is at DeLancey's stable. Austin can collect him there. I will write permission."

"Keep the money. Use it for bribes."

"Bribes make uncertain friends." Robert let the pouch lay and scribbled permission to take the bay.

Tallmadge was grinning knowingly now. "Spend it on Mary. I'll inform Brewster." He wrapped his massive palm around Robert's arm in a gesture of support. "I am grateful to you, Robert Townsend, grateful for the sacrifice that you make." He meant the horse but Robert knew he was thinking of the integrity of his soul. Tallmadge continued, "Philadelphia will fall! Not soon, but it is inevitable!"

"Rivington says so." There was doubt in his voice.

In an effort to lighten the mood, Tallmadge added, "And Rob, eat more. Strong passion devours the flesh."

Robert nodded blankly. His mind was elsewhere.

Benjamin Tallmadge smiled benevolently, "We are all human Robert. Yours is a particularly proud and perilous task." He added with gravity in his voice, "If you tell Mary you love her, the confession may bring you some relief." He left unseen by the narrow door to the back alley.

Robert sat for a long while, in the gloomy chamber, listening to the breathing of the horse and combating the demons that tortured his conscience. He must return to Oyster Bay tomorrow on the ferry, before more ice clogged the sound. But Mary, his passion and his hope, would have to remain in the city. His mother, Sarah, would never accept his mistress into her home.

Stewart was bent over the keyhole, his pink nose twitching like a rabbit's and his blue eyes twinkling, when Robert got up to leave. Stewart snapped his head up defensively, "In the holy name of the blessed Saint Andrew, sir, I hear no more than the wee wind singing in the eaves." Robert knew it was a lie. The Scotsman wasn't finished. "Captain Simcoe, sir. I've admitted him to the parlor....You'll want to bring an armload of wood to the ladies, sir, on a windy eve like this, from the box inside the door. The ladies and the Captain are taking tea." Stewart flung a scarf around his bony neck and clamped his teeth on the stem of his pipe. There would be no more discussion this day.

Robert's distrust simmered. Where did Stewart's sympathies lie? Scotland was a recent addition to the English realm, only lately subdued. Robert Townsend ripped his cape from its hook, slammed the door and stomped out into the sleet-filled wind. He turned his face deliberately into the stinging shards of sleet and stood for a moment in the middle of the street.

Stewart came up behind him. "Take this, sir. He makes a better entrance who has a reason for his absence." He handed Robert an armload of wood.

Simcoe had arrived while Robert talked with Tallmadge and Jack Rivington and Oliver DeLancey had come a few moments later. They had walked from the Gazette offices in Wall Street. It was a fair distance. Their cloaks and boots were covered with snow. Now, standing by the fire, they dripped like a melting snowmen.

Robert entered this nest of Tories and dropped the dry logs in the center of the floor. There was a loud banging on the door. Drake was there with a missive addressed to Culper Junior. It was a summons from Austin Roe. His horse had popped a splint. The horse was lame. He needed the bay. Robert scribbled another permit and sent Drake scurrying quickly on his way.

When he looked back into the room, Mary sat to one side. He did not like to see her like this, alone among enemies. Simcoe sat elegantly by Sally. DeLancey and Rivington hovered over Audrey who glowed with the attention. They had brought her a present, a bottle of Dr. Keyser's Pills which Jack Rivington vowed, infallibly cured every disease, even some too embarrassing to be mentioned in a lady's presence.

Robert left them to their trivia. He walked slowly out to the wharf. Farley was there. The Katherine had escaped the freeze and would sail with the tide, weather permitting, the next day, the 22nd. He would take them east up the sound into the bay. But Farley had a warning. "I was lucky to free her from the ice, sir. My men were chopping half the day. They say tomorrow will be fair but the winter will be hard, sir. The gulls are few this year and they fly inland and all the geese have departed."

Robert sensed something deeper in the concave furrows of the sea Captain's brow. "What is it, Farley?"

"I mean, sir, that anyone, Miss Audrey and Miss Sally, who wants passage to Oyster Bay, must sail with me tomorrow. Ice is building quickly in the shallows and will block the channel."

Tomorrow dawned springlike. The westerly breeze veered south bringing warmth and a clear crystal sky. Melting ice sloshed in chunks against the wharf and fell dangerously from the rigging onto the decks. Farley's ominous words were forgotten. Robert and John Graves Simcoe carried Audrey aboard and bed her down in the Captain's snug cabin in the stern. They sailed smoothly downwind on a broad reach, over soft, billowing swells, and quietly entered Oyster Bay.

22

Let songs of triumph every voice employ,
And every Muse discharge a feu de joie.

*I*t was raining a slow persistent drizzle, when they disembarked. They were wet and tired from the damp of the sea. Home, a hearth fire, dry clothes were waiting. Samuel stood near the door. He reached up to kiss each daughter and clasped John Simcoe's and Captain Farley's hands. When he came to Robert, he threw his arms around him. The grip was weaker than Robert remembered, but it held longer. Robert hugged back with every sinew and bone and an awful stabbing fear. He felt the protrusions of his father's shoulders, the slack of muscle, the thin drapery of skin. A vision startled him of a younger, active father whose skin was smooth and muscles taut. Robert Townsend had thinned too, his square face lined with a sharp definition of cheekbone and deep-set, cavernous eyes.

Beulah chided him like a fussy hen. "What you been doing, Mr. Rob? Fasting like a Papist?"

Robert's smile did not change the expression on his face. He winked, "I live like a monk in the desert, Beulah, without you to cook for me." The passage home, the walk up from the dock had exhausted him. He had learned to calculate every human expression and movement and stuff his true feelings into the back of his soul like used clothing in an old trunk. Sometimes fear of discovery strangled his words. Sometimes doubt clouded his thoughts and he lay awake like a prisoner on the rack, conflicts spinning in his head like logs in a whirlpool. Then he would think of Mary.

He followed his sisters, John Simcoe and Farley into the parlor to pay homage to Sarah who bestowed a hand to kiss on Simcoe and Farley. The girls received a thin smile, but Robert, only two sticklike fingers. He retired early to his garret upstairs. The larger room downstairs, which had been his, was now allotted to John Graves Simcoe of the 40th Regiment of Foot. Simcoe was the favored son of the house now. He had replaced Robert in the affections of the Townsend women.

Robert lay on his back which ached where the cornhusk mattress lumped like pebbles against the crevices of his spine. Cold nipped his toes and the tip of his nose. He had not lit the fire - he was too tired to carry the wood upstairs. Raindrops pattered lightly on the wood shingles of the roof which leaked. An icy drop smacked his cheek. A thin trail of water seeped down the beam from the peak of the roof and fell to the bed directly over his head. The water thudded on his cheek as steadily as a drumbeat, like the deceit which he could feel leaking into his soul, drip by cold drip. It had been a hard day, maintaining acceptable conversation, pretending enthusiasm, smiling when he would rather scream. Rather than face the effort again, he would sleep in a frigid room.

He got up, pushed the bed out from under the leak and shoved a basin underneath to catch the water. Rain! It was a bitter curse. Rain would wet the timber and puddle the shipyard. The blaze would sputter and die like the Continental Army. He felt the fire of his resolution dying. He saw his efforts, Brewster's, Tallmadge's, lying prone and lifeless. He and Brewster would be apprehended, jailed, executed. He stood up, shook himself in the cold air to clear the dreadful thoughts from his brain and sank back down on the edge of the bed, shivering and sweating from anxiety.

His thoughts rambled wildly. A victory! The rebellion needed a decisive blow! No more relentless, numbing retreats. It was up to him to provide the meager victory that the army could not produce. Tallmadge had ordered it. He pulled a blanket around him but it only absorbed the moisture from his clothing and gave little warmth. The whitewashed ceiling stared down in blank judgement. With the coming of night, he watched it change from dull white to hazy grey, then to black. He felt himself retracting from the cheerfulness that was his true personality, to a fearful, nervous isolation. He had allowed doubt to invade his resolve like the damp air that chilled his lungs. His future lay somewhere there in the blackness where he could not see. He had to grope to find it.

He closed his eyes and listened to the steady drip of water. Why had he heedlessly thrown in his lot with Brewster and Roe? Everywhere the British were celebrating. Parliament had knighted Howe. Would he, Robert Townsend, ever know that kind of reward? Would he ever experience the recognition and gratitude of his peers?

He laughed. It was a raucous cackling that rasped the lining of his lungs. What a clown he was, floundering like the ragtag continental army, running from his own demons, running even from the woman he loved! Mary, he couldn't erase her from his mind. Who was she? And the others with whom he had thrown in his lot, Drake, Youngs, Tallmadge, were they dedicated men or crazed, irrational idealists? And what of Stewart? The little Scot's defiant voice rang in his ears. He sensed a possible ally there. Could he trust the irrepressible Scot?

The water dripped evenly, slapping the surface with the measured regularity of a soldier's march. Later, much later, after he had counted a thousand drops, he realized he had dozed. The rain had stopped. He blew out the lantern and begged God for healing sleep. It arrived late in the next morning, like a stretcher-bearer, not able to give relief, able only to transport a man bleeding and screaming, from one painful resting place to another.

He awoke consumed by a compulsion to act. Before breakfast, he escaped to the barn and the safe, forgiving company of animals and Cob, the deaf slave. Cob was at work sinking the tongs of his pitchfork into soft brown turds, pitching them into a wheelbarrow. He hummed to himself, a habit left over from his youth when he could hear. The soft breathing of the beasts, their heavy, moist smell and the even motions of the slave quieted Robert Townsend.

He picked up a fork and started work in the stall next to Cob. The mare's wide belly filled half the long rectangle. The stall opposite stood empty. It was for the bay.

Suddenly, Cob looked up. "Where's the bay, Mr. Rob?"

Robert shouted back, "In the good care of a friend, Cob." He dared not mention Roe even to the deaf slave.

Cob nodded placidly. "That's my work, Master Rob!" He pointed to the pile of droppings.

Robert glared back. "No, I can clean out a stall. I can at least be of use to the beasts." The surprised slave did not understand and drew back. Robert stabbed the wet straw with terrifying force that made even the quiet mare shy back against the stall boards. He worked frantically until his muscles ached, then slumped numbly to a mound of hay.

He was there when Captain Youngs stepped into the triangle of light at the door. "Robert, the day is new and you sit idle!" He eyed the slave with apprehension. Youngs lowered himself to the straw beside Robert. "Brewster will land tomorrow in the marshes on the east side of Lloyd's Neck."

Robert covered his face with his hands. "Daniel, the Continental Army is scurrying like scared rabbits across the width of New Jersey! Sometimes I ask myself if we know what we are doing!" The concave curve of his spine, the tremor of his voice, spelled his fear.

Daniel Youngs snuffed back his own doubts. "This is not the time to hesitate. Rally man! Confidence and hope! You have friends and family!"

Robert laughed at the irony. "What family? My mother is a blithering Tory! My brother buys advancement with the best horse I own! My sisters have eyes only for scarlet coats and ears only for British courtesies!" His lips quivered. "Daniel, what will become of us if we lose?"

"We will find a new slice of land...like our fathers before us. It is not a terrible alternative. You are not alone. Your father is an honest man. Think of Solomon! Think of your Uncle Peter! You, Robert Townsend, cannot retreat now! Brewster has already landed!"

A pang of guilt shook Robert Townsend. Youngs was right. He, Robert Townsend, had to persevere for the sake of this stolid Captain who stood patiently before him, for Austin Roe, for Brewster, most of all for Mary. His head came up and his lungs filled, "Have you spoken with Prime?" Ebenezer Prime was the rector of the Huntington Presbyterian Church. "Prime will feed and provision Brewster's men before they strike the shipyard and find them safe haven after."

Youngs frowned gravely. "I thought they were to escape by sail, by cutting out a ship?"

"There is no suitable ship at the wharf. Brewster will have only a dozen men." Robert still wavered.

Youngs bit down on his lip. "They are men who can be trusted."

"Betrayal is easy with our army in full flight, too easy when success seems impossible." The words hung like icicles on Robert's dry lips. Robert shivered and Youngs placed a fatherly arm around his shoulder. He didn't speak. He didn't argue or encourage. In the silence, human sympathy seeped into the younger man's veins and Robert proceeded hesitantly to outline his plan. "When the Hessians drink their pints of rum...on the New Year, they will receive an extra gill. We will strike when they are drunk and sleeping."

The tuneless humming of the deaf slave broke the stillness. Youngs eyed Cob. "You're sure he doesn't hear?" He took a deep breath. "I have not yet stashed the powder and tar."

"Brewster doesn't need powder, only dirks and sabers. Success depends on silence, surprise and camouflage."

"Without sidearms, they will be vulnerable."

Robert grinned, "Must I now tell you to trust? Anonymity is their best protection. Their plans are well laid."

Daniel Youngs stared glassily into the darkness, then turned a terrified glance on Robert. He said, "I will kill myself before I am taken. You understand? I trust you to help my family, to tell them I died honorably."

"Don't speak so, Daniel Youngs! We are in the right. God will protect us. Fear is the devil's sword!" Robert Townsend stabbed down into the straw with his knife. It was a swift stroke and he looked up at Youngs with an eerie twist to his lips. "Go home, Daniel, shelter your family, keep them from danger, especially your boy. Youth is too curious." He stabbed the knife in the cushion of straw and jerked it out. "And I will do the same."

The interview was at an end, but Youngs turned back with a nervous flick of the wrist, "The aged spars on the west end of the yard have dried longest. They will burn fastest."

Christmas came and went. Robert attended the service. They celebrated the birthday of the Lord as they had marked Samuel's release from prison, joyfully. At Christmas dinner, Robert nibbled listlessly. At the carolling, he mouthed the words in a hoarse throat.

At Meeting, Christmas morning, John Simcoe stood, hesitated a moment to compose his words and raised his voice. "To all you good people, King George's loyal subjects. Your hospitality has made me appreciate your forbearance and sacrifice. You struggle every day on behalf of His Royal Highness. Wars are difficult times. Some of my countrymen have been harsh toward you, too quick to rebuke or punish, and for these I beg your forgiveness. His Royal Highness, King George III, will remember with munificence, all of you who have treated me, and the least of his subjects, with kindness. I am his and your most humble servant and I thank you with all my heart." His words were sincere, his bearing regal, and the red coat he wore marked an honorable man.

Robert Townsend listened silently. After Christmas, he counted the days. On the 26th, it snowed a few inches. On the 27th, the sun's rays on the whiteness were blinding. On the 28th, a dry wind that would feed an inferno, picked up from the south. Robert spent the day at the wharf with Farley.

Austin Roe emerged from the narrow path through Poverty Hollow, red-faced and breathless, on Robert's bay, on the 29th. The horse snorted and pranced. He hailed Robert on the road to Youngs, did not dismount, and waved his hat gleefully. "You've heard? Success this season! We bloodied some Hessian noses at Trenton!"

Robert wrenched his thoughts away from the horse. "A victory? Now? I thought the campaigning had stopped for the winter."

"So did General Howe! They drove the Brits into the icy river! Tell Youngs! Tell Brewster! And Happy New Year!" Austin spurred the horse who leaped to a gallop like a springing cat.

It was stirring news, good news, but Robert felt a pang. He watched the handsome bay gallop away.

23

Yet still remains an excellent resource,
Bring to the charge the continental force.

*T*he news inched slowly upon Robert Townsend's consciousness like the seep of low tide, then burst forth in a flood. He ran the distance to Youngs' farm.

Daniel Youngs placed his thumbs in his belt and laughed until his stomach shook. "Bloody tyrant bastards! Teach 'em what free men can do!" The laughter was infectious. Youngs broke open a fresh bottle of madeira and the two conspirators drank to the success and health of George Washington. The shred of good news was at least a hope.

Robert Townsend jogged eagerly back past Youngs' cornfield to the crest of Cove Hill, where he looked down on the shipyard, the place he would destroy. All was quiet. Stacks of lumber in various stages of aging, lay to either side. There were two buildings, a warehouse and a sail loft. Groups of men were hard at work.

It was a peaceful sight. Teams of oxen plodded back and forth hauling giant trees into the yard. Saw gangs worked the pits, turning raw logs into lengths of planking. The shipyard made yardarms, heavy blocks, dead-eyes and belaying pins. Broad axes chopped, adzes and chisels shaped and scraped the splinters smooth. Pit saws moved sluggishly with the rhythm of a man's swinging arm. So much of a ship was made of wood. It would burn well.

There were two ships on the ways, one whose ribs protruded from the keel like a giant skeleton long since scavenged. The planking gang stood by the other to nail the planks to the ribs. Caulkers drove oakum into the cracks which expanded when wet to make the hull waterproof. A third ship, had only a thin line of keel laid out.

Robert heard the cry, "Frame up!" Everyone dropped what he was doing to heave a giant rib into place. He recognized two of the workmen, Isaiah Tredwell and Ben Underhill. Ben had poor eyesight and had never learned to read but he was muscular and strong and an able man with auger and spike.

Two more ships rested at anchor in the deep water near the yard dock, one awaiting a new mast and bowsprit, the other new spars and rigging. The trunks of huge pines provided the masts. These were not air seasoned like the hull's timbers, but pickled in the brine of tidal creeks to keep the wood sound. A hundred-foot mast lay ready to be beveled to an octagonal cross section, rounded and smoothed and hoisted with block and tackle to its place midships. Dry sawdust covered the ground.

Robert studied the buildings. The sail loft was a wide rectangle. One end stored the coarse linen from which sails were cut. At the other end sailmakers laid out the yardage. This too, would ignite like a pyre. The flames would jump to the warehouse that stored the tar to stiffen the standing rigging and the casks of black powder and balls.

Robert Townsend had grown up around this shipyard. His father's ships had been fitted here. As a child, he had jumped the tree trunks that floated like islands in the creek. The huge pickled logs transmitted sound. You scratched one end and sent messages to a friend at the other. A pang of nostalgia seized his insides. But then he thought of the Massapequa swamps, of Mary and the horror of the hulks, and he felt better.

He walked on. The rope yard was busy too. There were giant spools of every diameter and length: rope for shrouds and halyards to raise and lower spars, and rotate the heavy yards around the mast. He spotted Charley White, the foreman, who had taught him to tie the bowline knot. He mimicked the motions now with his cold hands. It seemed a ghostly action from out of a former life.

He looked down at his hands and wondered how they would become agents of destruction and shoved them into the pockets of his coat, out of sight.

He walked back to the town where the Hessians and British prepared to celebrate the New Year. Drunken soldiers already crowded the streets. Sentries snored at their posts. Organized drills degenerated into ribald song and dance. Robert wove his way through the revelers to his door.

On the 31st, John Simcoe arrived with a goose. Sally slaughtered and plucked it, drained off the fat and roasted it to a crisp brown. Beulah steamed a plum pudding over a cauldron of boiling water. Robert slouched on a hard slat-backed chair. He did not usually smoke but gripping a pipe steadied his hands.

The Townsends sat down early to their New Year's feast. Samuel presided with Robert on his right hand. They drank and toasted and devoured the goose. Robert drank twice his usual quantity and ate sparsely. He watched and waited and tucked his shaking hands under his napkin. Audrey chattered innocently at his elbow. Finally, John Simcoe poured brandy over the mound of pudding and lit it with a stick from the fire. A river of deep cerulean blue flame danced around the base and leaped eagerly to the crest. The pudding flickered like a miniature pyre. Beulah stood by in triumph.

At the same moment another flame, not blue but orange, licked over the tar at the edge of the warehouse where the gunpowder was stored. The fire built slowly. Another flame sizzled in the sawdust by the stack of aging spars. The fires went undetected at first. The sentries were asleep or laughing drunk. The shipwrights had gone home for dinner. The seamen were on shore leave, singing in the taverns.

A soft southerly fanned the tiny flames. It lifted the sparks like feathers in an updraft and blew them across the shipyard. A second fire started in the sail loft and yet another under the keel of the largest ship on the ways. A sentry finally smelled burning tar and went to investigate. They all heard the first cask of gunpowder blow. An earsplitting clap echoed all over the village. The Townsends dropped their forks. Conversation stopped in mid-sentence. John Simcoe leaped from the table, grabbed his coat and ran frantically out into the lane with Kelly at his heels and Robert close behind.

The second cache of powder blew a few seconds later and shook the ground beneath their feet. Captain Hangar called out his groggy troops and marched them staggering toward the scene. They fell over gun barrels, tripped on their own bayonets and marched in sloppy ranks. They had no blankets and buckets with which to beat out the flames.

More explosions sounded. Burning debris took flight like flapping geese, up, over the trees and over the bay and cast glittering reflections on the black mirror of water below. Lieutenant Ormond tried to rally soldiers, shouting commands, to muster, to march, to fight - he meant the fire. The dumbfounded soldiers loaded their guns. A pitiful few civilians rallied to form human chains and relay bucketfuls of sea water to the flames. It was the solstice time, when the moon pulls the waters away from the earth. The tide was at its lowest and the water far away beyond the icy flats that rimmed the shore.

The shipyard burned brightly in the wintery night. It lit the horizon like the legendary Christmas star. The loyal townspeople could do little to stop it. The provisions that burned were the lumber and cordage and canvas gathered from farmers and fishermen and merchants who would never see the value of their possessions again.

When a fiery brand threatened Youngs' home, the neighbors rallied and diverted water from a free-flowing spring not 10 feet from the door to pour on the flames. Brewster himself and two of his men sloshed water on the boards and the house was spared.

24

Now war suspended by this scorching heat,
Springs from his tent, and shines in arms complete.

*J*ohn Simcoe reached the crest of Cove Hill too late. Flames leaped up the masts, devoured the tarred rigging and hurled orange tongues at the sky. The ships on the ways burned to blackened skeletons. The yards of sails burst in a mighty red vortex. No man, not the mighty English army, could stop it.

John Simcoe squinted at the searing heat. He rubbed his stinging eyes and turned abruptly. What he saw when he opened them, horrified him. A thin outline of a boy stood out against the flames. The wind picked up a brand and hurled it at the form. In the brightness, Simcoe picked out the shape more clearly. The boy gripped a dog, tripped and fell and screamed like an animal in pain.

John Graves Simcoe lunged forward like a lion from its lair. When he reached the boy, he was on his knees, hovering over the dog, coughing, eyes tearing and bulging in fright. Simcoe lifted boy and dog into his arms, and with his own body as shield, backed out through a wall of flame. He dashed the few feet to the gravel road where the snowmelt lingered, fell to the ground and rolled in the wet slush with the boy held tightly to him. When he rose, the boy lay limp and still as an empty sack. The dog jumped up eagerly and fled.

Robert Townsend raced to them. Simcoe had brunted the flames with his back. The golden braid of his dress uniform had melted into the seams of his coat. Tiny flames still flickered from his epaulets. Simcoe stood quivering and dazed and shouting wildly. "See to the boy! Is he alive?"

With his bare hands, Robert ripped the coat brutally from John Simcoe's shoulders and threw John Simcoe back to the ground into the smothering mud. John Simcoe struggled against him. Robert Townsend pinned him down while Daniel Youngs held his legs until every vestige of fire was extinguished and John Simcoe lay quiet.

But the figure Simcoe had carried rested unconscious on the snow. Robert ran to the boy and turned the young face skyward. He jumped back when he saw the face. It was Billy Youngs, only nine years of age! Robert rubbed cold snow on the cheeks, on the patches of hair. Billy seemed amazingly unscathed, in a deep sleep. There were no cuts, no obvious burns, only the unconsciousness. Remorse drove tears to Robert's eyes. Billy Youngs should not be lying here. He had told Youngs to keep the boy safe!

He looked up. John Simcoe stood over him. Mother Youngs came up behind him and pushed past to her son. Robert's mouth opened. Words flowed like water from a spout. "It's Billy! He's too young! Daniel, why didn't you keep him in? I didn't mean...."

Simcoe spoke suddenly. "He is not dead! See, he breathes! He will revive!" Miraculously, Billy coughed and blinked awake. Robert stared numbly from Billy's terrified eyes to the anguished, soot-streaked face of John Simcoe. He held his hands out before him and counted ten fingers, two palms, wrists and knuckles. Like pieces of putrid meat, he held them separate from his human form. Death or near death had resulted from these hands. He had almost killed the only son of his friend. The chill air made him shiver. He shook convulsively and sank down into the slush as the reality of what he had done engulfed him. Men had died. Property lay in ruin. If caught, he would be marched to the gallows and tossed into a pauper's grave, and Captain Youngs with him and he would deserve his punishment. He took no pride in the success of this night and shrunk into the welcoming shadows. That the boy would live because of the courageous act of his enemy was an irony he would have to bear.

Mother Youngs had wrapped Billy in a blanket and looked upon Simcoe like a Christ figure from heaven. "Thank you, Captain." She said it in awe.

A path parted for her as she turned to leave. It drew Billy, Simcoe and Robert with it. Simcoe called after her, "Teach him to respect fire and he will make a fine soldier someday. I will send a surgeon to dress the burns." The woman turned and stared speechlessly for a minute, then stumbled off with her son.

Robert gawked at Simcoe. "Captain, you are injured." Simcoe's burns were obvious.

"I am quite well, thank you Robert." John Simcoe was in shock. Patches of skin where the wool of his shirt had burned away gleamed an ugly red. But he seemed to feel no pain. Robert removed his own coat and placed it over Simcoe's shoulders. Sergeant Kelly arrived with the Captain's cape and together they urged John Simcoe to come away, but he would not leave. He stayed directing bucket and blanket brigades and beating the persistent flare-ups. He watched the flames devour months of toil until the last spark had blown to cinder on the night wind and settled on the quiet surface of the bay. Finally, he turned to Daniel Youngs. "We have done our best." He was satisfied.

Robert answered softly, "We are all poorer as of this night....Thank you Captain, for your valiant effort." He said it from under the weight of guilt.

They brought John Simcoe home. Sally was waiting with warm water and soft lint. Her red hair hung loosely without her cap, her eyes strained with the red webs of worry. They focussed on John Graves Simcoe. She pushed Sergeant Kelly away and took her place at his side.

They led him to a stool in the parlor but he could not sit. Beulah arrived with wet linens and lard. He lay face down upon his bed. Sergeant Kelly screamed in vain, "Give a heed to modesty, ladies!" and tried to push his way in. They ignored him.

They removed the clothing from his shoulders and the britches from his legs. It came away in shreds revealing charred raw flesh and blisters that flaked away like scales. Shivering, Simcoe reached desperately for Sally's hand. It was not a gesture of desire but a lurching grasp for relief from pain. The numbness of initial shock diminished. He held hard until her hand ached but he stared face down at the floor. His iron grip and a tightening of the tendons of his neck and jaw were the only visible signs of his suffering. Sally gripped back while Samuel held a glass of brandy to his lips.

Beulah swiped the brandy away, "Water, he needs cold water to quench the fire from the inside!"

Sudden spasms of pain distorted the stoic British face as he sipped the water though a straw. Beulah spread a cold wet cloth on the burns and shoved a wad of canvas between his teeth. John Simcoe chewed the heavy cloth in half, but he did not cry out. He whispered painfully, "Forgive me." like a penitent who has mortally sinned.

It was Sally who answered, "We've nothing to forgive you for. Tonight you are a hero."

His anguish echoed in his words. "I am the commander. I am to blame. The Hessians were drunk! I should never have permitted the drinking! And now I lay naked, helpless and in a woman's care!" He turned his face toward the wall.

Sally brushed his words away like so many cinders. "You forget John Simcoe, I have five brothers. I am not offended by the sight of a man, especially a brave man! I am inspired!" John Simcoe pretended he did not hear.

Robert crept out into the enveloping night. He wove his way back to the devastated scene, past wagons and buckets strewn in the road. A powerful magnetism pulled him back. Exhausted soldiers lazed by the roadside. A ghostly glow seeped from the last embers where the fire still smoldered. Brewster had done his work well. The sail loft, the rope yard, all the lumber, two of the ships on the ways, had been totally consumed. But Robert Townsend felt no joy, only the cold, sharp bite of remorse.

The door stood open at Youngs'. He looked in. Billy was sitting happily at table, slurping from a bowl of steaming chowder. When Robert entered, he looked up. "I rescued my dog."

Robert blinked back, unbelieving. "Yes." Here was the boy, breathing, talking. The dog was at his side, begging for the scraps of his meal. Robert pulled a package from his pocket, set it on the table and stammered, "I've brought you a sugar candy." He turned to go when Daniel summoned him back.

Youngs was cheerful. "The boy's fine, Rob, humbled a bit without my using the strap, and he's learned the danger of fire....Did you see Brewster?" He answered his own question. "I did, but only for a moment. Like a ghost, that one, magnificent! Saved this house! Hangar and his men were fanning flames in this direction. Bloody Hessians tried to burn me out! I have Brewster to thank for these walls and this roof over my old, bald head!"

Robert Townsend lay a hand on his friend's shoulder. He said simply. "I am glad, Daniel." He questioned quietly, "Brewster did not cut out a boat?"

"Where were you that you didn't see it, Rob?... Brewster, all handsome and wigged, like a foppish navy captain in lace and ruffles, and his men in whites like proper able British seamen! They rowed out to the Nancy, cute little fireship, slipped her lines and hoisted her sail like twenty-year men of the Royal Navy!" Youngs stopped to laugh. "Made out like she was coming to fight the fire but sailed out pretty as a swan under the guns of the Halifax and the fort at Lloyd's cliff.... I ran half way to Cooper's to watch, but they were too fast for me. Last I saw they were heading out into the sound. It was a coup worthy of Morgan or Drake!" He slapped his knee with pure glee.

"I didn't know." Robert replied weakly.

"The Brits don't know yet either. They're still too drunk. I tell you Robert, Tallmadge will love you for it!... Smile and be cheerful, man!"

"I cannot, Daniel....You forget I am a Quaker, unused to the violence. And my bay has gone to Roe who must use him cruelly for our purposes.... Did anyone die, Daniel?"

"A few damnable drunken Hessians and good riddance! As for the horse, Austin is sure to care for him well. I've a bottle. Drink will make you merry!" He poured out rum and handed the cup to Robert.

Robert smiled thinly and sipped. The liquor burned. Its sweetmess cloyed, but not enough to quench his remorse.

Youngs tried to sympathize, "Rattles you Quakers doesn't it, the killing?"

"Yes." Robert cast down his eyes and swirled his drink in its glass. The clear liquid slopped out over the rim. Youngs gripped his shaking wrist. "You have struck a blow for justice, man. God will bless you for it. That is what I believe. That is what you must believe."

"Then why won't God let me sleep?"

"God lets all good men sleep, Robert. It is war and tyranny and bloody, blind cruelty that torment your rest. You're a brave and good man, Robert Townsend. Don't doubt yourself." Youngs' strong arm braced Robert's shoulder.

"I will leave for Peck's Slip in the morning."

"So soon? That would smell like running, Rob. Only cowards escape the realities of war and you are not a coward. Think of all the good colonial men whom you saved this night. Count the ships and the powder and the sail that we have destroyed... in lives saved, not lives lost."

Robert Townsend nodded. His red eyes glazed and he turned to go.

Another reminder of the night's havoc awaited him at home. John Simcoe lay face down on a mattress of cornhusks in his old room behind the staircase. A covering of smooth buckskin covered his back where the skin was puffed and broken. Beulah sat with him. He was asleep when Robert entered.

"He shakes, sir, like he was lying on an iced brick... Sergeant Kelly went for the surgeon."

"Does he need anything? Can I...?"

"Water, Master Rob, he wants water. You could make a trip to the well. Mr. Samuel offered him whiskey but he spat it out. Says whiskey is to blame. Says that drunken soldiers sleeping on the watch let the fire burn."

Simcoe turned at the sound of voices, called out deliriously and awakened.

"He don't speak. He don't drink enough. He should take more water...." Beulah's eyes were large and liquid and revealed more than any words she spoke. "I give him this to bite like we do when the pain is great...It will save his teeth." She held a knot of pine - slaves bit down on pine knots during whippings.

Sally entered silently with a pitcher of water and a tin cup. When she lifted her eyes, they locked on the prone form of the Britisher. Robert stepped back. He recognized in his sister the deep caring that he struggled with in himself. Sally Townsend was in love.

Sally dismissed Beulah. "I'll wait with him, Beulah." Her movements were wooden. She filled the cup, tested it with her fingers and felt the icy cold. She bent Simcoe's head to the straw. He sputtered and the water splashed onto the mattress.

"You must drink, John, or you'll waste...and we must sit you up to do it."

He clamped his teeth and twisted up on his elbows. "I shall raise myself." But his lips braced back in a stifled scream and tears filled his eyes. Movement was too painful. He turned his head away to hide his embarrassment, "I must look an insufferable fool!"

"You are in pain. Only fools refuse the relief of pain... Drink. The water will revive you." He turned slowly. She reached out to him, gripping his uninjured hand in hers.

Robert Townsend backed away. He left two people sharing a suffering and a fortitude that were of his making. He was not a participant, not even a welcome observer in their private communion. "I will look in tomorrow." He muttered the words and walked silently from the room. Beulah followed.

John Simcoe lay exposed and humiliated. Sally did not release his hand. Her touch banished the loneliness of command and numbed the pain. Alone with her, his restraint evaporated. He whispered through parched lips. "I do not deserve one so beautiful."

She knelt beside him, "You have earned my gratitude and the respect of this entire village." His look was so intense, she turned her head away and walked to the darkened window. "Cob has not closed the shutters." Her quiet observation defused the emotion with the reality of the moment.

He was silent. His dark hair fell forward masking the contortions of his face. She combed and tied it gently back from his brow.

Conversation clung desperately to simple, physical needs. "Your wig is lost. Kelly will have to purchase another."

"And my sword, where is my sword? "

"It is here. It hangs on your bedpost." She moved it gently and it clanged reassuringly.

Kelly returned with the surgeon who did little. Rest, sleep and liquids were the proper remedies and rum or whiskey to kill the pain. He addressed Sally, "You will spend the night with him, miss?"

"Yes."

Kelly interrupted, "And I will be upstairs, sir."

Sally did not leave John Graves Simcoe during that night or for many nights after. She slept bundled in quilts, seated in an armchair near the hearth. They were long enveloping nights when John Simcoe ranted in his sleep. The slightest movement awakened him but he suffered without complaint. His sturdy shoulders lost muscle and his eyes sank deep into dark caverns. His strong legs thinned and weakened. His skin turned pale.

He watched Sally secretly from behind the walls of his helplessness, when she dozed, when she bustled around the room, when she could not look back at him. He traced the long straight line of the Townsend nose, the arch of her neck and the curve of her bust. He conjured the silky feel of her hair, the soft texture of her cheek and the smell of mint tea on her breath. He dreamed guiltily that she lay next to him on happier days when he was whole. And he cried. Unmanly and unworthy tears dripped through the husks of the mattress to puddle in a dark circle under the bed. But the inadequacy of his strength, his inability to act, made him shrink from her, while at the same time, her attentions evoked his deepest longings. While she slept, he let his mind run freely to the passionate thoughts that numbed physical agony and hastened the tedium of hours. When she woke, he withdrew into himself like a beast into the safety of its lair. Time dragged by, like dry sails without wind to fill them, inert, flaccid. Boredom condensed into frustration. He longed for the day when he could rejoin his unit and fight for what he knew was right and prove himself worthy of this woman by his side. Only then could he claim her with the honor and dignity she deserved.

The Townsends crept into the sick room to see him one at a time: Samuel to report the condition of Billy Youngs; Sarah to reiterate her own prescriptions for enduring pain; Beulah to clean and wash and stir the fire; Audrey with a sprig of green holly to cheer him. It was the color of spring, of new life, the green of hope and John Simcoe clung to the vision of the shiny leaves and red berries that refused to turn brown even now in the bite of winter.

But only Sally stayed. The meddlesome Sergeant Kelly frowned on the deepening attachment between his handsome commander and the beautiful Miss Townsend. He would not leave the two of them alone. But even he could not deny that Sally's presence brought John Graves Simcoe much needed peace.

Sally performed all the monotonous chores that Kelly refused, and she read to Simcoe, a duty that Kelly, who was near-sighted and had barely learned to read, abhorred. Each afternoon, she chose a book from the stack in the parlor. Her voice skimmed like music over the pages while Kelly twitched his pink rabbit nose derisively. John Simcoe did not move or give any sign that he heard in front of Kelly but when Kelly went out to attend to the inevitable chores, he studied Sally's every move. One day, he placed his hand over hers and kissed it. But that was all. It was an instant's impulse. He averted his face and bit back his lip, "Forgive me. I'm sorry."

Sally did not answer, but she did not drop her eyes until long after he had looked away. She placed her hand in his and he drew it against his cheek and he fell asleep.

Her thoughts rambled. What a strange man! Why did he persist in asking forgiveness? What peculiar guilt haunted him? She sensed in him desire and passion, intensified like the contained fire in a furnace. She thought back to DeLancey's ball when they had danced with happy abandon. Now he could not dance. He could not walk. He hardly spoke to her. The rub of the bedsheets opened new sores. Movement separated the cracks in his skin and left oozing, open sores. When he slept, she wept.

Weeks passed. Robert fled to New York and the business of Peck's Slip. Lord Howe did not prepare a spring campaign. The specter of an invasion of Philadelphia hovered. The dragoons mustered in Hempstead and Oyster Bay without John Simcoe, who lay abed, unfit for duty. Captain Sandford assumed command and came to visit and to garner John Simcoe's advice, but his visits were cursory. He followed his own mind and John Simcoe knew it.

It was March, before John Simcoe could sleep through the night undisturbed, and April before he walked alone. His recovery came fitfully, in tiny bits, like crumbs tossed to a beggar. He insisted on walking every day a little longer, punishing himself for some imagined weakness.

It was not the slowness of his recovery and not the pain, that tortured John Simcoe. It was the inadequacy of his comrades in arms, the same Hessians and loyalists whose discipline was lax and who had slept while on guard and allowed this terrible destruction to occur. It was his powerlessness to correct them, to insure that a similar event could not recur. It was the stagnant hierarchy and inertia of the officer corps, which lay like a wet towel over the most brilliant army in the world.

As the pain lessened, John Simcoe turned inward. Small defeats were numerous and each solidified his grim determination to master a movement here, a step there. Flexing a joint, buttoning his coat, pulling on his boots or jacking them off, chaffed. He steeled himself to each new effort until the tears dripped from his eyelids and his face lost all color. Frequently he failed. He would not accept defeat and God and nature and fate would not yield success easily.

Sally cried into her pillow at his stoic Saxon persistence. It overshadowed the sweet bloom of love. Where a few months ago, there had been laughter and caring, now she experienced a cold determination. His was a lonely effort that she admired but it did not admit passion, or even companionship. Robert had warned her to beware for her heart. He had not warned her that a soldier's worst battle would be private. He would wage it with himself.

This Simcoe was not like the others. He was too respectful, too noble. He inspired a distant passion, a worshipful love, like the stone statue of a saint or Caesar. In castigating himself, he fanned the embers of unrequited love, his own and hers. He loved her. She sensed it in every fiber. And she loved him. But she could not speak what she felt. That would be to invade John Simcoe's code of privacy, propriety and honor.

25

How could the tempest play him such a prank?
Blank is his prospect, and his visage blank.

John Simcoe lay abed in early May when the dragoons prepared to set sail without him. Cob and Beulah helped him into his full dress uniform and out to the beach, to watch the embarkation. They seated him on a stool on the wharf in the face of the wind but he insisted on standing, with two canes for support, flanked by Sally and Sergeant Kelly, like royalty with his retinue.

Ships lined the harbor. Launches ferried supplies aboard. Bales of hay, casks of ship's biscuit and rum, barrels of salt pork were hoisted aboard. Cattle, hogs, sheep, pigs and horses clambered up the gangplanks and into the hold like the animals into the Ark. Finally, the soldiers, hefty grenadiers, lithe dragoons, a regiment of foot, marched aboard.

John Simcoe watched in stony silence as the sails unfurled and the great ships swung downwind. It was a massive, inspiring sight, like Hannibal's departure from Carthage. His unit was aboard, Captain Sandford in command, and he, John Simcoe, remained here on a foreign shore, separated from his countrymen, abandoned by his fellow soldiers, discarded like a useless pebble into the sea. But he determined not to sink.

He cut a romantic, exotic figure. The wind turned up the corners of his red coat. He tilted forward over the canes, with red-haired Sally, the little Sergeant and the black slave behind him. To his troops looking back at the shore from the crowded decks, he was an object of envy. John Simcoe did not move from his position even as the last ships turned into the Sound beyond Plum

Point. The guns from Fort Franklin fired a round to bid them farewell, flocks of geese flapped in protest, then landed again as the smoke cleared, and a lonely silence hovered over the bay. John Graves Simcoe had been left behind.

Sergeant Kelly broke the awful stillness. "'Tis time we go in, sir. I smell rain in the wind."

Simcoe turned stiffly and flung his words in the wake of the departing ships like well-aimed darts. They fell short of their mark. "I will walk to the house, Kelly." And touching his canes to the ground, he pushed upright without a grimace.

The departure of the troops instilled an even greater determination in John Graves Simcoe. He would not stay down. The sores on his back opened and stuck to the linings of his clothes. Mean red patches still covered his shoulders where the rough melton wool of his coat chafed. His high-fitted boots rubbed the new skin from the calves of his legs.

Sergeant Kelly upbraided him, "Ye ruin your clothing! Your legs are raw! I'll never scrub out the stain if I rub my fingers to bony stubs! Give the time, sir, the time to heal! Time, and a dram to dull the pain, is the greatest healer of all!"

Simcoe snapped unmercifully at the fastidious orderly, like a dog at a pesky fly. "I am not one of your bloody Irish tinkers!" Sergeant Kelly recoiled at the insult but Simcoe continued unheedful. "I will shed my blood for my country and my king, fighting, to protect these good people! My duty and honor depend upon it!" Even Sally drew back from the fervor in John Simcoe's eye.

Kelly shouted back, "Act the lord almighty ye do! Ye should make your own bed, launder your own stinking, bloody clothes. Have ye no heed for your station? Ye risk your life in the burning flames for an urchin and a cur!"

John Simcoe could not abide criticism. He lashed at the Sergeant with an icy threat. "Silence, man! Or I shall have you court-martialed for contempt!" The outburst shocked even Simcoe himself who clamped his teeth quickly shut and turned his face away. Sally stared in disbelief.

John Simcoe never gave in. He strode out every afternoon, in the rain and cold, to the empty barracks, to the silent parade ground, to the shore to stare at the empty harbor. In bad weather, Sergeant Kelly accompanied him grudgingly. In good weather, Beulah was his escort. Sometimes John Simcoe summoned Kelly to walk out at night when he could not sleep, by the eerie light of the spring moon. It cast a silver swath across the black waters like the distant beam of a lighthouse. Stars twinkled like clear crystals. But a stiff norther could still blow the stinging mist off the surface of the waves. John Simcoe liked the wind and wet. It bit his nose and penetrated his bones and dimmed the memory of heat and fire. Kelly had to coax him home, make him sit by the hearthfire, towel him dry and spoon in hot tea.

Sally walked with him one afternoon to the beach and confronted him. "You torture yourself, John Simcoe, for no reason, and you make us watch your punishment. You assign yourself blame for faults that are not of your making."

His eyes flared widely and he launched into a bitter harangue. "Torture myself? It is you I've come to defend! You and all the other hapless, vacillating inhabitants of this land! I watch the rape of your forests, the theft of your crops and cattle, the burning of your ships! Foraging we call it! I've protested the senseless waste, the beastly Hessian conduct. We could at least repel the senseless rebel raids from Connecticut. It will be one year that we are here and there is no offensive, no struggle, no victory! Only gluttony, debauchery, torpor and waste! Loyalties shift because of it. These Hessians are as much slaves as the black men, sold by their Grand Duke to serve a foreign king! They owe our good king no allegiance. They enrich themselves." He stopped to breathe. His eyes blazed. "Even the Africans have a worth! They earn the value of their work! But Hessians loot and burn and destroy the riches of the land!" He hunched his shoulders, drew his head in defensively, and glared out over the empty bay. "Torture? What is the torture. It is pleading with my commanders, Kemble, Clinton, Montresor, to discipline, to stop the plunder, to mount an offensive. It is enduring Lord Howe who would rather add a title to his name and bastards to his brood than admit the wrongs we suffer!" He spat out the last sibilants in droplets of saliva. His spit landed on the fold of her skirt. Sally backed away. He recovered himself immediately. "Excuse me, miss. I did not mean to offend. I am agitated." He would not meet her gaze and the glance that he turned on the waves of the sea showed only bitter, repressed anger. He continued in a vicious whisper. "I have tried to tell them and they do not want to hear. This is my reward. They have left me behind."

Suddenly, he marched toward her and seized her brutally by the arms with two hands. His grip was strong and trembling. She shook from the force. "Sally, you must understand! I am a soldier! My honor, my rank, the possibility of promotion, these are what I live for! They think me deficient and infirm! I dare say you think of me so or you would not avoid me as you do!"

She fired her words back at him defiantly. "You drive me away, John Simcoe. Sometimes I think you quite mad! I flee from your tantrums but I do not avoid you and I have never thought you deficient!" She stopped suddenly. Her chest heaved. "I respect and esteem you, John Simcoe!" She almost confessed "and love you", but she bit off the words in mid-sentence. There was a brooding obsession in him that made her recoil. "I do not understand you! Go fight your wars! Embrace the wretched life you live for!" She was shouting.

A silence followed that punctuated the deep chasm between them. He drew up his shoulders and lifted his head proudly and retreated behind a barrier of stiff formality. Finally, he broke the silence, "And I esteem and respect you, Sally Townsend, more than I have ever esteemed a lady." He held his voice to a strangled monotone.

Sally let seconds intrude. She lifted her chin and arched her proud neck before she answered, "Thank you for the compliment, John Simcoe." There was a stain of sarcasm in her voice. Esteem fell far short of love.

A hardness congealed in Sally Townsend's breast. He offered her his arm to walk her home, but she refused. "John Simcoe, you must fill your own frozen sails. They are rigid and unyielding as the ice that clogged this bay." She whirled and walked unconsciously into the wavelets that lapped the shore.

He stiffened visibly at her distress, "Sally, please, you will wet your dress."

She walked on without turning. "And my shoes and my stockings and my heart shall feel the vitality of this world!" She bent to wet her hands and ran her fingers through her hair. "I am no child for you to mother, nor one of your troops to order about!... It is clear water. It will not stain. I will not drown!"

He spoke to her back. "I will send Kelly to accompany you home."

The water of the bay still bore the winter chill as it licked her toes. Sally Townsend enjoyed the cold. She took off her shoes and let the icy water bathe her feet. Her toes turned red until she felt them numb like flowers that deaden when picked. The zealous officer she had danced with at DeLancey's only a few months before, had disintegrated before her eyes with the ashes of the shipyard. In his place, was a frigid monument to manly endurance. She turned back toward the water and started to walk along the shore, weaving back and forth with the rush and retreat of the waves. There was an ease of motion here. There was comfort and hope that what was lost would return on the next wave.

Her path curved along the shore in a crazy zigzag of footprints in the sand. Her tears flowed suddenly and expanded into great sobs. She slogged on through sticky mud and over slippery rocks. The solitude of the beach, the even murmur of the water, the lifeless reeds left over from winter, reinforced her loneliness.

She bent to pick up a shell here a shiny stone there and looked up suddenly to find herself at the base of Cove Hill. Around the next bend, she would come face to face with the shipyard. She wiped her tears and started back.

"You'll find some good clams if you sift the sand with your toes. They make a good stew.... Darkness is falling Miss. It is not safe here for a lady alone?"

Sally jumped at the sound of the gruff voice. "Brewster!" Her nose wrinkled at the fishy smell.

Brewster did not answer directly, "Aye, 'tis me. Skulking around like a cat for a mouse in the dusk, come back to the scene of the crime, and you out here sobbing like a widow at a funeral! God knows it was not me that made you cry!"

She pushed her hair back and wiped her face clean on her sleeve. He pretended not to notice and took her by the elbow. "I found your shoes." He held them out to her. "This way. I'll tell Rob that I walked you home."

"You've seen Rob?" She dried her feet and slipped on the shoes.

"Aye, in the city." There was sympathy in the black eyes. "You grieve, miss. Tell me your grief. You will find relief for your heart and your secret will never pass my lips."

"You are kind, Brewster. I wish it were you who had touched my heart!"

"But it's him, the Britisher, Simcoe, is it not?"

"Yes." She breathed deeply. "But he will not allow himself the attachment of a woman. It seems by healing his wounds, I have injured his pride."

"Then he is a fool for his pride, miss. I would be honored to be loved for one minute by a woman like you." He took her hand and she gave it freely and she let it lay against his calluses because they each knew that any union between them was impossible, and because the touch of another human being loosened the vise of loneliness.

Brewster left her at the edge of the village. "'Tis not safe for me to go farther...And 'tis not safe for you to know I was here."

He turned to go but Sally held him back. "Caleb, tell Rob that I'm sorry, that he was right."

"Right? The older brother is usually the wiser. And you were wrong? A pretty head like yours should never be wrong." They laughed together.

"When the water surges in and stirs the mud, Caleb, it is hard to tell a pearl from a pebble.... This time, I was mistaken. But you have been a comfort to me, Caleb Brewster." She smiled. The odor of fish smelled good.

Sally spoke to John Graves Simcoe only twice more and then only in the presence of Audrey and Beulah. John Simcoe left Oyster Bay before the end of May. Captain John Montresor delivered his orders directly from General Sir William Howe himself, by coach and four, on May 21st. Montresor, *Monty* to his friends, was an old colleague of Simcoe's from Merton College, Oxford. It was a warm spring day with a hint of the brilliant summer sun to come, and Monty left the coach waiting in the lane. John Simcoe had one hour to pack and say good-bye.

The officer who left was not the same man who had arrived at the Townsends only a few months before. In appearance, he was thinner, more commanding. His singed hair had regrown darker with a speckling of grey over the ears. His new wig ordered from London, had not yet arrived. Sergeant Kelly brushed his hair back in a neat club. He had lost weight and muscle from the hours of inactivity and his red coat hung loosely but not ungracefully from the bones of his shoulders. His black boots, polished by Kelly, shone like mirrors, and his gleaming sword lay smoothly in its sheath against his thigh. He was handsome, perhaps more so, because the leanness chiselled his features, the fringe of grey at his temples added dignity and his deep blue eyes conveyed the poignancy of a man who had suffered.

Sergeant Kelly ran frantically packing boxes and readying the Captain's two horses for the voyage. Simcoe tended to military matters, to accounts of requisitions and forage, to the myriad reports which must be conveyed to the high command upon his arrival. Montresor entertained the ladies of the house and finally rose to help Captain Simcoe with his coat.

John Graves Simcoe bowed with deep gratitude to the family members standing in line in the hall. They were sorry to see him go and wished him well, all except Sally. She was not there. She arrived breathless and red-faced as he was walking out the door. He lingered a few extra seconds in front of her, but avoided her eyes. When he bent to kiss her hand, she looked boldly into the florid face of Captain John Montresor standing behind him. He held her hand tightly, unable to release it until she withdrew it. His voice was flat. "I will tell Robert you are well." He bowed deeply and walked out.

She stood immobile while the door to the coach slammed, the whip cracked and the horses trotted off. When she turned back into the empty parlor, she spied his books by the window in the corner. Tears welled up. She sucked in her cheeks, threw her head back and walked out to the beach, to the salt water and the mud and the flapping, squawking geese. She felt the wind blow her hair from her neck and sift the salt spray onto her face.

John Graves Simcoe rejoined his regiment on Staten Island, but when orders came for the 40th to proceed to New Jersey, he was retained. Montresor announced the news in Simcoe's garret room above the White Hart Tavern. He explained that General Sir William Howe did not think Simcoe strong enough as yet to command a full corps. General Sir William did not want to sacrifice such a valuable officer to the ravages of inclement weather, ill health, exhausting exercise etc. etc., before the surgeon general declared him ready. Captain Sandford would command temporarily in his stead. It was a feeble pretext.

John Simcoe's granite restraint cracked once more. He leaped like a tiger from his chair and slammed a fist into the wall. "I am as well to brave battle as I was to brave fire."

Montresor drew a curtain so passers-by could not see. He stated blandly, "The orders are written. They must be obeyed."

Simcoe appealed desperately to his friend. "I am a Captain in His Majesty's humble service and I am in line for promotion. May I at the least know the reason why I am to be furloughed?" He pleaded. "Monty, on God's honor, tell me the truth!"

Montresor pursed his pink lips. "You are mistaken, John. A furlough is not in question." He hesitated thoughtfully, weighing his words, "I tell you in strictest confidence because you are my friend.... Lord William Cathcart has newly arrived aboard the Phoenix, from England." He placed a hand on Simcoe's arm, "John, Sir William Lord Howe has no intention of going into battle with an unproven officer. He would take you, I'm sure of it, if he anticipated any real conflict."

Simcoe smelled a betrayal. "Lord William Cathcart?" He repeated the name; his square jaw clamped tightly; the muscles at his temples pounded steadily. "From England? What conflict?"

Montresor could not escape Simcoe's fierce gaze. He pinched the bridge of his nose to avoid Simcoe's eyes and smacked his lips mechanically, "I'm sorry, John, but Lord Cathcart has assumed the duties that would have been assigned to you had you been fully fit.... Cathcart will command the Queen's Rangers, formerly Roger's Rangers, but only for the present, while the army is idle. You will handle prisoner exchanges at headquarters."

Purple fury crept across John Simcoe's face. "I am correct in stating, Monty, that Lord Cathcart is to assume the command that was to have been mine?"

Montresor could not soften the sharp blade of truth, but he could not bring himself to affirm it. He declared blandly, "Lord Cathcart has paid dearly for the privilege.... John, he is a peer."

John Simcoe's handsome face went white. His hands balled into fists and he grit his teeth. He said coldly, "The bloody hierarchy of this mighty army will hamstring us all."

Montresor pretended not to have heard. "I've tried to lighten the blow, John. There will be other commands. Howe surely owes you one of the first and the best. He will not deny you again."

Simcoe's voice pitched higher. "Owes me, Monty? Billy Howe doesn't owe me. He owes these loyal people something more than casual leadership. He owes them protection from plunder, respect for the honor of their women, pursuit and destruction of the rebellious elements that prey upon them!" The months of anguish echoed in his voice. "Howe would sit on his hands and let a foolish peer play a game of chess with loyal subjects' lives! With his own soldiers' lives! He's had Washington between his teeth like a lamb in the lion's mouth! One snap of the jaws!" His voice fell and he muttered between his teeth. "We've a general who would fight a war from his bed!" He slammed his fist into the wall and splinters flew.

John Montresor dropped his eyes, embarrassed for his friend. In a few moments, John Simcoe recovered himself. "I'm sorry, Monty. I should not have spoken thus. We'd best pretend this meeting never occurred."

Montresor held out a handkerchief, "Your knuckles are bleeding. I admit it only to you, John.... You are right. And you have been cruelly wronged. Trust that the army has its reasons. Come, we'll go downstairs and drink black ale."

Montresor drank black ale while John Graves Simcoe stared darkly at his drink, nursing his injured hand, studying the column of liquid, turning it slowly, watching the glint of candle revolve in the fluid and turn around upon itself in monotonous continuum, like the endless sparring, like this colonial war that circled inevitably back to where it had begun. John Simcoe left Montresor asleep over his tankard. He stumbled up the stairs and collapsed upon his cot. He was drunk. The drink added to his frustration and anger. When Sergeant Kelly came to turn back the bed, he tore the piece of bloody handkerchief from his hand and hurled it at the Sergeant. Kelly jumped back with alarm.

26

'Tis done...Confusion sits on every face,
Inevitable ruin, foul disgrace.

Warm weather came in June, hard on the heels of a damp, rainy May.
Flowers budded, baby animals burst from the womb, and the earth smelled of
the sweet decay that precedes rebirth. General William Lord Howe lingered in
New York. News spread of a three-pronged drive south from Quebec, east from
Oswego down the Mohawk Valley and north from New York. Three armies
were to meet at Albany, splitting the colonies in half and destroying the Conti-
nental Army's lines of supply. It was a good plan, the brain-child of General
John Burgoyne, who had arrived fresh from a winter riding to hounds with his
Majesty the King in Hyde Park. But no official orders arrived from Lord George
Germain in London and General Howe advanced his own plans for conquest of
the colonies. Knighthood had bequeathed a certain comfort on the illustrious
General and a wide latitude of action or inaction. He hatched plans for an as-
sault on Philadelphia, seat of the Continental Congress.

John Simcoe's new office took him to Manhattan where he took up
residence at DeLancey's in a drafty maid's room. It was his task to arrange the
billeting of the more prominent prisoners, Gold Selleck Silliman of Connecticut, General Charles Lee and others who could be exchanged for valuable Tories
or held for ransom. Prominent prisoners were few. It was a desk command,
plagued by boredom and graft. By the end of the month, Simcoe's body was
healed but the debauchery of his fellow officers tormented his soul. Even his
beloved books could not distract him. He sought escape in the taverns and gam-

ing halls and race courses with Oliver DeLancey, Jack Rivington and Robert Townsend. Robert Townsend had redoubled his efforts to appear the good Tory since the shipyard fire. He laughed louder, danced longer and hailed King George in toast and song. But his first meeting with John Simcoe was awkward. Memories came flooding back. It was their fellow horseman, Banastre Tarleton, that eased them both through the initiatives.

Tarleton had arrived with the 16th Dragoons and appealed to Simcoe's stiff pride and Robert's guilt. He was brash and headstrong, but with a dash of brilliance and a predisposition to risk. His family were merchants from Liverpool and knew the Townsends but they dealt in slaves, which made him callous to suffering and loss. It was Tarleton's calm acceptance of slaughter and scourging of prisoners that banished forever Robert Townsend's remorse for the few Hessians who died in the fire. Tarleton shared Robert's enthusiasm for fast horses and inquired after the bay, and Tarleton instinctively sensed the importance to his advancement of Robert's reports in the Gazette. He too had lost prestige to a peer. Tarleton was responsible for the capture of Continental General Charles Lee but Tarleton's commander, Lord Grey, had preempted credit for the capture. Tarleton vowed that this would never happen again and promptly and faithfully informed the Gazette of his considerable successes. Short, athletic, perpetually active and ambitious, he was an easy conversationalist and enthusiastic extrovert.

Tarleton understood the advantage of companionship with John Simcoe. Word had spread of Simcoe's brave rescue of Billy Youngs. Simcoe was a popular hero. Tarleton allied himself with Simcoe, a consummate officer of scrupulous morals and spotless reputation, in the hope that the public esteem and trust should extend also to him. More important, like John Graves Simcoe, he longed to meet the enemy hand to hand.

Robert Townsend, DeLancey and Rivington joined the two officers frequently at Grace's. Robert saw in Tarleton an opportunist and braggart who masked his lack of scruples and discretion in such fanatic devotion to England that even John Simcoe forgave him. Tarleton drank freely, bragged of his exploits and talked loudly on all topics of military interest, especially before Jack Rivington. He was entertaining company and an informant's ideal. From

Banastre Tarleton, Robert Townsend learned how to act the loyal Briton. And he learned the inner machinations of the British military.

Of special interest, was Tarleton's description of the capture of Continental General Charles Lee of Virginia. They had been drinking the ubiquitous black ale. Tarleton leaned over the table and lowered his voice to captivate his listeners. "Lee's no rebel. He was expecting us to arrive like hungry guests for dinner. There he sat at table and offered me a glass of madeira which I accepted and drank of course. We toasted good horses, good hounds, good food, the King. When he finished dining, he came willingly enough."

"No resistance, no attempt to flee?" Robert pushed his drink away.

Tarleton raised an eyebrow, slapped his palm on the table and snickered. "He commanded my unit, the 16th Dragoons, in the last war with the French. We were not strangers. He knew us well. He didn't oppose us at all. He knew we would treat him according to his station and feed his mangy curs. When I laid hands on him, it was as if I had solved a great perplexity for him....I would say that he was relieved."

Robert sipped his drink to hide his excitement. Had he heard Tarleton correctly? That Lee was captured by the same unit which he commanded formerly? That Lee wanted to be taken prisoner? He spoke like a true Tory. "Congratulations Captain! Did you ask Lee to pledge his allegiance to His Majesty?" Robert's whole mind tensed for the reply.

Tarleton's eyes narrowed cynically. "No. We have other uses for him. We want him for exchange." His lips curled wryly upward. "But I dare say he's more with us than against us."

Simcoe added mildly, "And I had to find housing for his dogs! No kennel good enough for the beasts! No prison comfortable enough for Charles Lee! We put him up at Murray's, in more splendid quarters than Governor Tryon himself, and he complains because Mrs. Murray will not allow his flea-bitten hounds into his chamber! They have to live in the cellar where they can scratch and shed at their leisure."

DeLancey fired back. "We should exchange him quickly so he can sleep with his dogs and infest the colonial militia with their vermin!"

"They're already infested to capacity!" They all laughed.

Rivington reached for his glass, unfolded a long arm and lifted it high. "A toast my good fellows, to General Lee and his hounds who are better quartered in their imprisonment, than Washington's wretches in the leaky tents of Pennsylvania! To the loyal dogs of General Lee! May they scratch and thrive and grow fat!" They laughed heartily and clinked their glasses. When Robert Townsend got up to leave, he headed for Drake's and a hot mug of coffee.

The five friends, DeLancey, Rivington, Townsend, Tarleton and Simcoe, attended the races in Jamaica once a week. They talked of politics, horses, hounds and gaming. DeLancey owned some of the best thoroughbreds from England. Tarleton had built up a substantial string by foraging, and challenged DeLancey by raising the stakes. They all bet freely, especially Rivington who invariably lost. More often than not, Robert Townsend won.

At the race meets, Simcoe held himself aloof like an untouchable god, a red-coated arm flung casually over the rail. At these moments, conversation and betting proceeded without him.

His disinterest did not go unnoticed. "John, you will depress us all." Tarleton winked at Robert. "He needs a woman to put him right... I hear your sister is a beauty."

Simcoe glared daggers. "And she is eminently a lady, Ban Tarleton! Speak of her with respect!"

Robert headed off a dispute, "Ban only states the truth. We all admit to admiring Sally."

They prodded Simcoe to insist on a field command, to speak up for himself. But Simcoe drew back. "I should not be required to pay for a rank that I have dutifully earned."

It was Rivington who finally convinced John Simcoe to press for his own promotion. He appealed to Simcoe's sense of responsibility. "They need honest soldiers, John, who cannot be bribed, and who will treat the population with consideration and justice."

It was an astute evaluation of the British presence, but it came from a civilian. John Simcoe whitened in icy silence. He did not answer but he did make the appointment the next day. They accompanied him at the appointed hour to the Morris house which was army headquarters, past the sentries and secretaries, to the iron-studded door that housed the high command and they sat with him patiently on the hard benches that lined the walls. When his name was finally called, he walked woodenly through the doors to his audience with General Henry Clinton.

He emerged with a stony smile and written orders in hand to resume command of his unit. "But I do not have my promotion. It seems the quotas have been filled." That much was a bitter disappointment.

In the end, Simcoe's was a command of endless drills and tedious civilian policing. There was no campaign in the summer of '77, except far away in the north near Lake Champlain and Albany. The army in New York and Captain John Graves Simcoe sat idle.

Reports arrived of distant victories. General John Burgoyne had captured Fort Ticonderoga. General Barry St. Leger was advancing from Oswego down the valley of the Mohawk. John Simcoe itched to fight with them, but no orders came.

The officers spent their time deriding young General Johnny Burgoyne. They were jealous. "Gentleman Johnny" they called him and considered him a wag and a braggart. He was too young, too extravagant, too rich, too brash. Resentments seethed. He was a peer playing tin soldier, like Lord Cathcart. Robert Townsend thought him more like Tarleton, overconfident and rash. Burgoyne owed his victories to blind luck and to the invincible prowess and precision of the infantry. Given too much rein, he would defeat himself. His own fellow officers willed his defeat.

Robert Townsend repeated these thoughts to Mary and relayed them to Drake who sent them on to Brewster and Tallmadge. Mary went about her baking. Tallmadge himself had approved her involvement and Robert did not interfere. She delivered bread to Drake in the coffee house each morning. No one suspected a pregnant woman of spying. She lived on at Peck's Slip and busied herself with Stewart in the warehouse and Mrs. Burke around the neighborhood. Her proximity was enough to make Robert Townsend's desire for her flare.

He and Mary were sitting quietly at Peck's Slip on a lazy summer evening when John Simcoe came to call. Two lathered horses stomped at the hitch rail and Simcoe's voice ordered Kelly to walk and water them. He entered meekly, hat in hand.

"Robert, I would speak with you alone."

Mary rose immediately. "I will make some tea."

"No Mary, bring out the madeira. The Captain has had a tiring ride."

"I do prefer tea, Rob." Simcoe seated himself awkwardly across from Robert. "I've come..." He rubbed his eyes and began again with a non-sequitur. "You must think me callous."

Robert stared wide-eyed. "Callous? Because you obtained an active command?" The thought did not follow. He poured himself a glass of madeira and held it high. "To the King!"

Simcoe sipped his tea, "To His Estimable Majesty." He replaced his cup in its saucer and dropped his eyes before he spoke. "I have treated your sister cruelly."

Robert looked up in surprise. No mention had been made of Sally since John Simcoe had left Oyster Bay. That he should speak of her now, was oddly foreboding.

Simcoe's lips drew together in a thin line. His eye searched painfully for a reaction. When Robert did not respond, he picked up his cup and ran a finger around the rim. "I am aware that you did not approve of my attentions to Sally."

Robert nodded. He felt strangely sorry for the man. "No, I did not."

Simcoe twirled the liquid in the glass. "I do harbor fond feelings for Sally, as I think she does for me." His lips drew into a fine line and deep furrows creased his brow. "Too many of our soldiers dally too freely with colonial girls. I do not approve. I am not one of them. I have never unfairly sought her attachment. What affection there is between us is the product of conditions beyond our control." He stopped, pinched the bridge of his nose and closed his eyes. "I am here to tell you that I shall withdraw.... All I ask is that you not let her sadden. Distract her from any pain I may have caused."

"And if she will not be distracted?" Didn't Simcoe know how stubborn Sally could be?

"Look for one more handsome than I."

Robert laughed derisively, but John Simcoe stared him down. "Do not mock me. It is with great difficulty that I speak and my heart rebels at the thought."

Robert stared in disbelief. "Surely you know she is in love with you!"

John Simcoe looked up as if he had been struck. "And I with her.... " A deep silence followed. His voice floated away like the echoes of a dirge. "She has never stated it, nor have I confessed my love. When last I was in Oyster Bay, she avoided me. I want to do what is honorable and just, what I think will make her happy. I am a soldier. My life is uncertain. I am British. I sense a suspicion of us Britons in you, even among loyal colonials, even deep down... in Sally". He paused, looked away and continued haltingly as if he were scraping out the lining of his soul. "When this campaign is complete, I will return home. I would take her with me but she would languish. There is antipathy there, against any newcomers, be they forever loyal to our good king. I pray time will heal her distress."

Robert could feel only sympathy for this strange man. Simcoe suffered, like himself, from the war and from the perverse workings of his own will. He said simply, "Thank you for your honesty, Captain. I will do what I can."

Simcoe's lips trembled with words that did not translate into speech. Finally, he muttered, "I am in your debt". He flicked a fly from the rim of his cup, threw his head back and gulped what tea remained. "Tell her I am an ingrate, a scrub, that I have turned to strong drink."

"She is not stupid. She will not believe that." But Robert did not know what his sister would believe. Any deception gnawed at his soul. In the end he said nothing.

Simcoe added words in parting. "Ours was a silent understanding. It must be a silent parting. It is no less painful."

Preparations proceeded slowly for the invasion of Philadelphia by sea, not by land. Ships carrying men and supplies would sail up the Delaware River to the colonial capital, leaving most of the loyalist units with a reduced force under General Henry Clinton in New York.

Finally, on July 23, 1777, 15,000 troops boarded 260 ships. All New York came out to watch. It was the largest single embarkation that Robert Townsend had ever seen. Lord Howe took Joshua and Betsy Loring, John Simcoe and Banastre Tarleton with him. Robert watched closely as the dragoons led their mounts aboard. None matched the description of his bay. Austin had kept him safe. He and Mary waved from the crowded dockside as the tall ships spread their sails and swept out through the Narrows to the sweep of ocean. Life settled back into a quiet reality. Cattle, sheep, forage taken from the farms and villages of Long Island crowded the ships' sweltering holds. The island lay stripped.

The hot days of August inched by. Robert Townsend checked inventories dockside and in the warehouse with Stewart. He oversaw lading and unlading of the ships. Evenings he spent in the taverns with Jack Rivington or with Mary. Many nights, he would fall into a chair and fall asleep fully clothed, then wake sweating and snoring in the heat of the summer's night.

Mary laughed at the bumping of life inside her as her baby grew. She gave up carrying wood and water and delegated chores to Robert who turned them over to Stewart. It was Stewart who first gave Robert the first sign of alarm. They were in the warehouse, taking inventory of a shipment of Scotch whiskey when Stewart removed his pipe from his mouth and babbled, "The wee lady laughs no more, sir."

"She is near to delivering the child, Stewart. She has no energy for laughter."

"With due respect sir, I have not seen ye laugh in a fortnight. Laughter eases the laboring soul like the wine and the beer and the sweet smell of heather."

"Spare me your remedies, Stewart."

Stewart would not be silenced, "A draft of brandy would help ye sleep, sir. Ye do not recognize the symptoms."

"What are you saying, Stewart. I am not sick."

"Not ye, sir, I speak of the young Mrs."

Because of Stewart, Robert observed Mary more closely. The features of her face pinched tightly together, as if she were concealing pain. At night, she would lean far back in the armchair by the hearth, hands spread upon her mound of stomach and stare morosely into the dark.

Finally, he questioned her. "What is it Mary, are you in pain? Do you worry?"

"I have alerted the midwife." Her voice trembled when she spoke again.

"The life inside me is diminishing."

"What are you saying?" He was about to laugh at her foolishness but she turned wide eyes on his. They spelled raw fear. "Don't deny my worry, Robert Townsend. I am fully rational. The baby has not moved in the womb for the last three weeks." Suddenly her face went rigid. Her eyes clamped shut.

He rushed to her side. "Have you spoken with anyone about this? Mrs. Burke, who has borne many children?"

Her face smoothed again in a thin smile. "There, it was only a single pain. There should be many. Mrs. Burke says a woman frets by her nature... that it is too soon." She turned away to face the darkness.

Robert placed a hand over hers. "Perhaps it is a lazy child that it does not move?"

She shot back with a determination that bordered on anger. "He is Drake's child! Drake was a vital and forceful man! He could not sire a lazy son!"

Robert Townsend could not sleep. The image of Mary in pain taunted him. Near dawn he heard her cry out and rushed to her bedside.

Her eyes were huge; her hair, matted with sweat. "It is time!" Her face contorted in a sudden spasm and her whole body arched backward. A rush of fluid puddled the floor.

Robert Townsend shouted for Stewart who ran for the midwife. Mary's labor lasted only a few hours when she gave birth to a scrawny baby girl. It was an easy delivery. The midwife stayed with her until well into the morning, soothing her, bathing the infant, until Mary slept peacefully.

Before leaving, the midwife handed the infant to Robert. The effect on him was immediate. The baby had the same dark curls as her mother and the same pale complexion.

But Stewart issued the warning, "'Tis not your child, Mr. Townsend, and the child is feeble and thin. Be there any news of the father?"

Robert answered ominously, "No."

Nor was there news of General Howe and his massive flotilla until a merchant ship docked the third week of August and reported that the expedition had blown far off from the mouth of the Delaware, past the Delmarva Capes. Supplies had run short. Passing ships had seen bloated bodies of animals floating on the waves. The horses, oxen and sheep, that could not be fed, had been cast overboard. Whole herds, the wealth of Long Island, had drowned. Head of Elk on the Chesapeake Bay was the new point of disembarkation and supplies would be replenished at the expense of the Maryland Colony.

The Continental Army was too much in disarray to take advantage of Howe's misfortunes. Washington knew what was happening. Robert's powerful friends, who joined him at Rivington's, told all, and Robert dutifully passed it along to Brewster or Roe. But Washington retreated continually across the broad face of New Jersey. Disheartened, Robert Townsend continued his work. He noted the desertions, impressments, contents of warehouses, the arrival of new recruits, the disposition of Hessians, the caliber and range of British guns and the length of their bayonets. He exposed a plot to kidnap General Silliman from his home in Connecticut and to hold him for exchange. Brewster warned Silliman in time. But weeks dragged by. Hospitals and prisons and were filled. Another ship was demasted and added to the floating prison in Wallabout Bay off Brooklyn. It was the H.M.S. Scorpion, an appropriate name.

One early morning, late in August, Austin Roe jerked the lathered bay to a halt, ran noisily up the stairs at Peck's Slip and burst through the door. Mary cowered at the brazen little man, as Robert came running from the warehouse.

Austin's face was grave. "Rob, I had to come myself to tell you. It's from Sally." He handed Robert the message.

Robert tore open the seal and read. "She wants me home. Cob has been arrested. Father is helpless to deal with Captain Hangar."

Austin was nodding nervously. "Hanger is the thief who would have stolen my horse in the card game!"

Robert soulful eyes settled on Roe. "Why Cob? Why now?"

"Because he did not obey a sentry's command. The sentry was Hessian. Cob did not hear, could not read the lips of the German. You have Tory friends, influence. Only you can secure his release."

"From Hangar? I'm not so sure. I could bribe him with the horse...."
But he doubted the horse was prize enough to stop George Haugar.

"At least he will not end up drowned with the Philadelphia requisitions.

I will do everything in my power to help. Farley has a ship at the pier. Go quickly!"

"The tide and the wind are wrong. If your relays are in place, I will use them and my bay."

Robert left Mary and Austin Roe standing on the porch, jumped aboard the waiting horse and sank his heels into its flanks. The bay jumped to life and clattered away toward the ferry.

He arrived in Oyster Bay well after nightfall, but he was not tired. The injustice, the myopic stupidity and greed of the Hessians, the inhumanity, galled him like a canker. He knew why they wanted his horse. But what could they possibly want with an old, deaf slave?

"What happened?" He fired the question like an arrow at Beulah who had heard him ride up and held the door open.

"Cob went out after curfew. The dogs were chasin' the newborn calf. They say he didn't know the password. He said they never asked him for the password! Probably asked him in Dutch!"

"Where is he? Have they injured him?"

Sally came up behind Beulah. "He's to be sent tomorrow to the collection point at Bedford. He's in irons at Wright's Ordinary."

"I should have brought Jack or Oliver. Damn Hangar! Who is here who can talk to Hessians?"

Sally appeared, eyes wide with worry. "Thomas Barney, the village magistrate, the man who denounced father is friend to Hessians!"

"I will speak with Barney in the morning. Pray that he can be bought, Sal."

"Must justice always come at a price, Rob?"

"Justice and loyalty and love, Sal, they always do!"

Barney sat at his desk when Robert entered the following morning. He greeted Robert cordially and poured out a glittering glass of port, "Good day, Robert. Some port?" He passed a glass. "How's New York?" He leaned back in his tufted chair and folded his white hands comfortably on his paunch.

Robert took the glass, pretended to sip and remained standing. "New York thrives, sir, under the equanimity of British rule."

Barney smiled satisfactorily. He enjoyed watching Robert squirm. Finally, he invited, "Sit down, Robert, and what brings you here this fine morning?"

"Sir, my slave, Cob, has been unjustly imprisoned."

"Your slave?" Barney lifted a curious brow. "You seek justice for a slave?"

"Yes sir. He has been a true and faithful servant."

"For what cause has he been imprisoned?"

"He went to aid a newborn calf, after the curfew, and did not obey the sentry's command. He is deaf, sir. He did not hear."

Barney pursed his lips, hesitated and rubbed his round chin. "Captain Hangar is a difficult master. Can you offer an inducement?"

Calculations clicked in Robert's brain. "One hundred guineas, sir."

"A high price to pay for a slave."

"His wife and two children belong to us also. They are like family."

Barney nodded in understanding. Robert blanched when he realized what he had said. To call a black man family meant that the master had fathered him by a female slave. It was a simple way of increasing a family's wealth. Robert's remark could be interpreted as a dark blemish on the family name.

Barney replied with a wry smile. "I'll see what I can do. Where can I find you?"

"At home, sir. We will await news."

The family waited. Hours ticked by. They sat in the parlor with Beulah who hovered fearfully over her children. Sally and Robert performed the chores which would have been Cob's and Beulah's. About 3 o'clock, Barney rode up on a fat pony. He did not dismount. They walked out to meet him in the shade of the whipping tree.

"Captain Hangar wants you to understand that he has need of three kegs of rum and two fattened beeves." Barney could scarcely disguise the venom. "Since the prisoner is a family man...."

Samuel started. Robert put out a hand to hold back his protest. He spat the reply. "Where should I deliver them, sir?"

Barney averted his beady eyes. "Bring them to Wright's Ordinary. Upon their delivery, Captain Hangar will set your slave free after one hundred lashes, to be well laid on his naked back, here at this tree, tomorrow morning at eight o'clock." One hundred lashes could kill a man.

Robert's jaw dropped then locked in anger, but it was Sally who shouted protest, "The price was for his freedom, not his punishment, and you'll make us witness the man's suffering!"

Barney wrinkled his pink nose. "The price was for his life. You have that, but he is to be made an example. Prepare yourselves with clean wool and grease. He will heal.... Deliver the guineas to me. It is the best that I can do." He pulled the pony around and bounced away down the lane.

Sally and Beulah froze. Robert cursed. Old Samuel took charge. "Don't condemn yourself, Robert, my son. Barney is a hateful man. God in heaven knows that I or my father have never profited in human souls. By this we shall know our true friends." The old man smiled. "Sally, take the children to Youngs. They should not witness their father's scourging. Here, now, we will do as Barney says. We will deliver the ransom. Beulah, I advise you to go too, but I will not force you."

There was anger in the black woman's eye. "I go to see if there's anything Cob needs."

"Tell him, Beulah, that I will send a clergyman, and tell him he must bear up and survive and he shall live as a free man."

Beulah voice rang flat. "Thank you, Master Townsend."

No one slept. At eight o'clock, Hessian guards marched Cob in a neck iron to the tree as scheduled. They gave him a pine knot to clench between his teeth, tied his arms against the shaggy bark of the locust tree and ripped the shirt from his back. Hangar nodded his fat chin and the executioner raised the cat. Cob closed his eyes and bit down hard. Beulah turned away. The nine studded lashes descended. Sally and Robert watched the keen white eyes of the black man. The sharp tongs lifted the skin from Cob's back. He never cried out. Beulah stood like a column of stone. Only her eyes glared her hatred.

A crowd of brute, impassable Hessians had gathered around to watch. A few townspeople were present. Daniel Youngs turned away in disgust. A sergeant counted the stripes like the tickings of a clock. Minutes stretched to eternity. At each count, Cob sank a little lower. The ropes binding his wrists ground deeper into his flesh. Finally, it ended. They cut him down. Cob lolled like a dead fish, bloody and unconscious. The impassable Hessians walked away.

Beulah and Robert ran to cut his bonds and give him water. They rolled him onto a tarpaulin, carried him inside and lay him on the bed where John Simcoe had slept. Blood soaked the tarp and the bed. They wiped and washed and bandaged his wounds and gave him water to drink. For two days, in a fever, he hallucinated. Then he woke. He would survive. Robert walked the distance to Barney's on Hog's Neck and hurled the guineas onto his desk. Barney nodded quietly. Robert never uttered one word.

That afternoon, he rode to the swamps to search again for Drake. Conditions were worse, food more scarce. Dunned by their losses to the British foragers, people concealed what they had left. Shipping dwindled and goods that did arrive were heavily taxed to support the vast army. Smugglers charged exorbitant sums. Raiders crossed the Sound continually to wreck havoc on British-held territory. Whole forests were felled. Raw stumps dotted the landscape where once great trees had spread their shade. Wild game disappeared. The wheat crop lay devastated; the salt hay cut to stubble, in the name of war. And the brutal Hessians roamed unchecked. Robert returned from the swamps to find Cob better. But Cob refused the offer of freedom for fear he would be kidnapped like a prize bull and sold again to a harsher master.

Austin Roe delivered another letter to Robert in early October, from Solomon. Solomon predicted French aid if the Continental Army could produce a decisive victory. Victory? The word rang like a hollow bell, loud but without substance. But news arrived that Herkimer's militia had stopped Barry St. Leger and his Iroquois, along the Mohawk. Burgoyne would not receive expected support. There was faint hope. Austin was ecstatic. But Robert Townsend laughed at the idea of victory.

General John Burgoyne had captured Ticonderoga without a fight and advanced down the Hudson Valley with an army of over 8,000. Opposing him, the rebels had divided their loyalties. New Yorkers favored the haughty commander of the Northern Department, Philip Schuyler. New Englanders hated Schuyler, a Dutch patroon, who had contested Massachusetts' claim to the Hampshire Grants. They preferred the hook-nosed, spectacled, Horatio Gates.

The contest was far removed from Long Island but it held small seeds of hope for Robert Townsend whose task it was to prevent General Clinton from leading troops up the Hudson to reinforce Burgoyne. It was not difficult because Clinton had barely enough reliable troops to administer New York. Robert Townsend knew George Washington had less.

General William Howe landed in Maryland at Head of Elk on the Chesapeake on August 24th. More news arrived of more British successes at Chadd's Ford on the Brandywine River and at Paoli in the Pennsylvania Colony. Paoli was a massacre. Austin Roe related the bitter news. "Your friend, Ban Tarleton, led that one, bayonets only, like Cromwell at Drogheda. He hacked Wayne's Pennsylvanians to bloody little pieces."

Robert was not surprised. "Banastre Tarleton is not my friend. He is an expediency, the source of my intelligence... he will do whatever bloody business brings him glory." He added coldly, "Mercy and quarter are of no consequence to him. He will win at any cost."

"Strange friends and bedfellows you have, Rob!"

"I am the jester; I am without friends among them..." But he thought of one friend. Mary!

Austin had come to take back the bay and he watched Austin gallop away down the lonely road to Poverty Hollow.

On September 26th, General Cornwallis entered Philadelphia in triumph. Loyalists cheered. The long months of inactivity had borne fruit. On October 6th, more news arrived, another British victory at Germantown. Washington continued his retreat. Austin Roe did not come; Brewster was silent. The successive American defeats filled Robert Townsend with grinding pessimism. *Vic-tory*, the very event his heart craved, echoed the name of his enemy.

He accompanied Sally to tend the sick at the Meeting House which had been converted into a hospital. There was a greyness to her complexion, a sag to her cheeks. Dark circles encompassed her eyes.

"Sally do you watch your health? There is too much illness here... You're thinner than a thorn tree. You work until your knuckles are raw."

Sally did not answer at first. She stared glassily at the wall and seemed to read his thoughts. "You never liked him, did you Rob?"

Her question confirmed his suspicions. Robert answered truthfully. "I like him but not as a brother."

The hospital was a busy place, filled not with war casualties but with the injuries of life in damp barracks and crowded ships, and the inevitable victims of demon rum. It smelled of sweat, vomit and dried blood in the damp autumn heat. Sally wore a stained white apron, her hair tightly coiled at the back of her neck and covered in a linen cap. She looked ascetic, like a hermit fasting in the wilderness. She stood over a young boy of about twelve years, whose fearful eyes peered out from a rosy face and spoke softly, "It will hurt when I pull. Drink this." She handed him a mug. For a moment, Robert stood in silent admiration of his sister. She was not pining away. She was doing useful work, relieving pain. He thought that it was better work that his own deceitful pursuits.

She pulled. The boy's eyes closed. His muscles went limp and he breathed more easily. She stroked his brow. Robert walked up behind her. "Can I help?"

"Yes." He knew by her smile that her animosity had diminished. "He fell down an open hatch and broke his leg! Hold it in place while I splint it tightly."

Robert did as he was told. "Sally, I have seen him, John Simcoe." She continued unrolling the length of bandage around the splint.

When she finished, she looked up coolly. "John Simcoe? When? To what purpose?" She dropped her eyes to the grey face in the next bed. The sick man was delirious, mumbling incomprehensibly - a camp fever from sleeping in wet blankets and eating rancid food.

"He asked for you."

"Is that all?"

"Sal, come home."

She answered evenly, "I will be there before dark. Home is not a happy place for me as it was not happy for you, but I am a woman. I cannot leave freely." Robert did not pressure but he did not leave without her.

"You could come to New York, Sal. There are officers there who will not repay your attentions with disdain, who will at least make you smile again and dance and sing."

She snapped back. "And who will repay my attentions with silks and laces and French perfume and lie to me like Judas Iscariot if I will jump to warm their bed!" Her voice cracked and she averted her eyes. "Rob, I don't know whom I should believe, where to find a shred of happiness. This work at least distracts me. I feel better when I see ones who suffer more than I."

"Come to the city, Sal, for a while. The weather is fine and there are no casualties of war."

"Maybe... I believe I will."

New reports arrived of the plight of Burgoyne, of Colonel Baume's dragoons, slaughtered by a brigade of shirt-sleeved, New Hampshire men at Bennington. Austin Roe galloped in with the news and took lunch with Sarah and Audrey in the garden. He winked at Robert. The news smelled of victory. Robert tended the horse himself. He stroked the silky coat. The bay was still safe, still fast and still beautiful. How long would he escape the requisition? How long would his legs hold up to the pounding gallop that Austin's rides demanded?

Burgoyne needed his own relief and on September 21st, appealed to Sir Henry Clinton. Again Austin carried the news at night on the lathered bay and this time he summoned Robert to meet him at Youngs Farm. They drank sweet cider as Austin related the story of Burgoyne's wanderings to Captain Daniel and young Billy whose mother ordered him to bed.

Captain Youngs contested his wife, "It will be a great victory, Mother, and the boy must remember the day and the hour."

"And he must remember to keep his knowledge to himself in front of our Hessian guests! He is young, Daniel for such dangerous knowledge."

"He's not stupid, Mother!" He tousled his son's hair.

Austin began slowly. "Gentleman Johnny Burgoyne sent an idiot courier who wandered across the Connecticut line and fell in with a party of our militia. They were some of old Putnam's men in captured British togs. Their own uniforms had rotted to rags. They took him to Schuyler who found his message encapsuled in a silver ball." He stopped to laugh. "A waste of good silver for words that the man should have carried more safely in his brain. But that's Burgoyne, flaunting his riches, parading around the wilderness as if he would take an afternoon ride in Hyde Park! He has cavalry he doesn't use and baggage he doesn't need and how many thousands of troops who have yet to fight a battle! Three months he's been marching! He's learned to chop trees and ford rivers and go hungry and shiver in his silken bedsheets!"

The next week, Austin came again with news of St. Leger's defeat along the Mohawk. Now Burgoyne's Army was locked in deadlock in dense woods that prevented movement. They could not forage. They could not advance and Burgoyne vowed never to retreat. Horses starved. Salt pork and flour ran out. Clothing shredded and footgear disintegrated. Still Burgoyne would not retrace his steps or relinquish his thirty wagonloads of personal effects. Robert Townsend, Austin Roe and Daniel Youngs clinked their mugs together and toasted "the pride of fools in the wilderness." It was a happy time, the first in a long while for Robert. He drank too much and slept that night at Youngs'.

The next day, Robert sailed with Sally back to the city. They stopped to see Jack Rivington on the way to Peck's Slip. Rivington sat slumped over a table with his back to the silent press, a bottle of rum in one hand, a crust of bread in the other, mumbling to himself the horror of defeat. Sally's presence and news of Audrey elicited a weak nod. He signaled them to chairs opposite without a glance, and poured out another glass for Robert. "You've heard?" He bit down on the stale crust and washed it down with a swallow of rum. "Gentleman Johnny's lost the lot! Surrendered the entire army to toady little Gates! Saratoga! It's a black name in the annals of Britain!"

It was October 15th. Robert Townsend swallowed his joy and said nothing. His friend, Jack Rivington, was in one of his dour moods. He pulled a jug from beneath the press, took a long swallow and slammed the cork back in. His slurred speech poured out like heavy syrup, "And Gates gave a victory dinner! Filthy little commoner, Horatio Gates, sat with His Majesty's General John Burgoyne before two dirty planks, set on two empty barrels that smelled of rancid beef. They drank from the same glass because it was the only unbroken one Gates possessed.... And Johnnyboy lifted his glass to George Washington!" Rivington burped and his whole body shuddered. "General John Burgoyne, who last winter rode to the hounds with the King!" Rivington lifted his glassy eyes in disgust. "The fox got away! Samson toasted the Philistines! Cromwell blessed

King Charles instead of beheading him! Queen Bess bowed to Popish Mary, Queen of the Scots! Johnnyboy should have sliced off Gates' head and served it to King George like John the Baptist on a plate!"

Robert took the jug from his friend. "Enough Jack, you're drunk. Your ravings have no place in tomorrow's edition!"

Rivington raised watery eyes to Robert. "Tomorrow's edition be damned! And just what brilliant conquest am I to print in tomorrow's edition?"

Sally answered quietly. "You will print a brief note of sympathy for General Burgoyne, like a funeral announcement. Edge it discreetly in black. Follow with a eulogy for General Howe who has conquered the rebel capital and banished the Continental Congress to Lancaster and the Continental Army to the wilds of Pennsylvania."

Rivington threw his head back and toppled into a chair. "Praise and glory be to the King of Philadelphia!" He shouted it to the rafters. Then his head bobbed back forward and his eyes bugged. "Brave Howe! Mighty Howe! How can I tell my readers what they know to be false? The news has spread like a fire in a haystack! In two days Gates has captured an entire army. Howe has not accomplished the like in two years. He scurries off to spend Christmas with his mistress who warms more than his toes between his sheets! He let an entire army escape!" Rivington's fist slammed down in drunken anger on the black metal frame of the press. He shrieked with pain. "I have broke my hand!"

Sally stepped in. "It's not broken. Flex it a little."

Jack Rivington worked his sore fingers and continued more somberly. "Pain does sober a man. Howe was jealous of Burgoyne. How would you feel? A flashy young upstart arrives from winter in Hyde Park with the King and tells the Commander-in-chief how to win his war. Burgoyne's was a good strategy, Rob, but Howe did not want to be told, so he left Burgoyne to the wolves in the wilds. They severed his hamstrings and closed for the kill and the Whigs in Parliament are shouting foul!" He rubbed his eyes and made a rude attempt to stand. "Help me, Rob, Sally." He fell back and his voice turned to a suppliant whine. "Help me up. Read the type for me. The letters are a blur. Spell out the word... *Phil-a-del-phia*. It is Greek; it means loving... We must love Philadelphia and hate Saratoga!" He pulled too hastily at a drawer of type and spilled the letters onto the floor.

Sally stooped to pick them up while Robert helped Jack Rivington to a lonely chair. "Tomorrow's edition will be a day late."

"No, never late, Sal! But don't you be checking it for spelling and punctuation!" Rivington's eyes rolled and he bellowed like a hawker, "We have lost more than a few commas over John Burgoyne!"

Robert patted his friend on the shoulder and nodded to Sally. It was time to leave. Rivington would start drinking again as soon as they were gone, or he would muster the will to collect his thoughts and print the paper. There was nothing they could do.

They left Rivington glaring bug-eyed at his presses. They walked silently through the streets to Peck's Slip.

When they came to number 41, Laddie growled then jumped as they came through the door. Stewart called him back.

Robert reacted angrily. "Get this bloody beast out of my house!"

Stewart ignored the complaint. "Quiet, sir, the Laddie watches like a guardian angel. The wee one is not well." He pointed. "They are there by the fire."

Mary stood in the shadows by the hearth, holding her baby. Mrs. Burke stood at her side. A huge kettle belched steam as Stewart resumed his post, wafting the hot steam back into the room with a blanket. Mary's face was milk pale.

It was Stewart who raised his voice to explain. "The wee one cannot breathe, sir."

They heard it then, the rasp of inhale and exhale, as the tiny lungs sucked for air. Sally hung back but Robert moved closer to see the little blue face. Sally placed a quiet palm on the child's dry cheek. It was burning up.

Robert whispered the good tidings that should have made Mary's heart leap. "Burgoyne has surrendered."

No one seemed to hear or care. The baby coughed and Mrs. Burke spoke up. "She does not eat; she does not sleep; without air and water to cool the fever, she will not live the night."

Sally stepped up, "Let me. Mary, your milk will dry up if you do not rest."

Mary gave no sign that she heard. She grasped the tiny form to her breast through the long dark hours with Robert, Sally and Stewart standing in mute witness. Gradually, near the dawn, the child's breathing slowed, sputtered and stopped. When daylight finally shone a faint grey out of the blackness, Sally held a feather to the little lips. When it did not move, Mary relinquished her charge. Robert took the small body wrapped it in a white cloth and placed it in the cradle. He returned and wrapped Mary in his arms. "Stewart and I will see to the burial when the full light dawns."

"Please, not in an Anglican churchyard, rather a Presbyterian or a Quaker burying ground. Tom Drake would want his daughter in a free man's soil."

Tom, that name again! When could he call Mary his own? He murmured softly, "In the yard by the Meeting House, I will bury her myself."

"You are a kind man, Robert Townsend."

Kind, cruel, sad, lonely, Robert didn't care. He held Mary close and rocked her until she lay limp against his breast and Sally took her by the shoulders to lead her to a pallet and some sleep. Only then did Mary cry out. It was a strident yell, more the wail of an animal than the expression of any human grief.

27

Does lordly Congress relish this defeat?
Say it is pleasant to their souls, and sweet?

A cold, damp day dawned with the smell of snow on the air. Robert and Stewart broke the surface freeze to loosen black earth. They dug a small hole for a short life and placed the corpse in the grave. Robert read briefly from the Psalms. His voice croaked with grief and doubt. "To what purpose, God, did you give this one breath and to what purpose have you snuffed it out? There are green pastures even in this dying season... in the house of the Lord." Stewart bowed his head reverently as Robert passed his hand over his eyes and cut short any further prayer.

Stewart sensed his despair, "Ye have to believe in a purpose, sir, that man is born for a reason. Faith is harder than the granite of these headstones when they mark the dust of ones we love." His voice trailed off.

Robert hardly heard. He stood numbly listening to the scrape of the shovel and the sift of the earth as the Scotsman refilled the grave. It filled swiftly because it was small. Stewart shouldered the spade and started away. Robert followed. When they reached the narrow gate in the cemetery wall, a tall man in a voluminous cape stepped out from a shiny black coach. He was well-dressed, with spidery arms that held the cape tightly around him. He walked with splayed feet in wide silver-tipped boots, not unlike a duck. A servant followed and carried a spray of evergreens under his arm.

After they disappeared through the gate, Stewart drew Robert Townsend back. "Sir, the man who just entered, I know him. He is a general in the Continental Army. My old brain wonders what he is doing here." When Robert did not react, Stewart grew urgent, "Did ye not hear me, sir? Conway is his name sir, an Irishman. What has an Irishman and a rebel to do in British New York with a coach and servant to wait him?" The little Scot's customary cheerfulness had narrowed to a snuffling suspicion.

Robert muttered a reply, "There are Irishman who will sell their souls for silver or a fast horse." He thought of his beautiful bay and muttered, "Greed makes Judases of our friends as well as our enemies."

"In the last war, sir, that man was a mercenary soldier, one who preferred his own advancement to all else."

The bitter tone of the Scotsman's voice brought Robert to a halt. He drew his hand across his eyes and quizzed Stewart warily. "You talk like a rebel, Stewart. Is that where your Scottish loyalties rest?"

"Aye sir, in the same fold as yours. I am loyal to no bloody tyrant. I would till my own soil with my own gnarled hands and the sweat that stains the rags on my back." He clamped his teeth shut. His blue eyes shone red like hot coals. "We tradesmen and laborers have our own mind. They have whipped and kicked us and burned the fruits of our labors and now they would charge us the price of inheritance in bloody tax!" He stopped and stared with hard blue eyes at the stony face of his employer. "We will not let them do it again.... The carters and the dockers, the little people in the port, we listen like owls in the night. The officers, sir, they talk as if we are too stupid to understand what they say. We listen.... Do ye know why no wagons enter the Valley Forge, no blankets, no flour and no meat? The wagons are here, sir, diverted to the English lords! Or they rest abandoned on the roads! The drovers are greedy. They take the cargo for themselves and sell it for profit to the British who line their pockets with sterling."

Robert stood transfixed. It was fantastic, but if it was true? Robert Townsend wavered. How far could he trust Stewart? How much did Stewart know?

The little man stood hunched like a gnome beneath pick and shovel. "Believe me sir! Follow the man and ye will see! See if I am right." He turned stubbornly and walked away.

Robert Townsend pulled his hood high over his head and hung back in the shadow of the wall. The coach waited. When the caped man returned and the coach drove away, Robert followed. He had to run to keep up. It stopped not far away in front of a brick house in Maiden Lane. The man entered and did not come out. A red-coated officer climbed into the coach and drove away. Robert knew the house. It was the Morris mansion. It quartered the British military high command.

Robert returned to the cemetery and stopped by the grave where the stranger had deposited the evergreen boughs. The stone was worn and inscribed with the name "Conwell". Could Stewart have mistaken the name? When he stooped to pick up the spray, a rawhide pouch slipped out. Robert seized it, hid it in the folds of his cape and headed back to Peck's Slip.

Stewart and Laddie were waiting at the warehouse door. "Please sir, what did ye find?"

Robert held his voice flat. "He went to a lodging in Maiden Lane. I see no reason to suspect...."

Stewart cut in with a sharp edge of anger in his voice. His nostrils flared; his eyes narrowed. "Because I wear homespun and cannot read, and speak wi' the lilt of the moor, my words are like the chaff that blows away and ye do not believe." He shouted now as if volume would prove the truth of his words. "He is Conway. I tell ye, and I would swear it on my judgement day, in front of the Lord Almighty!

"Be quiet, Stewart! The neighbors have Tory ears!" The acknowledgement of his own spying stuck deep in Robert's throat. But Stewart knew. Robert knew that Stewart knew. Still Robert hesitated. To what extent did Stewart's knowledge endanger Brewster and Roe? And Mary? Could Stewart cause her harm? It was too late for worry. In the end, he blurted the truth. "Conway left this by the Conwell grave, hidden in a spray of holly boughs." He pulled out the billet.

"Should I summon Tallmadge, sir?" The mention of Tallmadge shocked Robert. Stewart had known all along.

"We should open it first. There may be nothing to report." At Stewart's rough table, they unsealed the packet. It contained a letter. The script was pretentious, inscribed with a wide quill, with flourish. No effort had been made to disguise the meaning. Robert read it aloud. "Mifflin respectfully accepts your gift. Gates will respond to flattery. Need L 1,000 doubloons or pistoles, in gold for Rush, Lovell and the Board of War. The votes are assured in Congress and they will dismiss Washington and send Lafayette to Canada and his Gallic cousins." It was signed Conwell.

Robert sat at table and held the paper to the light. Stewart reacted in horror, "I told ye, sir, he is a spy. The bloody English are issuing bribes, sir!"

Robert refolded the billet. His face turned dark. "It is far worse, Stewart. They try to influence the actions of our congress and the choice of our commander." He smoothed the paper flat with the palm of his hand and frowned. The muscles of his face contracted. "They want to replace Washington! That would hamstring the Continental Army!"

Stewart raised his voice, "With Horatio Gates, sir! Horatio Gates is the son of a serving man!"

Robert smiled at Stewart's blind prejudice. "You are a serving man, Stewart! Benedict Arnold is the son of a druggist and Daniel Morgan can hardly read! Serving men fight as bravely and die as nobly as lace-cuffed, sweet-smelling aristocrats!" He ended with a self-satisfied grunt. "But you are right. Gates is a pigeon... and the British are wise enough to wish us feathers instead of heart for leadership. Gates as commander would mean the dismemberment of the army."

Stewart snorted indignantly. "When shall I summon Tallmadge, sir?"

Robert pushed out his chair and rose slowly. "Not Tallmadge, rather summon Brewster but not yet! Stewart, can you recognize this man again?"

"Could I ever forget the way he walks, like a web-footed booby. He kicked me with those boots once for stealing a button from off his coat. I was his orderly."

"Did he recognize you?"

"Today? He didn't see me and I was beardless and young when he saw me last, and the hair that topped my head was black." Stewart's hair was salty grey.

Robert took command, "I will contact Tallmadge and Brewster. It is too dangerous now for Tallmadge to cross over." He left Stewart and raced to the Swan and ordered coffee. Drake sensed his urgency and hovered like a hen over her chicks.

Brewster arrived the following day in the alley at the warehouse door. Stewart summoned Robert immediately. They sat at Stewart's rough table, arms folded, heads together. At first Brewster did not believe that a major general could so easily break faith, but as Robert spoke, his hawklike face clouded. "We must first verify his identity."

"I submit, Caleb, that we send Stewart to Valley Forge, to Washington, to identify the imposter." Robert eyed his servant who was grinning widely with assumed importance.

"Are you willing, Stewart? I will find you a guide."

"The Stewarts are a fighting clan, sir. I be honored."

It was a dangerous assignment. The Jerseys comprised rich lands where Briton and Hessian foraged endlessly and the colonial militia took back what it could by whatever means. Thieves abounded.

Brewster clapped his hand over the Scot's stubby fingers and exited silently back into the alley the way he had come. Robert walked to the front of the dark warehouse. His boot caught the edge of a bundle where the open aisle should have been. He tripped and fell. "What's this baggage laying in the aisles?"

Stewart approached sheepishly holding a lantern which revealed more bales stacked high in the aisles. He held out his hand to help Robert up. "Ye're not hurt, sir?" Robert shook himself off. Stewart continued, "It's how I know the supplies did not arrive at Valley Forge. These are blankets, and kilts for our brave soldiers... and shoes. They have great need of shoes at the Forge. Men are walking barefoot, feet bleeding in the snow."

Robert jaw dropped. "You mean this," he pointed to the bundles, "is destined for the Continental Army?"

"Aye, sir."

"Kilts?" His eyes narrowed. "You've stolen kilts?"

Righteousness colored the little man's face. "Aye, sir, thick and warm and woolen. None better for to brave the winter... but not the Stewart plaid. 'Tis too visible a red. We took only the Black Watch, green as the forest, and blue like the night sky, from the miserable traitors who allow an honorable plaid to color an English rank!"

"The Black Watch is visible as the Stewart, man! Everyone knows they are King's men... If they raid the warehouse! If you are discovered...."

"But I shall not be caught, sir. The Laddie dog watches like ten of me. They think ye a high and mighty Tory. They would lick your boots clean to read their names in the Gazette! They'll not touch what is yours. They'd not dare." The dim light accentuated the bold innocence in Stewart's face. "We take only from those who can do without, from the commissary, from the provost. Mere pilfering, sir, not enough so's they notice. Mr. Brewster comes each week, on Fridays, to ferry it across the river to the Jerseys... but too much is lost to the brigands and the freighters. It does not arrive at the Valley of the Forge!"

A mixture of shock and anger struck Robert Townsend. He lashed out. "Stewart, you are a thief like them! Worse you are a stubborn and a stupid one!"

Stewart stiffened in self-defense. "I am not stupid sir, though stubborn I grant ye, and I am cunning like the weasel! But I am not a thief! Forager would be a better word, same as the Britishers and the Hessians who take from us. We take back what is rightfully ours, from the giant warehouse on Water Street."

"Stewart, you are stealing from Cunningham's and Joshua Loring's own stores!"

"Cunningham is a lout! Not *cunning* if he cannot discover the theft, although I will grant him the *ham* and a kinship to the pig!" Stewart was proud as a hound with a bone. He looked at Robert eye to eye.

Robert frowned. He had lost the argument. He tried one last plea. "You place us in great peril, Stewart!"

"Ye put your own self in peril, sir." When Robert reacted with a leer, he continued, "And 'tis only while there be need. In the spring, when the crops increase and the weather warms, there will be no more need."

Robert's anger raged. Stewart had used the warehouse to store contraband without his permission. But he admired Stewart's daring while deploring his lack of prudence. He could dismiss the brazen Scotsman but that would not dispose of the stolen kilts. And Brewster was involved. Stewart stood somewhere between hero and fool.

Robert Townsend shoved his hands in his pockets and issued a warning, "Discretion, Stewart, and strict secrecy if you please, if you are to remain in the Townsend employ."

"As always, sir. I would have it no other way."

Robert walked back across the street in a black mood. He was not adept at hiding his annoyance from Mary. It showed in the glare of his eye and the set of his jaw. She was quick to discern it. She smiled up at him and did not seem in the least despondent at the loss of her child. "Are you hungry? I've mutton stew just come to a simmer. There's enough for Stewart too.... You might ask him to join us."

Robert muttered testily, "Damn Stewart."

The curse surprised Mary. "What has Stewart done, Robert Townsend, that you come swearing like a whaler?"

Robert glowered. "He's stashed bales of clothing, kilts from the Black Watch, all stolen, all damning, all over the warehouse!"

"They will not be there long." She bent to stir the pot, lifted out the dripping spoon and licked it. She was smiling like Stewart.

Robert's coat was half off. He stopped, stunned. "Not you, too?"

"Did you think I've sat idle. Mourning does not console me. The silence, the weeping, I look frightful in black. I am a doer, Robert Townsend. You must have noticed...."

He had. She was always baking, sewing, cleaning. But smuggling and stealing? He bit his tongue. "Have you not enough to do without meddling in a man's work?"

"I am bored with woman's work."

"Are you mad, woman? You are a thief and a smuggler! If Loring finds out, if Cunningham orders his men to search...."

"We shall explain that Captain Simcoe has requested clothing for the prisoners. I have a copy of his requisition."

"Simcoe! Then you've forged his signature! They know better than to think him involved!"

"Just so, he is above reproach. As for the signature, it appears authentic." Mary tossed her black curls defiantly, "Kilts are sturdy, thickly woven sheep's wool, what our poor soldiers need. They can sew them into britches or cut them into blankets! You needn't worry. They will disappear day after tomorrow when Brewster comes to collect them.

"And Brewster too! I cannot believe he permits this! Common blankets would be less conspicuous!"

"They are not conspicuous in the warehouse. As for Stewart, I am proud to share his efforts."

"You are an impetuous, stubborn woman!"

"When I am doing what is right, yes, Robert, I am."

Robert had no answer. She watched the red flush of suppressed anger settle into his face. She continued to look at him until he turned away. Over his objections, she summoned Stewart for dinner and they ate in stony silence.

28

The merchant trembl'd for his crowded store;
One dreadful pause, and all perhaps is gore.

*T*he kilts disappeared on Friday and so did Stewart. He accompanied Brewster across the river to Jersey and on across the Raritan River to Valley Forge. Robert took up the guard and inventory duties himself. He settled comfortably into life with Mary in the little house, until the third week when there was an unexpected knock at the warehouse door. He opened to two burly ragamuffins who stood near an open cart piled high with wooden casks. Mary marched up the alley in the mud behind them. They went into action as if by rote, backed the wagon to the alley door and began to unload casks of salt beef. Mary explained, "Salt beef, sustenance for the winter months!" Robert barred the door and confronted her angrily. "Where did they come from? If they are stolen, you cannot bring these here." His voice was shrill with determination.

The men stood dumbly, each with a heavy cask across his shoulder. Mary planted her hands on her hips and answered for them. "Shall we leave them in the street for the British sentries to stumble over?"

"Mary be reasonable!"

She confronted him brazenly. "Robert Townsend, have you lost all courage?" She seemed to grow in stature. There was a fire in her brilliant smile that he had not seen before. "Yes, there is risk. There is a risk in all we do, in what you do, Robert Townsend. There is risk in any deceit. I am happiest when I risk. Risk invigorates my soul and dulls my darker emotions. I dare say it does the same for you!"

"But I am a man!"

Mary reddened and raised her voice. "And I am not! Giving birth, Robert Townsend, is as great a risk as any man can take." A horse's hooves clattered on the cobbles of the street. Mary jerked around. She turned back with eyes full of urgency. The two workmen set their barrels down and palmed the knives that they carried in their belts. Mary edged quickly by Robert, "You must let us in now!" Her voice quivered. Robert sensed her fear.

He held the door wide while the two men picked up their burdens and followed her. He closed the door, ran after her and swung her around to face him. "Mary, you must put a stop to this!"

She jerked away but he held her firmly. "It is too late for that."

The clatter intensified. The dog barked. Mary trembled beneath his grip. A rag picker with his cart clambered by in the street, before a high-seated phaeton with a red-coated officer on the box. The officer flicked his whip at the rag picker who fell onto the cobbles. The rag picker cursed but stayed down where he had fallen. Another lick of the whip laced his mangy horse. As the clatter died away, he picked himself up and stroked his frightened horse. Blood ran down his cheek.

In the warehouse, there was absolute silence. Mary was first to speak to one of the workmen, "See to Cheever, if he is hurt!" The shaken rag picker was getting up, shouting invective at the officer. "Devils in red, think you own the streets!"

Robert had not diverted his thoughts from the smuggling. "You trust your secret to common laborers!"

Mary was unperturbed. "He shadowed the alley! I for one am grateful."

The workman returned with the bloody-faced rag picker and addressed Mary. "It has laid his brow open, mum. He's frightened."

"Take him to the house."

In the warehouse, Robert drew back a tarp on a bale - blankets. In a fury, he threw back more tarps.

Mary explained softly. "I'm sorry, Rob. I did not think that you would object. These are only blankets. There are no more kilts."

The apology softened his anger. He breathed more evenly but he did not reply.

"You are so particular, so careful, Robert Townsend, and you are much better looking when you smile..." Mary was teasing him.

He would not be teased. His blue eyes drilled like an augur straight into her gaze. Emotions suddenly burst forth like water from behind a dam. "Don't mock me, Mary Drake!" He was not aware that he was shouting, "I am thinking only of your welfare. I care too much for you to withstand your mockery! These wily English have cast you as my mistress and me as your lover! I am tired of pretending, tired of censuring my every word, tired of trying to be what I am not. I wish that this lie I live were true! I want you safe and happy! God knows I want you very badly!" He stepped back, shocked at his own performance, half expecting to be slapped.

Her mouth opened. The workmen returned with another load before she could form the words. Robert whirled and stalked out the door before a second outburst overwhelmed him. He charged across the street and up the stairs two steps at a time. He was breathless and nauseous when he stomped into the room, as if he had run a hard race, then drunk cold water from a slough. He took off his jacket, loosened the collar, unbuttoned his shirt and shouted in the caverns of his soul, "Fool! Blockhead! Idiot!" He threw open the window to breathe the cold air and stood with arms braced against the frame, head hunched between broad shoulders, brooding, while the winter cold gushed in around him. He turned suddenly back into the room to come face to face with the wounded rag picker.

Blood dripped down his face. He stood meekly, hat in hand. "Beg pardon, sir. I don't mean to cause you trouble."

"Come, I will clean the wound. What's your name?"

"Cheever, sir."

He washed the wound and covered it with clean cloth then opened the rear door to let Cheever out. He was standing with lungs still heaving, when he heard Mary's footsteps. She entered slowly, pushing the door to reveal a widening triangle of brightness behind her. She stood for a moment like an angel in a halo of light, then closed the door gently. She almost whispered, "You'll catch yourself a chill, Robert Townsend. Close the window."

Robert Townsend breathed in deeply. As he turned toward her, his words gushed like a flood. "Mary, you must listen! I have felt for you from the bottom of my heart, from the first time I saw you, but I dared not reveal myself. There was your husband, then the baby. I have fought battles like no brigadier has ever conceived, here in my heart." He whirled to face her and pounded his chest with his fist. "I withdrew and retreated and re-deployed. I have no more defenses, Mary. I must hide my feelings daily, act the zealous Tory! I must pretend to be what I am not every minute that I live! I cannot continue this farce in front of you! I am quite mad about you!"

"I did not know."

"Have I have become so very good at deception?" Sarcasm strangled his words. He turned again to face away from her to look out the open window.

"You are a good spy." She walked up behind him and lay a hand on his shoulder. "Robert Townsend, I'm overwhelmed. You surprise me, but you do not displease me."

He grit his teeth and continued to stare, as if he had not heard. "I love you Mary. I have loved you from the first." The chilly wind blew through the window ruffling his hair and cooling the heat in his face. "I do not expect you to return my love, but I cannot remain here under this roof and deny myself any longer. I admit that my intentions are not pure.... I will find other lodging."

He felt pressure on his shoulder. It was a light touch, like the brush of a cloud, but it coursed through his veins like swift tongues of fire. She pushed harder and he leaned to her. Suddenly her other hand was on his sleeve pulling him gently, quietly, toward her. She placed a hand on each cheek. She moved up on her toes to reach his lips. A delirium shook him. When their lips met, months of frustration flooded away like wine from a barrel when the bung is pulled.

Their love-making was jubilant and passionate, like the howling wind that blows out the tempest and blows in the sun. It quieted at dawn. The sun rose red in a blazing sky and Robert Townsend slept the sleep of the blessed or the damned, he didn't care which, because Mary slept in his arms.

The sound of the dog barking and men shouting in the street startled them awake. Robert scrambled into his clothes and rushed to the door. Cheever, the rag picker was back, shuffling drunkenly beside his wagon. Two sentries came up behind him and clubbed him down with the butts of their guns. "The password or the toll! You forget one, you pay the other!" Cheever slid numbly to the icy cobbles. This time he did not get up. Robert rushed out as the sentries fled. The man bled from a blow to the back of the head. He was unconscious. Robert carried him to the house where he revived and looked wildly around, "Me horse, me Nelly girl, did they take her?"

Mary looked out. "She is standing in the street."

Cheever glared at Robert worshipfully, "God be praised ye came when ye did sir. They be no true sentries. Bloody thievin' devils! I told them the password, I did, but they did not heed. Go to me Nelly girl, sir! She be an innocent mare, me friend and me livelihood!" The eyes blinked, "And do ye have any whiskey to kill the ache in me head?"

Mary stood by with a bottle and cup and poured generously.

The man ranted on. "Not wine, mum, I crave good rum. The stronger the nectar, the duller the pain!" He passed out again and awakened a few moments later. "Take me Nelly girl to her stable at the end of Wall Street. Knock twice, then thrice more. There is a man, Hickey, who will bed and feed her. Take her now before they lay hands on her and use her cruelly. An' gi' me more sweet rum before I die of pain."

Mary took charge. "Go! I'll tend to him."

Robert Townsend tugged the swaybacked mare, Nelly girl, the whole length of Wall Street until his shoulders ached. He knocked as instructed and Hickey opened furtively, led horse and cart inside and closed the door. His voice croaked. "Where's Cheever? That's his beast. Did he fall down blind drunk?" Hickey wore rags and squinted through hooded, secretive eyes, like a vulture. He eyed Robert's unpatched, clean clothing.

"They tried to steal his horse."

"They who?"

"Sentries. I don't think he remembered the password. He thought them common thieves."

Hickey turned to unbuckle the harness. "He knew the password, unless the drink dulled his brain, or they did not give him time to think. Cheever's mind is slow, even without the drink."

When Robert's eyes adjusted to the dim interior of the stable, he noticed bales piled in the stalls like those in the Townsend warehouse.

Hickey mumbled while he unhooked the traces, "They were desperate or blind greedy, steal a splinty nag like her... Wagon's worth more. Can't no more use a good horse on the streets of New York! Brigands steal the shoes off a horse's feet and the hairs from his tail!"

The harness was unbuckled and Robert started to back the wagon away. Hickey held his arm. "I'll do that. It's heavy work for a man what can hire another to do it for him. You say Cheever sent you here? I know by your clothes, you're a rich man, that or a thief, and Cheever knows no rich men." It was as clear a challenge as the slap of a glove.

Robert held his tongue. He shoved balled fists into his pockets. "I work according to my station and you according to yours. We both work as free men for Brewster!" He repeated as if the name carried a sacred meaning. "Caleb Brewster!"

"Brewster?" His laugh had the sound of steel on a whetstone. "I know only one named Brewster!" His ugly stare threatened. "There you stand in gentleman's clothes from Mulligan's Thimble and Scissors no less! You want me to believe you take orders from one what smells like Brewster!"

Hickey was not convinced. The horse was safe. Robert Townsend thought better than to challenge, turned on his heel and walked out.

It was one of those clear cold days with the sun so strong it portended not spring, but the heat of the coming summer. Yet the darkest days of winter had not yet arrived. People were sauntering in the street, singing, laughing enjoying the light of a brilliant afternoon. Robert Townsend squinted at the bright blue sky that would darken very early. There was a latent thorn pricking his consciousness like the early advent of night on that glorious day. Suspicions tortured him and suppressed his natural optimism. He could not trust people and others could not trust him without questioning his allegiance or his religion or the clothing he wore or the status of the woman he loved. Would independence change the perceptions of men? He doubted it. He kicked a pebble. It rattled across the cobbles.

He imagined a cottage beside a stream with an apple tree in the yard and a milk cow in the pasture and a few sheep and some chickens and geese, but he walked to the cramped little house near the wharf at Peck's Slip in the shadowed, rutted street and he rubbed his bloodshot eyes to hold back unmanly tears.

He had heard John Simcoe speak of an ancient Greek named Sisyphus. It was a peculiar name for a man who spent his life trying, never succeeding. He felt like that man now, trying to hold a tiny pebble in place. A gush of water, an angle of hill, a puff of wind, and it slid so easily backward, like this forlorn cause he had pledged himself to. His felt his own life slipping backward.

29

Seen or unseen, above, on earth, below,
All things conspire to give the final blow.

Christmas came. It was weeks away, then in a moment, it had arrived. There were no celebrations. General Howe was snuggled safely in Betsy Loring's bed in Philadelphia. The wood, hay, beef, flour, that should have provided an easy winter in New York went to supply British extravagances in Philadelphia. Joshua Loring, Commissary General and William Cunningham were left to collect and distribute what was left in the city. They sent out gangs of brigands who took whatever they wanted and kept much for themselves. They portioned out what was left to whoever would pay the highest price. The poor who could not pay, or anyone suspected of rebel sympathies, had to steal to stay alive. Prisoners in the Sugar House or aboard the freezing hulks, died.

The British enthusiasm of the previous year had evaporated with their crushing defeat at Saratoga and the effort to feed, clothe and fuel the huge army. But the weather was milder than the year before. The sleet and snow did not arrive but was replaced with cold, pelting rain. Disease spread. Robert heard the hacking cough of consumption on every street corner. And there was smallpox in the city. When Captain Farley's Promise docked at Peck's Slip with a cargo of dry wood, the queue backed all the way to Pearl Street, a shivering, threatening mass of greedy, cold humanity. Captain Farley apologized to Robert that he could not set aside more wood for the family.

"We will do with one less log on the fire, Farley." Robert retreated to Peck's Slip with Mary and made do with very little. He and Mary closed off the upstairs and snuggled together in comfortable warmth in the front room and kitchen. Farley promised to return with more wood the next week, but there was never enough.

Stewart had not returned. Cheever replaced him in the warehouse but Cheever's could not write and keep accounts and the dog, Laddie, whined for his master. But Cheever joined them for the Christmas dinner. He tied a towel around his neck, slurped his wine and devoured his meal with his fingers. His conversation consisted of grunts and snorts. Robert ignored him. Mary smiled sweetly and heaped more food on his plate. There was turkey and venison with turnips and onions and a fine madeira from Martinique. When Cheever loosened his belt and started to belch, Robert pushed him out the door and watched while he vomited the whole of his dinner into the street.

Brewster arrived the day after while Robert was dozing in the armchair by the fire. He jerked awake when the whaler entered. Robert almost didn't recognize him. Brewster was clean-shaven, dressed in clean brown homespun, tailored britches and tricorn hat. He reeked of French perfume. His dark face was grim. He entered without a word and sat himself at the kitchen table. Mary poured out a glass of cider and teased, "Caleb Brewster, you've washed the smell of whales from your skin! Are you in love?"

"We took Colonel Hargraves from Sag Harbor for exchange. He had a supply of scent. I thought it would impress you." He answered genially enough but did not change his expression. He waited before he announced the reason for his coming. The pause stressed the gravity of his news. Stewart, he announced, had identified Conway but he had been seized by Gray's legion on his return near Camden, in the Jerseys. "Gray's men. They are the same murderers who butchered Wayne's boys at Paoli! The Board of War in its supreme wisdom, has appointed Conway the new Inspector General of the Continental Army! Imbeciles and madmen, we have elected to rule us! General Washington swore like a sailor when told the news. He has protested vigorously to the bloody Congress!.... Me, I think it a conspiracy, one that involves more than Conway.... Mifflin, the Commissary General, Rush, Lovell are suspect, and Gates is denying all and laying the blame to his aide, James Wilkinson." He raised his shaggy brows to look sullenly at Robert. "What do you think?"

Robert was silent. Mary answered with a question. "Think? Tell us first what has become of our shipments?"

"Bogged and rotting in the Jersey mud. That's why I come tonight. It's why I've shaved off my beard and dressed myself like a London dandy.... Tallmadge says we must be careful. You must stop the collections for a while." He addressed his next words to Mary alone. "You hear me Mary Drake! Distribute what you already have to the needy. Hide it. Destroy it. Amass no more. Cunningham is sniffing like a bloodhound on a scent!" He turned to Robert with an ugly frown. "You see to it that she listens to me. How is Cheever?"

"Healthy, hungry and useless."

"I thought as much."

Caleb Brewster spent the night and left the following day at dusk. He took Cheever with him. Robert and Mary were left to care for Stewart's dog, pack and distribute or destroy the remaining contraband. Captain Farley of the Promise agreed to transfer the stores secretly to whaleboats at an appointed cove east of Throg's Neck for shipment to Connecticut. It was dangerous work. On his third run, between Hellgate and Flushing, a schooner captain hailed and boarded him. Farley dumped the remaining bales overboard, into the Sound.

Robert slept more easily after the contraband was gone. He and Mary settled into an easy existence. He gave his full attention to business and his profits rose. The wood shipments continued and he fitted out the Katherine and the Weymouth for the Barbados run. They returned with ships' holds full. Robert sent a barrel of rum to Colonel Cunningham to curry favor, one to his friend, Jack Rivington to loosen his wagging tongue, and one to Angus MacRae at the tavern out of the goodness of his heart. He met Jack at the tavern on a rainy evening. Angus ushered them into a back room where the walls had no ears.

30

O save yourselves before it is too late!
O save your country from impending fate!

*I*n April, Stewart returned. He was thinner and his skin was grey but his feistiness was unshaken. He had remained in British custody for two months, in a tavern in Germantown in an inner room without light. Sergeant Kelly, John Simcoe's orderly, had saved him. The Irishman had greeted the guard as he passed and Stewart had recognized his voice and called out. Kelly had vouched for Stewart's good faith. The following night, the bolt came loose and Stewart had walked out. He made his way across Jersey as a fugitive to Paulus Hook where he met with his smuggling friends. He was lucky. Physically, he was not unhealthy. He had eaten clean food although not enough of it, and he had slept in a dry bed. But he was pale and weak. Most of all, he missed his dog.

Mary insisted Stewart rest when he arrived home. He lay down for three days. When he awoke, he was hungry. He ate until the cupboard was empty, then went back to his warehouse and his beloved dog. To rebuild his strength, he began to take long walks with his dog. The walks gradually became daily ritual.

April came and went. It was May when Robert walked with him down Greenwich Street, along the banks of the Hudson River. Buttercups bloomed in sunny meadows and the white bells of lily of the valley filled the shade under wide tree branches. Green mint grew wild and scented the air. Soldiers on horseback passed them by on their way to armory or tavern.

Robert and Stewart chatted while the dog darted back and forth across their path. Sometimes Laddie ran ahead after a grey squirrel or splashed into the marshes to chase ducks. Today the dog bounded into a flock of pintails then shook himself and waited near the entrance to a narrow path that wove inland to Harrison's Wood.

"'Tis there where I used to wait for the boats to Jersey, sir, and here where I set foot again on beautiful Manhattan after my captivity. The Laddie remembers." Stewart eyed Robert furtively and continued. "The boats that took the goods put into shore there. We had wagons in Jersey that carried them on to the Valley Forge. Do ye want to see the place?"

Robert was curious. They walked down the path to a wide clearing behind a wall of twiggy sumac. Lengths of bailing cord lay among the grasses and Robert spotted two casks with the stamp of the British commissary in plain view. "Discovery of this will earn you a hangman's noose, man!"

"The place was clean when they arrested me, sir! I swear it!" Stewart's eyes bulged as wide as Robert's.

A sudden realization struck Robert. The smuggling must have continued without Stewart. It had moved away from the warehouse to this lonely place. Stewart's words confirmed his suspicions. He answered, "Do not swear!"

"Not to worry, sir, they will not trace the supplies to us!" Stewart clamped his mouth shut and shot a glance into the trees. More bales were there. "Unless your mistress Mary...."

Robert's anger mounted. His jaw went rigid. "Brewster has ordered you to halt collections, to destroy what you have! That was months ago! Think man, of what could happen if you are caught! If Mary is caught!"

"I think about it daily, sir. The wee lady is very brave, braver than I! She fears nothing!"

The truth shook Robert like the slap of a dead fish. The muscles of his face pinched as he cringed at the thought. It was so like Mary. She refused to give a thought to the unpredictable future, even to consider dire consequences. She was careless, even rash.

Robert Townsend turned his rage on Stewart. "Stay here until every scrap is buried, banished, burned to black cinders. If I hear you are any more involved in stealing or smuggling, you'll seek employment elsewhere!" Stewart shrank from the lash of Robert's tongue.

Robert Townsend dashed home. His route took him past the Commons, Bridwell Prison and the Debtor's Jail with their barren, threatening walls, iron-barred windows and nauseating smell. His mind raced. His ears rang with the cries of inmates for food, alms, mercy. Didn't Mary hear their howls? How could she risk jail? How could Stewart abet her? At the head of Ferry Street, he stopped to catch his breath and he came to a decision: he must separate Mary from her accomplices before she was caught. He must remove her to a place where she would give up this perilous work. He thought of exiling her to Connecticut. His heart rebelled at their separation and he knew she would not go. He thought of the swamps at Jamaica or Massapequa, but he doubted a woman would bear those frightful conditions. Finally, he decided on Oyster Bay, if his righteous mother would have her. If not, he could find another accommodation. He forced himself to walk the last few blocks to Peck's Slip to calm the beatings of his heart. The mad thumping would not quiet. The hands that he shoved in his pockets were fists of explosive energy.

He confronted Mary as soon as he arrived. "You are careless and foolish! Mary, you are a woman! Do you know what they do to women in the gaol? Do you think your feminine form will protect you from Cunningham? He is English! They burned Joan of Arc at the stake and she was only a girl of fourteen years!" He was shouting.

Mary stared back stubbornly. "You sound more like the fiend than they, Robert Townsend!...Please lower your voice!"

"I try to impress you Mary, for your own good, for the sake of reason and some vestige of prudence! How else can I make you understand? I want you to survive! I want us all to survive! I want this effort of ours to succeed!"

"And so do I." There was an iron set to her jaw. She turned on her heel, grabbed a shawl and headed for the door to the alley. It had started to rain.

"Where are you going?"

She did not answer. He wanted to grab her forcefully, slap her, make her listen, make her admit the folly of her behavior. The door slammed. He balled his fists, and slammed them into the hard oak panel of the door. An hour passed and she did not return. He paced the floor.

Finally, he set out to search. He stormed into the street where Stewart was standing, bareheaded in the rain, calling his dog.

"Have you seen Mary?" The fire in Robert's eye shocked even the gritty Scotsman.

"Aye, sir, she's at the tavern with Drake."

"When does the next ferry leave?"

"Farley will depart Thursday noon, sir."

"Not Farley, the public ferry to Brooklyn!"

"At two o'clock, sir.... "

Robert slapped five guineas into Stewart's palm. "Book passage for two. We will be on board!"

"You and the wee lady, sir?" Stewart eyes bulged incredulously.

"Yes. I am taking her away for her own good and for yours! After we leave, there is to be no further smuggling from the Townsend premises or anywhere else! Do I make myself clear?" Robert's voice sliced the hot air like a knife.

"Yes, sir." Stewart cringed at the swipe.

No more was said. Robert stomped home, took down a large trunk and began to pack. Mary came in as he worked. "Where are you going?"

Robert compressed his voice into a dry monotone. "We," he paused to emphasize the plural, "are going to Oyster Bay. Prepare what you will need. We shall pass the summer in the country."

Her chin came up defiantly. "Do I have a choice?"

"No." The word cracked like a whip.

At one o'clock, Robert locked the house at Peck's Slip and took Mary firmly by the arm. They headed silently across the cobbles down to the wharf. Stewart stumbled behind carrying the heavy trunk. They stopped at the end of the gangplank where Robert gave the ship's boy a guinea to stow the trunk safely. He escorted Mary aboard the ferry like a lord with his lady and never turned once to say good-bye.

At the Brooklyn landing, they mounted the post chaise which clattered down the dusty road to Jamaica. There they spent a night in the upper room of a tavern. They continued on the next morning with three other passengers. One was Thomas Barney, the rabid Tory from Hog's Neck. Barney did most of the talking and never addressed one word to Mary. His beady eyes appraised her tiny form. Robert could read the lascivious glances and the thoughts that tickled his Tory brain: scandal and disgrace for the Townsend name. Mary sat in polite silence while Robert sat on his hands. He would have liked to have punched Barney in his haughty nose.

The coach deposited them at Wright's Tavern late in the afternoon. They walked the short distance to the Townsend door. Samuel himself answered. The white house seemed greyer, more forlorn than when he had left, but Audrey jumped up when she heard her brother's voice and welcomed him with a hug.

Samuel Townsend did not smile at the sight of his son with the strange little woman. He stooped over a cane and muttered a cursory greeting while the old blue eyes darted like a hawk's from Mary to his son.

Audrey invited them to the parlor, but Samuel stood his ground stubbornly at the door. "Robert, come to my room." It was an order.

Robert walked rigidly after the old man. Samuel closed the door behind them and sat himself at his desk. Robert remained standing and waited for the older man to begin. After a long pause, Samuel spread his palms on the smooth surface and leaned forward in judgement, "Robert, are you living with this woman?"

"Yes father, but it is not as you think. I love her."

The old man grimaced. "And does love permit promiscuity? When I gave you my blessing it was not to enable you to flaunt the commandments of God!"

Robert's face never twinged, "Father I would willingly marry her but she will not have me! She has a husband who was sent to the H.M.S. Jersey a year ago and has not been heard from since.

"The Jersey is a prison ship?"

"Yes sir. She lies fouled in the mud of Wallabout Bay. Her prisoners die like flies in a web." Robert looked away to a dim corner of the room and muttered, "Benjamin Tallmadge himself has asked me to protect Mary! She does not know whether her husband is alive or dead, whether she is married or free. Father, this war makes a mockery of God's commandments! I should have taken up a musket and gone out to fight!"

The older man sat rigidly. His face was pale. The furrows etched deeply into his brow. "Do not talk so. You have not taken up arms. That is to your credit. You have held at least to that much of your belief."

"Have I?" Robert met his father's glare. He swallowed once to settle the cramping in his chest, tucked in his head and retreated under a canopy of silence.

"Is she in danger of arrest?" The old man's voice croaked.

"Yes."

"Are you in danger of arrest?"

"I don't know. Possibly."

"Sit down." Robert sat stiffly, arms folded, shoulders braced, his fierce gaze anchored to the dimness. There was a pause while the old man ran his tongue around the perimeter of his lips and studied the tips of his fingers. "And you are less in danger here in Oyster Bay than in the city?"

"Yes, sir. Colonel Cunningham is in the city. He will not seek out prisoners as far away as Oyster Bay."

Another silence while the father folded his hands. "Have you any thoughts for accommodation besides this house?"

The question surprised Robert who unfolded his arms, squared his shoulders and returned his father's grim stare. "No, the decision to come was in haste. Mary cannot continue her activities as she would have in the city, here in the countryside."

"What activities? Is she a prostitute?"

The word rolled hideously, like sour spittle, from his father's lips. Robert's own lips quivered as he framed his answer. "She has been smuggling provisions to General Washington."

Samuel's eyes dropped before Robert's rude glare. "At least she has chosen the honorable side of the conflict! Have you thought of your mother? If she learns you are living with a woman without the blessing of marriage, it will exacerbate her condition. Did you think at all, Robert? Or was your decision the result of baser emotions?" The old man paused, then almost whispered. "You are my son. I have brought you up to be God-fearing and moral, and you are keeping a mistress! Like General Howe! Like infamous Tarleton! Like some lusty grenadier in gold braid and lace cuffs, come to America to populate the land with bastards!" The old man's eyes flared and filled with liquid. "You are a Townsend and you dishonor your good name! You have incurred my displeasure. You will incur your mother's wrath. She will forbid you to enter this house!" The words thrust brutally home.

Robert's recoiled at the accusation in his father's eyes. His jaw tightened and he replied stubbornly. "I had not thought on those possibilities, sir." Anger boiled up in his breast and he shut his mouth before the bitterness burst forth.

"Your mother would do that and more. I am too old to stop her. She listens only to the New Light minister and he does nothing but breathe fire like a dragon and embitter her further." Robert retreated into stiff formality. The father's staccato syllables echoed in his brain as Samuel's voice rose. "You embitter me. Mother is a hard woman. I can no longer accept her opprobrium. I extend my sympathy to you, my son, but I cannot disturb the peace of this house. You may stay in this house if you wish. It is your childhood home and I will uphold your right, but your Mary must live elsewhere. Youngs may take her in for a price or there is the room above the tavern. Wright could use the help."

"She is not a serving woman! The Hessians would abuse her!"

"And you do not abuse her already?" Robert blinked at the accusation and Samuel continued, "The Coe house is vacant. The family died of the pox. Coe was imprisoned in one of the hulks you describe. He escaped, was exchanged and came home to deliver the disease to all his family. It was a great tragedy."

"I'm sorry for them." In fact, he had ceased to feel. Events were spinning away from him, out of control. His father was receding like a shadow in a mist. He wanted to reach out to stop him, but the effort was like grasping at a handful of air. He repeated dryly, "Then our choice is an infected house, a smelly tavern or return to New York and risk a British prison."

"You have nothing to fear from the house. You were inoculated. The Coe uncles will be glad to have the house occupied lest a company of Hessians learn it belonged to a rebel and tear it down for firewood. Has your lady been inoculated?"

"I don't know."

"If not, she can apply to John Simcoe's surgeon. He has stayed in the city."

Robert squirmed under the old man's gaze. He wanted to leave yet the old man held him there. Samuel lay a hand on Robert's arm. Robert muscles tightened at the touch. Samuel's scratchy voice filled the silence. "I'm sorry, son.... Let her stay at Wright's for the night. We will make the arrangements with Elias Coe tomorrow."

Robert had to force his gratitude. "I appreciate your efforts, sir, but it is not safe for a woman alone at the tavern. I will stay with her." He wanted to add *since I am no longer welcome in my own home.*

Samuel bowed his head. "As you wish. You are a proud boy." He lifted his steely eyes. "You realize you will create, you have already created, a great scandal."

"You have insured that the scandal will not extend to this house. I am doing that which, in my soul, I think right." The muscles in Robert's face relaxed. He faced his parent impassively. He had drawn his line in the sand. He turned to walk away.

The old man called him back. "I believe you, my son.... Are you ready to stand before God in the face of your actions? If so, I will not withdraw my blessing."

Robert nodded. "I am prepared to do just that, sir."

Major Edmund Fanning investigated the disappearing commissary stores. He found the freshly dug earth where Stewart had buried the stolen provisions. The place looked like a mass grave. There was smallpox in the city and burials were many, even burials in unfrequented places like the quiet clearing. People feared decaying corpses and the loose earth around them. The soldiers stayed away from Stewart's diggings. Fanning reported the digging to Cunningham who reported to General Clinton who dismissed the inconsequential loss of a few more rebel souls to the pox. The buried goods remained undiscovered.

General Clinton issued a proclamation. Jack Rivington's Gazette printed it on the front page: *All citizens who determine to deny provisions to His Majesty's occupying forces will witness the confiscation of their property and will be brought before a magistrate for further disposition.* The words *further disposition* sent icy splinters down Robert's spine. There was more: *Any Citizen apprehended while in possession of His Majesty's duly collected military provisions, will be tried as a thief and hanged.* The punishment for theft was usually whipping, and if the value of the stolen property was great, hanging by the neck. Wartime had increased the penalties. When Robert Townsend read the news, his hand shook. But when he showed it to Mary, she dismissed it with a laugh.

31

'Tis an honor to serve the bravest of nations
And left to be hanged in their capitulations.

*T*he tavern was nearly empty when Robert and Mary arrived. The officers had all departed for a horse race at Hempstead. Wright, the tavern keeper, showed them to an outside stairway which led to a tiny room under the eaves, and hauled their trunk up after them. The room had been used to store ale and the aroma lingered. There was a single bed under the slanting roof and a chair shoved back beneath it to prop up the crossbeam. Robert could not stand straight without hitting his head. There was no window. Light shone obliquely from a single candle which stood on the floor. Wright mumbled an explanation, "'Tis the best I can do. Hessians are stingy bastards, like Shylocks. They think beer is as plentiful as sea water! They refuse to pay! At the least, the room has a key and it will be a warm night." He handed Robert the key to an old padlock, averted his eye and backed away muttering, "Ye'd do right to bar the door as well."

Robert's head hit the beam and he cursed. His comment came a few seconds after Wright had closed the door behind him. He was angry. "Barred from my own house, treated like a servant in the town where I was born! I'm sorry I ever brought you here."

"Most of us are born to servitude, Rob. The British think of us as such, servants who will jump to their bidding and satisfy their greed. I don't envy Wright."

Her sympathy did nothing to soothe him. "I treat slaves better than my family treats me!"

"Do you, Rob? Do you treat them better than the soldiers treat Wright? Do you allow them the choice of a life? You did not allow me the choice to refuse when we left the city."

"My haste was for your own welfare and protection." He sat numbly on the trunk. A red lump expanded over his right eye where he had hit the beam.

Mary sat beside him. "Rob, I do not want or need protection. I am responsible for my own welfare." She put up a hand to assess his injury.

He caught her wrist. "Mary, I cannot risk losing you."

"You can let go my arm, Rob. You don't need force. You're hurting me."

He released her, shocked at his own brutality.

She lay a hand on his cheek. "I cannot stay angry with you, Robert Townsend.... You are a man of commitment and passion." She touched the spreading bruise over his eye. "It has broken the skin. There is blood. Ice will stop the bleeding." She motioned toward the door. "Shall I ask Wright, in the taproom."

"I will not stoop to ask him for one drop of water!" He clenched his teeth.

"The man has troubles, too, Rob. Have patience with him." Her voice washed over him like a spring shower. "And I will have patience with you. You brought me here against my will. I, too, was very angry." She stopped and mused, "Why is a woman not allowed the expression of her anger?" He had closed his eyes and lay back on the stiff husk mattress. She continued, "I have encased my anger like an egg in a shell and I am careful not to crack it. I have learned there is too much in life that I cannot foresee, that my anger only drains my own energy if I let it escape. But you, you try to predict a future you cannot possibly foresee and you suffer for it." She laughed lightly. "I work for a simpler goal, to alleviate the suffering of my human brothers. I will survive, Rob. You will too. If we lose this struggle, we will find another home. If we win, what kind of devastated place will we inherit? I have not the courage to think on such things, Robert Townsend. Today, we have a warm bed. We trust each other. It is more by far than Thomas Barney or Sir William Lord Howe for all his prestige, will ever enjoy."

The sight of her cooled him like shade in summer heat. Her violet eyes crinkled and she continued, "Maybe if I were more careful like you, Tom Drake would be alive and a free man today. But I do not allow myself regret, Rob. Regret is a thief. It robs the soul of happiness. I have met you and put away the past... I love you, Robert Townsend, and I want to be happy."

He put his hand over hers, kissed her, then jumped up suddenly. "I forgot to ask. Have you been inoculated?"

"Sit down before you crash into another beam. The answer is yes." A smile lingered on her lips. "We will do well, Robert Townsend, and if I cannot smuggle and spy, at least I can create a glorious scandal!" The sound of her laughter echoed sweetly like the song of a lark.

Robert loved the persistent optimism of this diminutive woman! It was infectious. He felt his heart expand to fill the cavity of his chest. He pulled her tiny form against him hard enough to stop her breath, then released her slowly. "I will love you, Mary Drake, more powerfully than armies on the march, more than I have ever loved a woman." Yet his mind wondered about her past, her upbringing, her family, her life before Drake, with her husband, before Tallmadge had brought her to him. He smiled gently and said, "It's a steamy day for a glorious summer! Mary, let's rub their itchy noses in scandal!"

The sound of horses trotting up interrupted them. The noise filtered easily through the cracks in the floor. Boots tramped, swords clanked and gruff voices commanded ale and beef. They were American voices, loyalists, and something was terribly wrong.

Robert started, rose halfway to avoid the beam and headed for the stair. "Lock the door behind me, Mary. I'll fetch the ice."

Two orderlies stood outside walking five lathered horses. The officers had dismounted and entered the tavern. They seated themselves at a rough, round table as Wright came running with a tray of mugs and a pitcher of ale. At the sight of them, Robert retreated to a corner by himself. He could not make out their faces in the dimness.

They grumbled an impertinent command. "Innkeeper, bring us cold drink!"

Wright snapped back, "I cannot afford ice or good ale at the prices they ask! Use all our wood for the stocks of your guns and masts of your ships and drive the price of ale beyond the reach of an honest man!"

A red-faced captain swore and unbuttoned his collar. "The man is right. The war devours the grain. The broad-axe thunders over the forest." From the sound of him, he was an American loyalist.

Another officer complained louder. "And us layin' out in the damp and the dark with the howling beasts while bonnie Billy Howe retires to London with 'is medals and 'is wenches and 'is sterling teapots and lace cuffs! Leaves us behind to mop 'is mess and tidy 'is ships while hogs root in the commissary and rats in the shipyards. Our forests cut to stumps and not a guinea left for the bloke to buy a stick of firewood!"

"Quiet Adam, before the Colonel hears."

Adam would not be quiet. Sarcasm echoed in his voice. "We beg shoe leather and wood - my wife writes me they took the cow - while the general tailors his uniforms from velvets and silks!" He puffed out his cheeks and stuck out his stomach in mockery of portly General Howe. His companions laughed heartily. "The General must have his amusements! 12,000 pounds sterling worth!...I read it in the Gazette! 12,000 pounds so's they can parade like knights and ladies and turn the cornfields of Philadelphia into medieval lists! They gave a ball whose bloody Popish name I cannot pronounce! Should be buyin' britches and boots, horses and powder and replacin' my cow and the rails they stole from our fences and the siding from our barns!"

A second officer took up the thought, "Adam is right! Billy Howe couldn't chase a fox into his hole if it left a mile of scat trailin' over the countryside! And he leads a life that would outrage a London prostitute!"

The group fell silent. A tall, hefty officer entered. Robert recognized Oliver DeLancey and rose to greet his friend. "Oliver, you've been promoted. My congratulations!" A General's epaulets adorned DeLancey's shoulders.

But Oliver DeLancey's normally jovial face was grim. "Rob, good to see you." He took off his gloves and threw them onto the table. "Gentlemen," he announced, "I've sour news. France has entered the war." They stopped to stare. "February last, they signed the treaty. France has recognized the colonies as an independent nation."

Silence. Mouths hung open. They sank lower into their chairs and drank warm ale. Adam's voice bellowed, "So now my fine gentlemen, we will have to buckle down and fight or have His Most Christian Majesty, Louis XVI, with his catholic Pope for masters! Then they should complain of tyranny!"

No one laughed. A black mood descended. The warm ale cloyed. When Wright served a watery stew, Robert excused himself and took a tray and a bottle of wine upstairs to Mary. Over the lonely candle, they hugged each other and whispered their hopes to the spiders in the eaves and fell onto the scratchy husks of the mattress.

About nine o'clock in the morning, there was a knock on the door. DeLancey's men had left. Songbirds were chirping in the eaves. The sun had peaked in a blue sky and Robert and Mary awoke to an insistent pounding. Robert rolled over, pulled on his britches and unbarred the door.

It was his sister, Sally. "Audrey told me how father turned you out. I'm sorry for you, Rob. I want you to know I spoke no word against you. I want peace between us."

"Come in, Sal, unless you're afraid the smoke of scandal will blow over you. I'm glad to see you."

Sally laughed. "Afraid? Not me, Rob! I came to see Mary to ask if she will help at the hospital?" She bent to enter the low-ceilinged room. "Father says he will take you to Coe's about the house today at noon.... and Beulah sent this." She handed him a basket. He pulled back the cloth to reveal fresh bread, hard-boiled eggs, a jug of cider and an apple pie. "She says Wright's cooking is only good for pigs and soldiers."

"Thank her from the bottom of my heart, Sal."

Mary sat up in bed.

"Will you come, Mary, to the hospital? The sick there are loyalists and I suspect you would rather minister to rebels, but all men hurt the same and they will not spread rumors and will not care with whom you sleep."

"Tell me where and when." Mary jumped up.

"Now, as soon as you're ready, at the Meeting House." Sally turned to go. "I almost forgot, Rob. The Promise, father's ship, is in port. Captain Farley has a letter for you from Solomon."

Robert followed Sally out onto the landing, but Sally chased him back. "Go to your Mary, Rob. You are fortunate."

Samuel and Robert visited Squire Coe to request use of his house. Coe questioned their wisdom. "'Tis a death house, Samuel. The ghosts of Annie's children will be screamin' in the gables. Don't say I didn't warn you!"

"It's only a death house as long as it has no life within its walls." In the end, Squire Coe gave Robert the key.

Coe's was much smaller than the house at Peck's Slip, two rooms down and one gabled bedroom up. It sat on a side hill east of the village, a weather-beaten little speck of dwelling. The grass grew waist-high at the front door and tall weeds choked a vegetable garden in back. But a sturdy fence surrounded the property to keep out the predators and lilacs grew along the sides. They were in bloom and their sweet scent permeated the air. A windbreak of hardwood trees separated it from the south road.

Robert liked it immediately. It was a perfect refuge because the thick foliage kept it secluded. But what drew Robert to the tiny dwelling most was its cheerfulness. The roof sagged a bit at the center, giving the whole the shape of a smile. The windows were large and would let in the light and beans and pea vines proliferated in the fenced garden in spite of the weeds. Robert collected Mary that afternoon. They walked the 500 yards from the tavern to Coe's. Cob brought the trunk. Robert Townsend whisked Mary into his arms like a newly-wed and carried her over the threshold.

July and August of 1778 were happy times. Robert and Mary lived quietly as man and wife but unmarried, and let the village tongues wag. They had few worries and made no effort to deceive. They talked only to friends like Daniel Youngs and Austin Roe. Mary weeded the garden and planted pumpkins and sunflowers and busied herself at the hospital. Robert threw himself into menial chores, hauling the water, chopping wood and helping Cob. The summer was wet, the sun strong and the crops grew. In the evenings the two lovers read the histories of wars that John Simcoe had left behind. Sally brought them over after she had finished reading them.

News filtered in. General Lord Howe departed in a blaze of unearned glory and the British evacuated Philadelphia. They slogged across New Jersey in the rain and steamy June heat, with 1500 wagons. The Tory population of Philadelphia accompanied them in an orderly march, marred only by the Battle of Monmouth, for which both sides claimed victory. Washington harassed them all the way. The population of the city of New York swelled again with the arrival of the soldiers and the loyal citizens of Philadelphia who feared for their lives if they stayed behind. Their hopes to return to Pennsylvania receded with the entrenchment of Henry Clinton in New York and new orders which arrived from England. The French presence had shifted attention south. Britain feared the loss of naval bases in the West Indies which could be better protected from Savannah or Charleston. Offensive action was to cease in the north where the British would maintain a naval station at New York. The British had abandoned Philadelphia forever.

Caleb Brewster's raids across Long Island Sound increased. On a stormy day in August, he appeared at Youngs' Farm and sent Billy for Robert Townsend. Robert stared in disbelief when he saw the big whaler. He was clean-shaven, fatter and dressed in neat Quaker garb. They sat at a wide table and listened to the news he brought of the city. "I saw Stewart a week ago, Rob. He's lonely."

"For me or for Mary and his smuggler friends...or for his damned dog?"

"He's running your store at a tidy profit. Farley keeps him stocked. The dog barks when anyone knocks."

The three men fell silent, leaving unanswered questions hovering in the air between them. Caleb Brewster spread his long arms wide. Daniel Youngs prodded the big whaler. "Why did you come, Caleb? You find something else to burn?"

"Something, yes. But not to burn." He took his time explaining. "We shall lay siege to Newport." Nathaniel Greene was to conduct the siege on the island city. The French fleet would bombard the island from the bay while Greene and the army attacked from the rear. "What we need from you folks, is a quiet diversion to keep as many British ships as possible here in port and away from the scene of battle. I leave the details to you. Nothing dramatic, just effective." Youngs grinned widely.

The three conspirators discussed possibilities. Installation of faulty rigging, recalcitrant work crews, shortages of materials to slow the pace of repairs could all retard the ships. In the end a hurricane swept out of the gulf and spread greater havoc than any mere human effort. It was a swift swirling storm that hurled its winds around its vortex, snapped masts, ripped canvas, dragged anchors and ran ships aground. When it was over, the British fleet withdrew to New York. The French commander, Count d'Estaing, retired without firing a shot, to Boston, for repairs. Nathaniel Greene in command of the Americans, had to withdraw. He blamed French snobbery for the defeat. Count d'Estaing returned to France outraged and insulted. Newport remained British. The French alliance wavered. Rivington's Gazette rang with accounts of Admiral "Black Dick" Howe. The General's brother's timely arrival and swift action caused the French to withdraw! Jack Rivington cursed the story as another British lie, but he printed it anyway.

Robert Townsend watched from the sidelines. The summer passed by in a passionate blur. Gossip peaked then died. Sally and Audrey and Daniel Youngs came to visit, but most often, Robert and Mary were left to themselves. Robert traveled to Setauket twice to see Roe. He frequented Wright's tavern to share a bottle of port with his friend, DeLancey, and he went home early to the conjugal bed. Thoughts of Mary consumed his days and her presence ignited the ecstasy of his nights.

32

I would not keep a cat, or feed a bird,
That pip'd ungraceful, or ungraceful purr'd.

*I*n September, John Graves Simcoe returned. He had been wounded at Brandywine, but not severely, and he had been promoted. He wore the epaulets of a Lieutenant Colonel and he commanded a crack loyalist unit, the Queen's Rangers. He made his entrance like the prodigal son come home and sought out Sally immediately.

Sally Townsend was not there. She was on her way home from the mill, carrying a bolt of cloth, when she spotted the figure in a forest green coat entering the house. She knew it was him. She remembered the curve of his shoulder, the rhythm of his walk, the free swing of his arm and the carriage of his proud head. She bit her lip. More memories came flooding back: his brown wavy hair, his ramrod straight spine, his quiet, thoughtful presence. But there was a difference. He walked with a new fluidity and confidence.

She spotted Sergeant Kelly, Simcoe's orderly, who held a grey horse. Her heart pounded. She moved forward tentatively, then with a rush.

Kelly was leading the grey horse to the barn. There was another mounted officer near the gate and a strangely familiar third bay horse, under the tree. A repulsive, pockmarked gnome in the white uniform of the British Legion, held this horse firmly and blocked the gate to Raynham Hall. Mud had splattered his waistcoat, the fronts of his boots and the shaggy legs of the horse that gnawed the bit nervously and spit foam. In the strict class divisions of the British Army, he was an underling, lacking in cleanliness and discipline. As she drew closer, her repugnance grew. She recoiled to avoid touching the man. He was Hessian.

The mounted officer stood opposite the Hessian, also in white but his uniform was clean. Sally recognized the rank - major. As she drew closer, he leered wryly, lifted one suggestive brow and introduced himself. "Major Cochran, British Legion, lately billeted to Jericho, Miss." He ran a tongue over his lips. The hesitation implied greater intimacy. "We are to be neighbors; I hope we should also be... friends!"

Sally ignored the remark. "That's my brother's horse!" She pointed to the animal the Hessian held.

"You are mistaken, Miss. The horse has been in Colonel Tarleton's string for two months. He was taken from Setauket, part of Selah Strong's allotment and a gift to the Colonel. I know. I am his adjutant."

"The whole village knows that animal! He was on loan from my brother to Austin Roe!" She tossed her head back. The red hair flashed in the sun. "My brother will not be pleased. I hope at least, that Selah Strong has received compensation equal to the animal's value!"

Cochran heard the challenge in her voice, but could not be sure of her meaning. He spoke with oily politeness, "Compensation? The requisition is small payment for your safety, Miss."

"Only when what is requested is offered without rancor and given freely, Major."

She started suddenly. The dirty Hessian who held the horse was edging closer.

Sally placed the bolt of cloth between them. "This is my house. Get out of my way!" She nudged him with the bolt of cloth.

The Hessian's tongue ran across his lips and he moved forward again. Cochran made no effort to correct him.

Sally raised her voice. "Major, call off your hound!" The major did not move a muscle. She whirled, smacking the horse's shoulder with the heavy bolt. The horse jumped back pulling the Hessian off his feet, but he did not release his grip. He squeezed the animal's jaw between the D-loops of the bit only exciting the animal further.

Sally marched ahead. The Hessian's grimy fingers dropped the reins suddenly and reached for her like ugly pincers. She jumped away and swung again. The bolt unfurled as she snapped it back and the horse wheeled away and galloped up the lane. The Hessian rolled to the dirt and came up clutching the hem of her skirt.

Major Cochran laughed uproariously. "A mouthful of dirt for a piece of skirt! And you've lost the horse in the bargain, Sergeant Bayer! She's as slippery as a fish in bare hands!"

"My bare hands cling better to bare breasts, mein major!"

The major laughed with perverse pleasure and trotted off to collect the bay horse.

The Hessian's eyes gloated. He tightened his hold, "You make mein Major laugh, fraulein! Do not run! You will haf hot rum to brace you and a major to warm your bed. Silks and soft down instead of husks and coarse linen." He licked the dirt from his lips and dried them on his crusty sleeve. Sally kicked the cloth between them. She smelled the stink of rum on his breath.

Cochran returned, leading the horse. "You make a better groom than a suitor, Sergeant!"

Suddenly, he stopped laughing. The door to the house creaked open and two men stepped out: John Graves Simcoe, and his orderly, Sergeant Kelly. Cochran saluted. The Hessian snapped to attention. Simcoe comprehended at a glance what was happening and his face purpled in anger. "I should have you thrown to the sharks, Sergeant!" He unleashed his full wrath at Cochran. "As for your conduct, Major, it is disgraceful! I have a mind to draw up charges!"

A tremor shook Cochran's jaw. "Sergeant Bayer!" The name and rank echoed a shrieking reprimand. He turned apologetically to Simcoe. "It was all in good jest, sir!"

John Simcoe's voice leveled Cochran. "An Englishman does not amuse himself at the expense of a lady! It is your duty, Major, to foster good conduct by the strength of your example."

Cochran blanched and tightened his hand on the rein. His horse stepped obediently backward. But the Hessian bristled like a cornered beast. He turned and slammed his fist into the barrel of the bay. The terrified animal jumped backward the length of its rein.

Simcoe wasn't finished. "And Cochran, noble example is paramount when you command barbarians. Hessians have advanced little since the days when the tribes invaded Gaul! Order the brute to stop torturing that horse!" He stooped to retrieve the bolt of cloth.

Major Cochran signaled the gnome away with a wave of his hand. "You are dismissed, Bayer." Simcoe took the rein. Cochran assumed a pose of stiff formality and clipped each word in formal, aristocratic English. "Dispatches for Lieutenant Colonel Simcoe, from Lieutenant Colonel Tarleton." His eyes did not blink. The muscles of his face did not move. He handed Simcoe a brown leather cylinder and recited his formal directions in a precise monotone. "Lieutenant Colonel Tarleton begs the Colonel accept this fine animal as a gesture of his respect in the hope he can count on the Colonel's cooperation and support, sir, in the future." He added with more calculation than remorse. "We are to be neighbors for the duration of the year, sir. I hope this disturbance has not created animosity between us. I apologize, sir."

John Simcoe's voice sliced the air. "I accept your apology, Major. Convey to Lieutenant Colonel Tarleton my deepest gratitude and tell him that my support and cooperation are as forthcoming today as they have been at Hancock's or Monmouth or Quinton's Bridge. He can depend on me." Simcoe snatched the dispatch case. "And Cochran, mark that you address ladies with respect in and out of my hearing. And tell Lieutenant Colonel Tarleton that I always welcome brave and disciplined troops as neighbors. I would hope that my rangers are equally well-behaved." The sarcasm was only thinly veiled.

Cochran saluted in silent fury, reined his horse furiously around and galloped up the street.

John Simcoe turned to Sally and bowed. "My apologies, Miss, for the unruly conduct of my countryman."

Sally Townsend met his gaze. "Thank you, Captain." She hesitated a moment, then smiled radiantly. "But you have become a Colonel!"

He corrected her. "Lieutenant Colonel. It is a lesser rank. Is it because I have gained promotion that you address me so formally? You used to call me John. I am the same man." He said it meekly, not boastfully, as if there was no great import to his success. He continued, "I have been fortunate to draw your home again for winter quarters." He stepped aside for her to pass. His eyes lingered on her face. "It warms my heart to see you looking so lovely." His lips came apart. He had more to say but withheld it.

Sally's heart pounded. She dropped her eyes and recited a platitude to fill the silence. "We welcome you, Colonel. The man is forgiven. It would take generations to teach Hessians the manners of English gentlemen." She looked up suddenly.

John Simcoe blinked. She had caught him staring. He stammered, "Hessians are like wild colts. They lack good breeding."

Mention of horses reminded her. "You heard? I did not lie. The horse is Robert's."

"Then he shall be Robert's again. Is Cob here to take him?" Cob shuffled around the corner of the house.

Sarah Townsend's shrill voice interrupted, "John, Sally, come to the garden! Beulah will serve tea. The Colonel must be tired after his grueling ride."

John Simcoe bowed again. "Lieutenant Colonel, Madame, not full colonel.... The ride was not grueling because I was on my way to Raynham Hall. I feel as if I have come home." From John Simcoe, this was not flattery but the truth. He handed the horse to Cob but did not take his eyes off Sally.

He offered her his arm and they walked to the garden where he took his place beside her on the bench. He spoke softly, beyond the hearing of the others. "I want you to know that I requested this billet, that I have missed your warm hospitality, that I especially have missed..." He turned the full force of his dark eyes upon her... "you."

Sally's head swam. She dropped her eyes, "Surely you exaggerate, Colonel. Philadelphia has treated you admirably from the looks of you." The desire in his eyes choked off her speech. She corrected herself, "Lieutenant Colonel, John. What a mouthful of rank!" They laughed together at her fumbling.

Silence. His fluid voice filled the vacuum. "John is a simple name." His eyes flicked uncertainly from her face to the ground and back again. Finally he blurted, "Will you ride out with me if I order the carriage, as we did the day after we met?"

Sally did not answer. She followed her own thoughts. "You've recovered completely."

"I never thanked you properly for your care."

"It was freely offered."

"I came back for good reason, Sally." John Simcoe who was usually so eloquent, searched for the right words. He repeated, "You did not give me an answer. Will you come for a drive with me tomorrow?" He was struggling like a stuttering child, mouth open, words hanging in tatters on the tip of his tongue.

She swallowed hard. "Of course."

He stammered on, "I have been brave in battle but today simple words make my courage quake." He placed his hand over hers, "I have come back to ask your forgiveness, hoping that my actions have not quenched every spark that was in your heart."

She was shaking her head. Her hair shimmered; her eyes welcomed. He felt the pressure of her fingers where they closed around his. "Sally, if your father will permit, I have come back to ask you to be my wife."

Sally Townsend gripped her throat. Her mouth opened. After a stunned moment, she choked out the words, "Colonel Simcoe, you do me great honor!"

"Only honor? I would hope I could inspire passion!"

"But you do!" She hesitated, swallowed hard and continued. "There was a time, I struggled to blot out all thought of you. I threw myself into my work and numbed the very part of me that sees beauty and light, and now you come back like Phoebus in a fiery chariot...." Her thoughts tumbled together like grains of sand in a bucket.

He put a hand to her lips. "I love you Sally." He pulled her to him. "I have been so long away and I have done much thinking. England is no longer my home. This is! These shores that have welcomed me like a son! I bless the rebellion that brought me to you or fate or the will of God. I cannot alter my past. I only know that I want to live my future, the rest of my life, with you... if you could find it in your heart to love me." His eyes pleaded. His broad hand covered hers. His speech ran on like a river spilling over its banks. She felt his grip tighten as his voice poured over her. "I can only imagine a good end to these present difficulties. We will win the war, Sally! I will win it for you! And we shall share a home and beautiful children with hair the color of the sunrise like their mother's, and they will populate this glorious land! I love you, Sally Townsend.

Townsend. I shall love you as long as I live."

He kissed her lightly at first and then again with passion. She curved against him languidly, like a swan on a gentle wave. They lingered in the garden behind the lilacs that screened them from the lane until Sergeant Kelly poked his pink nose around the hedge. "You've to meet with Major Sandford and Lieutenant Ormond at three, sir."

John Simcoe was not angry. He muttered, "Thank you, Kelly." and smiled radiantly at Sally. Tears ran down her face as he rose. "And now, Sally, I have duties to perform. May I use Robert's horse or should I saddle another?"

"By all means use him, Colonel... John. No one will dare to steal the Lieutenant Colonel's horse!" They parted laughing.

Kelly held the off stirrup as John Simcoe pivoted on his heel and sprung gracefully into the saddle. Astride the horse, he was even more imposing, a Caesar at the Rubicon, Alexander at the Granicus! Sally Townsend remembered the stories of heroes as she watched him ride away. Silver epaulets twinkled against the forest green of his coat; polished black boots gleamed brightly like a starry night against the glossy red dapples of the horse. Sally stood motionless after John Graves Simcoe had disappeared. She shook uncontrollably at the thought of what she had done. She had written a new future. She had followed the urging of her heart like the geese who follow their course south. It was not a choice. It was a driving, inescapable instinct and she was happier than she had ever been before in her life.

She didn't hear her brother, Robert, come up behind her. She only heard the bite of sarcasm in his voice. He grabbed her arm. "So he's back, Sal! Did he whisper his Tory temptations in your eager ear?"

"Let go my arm! You're hurting, Rob! Has the devil got you? John Simcoe is a fine man!"

But Robert Townsend spoke his mind. "And well-dressed and well-educated and well-mannered and handsome and twenty-seven years old and unmarried and as haughtily British as they come! I'm surprised one of the Philadelphia strumpets didn't snap him up. But yes, I'll grant you, he is a gentleman and an honorable man, the swan that snaps the duckling from off the surface of the pond."

"Stop it, Rob!"

"I thought you had got over him, Sal!"

"You are not privy to the workings of my heart. I love him!"

"Then pardon me! I did not know." Robert groaned, exhaled and changed the subject. "I have been speaking with Farley at the dock. He has much to report. Sally, we've Tarleton to contend with - Banastre Tarleton! Do you know who that is?" His brows knit together and his lips turned down in a fierce grimace.

"The one who sent the horse? Have I met this Tarleton?"

"You will very soon. He's the greatest womanizer in the British Cavalry!"

Robert reminded her of an angry tethered dog barking and charging at the end of the rope that held him. She avoided the perimeter of his bite. "You exaggerate like an Irishman, Robert Townsend!"

"Stop acting the virtuous saint, Sal. I am your brother and wiser by seven years, Sal. Banastre Tarleton commands the British Legion who've spilled enough rebel blood to fill this bay! They are bayonet experts, the cruellest devils in the British Army. That Bayer and Cochran are perfect examples. And they parade around in white uniforms like bloody blessed angels and bathe their hands in gore…. Sally, Tarleton will come after you. I know him. Jack Rivington knows him. He had a mistress in New York not two weeks after deserting another in Philadelphia!"

"Good for him! Go shout your warning to the Barney spinsters!"

Robert glared blackly. He chewed his words as if to relieve the tension in his jaw. "Don't bait me sister Sally! I will be returning to New York. I shall ask Austin to keep an eye on you."

Sally Townsend fired back. "I am not a sheep in your pasture, my brother! John Simcoe is our friend, or have you forgotten? He has just returned your horse! You should thank him but no, you deride the man! But for him, our father might have died in the hulks!"

At mention of the hulks, Robert Townsend's anger flared. "I am to thank him for my own horse!" His broad face went white and his lips drew back against the white of his teeth. "What do you know of hulks, Miss Sally Townsend, cavorting about the countryside with your Colonel in his fancy coach and his bloody red coat? He and his ilk stole the horse and invented the hulks!"

"His is a Lieutenant Colonel and his coat is green!" They were both shouting.

Blistering rage coated the whites of Robert's eyes. They masked deep turmoil within. His chest heaved. His square jaw clenched like a vise. His brows locked in a fierce, barbaric glare. Sally drew back. "What is the matter with you, Rob? Something is terribly wrong!"

Robert Townsend's lips came together in a blue pencil line and a shiver shook him like a sapling in a storm. His mouth opened and closed several times before he regained a struggling composure. "You know, my sister, that I've no special love for Mother England. She's stripped our land, killed our livestock, stolen our horses, devoured our crops and sent hordes of Hessians to patrol our streets. She's stubborn and proud and hamstrung by her precious conventions." He stopped to catch his breath. His eyes shot fire. "But yes, I do like John Simcoe, as a man... But I detest his associations and I feel sorry for him. And I am not afraid to say that he will bring you to grief, my fine sister!"

"Don't patronize me, Rob! The British are winning! If you hate them so, why do you drink their wine and dance at their parties and sing their thumping victory songs with DeLancey and Rivington and all your foppish Tory friends? Why don't you fight them, Rob? Go to Connecticut like Micah, like our Peekskill cousins! Or perhaps you are too feeble a lily on a stalk!"

Robert recoiled like a whipped animal who knows it is outmatched. She was intelligent, too far along the trail of the scent, too close to the truth. She would sniff him out as a spy. He had to withdraw but his whole being resisted. He longed to jump to the challenge but he wrung the passion from his voice. He said dryly, "DeLancey and Rivington were born on this side of the ocean. Simcoe was not. He can never be one of us. By instinct, by loyalty, by duty, by privilege, by birth, he is different!"

Sally Townsend no longer understood her brother. He had changed like John Simcoe had changed, like she had changed, like her family, the village and the whole island had been transformed, since the rebellion began. "Before the war, Robert Townsend, you would have thought John Simcoe the perfect match for me! I no longer understand you. And I am not the woman I was. You drive me to him, Robert Townsend, by your aversion! I should say by your hatred. She turned away and her voice came in a loud whisper. "You are no longer a brother to me!"

The arrow was well-aimed. Robert Townsend silenced, bowed formally, spun on his heel and pushed open the broad Dutch door. When it creaked on its iron hinges, when Sally moved to call him back, he did not slow his step or speak one word, but stalked off down the lane, hunched like a child who does not know why he is rebuked. He had left a piece of his heart in that house, lashed to the shaggy bark of the locust tree. Like Cob, he felt as if the skin had been stripped from his back.

33

The wretch that is not fit to live
To kill can be no sin.

*R*obert's final words disturbed Sally Townsend. She lingered at the door, glanced once up the hill through the twisted branches of the locust tree and shivered. The leaves had yellowed early and dropped in a wide circle in the street. She could see beyond the branches. Sentries stood on the hill like statues and looked down on the village and the harbor. They protected the village and held it secure from rebel raids.

Her mother's voice intruded on her thoughts. "I have loaves for Joseph Cooper, Sally." Sally did not react immediately and Sarah bellowed impatiently. "The loaves, Sally, did you hear?"

Taking loaves to Cooper was an act of kindness. Joseph Cooper had no woman to bake for him. The bluff where he lived was the windiest and coldest place that Sally knew. It faced north and east and braced against the fiercest storms. But it was wildly beautiful, a massive slab of glacial granite that hung over a maze of rocks like a eagle over a water hole watching the movements of its next meal. No ships came near. The British had built their fort on the opposite shore of the harbor, in Joseph Lloyd's high forest. They named it Fort Franklin after the Tory governor of New Jersey, William Franklin. Joseph Cooper's bluff hovered beyond the range of their guns.

Cooper was the brother-in-law of John Townsend, cousin to Samuel. The Coopers, like the Townsends, were original settlers of Oyster Bay who had purchased their land from Chief Mohenes of the Matinecock Indians. It was rich land, with clear springs and great spreading trees, seabirds and shellfish, deer and wild turkey. Of wild game, Joseph Cooper had plenty, but he did not have the will to hunt. And he lacked completely the processed flour, sugar, coffee and baked goods.

Sarah Townsend's voice sounded more harshly in Sally's ear. "The wind blows from the east, Sally. A storm's coming. Take Cob with you. And take your warm cloak with the hood."

Sally's head jerked up. She was thinking of the drive she took with John Simcoe to Cooper's the day after his first arrival. He too remembered. That was two years ago.

"Sally, Be home by dark!"

Sally grabbed her cloak from the hook in the hall, picked up the basket of loaves from the kitchen and left before resentment of her nagging mother surfaced.

Cob was in the barn. Since the whipping, he was reluctant to venture out, even to the pasture. He knew why Sally came for him and found an easy excuse. "The mare is nervous, Miss Sally, goin' to give birth soon, but I saw Billy Youngs down by the beach. He'll go with you as far as his house." Billy Youngs was only a boy.

The path to Cooper's wove past Parrish's Store, Wright's Tavern and the ghostly chimneys of houses stripped and burned in a Yankee raid. It used to hug the shoreline in full view of the ships at anchor. Because of the rebel raids, because of the warships and their powerful guns and of the predatory seamen who manned them, the villagers had moved homes and businesses back from the waterfront. They had re-directed the road away from the shore. The new road plunged into a half-mile of virgin forest before the trees thinned out again near Daniel Youngs' rope and sail yard. From Youngs' Farm, it was another good mile to Cooper's.

Sally found Billy Youngs at the water's edge. She loved the places where the tall trees swept down to the very edge of the water that lapped in wavelets at her feet. So many creatures, the fiddler crabs, loons and pipers, eels and shellfish, the sand worms with their thousand legs and the spike-tailed horseshoe crabs that trailed up the bank at the summer solstice to lay their eggs, fascinated her.

Many of the trees were raw stumps now. Their roots had released the black fertile banks to the invading sea, smothering the life that lined the tidal flats. The sea creatures had died or retreated to more elusive basins and the army had trampled the banks and hauled away wood by the shipload. The locust trunks stood now as masts in the harbor and the walnuts squeaked as axles beneath the wagons. Barracks, fortifications, ships, had devoured the forests of Long Island.

Seamen and scavengers stalked the stubbled shore for any scrap the army might have missed. Sally hated them. They were leathery, unshaven rascals and smelled worse than Brewster. Their enthusiasm for the red of her hair and the curves of her figure was coarse. Sally sensed them undressing her with their eyes. Some broke curfew and came to the shore marshes to drink stolen rum and threatened anyone at the point of a knife. They reacted to drink like a wild colt to the whip, and to women like vultures to carrion.

Sally neared the shore with caution. The tide was in and Billy Youngs was at the high water mark. He was gathering mussels.

"Billy, these are not to eat! The inshore mussels are poisonous!"

Billy's bare feet were covered with mud. He seemed immune to cold and wet. He had filled a bucket with the black fluted shells that grew high up the bank, above the swift flow of tide. He brightened at her voice, then laughed. "The Hessians'll eat 'em and they'll pay me in silver and vomit their guts back out with the tide and blame the English beer that made them retch." Sally laughed too. Billy picked up his bucket and started walking at her side. He knew where she was going. He was a long-limbed, skinny boy, but short for his age. Brown hair fell over his eyes and freckles spattered across his nose. His blue eyes peered at her basket hungrily.

"Billy Youngs, put your tongue back in your mouth!"

"I have a bite?"

She handed him a loaf. He stuffed a chunk into his mouth and stuffed the rest of the loaf under his shirt.

"I'll shuck you some mussels so's you can take 'em to Mr. Cooper, the good kind of mussels!"

"Not today, Billy, it's getting cold. I should hurry."

They passed the New Light Baptist Church and entered a deeper wood.

A gull squawked. He had come inland, on the updrafts of a coming storm. A flock of geese ranged overhead, honking their way south. Field mice and chipmunks and a grey squirrel scampered amid the thick undergrowth.

Abruptly, the path turned from the shore into a dense stand of uncut hickory. Heavy vines shrouded the limbs, high up into the canopy. A few leaves still clung to the vines, pointed and shiny in groups of three, and red as blood with the coolness of autumn. Other vines were berried and thorned and cut grooves in the massive trunks. Rather than tackle the poisoned vines, woodcutters had let these trees stand.

Billy ran ahead noiselessly but Sally's cloak blew open in the stiff breeze and caught on a thorn. She turned to untangle it.

"You haf a smile for me now, mein Fraulein? There is only a boy who runs away to protect you?" The words were guttural and blended eerily into the sounds of the forest.

Sally froze. She remembered Bayer's voice. "Release my cloak!" She imitated John Simcoe's strong voice of command.

"Where is your Colonel now, mein liebchen? You haf a password for Bayer!" The password was required of anyone who traveled the roads after dark.

"I need no password in daylight!" She spoke up loudly across the dull hum of the forest.

Bayer grabbed her wrist. "I do not know what time of day it is." His bald head nodded; his beady eyes leered. "I follow you. I am careful. I am quiet." With his free hand, he unbuckled his belt. It fell to the ground. His white tunic opened and a hairy pink belly spilled out.

Sally stared at the bloated stomach, the round knob of head, the wet, fat lips, the nostrils wide, like a hound's. "Go back to the alehouse! They will give you drink!"

"Where is de woman in de alehouse, de woman mit flaming hair like you?" He pulled her toward him.

Sally pulled away and struck out vainly with the only weapon she had, the basket of bread. Loaves pelted out among the vines. Bayer's fiendish laughter echoed. "Such a weapon, not hard, not sharp, soft like de mother's breast!" He held her wrist in his iron grip. Now she eased toward him slowly and his lips curled upward. "Ya fraulein! Come!"

Silently, she unclasped the cloak from her neck and let it fall seductively to the leaf-covered ground. When his grip loosened, she hurled herself at him. The awkward Hessian slipped on the damp leaves and heeled over backward as she pulled free. He shook his head, rolling sideways to bring his knees under him. She had a glimpse of Billy Youngs leaping like a nimble cat along the path. He came up behind the fumbling Bayer. She saw the rock in his hands, ready to descend. She cried out too late. Billy Youngs had brought it crashing down into the Hessian skull. There was a crack. Bayer fell.

The boy smiled. "I take good care of you, Miss Sally, better than Cob!" His boasting lasted only a moment until he looked down at what he'd done. Bone fragments pulsed out red liquid, redder than the holly berry and the poisoned leaves in autumn. Billy's eyes grew to saucers. The rock thudded to the ground. His hand shook, then his whole body. He mumbled incoherently, "He's dead! O Miss Sally, they'll kill me for this!"

Sally hid his face in the folds of her cloak. "No Billy, you are too young. It was a brave thing you did....He would have killed me."

The boy would not quiet, "He's a soldier! They'll come for me! They'll hunt me down!... I don't want to die!" The words seeped out from deep in his throat, in spasms like water wrung from a towel.

Sally dared to look around. The Hessian's blood was pouring out like a calf at the slaughter pit. For far lesser crimes, men were thrown into prison, beaten, starved, hanged.

"Billy, give me your knife." He handed her a blunt clam knife. She ripped out a stout length of vine and whispered a silent prayer. "Lord, preserve me as your servant Judith was preserved." With that, Sally Townsend crouched behind the Hessian, lifted the bloodied head to her lap and pulled the vine tightly across the windpipe. Billy watched in stony silence. The man sputtered, lifted a weak hand as if in reflex, kicked and fell back. She held a leaf to his lips. It did not move.

Sally stood up and wiped her hand on her skirt. "You did not kill him, Billy Youngs. I did." She breathed deeply. "Now we will hide him. He's not big, just fat. Roll him into my cloak and we'll pull him into the trees." The boy stood anchored to the earth. "Come, he is too heavy for me alone!"

Billy grabbed the stocky legs. The shock in his blue eyes faded with the immediacy of action.

They dragged Bayer off the path. With their bare hands, they cleared the covering of leaves that blanketed the forest floor to expose a black patch of earth. They smeared the white of his uniform with the wetness of the earth. Sally rolled the body into a depression and piled on handfuls of sticks and leaves. No one would know there was a man there until the wild beasts sniffed out the man-smell and feasted on the traces of the deed.

Sally stood up and wiped the sweat from her face. "Pick up the bread, Billy, and the basket. I'll get my cloak." She felt her body shake from the cold or from fright, she did not know which.

Billy stood stock still, eyes wide, glued to Sally. "Billy, you must swear before the Almighty never to tell." She took the boy's face in her two hands and held him face to face. "And now listen to me.... The bridge by Cove Creek. I shall miss my step and fall into the swamp. When I scream, run home, summon your father to come and he will bear witness that I fell this fine afternoon.... You understand?" He nodded weakly. "Be brave now and you will grow to be a strong man!" She turned and pushed and he ran.

She ran too like a hunted animal, past the tall tulip trees and through the creeping vines. Thorns tore at her skirt. She ran past the rope yard to the boggy river and the rickety planks that formed the bridge. The water was black and cold and sloshed angrily in the decaying reeds. A fish jumped. A muskrat slithered into the water. Sally hesitated only a moment and jumped. Waterfowl screeched in protest. The mud sucked at her skirts, at the thick folds of her cloak. But the swamp was not deep. She ducked her head into the murk; she ground the mud into the cloak, over her arms, into her hair to wash out the telltale blood. She remembered to scream.

Billy came with his father and sister, Peg. Together they pulled Sally Townsend from the slime. Peg Youngs wrapped her in a blanket.

Mother Youngs saw them coming from the porch, and rushed to draw clean water from the well. "Set the chowder on the hearth, stoke the fire higher and pray she doesn't sicken. There are evil humors in the marsh!"

"Curse the Hessian devils stole the planking from the bridge!" Daniel

Youngs drew out a cup of the steaming broth and held it to Sally's lips. "Drink! It will warm the insides of you, girl."

Sally sipped. Peg and her mother stripped the fouled clothing, washed and dressed her in a clean nightshirt and wrapped her in blankets. Finally, her shivering stopped and Mother Youngs could withhold her curiosity no longer. "What happened, child?"

"I slipped."

They assumed the rest. How many times had Sally Townsend crossed the bridge without incident? "You should never walk alone, child."

"Billy walked with me."

"He's a good lad but too small and too young when danger strikes! You need Cob."

"Cob had a mare in foal."

"Your life counts for more than a horse!" Mother Youngs was indignant.

"Cob is afraid." Daniel Youngs understood.

The night was cool. Sally sat quietly on the settle in front of the blazing hearthfire. She dozed. She awoke to the hum of conversation and the faint yellow flicker of candlelight. Mother Youngs was whispering to her husband. "Sarah Townsend worries more for that hermit Cooper, than she does for her own fleshed daughter. This one's too pretty to be allowed out unchaperoned."

"Sarah does her best. She can't tend to Cooper with her hip. Audrey is naive. Samuel is infirm. Sally is quick witted and responsible enough to take care of herself. 'Tis the bridge that is unsafe since the Hessians ripped up the planks. The beams are all crusted with mosses and slime."

"Audrey's not so frail she can't shoulder a chore now and then!" Mother Youngs would not be silenced. "I heard Robert was home. He could have accompanied her."

"Robert lives apart and has duties in New York."

"I've heard of his duties, important duties that enable him to keep a mistress! Robert shames the name of Townsend!"

"Sarah, be kind!" But Daniel Youngs smiled inwardly. Mother Youngs did not suspect that Robert was a spy.

34

But whence arises in the dead of night
This horrid noise to fill us with affright.

Sally Townsend lay awake. Daniel, Mother, Peg and Billy Youngs had gone to bed. Pounding rain thudded against the clapboards. The wind howled. It would continue through the night into the grey damp of dawn. A flame flickered weakly. The hearth fire hissed from water that dripped into the chimney. It shed only a faint light.

Sally could not sleep. Faces loomed up in her imagination. There was Billy whose freckled cheeks were pale, eyes bulging in fright. Bayer's beady eyes stared from his dead visage, his lips open and tongue lolling from his bloody skull. John Graves Simcoe's mouth was taut. Deep furrows edged his eyes. Sally saw him reaching for her, beckoning and she was running toward him, but the dream faded and she began to cry.

Sally Townsend thought about her own impulse of the moment. Events had raced beyond her control and she had killed. She harbored a feminine revulsion to the physical messiness of the deed, and the disgusting behavior of the ugly German, but she felt no guilt. Most of all, she feared the rejection of John Simcoe. She pulled the blanket around her while a cold sweat made her shiver from the inside. She listened to the noises of the night, the creak of a shutter, the thud of the rain, the barely perceptible lapping of waves on the shore, the eerie howl of a wolf. She willed the wolves to devour the body and scatter the bones. She contemplated her explanation to her family and to John Simcoe. Courage, discretion, prudence, secrecy, she would need all these to define her actions and protect Billy Youngs.

A new sound echoed in the darkness. Horses stomped and heavy boots sucked down in the mud. A sword clanked and a hard fist banged the planks of the farmhouse door. Soldiers!

Sally shrank back in fear. Had they discovered the body? Did the soldiers come for her in the stormy night? Had they come for Billy? Young men were especially vulnerable. Younger boys than Billy had been taken, kidnapped, to serve as cabin boys on board ships or orderlies in the army. And young women were vulnerable to the lusts of ranking officers or worse to the lurid whims of underlings like Bayer.

The rapping on the door increased. Daniel Youngs appeared and struck a light. His voice was quietly resigned. "I'm coming. Wake a working man from his sleep, you must give him time to rouse."

Mother Youngs rose behind him. She placed a hand on Sally's shoulder. "Go to the back room, with Peg and Billy!" Her touch was light, trembling. "It will be as if you were not here."

"No deceit, Mother! We have not violated the curfew or incurred any penalty. We shall admit them with grace and decorum. Stand aside while I open the door."

"You are too trusting, Daniel." Mother Youngs grumbled but did as her husband directed. But she shielded Peg and Billy with her wide body and ample robe.

The heavy door squeaked on its hinges when Daniel Youngs pulled it back. A rush of wind ripped it from his hands and extinguished the candle. A British officer stepped into the darkened room. Water dripped in a dark circle from the folds of his cloak.

Daniel Youngs lighted another candle and reacted with surprise. "Lieutenant Colonel Simcoe, sir!" His voice rang with relief. "We thought you were Hessians. Mother, put the kettle on...and bring refreshment!"

Simcoe spoke with urgency. "I did not mean to scare you, Youngs. Forgive me for waking you in the dead of night. We come on a vital errand. Miss Sally Townsend did not return home before curfew and has been missing since this afternoon when she left for the hermit, Cooper's, farm on the Neck. She never arrived at Cooper's. I thought perhaps you or one of your people might have seen her. She should have passed this way."

"She is here, Colonel," Mother Youngs spoke up while Squire Daniel stepped aside and fumbled with a match to light another candle. "There by the fire. Daniel pulled her from the river."

John Simcoe glanced at the muffled form in front of the fire which sparked suddenly. "I...was worried for you, Miss Townsend." Sally sat silently. The folds of Peg's nightshirt billowed around her. John Simcoe averted his eyes. "I am much relieved that you have not come to grief, Miss."

Sally nodded, caught his eye and held it. She did not speak.

Mother Youngs pulled up her best mahogany chair. "Please, Colonel Simcoe, sit. The tea is coming to a boil. Warm yourself before you return."

"Thank you, Madame. My adjutant, Lieutenant Ormond, is waiting outside. I would bid him to warm himself too, before starting back."

"By all means, sir."

John Simcoe turned to Sally. "When you didn't return, I sent Ormond to Cooper's... You weren't there and you didn't send word." He poured out a cup of tea and carried it to her.

Sally lifted her chin bravely. Her mouth opened tentatively and she finally spoke. "I started but I fell from the bridge. My clothes are ruined."

Mother Youngs complained, "The bridge is rotten, what's left of it, sir! We need a good British squad to set it right! Only the round struts are left, slick as spilled oil! The Hessians laugh when they see us flounder."

"I'll send a detail in the morning, Madame." John Simcoe marched to the door and called to Lieutenant Ormond who clomped in eagerly. Ormond was shorter, with a ruddy, round face and muscular, stubby limbs, that reminded Sally of Bayer in the gloom. But his attitude was courteous and his manners urbane. He stood inside the door and shook the rain from his clothing until Captain Youngs invited him to sit and eat. Ormond had a voracious appetite.

"Peg, bring Sally more tea. Sally, drink. The tea will fortify you. Take some sweetcake, girl, and some cheese. You needn't be shy with Colonel Simcoe!" Sally seated herself with the family at the table. More than once, she felt John

Simcoe's keen eyes upon her. More than once, her heart stirred. She met his glance with a faint smile. What must he think to find her so disheveled and pale, sleeping on a pallet in a farmhouse, and he, a Lieutenant Colonel in the King's Army! She held the teacup with both hands and smiled. The hot liquid seeped in and gave her courage.

Simcoe straightened, aware suddenly that he was staring and that he attracted the intense scrutiny of the Youngs and Lieutenant Ormond as well. He sliced the bread and stuffed it in his mouth.

Youngs questioned him with a wink. "And where is Sergeant Kelly? I never see you without him."

John Simcoe laughed. "Wake Kelly to go searching for a lady in the depth of night! He would denounce the errand! I would sooner snatch a lion from his lair than brave his wrath! And his tongue would wag like a hound's tail!"

Daniel threw a glance across the table. "You hold your own tongue, Mother!"

Ormond chuckled agreeably. He understood the discretion necessary to the courting of a woman and he sympathized with Youngs. He was a married man.

John Simcoe sipped his tea politely, rose suddenly and turned, red-faced, to Mother Youngs. "Pardon Madame, we have overstayed our welcome. You must be tired. I didn't mean to interrupt your slumber. We will ride back warm and at ease in spite of the rain. I am relieved to know Miss Sally is in your capable hands. Mrs. Townsend was very anxious."

Mother Youngs snorted at the mention of Sarah Townsend. Her words were not kind. "Mrs. Townsend fears for her own health and occasionally for Audrey's. Sally's welfare has never troubled her more than the passing clouds in the sky."

John Simcoe eased the embarrassment as best he could. "I can assure you, Madame, that Sarah and Samuel Townsend care for Miss Sally very much. But for the curfew, Mr. Townsend would have come himself." His tone turned apologetic. "Hopefully, the curfew soon will no longer be necessary and hostilities will cease. But you are right, Madame. A young and beautiful lady should not go about unescorted. I shall personally attend to Miss Sally's homecoming in the morning."

Simcoe moved to the door and Sally watched him go. Her heart cramped tightly in her chest. There was another gust of wind and creak of hinge as Simcoe and Lieutenant Ormond edged out the door and into the rain-soaked darkness. The heavy bar thudded back into place.

The Youngs family and Sally Townsend did not go back to sleep that night. They sipped their tea, and munched their cake and listened to the hammering of the rain. Its ominous rhythm rapped the shingles like the war drums of the native tribes.

Mother Youngs was first to speak the thought that was in all their minds. "He's a handsome man. I think he cares for you, Sally."

It was a blind-sided remark, the careless matchmaking of village matron. Sally could read it in her eyes. Mother Youngs was clicking off the possibility of courtship and marriage to the dashing Britisher. Sally hated the speculation that would ignite village tongues and subject her to scrutiny and gossip. She spoke up in her own defense. "There is no sympathy between Colonel Simcoe and me." The denial rang hollow but Sally Townsend knew her prospects had dimmed. John Graves Simcoe was too good and moral a man. How could she confess to murder? He would break their troth. One of the other officers might have dismissed the loss of the burly Hessian, but not Simcoe! His deep sense of honor and right would object. He was not a rake or a gambler like this Tarleton Robert spoke of, or a brute like sadistic Cunningham. He was a good man and she loved him for it. Now she had denied that love. Silently, she cursed the bitter war that severed families and made enemies of men of like mind, that paired the noble with the foul, that prompted her to kill, and squandered the love she bore for John Graves Simcoe. It blew away like chaff before the wind.

She covered her face with her hands. Tears seeped through her fingers until she thought of Billy. Such a young lad, he must not suffer. She would have to bury the knowledge of the dreadful afternoon like a deadweight, deep in the bowels of her soul. No word, no breath, no sound of the truth must ever surface.

Mother Youngs heard her gasp and placed a cool hand on her sweating brow. "Finish your cake, Sally! By the good God, girl, I think you have a fever!

Sleep will make you well and send you your cavalier in the morning!"

Sally swallowed the cake and closed her eyes but precious sleep did not come. Her conscience prickled like a burr at the base of her brain. The Almighty had witnessed her act. Would he damn her to the fiery torments of the Baptists or was he the kinder, more reasonable god of the Quakers? Surely he would not damn the boy! And what was this hell that Christians threatened? Sally could imagine no worse fate than existence in the hulks or rape by the ugly Hessian. She could not endure the thought of coupling with the ugly man. If this was hell, then war was the greater evil and hellfire no more than a puff of ash.

The Youngs had rekindled the fire and gone off to bed. Sally shivered alone in the darkened room. Her thoughts rambled. If there had been no Hessians, if John Simcoe had been fat and unattractive, if Robert had been here to accompany her, if Joseph Cooper had come to live in town! *If* - it was a tiny word and controlled so much. *If* - reality did not allow for the possibility.

She thought of Joseph Cooper who had withered even before the coming of the army. His wife, Mary, had born six children. They had watched their family grow. Mary Cooper died two years ago, after their sixth and last surviving child, a daughter named Esther, had succumbed to smallpox. Six dead children and a wife had made seven graves that poor Cooper had dug on the windy bluff that overlooked the bay. So much hardship for such a beautiful place!

The thought that Cooper's misfortune was far worse than hers, renewed Sally's strength. She had been doing God's work, taking bread to the hungry, bringing a small respite to Cooper's suffering. It was Bayer who hindered that work, who deserved to die. She questioned the God who created such a fiend. Was Bayer's death by her hand in his omniscient order of things? Why had God sent John Simcoe, who, of all the officers, was the one among many who hated Hessian depravity and the one of all of them who might understand the desperation of her act. Would that same John Simcoe find forgiveness in his heart? Or would his love disintegrate into righteousness? The questions tortured her soul. She resolved finally to confess her guilt to John Graves Simcoe. It would be a test of their love. If the test ended in failure, she did not fear the future. She wished there would be no more time to endure.

35

What remedy for this unlucky job?
What art shall raise the spirits of the mob?

*L*ieutenant Colonel John Simcoe rode back to Raynham Hall in the driving rain. He swayed gently in the saddle, a dark caped figure, head down, body slanted into the wind which drove the icy water under his collar. He was so deep in thought, he hardly noticed. His joints ached with the cold and each deliberate motion of the horse.

"With the Colonel's permission, sir, the left fork leads to Raynham Hall." Ormond had to shout over the pelting rain. They had almost passed the fork in the road that led to the village.

Simcoe jolted upright, the rain slapped against his face as he turned the beast left toward the village and the Townsend home. They came to a halt at the gate under the bare black branches of the whipping tree. John Simcoe shouted above the clatter of the rain. "I'll stable the horse myself, Ormond.... And Ormond, sleep late if you wish. You are excused from the morning muster, and please not to speak of tonight's mission, to anyone, especially your fellow officers or Sergeant Kelly."

Lieutenant Ormond smiled and nodded. "A good morning's sleep shall erase my memory, sir. Thank you... Should I strike a light for you, sir?"

"In this downpour, it will do no good. But thank you. Go home. Dry and warm yourself. Kelly will be about in the morning."

"Then good night, sir."

John Simcoe led the bay horse into the blackness of the stable and struck a lantern. The light leaked a sick yellow glow into the recesses of the stalls. Water dripped from the roof in more than one place and the air stank with the hot breath of animals. Simcoe's head ached. He was wet and cold. He had been awake since six o'clock in the morning and it was now past midnight. He lay an arm across the saddle and his head upon his arm and let exhaustion consume him. It felt good to be alone. It felt good to shed responsibilities like a duck's feathers shed rain. Sally had been unusually quiet at Youngs. He worried for her health; he worried for her spirit; he worried for the future he had so carefully constructed in his mind. The war was not going well since the French had entered. Saratoga was a disaster, a Hessian fiasco. His own Rangers could have rolled over Gates' Army like a storm wave but the high command shunned the best loyalist recruits. Simcoe had spent his days scrambling to maintain their morale during endless musters and foraging forays and drilled them doggedly to attack by horse or foot. One bayonet charge would have sent Gates' scoundrels running like rabbits for the dunghills, except maybe for Arnold! There was a man who was a true fighter. If only Arnold had fought with Burgoyne! But he was dreaming, asleep on his feet. The animal moved away suddenly from the pressure of his weight and he almost fell.

Simcoe had forgotten the rain-soaked beast. The bay horse shook himself and spattered water all over the aisle. Gently, he released the buckles of the girth and lifted the saddle from the horse's back. This horse of Robert Townsend's that Tarleton had claimed, was a noble steed, perfectly schooled, tall at the withers with broad chest and deep heart. But the horse was a symbol of the kind of assumed superiority that John Simcoe detested. Tarleton had a stable full. He could requisition the horse with little remorse, then offer the prize to his superior to buy promotion instead of meriting it, to exalt the less deserving at the expense of those who truly merit. Simcoe, himself, had suffered because of it.

He attached the horse to an oak partition and mumbled to himself. "We tie our best men. We attach blinkers to their eyes and hobbles to their legs so they cannot see to left or right and they stumble when they should walk..." He smacked his lips. There was a sour taste in his mouth like wet cotton. He was thinking of General John Burgoyne who could have saved himself and his army, but refused to sacrifice one wagonload of his personal effects, refused to retreat even when reason dictated.

A voice startled him from out of the blackness. "Please, sir, I'll do that for you." It was Cob.

"It's late for you, Cob! The curfew!"

Cob read his lips. "I was asleep in the stall with the mare, where I can watch the foal, sir." He took up a brush and began to swipe the dried mud from the horse's legs.

Simcoe followed the slave's line of vision to the foaling stall where a brown mare stood licking her new brown babe. They were hardly discernable in the gloom but John Simcoe smiled at the silhouette that wobbled on spindly legs and suckled its dam. Life was very precious to a soldier whose life could vanish in an instant's blast from a cannon and who spent his days promoting ways to take another's life. He pinched the weariness from his eyes. The mare reminded him of the comforts of a wife, mother to his children, a quiet home. It was a distant dream for him but the presence of the animals brought it into focus. He was getting older. The glory of battle faded with each year. He did not want to die without human offspring. He wanted a son, a son by Sally. The craving sucked the air from his lungs and the blood from his heart at times like tonight when it was dark and he was lonely and tired.

He shook the rain from his cloak, wiped the mud from his boots and watched the slave pull the bridle over the horse's ears. The bay stretched his neck and shook himself. The lantern sputtered. Cob led the horse to a stall. He picked up a rag to wipe the wet tack. The horse had a humble stall; the slave had his cell and the warmth of this stable. John Simcoe had neither. He felt the need for companionship and lingered.

There was fawning reverence in the black man's voice when he spoke again. "Colonel Simcoe, sir, did you find Miss Sally?"

"Yes."

Cob's corniced brows locked together. "I should have gone with her, sir, in spite of the mare. I'm sorry."

John Simcoe looked up. Cob's expression showed deep concern. He had his place in the emotional bonds that tied this family together. A pang of sympathy struck the Britisher and he answered softly, "She's at Youngs'. She's fine."

He added after Cob's eyes had turned away. "I do not blame you, Cob."

The slave did not hear. Cob's head bowed in submission. He hung the bridle on its hook, picked up a broom and swept the wet straw from the aisle.

John Simcoe watched from the shadows. Cob swung the broom casually from side to side, with grace and ease, without complaint at the drudgery or uselessness of his task. The British Army, where each act had its prescribed exactness, and tradition dictated manner of performance, was very different. John Simcoe felt suddenly like the slave. He too must submit to masters, but he could not accept their folly and intransigence.

He was about to ask for grease for his wet boots and wondered silently what would have been Cob's treatment at the hands of other officers, Colonel Tarleton or Lord Cathcart. They would have struck Cob down as a malingerer for laxity of execution or slowness of his deaf response. Tarleton carried a whip for that very purpose. And tonight Tarleton would have accused John Simcoe of inattention to discipline. A black man must be made to know his place! That there was another kind of discipline, the discipline of good example, Tarleton could not conceive.

Simcoe slogged across the muddy yard to the kitchen door. Sergeant Kelly was slumped over the kitchen table, sleeping. He placed a shawl over the little sergeant's shoulders to ward off the dampness of the night and slumped into a chair.

His thoughts reverted to Sally. Their meeting had been too public at Youngs. He had detected a tremor in her voice, an undercurrent of doubt and could not reason why. Where would it all end? The high command feared losing Canada but was withdrawing troops and sending them back to Europe or the West Indies. Where would London's far-off decisions leave him? Where would they leave Sally? Loyal colonials like Edward Shippen and Joseph Galloway had complained bitterly to powerful men in London of the conduct of the war, in vain. In the lonely night, he wondered why he was here and what he was fighting for.

Despondency rolled over him like a heavy smoke. What had the loyal Americans gained for their trust and perseverance? An army of parasites that devoured their forests and the produce of their fields, slaughtered their livestock, and razed their houses; a prolonged war that consumed the loyal sons of loyal fathers! Galloway had lost his entire estate with the evacuation of Philadelphia. Shippen too. They lived in London on a pittance now. How many more loyal Americans had met the same fate? The honor of mother England was withering like the seeds sown on rock. John Simcoe heaved a sigh and pulled himself up. The only sound was Sergeant Kelly's intermittent snoring. It was a sniffling, satisfied rumble but reminded John Simcoe of sniveling London ministers who manipulated the colonies with turned up noses, in a series of self-serving, sporadic grunts. He dragged himself to bed.

When he awoke late in the morning, he felt better. The sun was high and Raynham Hall held the smell of damp earth and baking bread. Smoke from lighted hearths was swiftly sucking out the moisture.

Robert was in the parlor poking a fire to new life and looked up when John Simcoe walked in with his collar unbuttoned and red flecks in the whites of his eyes. There was a decanter of port on the table and he poured out a glass and handed it to John Simcoe. "Are you well, Colonel? Take some port. It fortifies the blood."

John Simcoe sank to the settle and leaned forward to warm himself. "I was to Youngs' late last night. I did not sleep well." He had not slept at all.

"Ormond told me you went out in the midst of that squall. He did not say why?"

"I went after Sally. She was caught away by the curfew."

A shadow passed over Robert Townsend's swarthy face. He seized the poker and stabbed the smoking logs. "Don't ruin my day with tales of my sister's follies!"

"She fell from the bridge on her way to Cooper's. Daniel Youngs rescued her." He added because he felt Robert expected an explanation. "She's a beautiful woman, Rob. You know I honor and respect her." The words descended like a weight in shallow water. They did not strike bottom.

Robert sensed the uncertainty in John Simcoe's voice. He sensed the passion that moved forward with utmost caution, so as not to alienate the brother, not to create any possible contest, and endanger his precious construct of the future. He replaced the poker silently, stamped out a spark that had sputtered to the floorboards and stood warming his hands over the fire with his back to John Simcoe and a face hard as granite.

John Simcoe continued, "Respect is a prelude to love. I count you my friend, Robert Townsend. I hope soon I can count you my brother! I have asked Sally to marry me."

Robert Townsend whirled on his heel and turned eyes like daggers on the green-coated officer. "Has my father consented?"

The Britisher snapped back at the onslaught, "I have not yet approached your father!"

Robert lowered his voice. "Forgive me, Colonel, if I did not imagine that an English officer and gentleman would choose a humble colonial maid for a bride! You withdrew as her suitor once before, or have you forgotten?"

John Simcoe parried and defended himself. "We are not all rakes like Tarleton and Howe. I withdrew because I did not think myself worthy. I was an invalid in this house. I felt I had unfairly excited her sensitivity and devotion.... I was mistaken. We have a new commander. I have my promotion and the prospects of victory are favorable." His chest heaved and fire lit the deep pupils of his eyes. "Her love for me has not diminished with time and distance. I count myself among the happiest of men!"

Silence! It enveloped them like a shroud. Robert turned back toward the fire. Flames crackled from the red-hot coals and wrapped like pincers around a huge maple log. Seconds slipped by.

Simcoe's smooth voice stammered, "As her brother, can you at least wish us well?"

Robert answered truthfully. "You are an honorable man, John Simcoe, but I don't think Sally will make you happy. I don't think you will make her happy. You are British born, Oxford bred. She is not a docile English girl. She has spirit, intelligence, independence!"

"And English girls do not? I grant that English girls know their place!... But independence!" He laughed at the irony. "It has a rebellious ring. That is part of why I love her. She has spark and verve and independence enough to choose me freely in spite of our differences and I will do all in my power to make her happy. Surely you are not so cynical that you cannot share our joy."

Robert looked away. "I too, have known love, John Simcoe. It is not a simple word. It is not always twin to happiness. It has confounded philosophers and kings and better men than you or I. I only hope that you and Sally have been circumspect enough to consider the difficulties that are sure to emerge." He looked away. The words sounded flat, like the memorized parsings of a schoolboy.

John Simcoe's words sparked fire. "I propose to wed her as soon as I have your father's blessing and the blessing of my family in England....I have come to love this continent enough to make it my home. A home with Sally is the object of my deepest desires."

Robert withdrew. He tucked his head like a turtle into its shell. His words floated, like a feather on the wind. "Then I wish you and my sister prosperity and long life."

"No happiness?"

"That too, if God wills it. Happiness is yet another complex word but I will drink to happiness for you both." He poured himself a glass of port. The glasses clinked sharply and Robert downed his drink. Simcoe only sipped. Like a mismatched team, they pulled at different speeds, in different directions and the carriage tottered between them.

Robert stood up abruptly. "And now Colonel, if you will excuse me... I have duties." He turned on his heel and stalked out.

John Simcoe was left with a half-glass of port in his hand, like a castaway upon a deserted shore. He tossed it into the fire which sizzled its complaint, then sank back on the settle. There was a growling in his chest, a pounding in his head and a tight apprehension in the pit of his stomach. So much for the brother. He buttoned his collar and hoped for a better reception from the father.

When Samuel walked in presently, John Simcoe jumped up like a springing cat from his chair. "I would speak with you sir, in private."

Samuel led him upstairs to his bed chamber where he kept his personal papers and desk, "Colonel, what can I do for you?" He motioned Simcoe to sit. The chair was hard and the soldier perched stiffly, straightened his arms and gripped a knee with each hand. The old man lowered himself slowly to his own cushion behind his desk and folded his hands neatly in front of him.

John Simcoe began nervously. "Sir, I come on a personal mission."

Samuel nodded encouragingly. "Then join me in a brandy, Colonel? It eases the aches of age and loosens the tongue."

John Simcoe had not eaten since the night before and the glass of port still soured his innards. He fumbled a refusal. "Thank you sir, but I am to inspect the corps presently and I cannot smell of brandy" He paused, drew himself up and spat out the question. "Mr. Townsend, sir, I come to ask the hand of your daughter, Sally, in holy matrimony."

Samuel gave a snort. His head snapped up with a twang and his nostrils flared. His lips moved before any sound came. "Forgive me, Lieutenant Colonel Simcoe. Your request is totally unanticipated. I had not considered Sally marrying at this juncture....Most of the young men she knows have joined one army or another." Samuel's old head bobbed but his sharp gaze pierced the dim interior light. "You are a soldier. I had not considered Sally marrying a military man. Yours is a dangerous profession and we are Quakers." He pursed his lips. "I assume you and Sally have declared your love, else you would not have come to speak with me?"

Simcoe straightened. "I submit, sir, that other occupations are equally dangerous. Your eldest son, Solomon, is a ship's captain.... My own dear father was lost at sea. I am not unaware of the perils of the ocean." John Simcoe studied the old man intently. "But yes sir, Sally and I have pledged our love, each to the other."

Samuel nodded. "Sally's mother will be delighted to have you for a prospective son-in-law, Lieutenant Colonel. However as a Quaker and her father, I confess I cannot immediately offer my blessing or express my congratulations with enthusiasm. And you realize that if I assent to the match, I cannot promise much by way of dowry. I was a richer man before this unfortunate conflict."

"I understand, sir. I have a small inheritance of my own."

"Enough to maintain her in the manner to which she is accustomed without intruding on her own inheritance?"

"I believe so, sir."

The old man nodded agreeably but his voice trembled when he asked, "And where would you and Sally make your home?"

"I will request a post here in the colonies, sir. I have learned to love the wild lands." Simcoe shuddered involuntarily at the realization of how little he controlled his own destiny.

Samuel Townsend rubbed his chin, and stood up. The conversation was at an end. "I have not refused, Lieutenant Colonel. There are many matters to resolve first. We will speak again." Samuel's was a cool, not a warm, reception. Samuel Townsend smiled broadly and John Simcoe reciprocated with ice in his heart.

36

Yet must on every face a smile be worn
Whilst every breath with agony is torn.

*J*ohn Simcoe went in search of Sergeant Kelly and a gig . The Sergeant stood outside in the noon sunshine, brushing Simcoe's green coat with the concentration of a cat preening. "I fear the coat has shrunk, sir. Ye must never hang it so near the fire...and every speck of dust shows itself against the infernal green... a snotty color, green!"

"Where are my boots, Kelly?" Simcoe interrupted impatiently.

"I've given 'em a dousing of oil, sir, lest the leather rot and crack." The sergeant's rabbit nose was sniffing. "And I've ordered new woolens, sir. Ye must have a new cloak and a waistcoat cut. There's a good tailor in Jericho from London, but I hear that the Thimble and Shears in New York City is the best for a senior officer like yourself. Mulligan, the tailor, is a friend to Mr. Townsend, a tinker of an Irishman, sir, but with a very grand given name!" He laughed mockingly. "Hercules! A god almighty name for a tailor!" When he realized Simcoe was not listening, he switched to a more compelling topic. "'Tis a fair lass, sir, lovelier than any in Philadelphia or London!"

Simcoe's eyes shot daggers, "Restrict you comments to your duties, Sergeant!... I'll want a gig presently to fetch Miss Sally home."

"The phaeton or the dog cart, sir?"

"The phaeton, Sergeant, and I'll drive myself."

He drove slowly, letting the horse meander in the sunshine. Sally climbed silently from Youngs' porch into the high carriage. There was a spark in the depth of her eyes, a quiver to her mouth, that had not been there yesterday. John Simcoe sensed a subtle hesitancy between thought and word. After the first greeting, their conversation ebbed. She gave a slight start when they drove through the stand of trees, took hold of his arm and clutched it against her. The gesture delighted and perplexed him.

The road curved to the water's edge. She smiled up at him, "Stop here, John. It is quite beautiful. There is a peace and comfort about the shore."

Her smile encouraged him, "I spoke to your father this morning. He has taken my request under consideration. I trust he will consent. I will write to my relatives in England this evening. They will surely send their blessing." He pulled her to him and kissed her lightly. "Not now, John, we are too visible."

At the wharf, they watched the H.M.S. Honor disgorge a troop of dirty prisoners. Townsend's sloop, the Promise, had a more cheerful cargo - Tobago rum. Longboats carried the huge hogsheads to shore amid the hoots and shouts of boisterous seamen. It was a happy, noisy sight, filled with rambunctious life. Sally brightened.

When they reached the village, Sergeant Kelly ran up. "Sir, General Pattison is here with orders!" General Pattison was Adjutant General of the British Army, not a man to be kept waiting! He did not usually deliver orders in person. John Simcoe whipped the horse to a swift trot.

Pattison was waiting at the gate. He handed John Simcoe a dispatch case and winked suggestively at the sight of Sally. "Gone a courting, Simcoe! With a lass whose hair is the color of flame, the proudest color of war and the color of the heart, no less! Good luck and good cheer!... I've a project should allow you to pursue your amour for at least another month!" He bowed to Sally sitting in the gig. "General Clinton has chosen you personally for the assignment, Lieutenant Colonel."

"I am honored, General." John Simcoe nodded graciously and made introductions. "Miss Sally Townsend may I present General William Pattison, Adjutant General of the British Army." Pattison held out a gloved hand to help her down.

John Simcoe opened the dispatches on the spot and read the orders. A cloud settled over his face.

Pattison placed a hand on his shoulder and directed him to the privacy of the lane. "Sir Henry specifies you to build a fort to insure the safety of his supplies." His tone was patronizing.

"We have Fort Franklin which cost great expense and effort to build.... It guards the entrance to the bay."

"Fort Franklin is too far from the storage bins and shipyards of this village, and is effective only for larger ships. The shallows are out of range. The whalers skim across with impunity all too regularly. Just last month, the pirates made off with the H.M.S. Fox and we lost this shipyard or have you forgotten? You were the hero of the hour! We've lost the yards at Mastic and Setauket. Rebuilding a shipyard is costlier than building new. Worse, the rebels pilfer supplies perennially. Sir Henry intends to stop the depredations once and for all."

To John Simcoe, a second fort was wasteful duplication. He queried delicately. "Fort Franklin was sufficient until now?"

"Orders have arrived from Lord Germain in London directing Sir Henry to send Lord Cornwallis and an army south with naval support, to take Savannah and Charleston. The King and Lord Germain feel that we have so far neglected the southern loyalists but that they will rally zealously to our cause and in the end, add to our strength. Oyster Bay has been chosen as one of the army's embarkation points. We will be amassing supplies here and supplies need protection." He stopped suddenly, removed his glove and scratched his twitching nose. "As a consequence of Lord Cornwallis' departure, General Clinton's forces in New York will be halved. Lord Cornwallis will attack General Washington from the south while General Clinton will pursue him from here. Together they will squeeze the rebellious rabble from North America, as the pulp from the rind so to speak." He wrung his glove in a tight coil. "And as you know, the southern colonies are important at this juncture because of French threats to Bermuda and our bases in the West Indies. General Clinton wants to entrench here in New York as firmly as possible before Lord Cornwallis' departure. He believes good fortifications will make up for lack of men. Thus, the fort.

"I see." John Simcoe lied.

"I'm sure you do." Pattison smacked his puffy lips, replaced his glove and raised a looking glass to his eye. "I looked over the topography while riding in. You've a perfect prominence for a fort right there." He lowered the glass officiously, and raised his shiny gloved hand. He was pointing to Samuel Townsend's hill which overlooked Raynham Hall. He walked off and motioned to Simcoe to follow. "Come, I'll show you."

John Simcoe's mind raced. The fortifications Pattison described would devastate a large section of Townsend property and construction of the fort would not endear him to the Townsend family. He climbed after Pattison stumbling like a distracted schoolboy. The hill was wooded and steep.

Pattison was exuberant. "You've all the materials for a fine installation near at hand, even the fruit trees for your abatis!" Pattison swept an arm over the Townsend's orchard like Joshua over the Promised Land.

"There is a higher hill there." John Simcoe pointed east to the Parrish farm. "You cannot see it through the trees."

Pattison unfolded his glass and looked. "Too far from the village and the moorings. Your prime objective is to protect the ships and storehouses. Better to keep the guns close in, better for aim - Hessians will probably man the guns and they are notorious for missing targets. Your guns have already arrived aboard the Jackal from Liverpool and been off-loaded at Burling's Slip in New York. They will be here in a day or two. If you begin tomorrow, the fort will be finished before winter sets in." Pattison nodded with self-importance and turned to descend back down to the lane.

John Simcoe dared question the details and called after him. "Are my rangers to do the digging, General?"

Nothing could deter Pattison's assurance. "Lord no, man! They are cavalry! I would never despoil the glorious honor of mounted cavalry by having them dig holes! You are authorized to employ as many contingents of Hangar's Hessians as you deem necessary. Hessians are like moles, good for moving earth." Pattison clamped his pink lips shut and folded his glass. "Any questions?"

"No sir. My orders are plain. Please convey my highest regards to General Sir Henry and assure him I will do my duty to the letter." John Simcoe bowed his head but he tasted blood on his lip where his tooth had broken the skin.

"Good-bye then. And good luck." Pattison bowed formally, but his voice babbled on. "General Clinton bid me tell you that he has chosen you because of your ample administrative ability and keen sense of duty."

"The General is always generous with his praise."

"Then good-bye again, Simcoe. Bid my farewell to your pretty redhead and pleasant dreams." The General's light laughter and casual wave of hand was like the slap of a glove. John Simcoe bristled. It was a hard order from a presumptuous superior. He had no choice but to comply. His blue eyes narrowed and bile churned in his stomach as he watched Pattison mount and ride away.

He turned on his heel and went to find Sally. How could he tell her that he must seize Townsend property? And Samuel, how was he to tell Samuel Townsend that he must raze the timber from his land and place guns on top of his proud Quaker hill?

Sally was in the parlor with Audrey. He burst in unannounced. "Is there some place private where we can speak?"

Sally reacted immediately to his unblinking stare. "The orchard. I will fetch my shawl."

He followed her out through the kitchen across the yard. The orchard was peaceful in the afternoon sunlight. The harvest was in; the apples picked. Yellow leaves clung to the twisted branches. Some had fallen and outlined circles of gold on the ground while sunlight filtered through the branches and dappled the earth. The green of John Simcoe's coat gleamed like an emerald.

He held her gently by the shoulders, stopped once to let his deep passion spill over him, breathed deeply and began. "Sally I have just received orders. You are the first to know."

She paled. Was he leaving again as he had before? "You are going away?"

He shook his head. "No." The look in his eyes intensified and seemed to suck her into the depth of his soul. "What I have to tell you is nothing that I could have anticipated. I pray it will not change your or your family's opinion of me."

"When a woman loves a man, she is not ruled by opinion...but I cannot answer for my family."

"I would do nothing to hurt you." His eyes locked on hers then flicked away. He paused to watch a grey squirrel scamper by and stammered, "Look at him! He buries his nut and builds his nest as I am ordered to secure this village, to dig, to build a fort to insure the safety of our forage." Sally shrugged. She did not understand. His voice broke. "To build it there, overlooking your home."

Silence. He took her hand, stroked it mechanically, and stammered on. "I must employ Hessian laborers. I am to raze these very trees for the abatis. Sally, do you know what that is? Their branches must rim the perimeter of the fort to slow an assault." One hand reached up to stroke the smooth grey bark. He picked out a leaf and rubbed it between his fingers. "Sally, do you understand? These will not bloom again! I am so dreadfully sorry!"

Sally stared back in disbelief. "The apple trees? They are our fruit. The cider is our drink."

"They are thickly branched and will form an impenetrable barrier. General Pattison delivered the order himself!" He took her by the elbows and held her gently at arm's length. "Sally, I will replace the trees with the best of nursery stock from England...at my own expense. Please do not think ill of me!... You have my word!"

"I know your word is sacred, John Simcoe, that you will stand by your word like a rock that bucks the tide, but there is other..." Her voice cracked.

He pulled her to him. She lay her head against his broad chest and he stroked the flaming hair until the question in his mind finally translated to speech. "Will your father refuse our union because of it?"

She stiffened and pulled softly away. "I don't know." And she braced herself against the tree to hide the shudder that ran the length of her spine.

Suddenly, she stepped away and turned her face to the sea. "It is not my father. It is you, John Simcoe, who will refuse our union, when you hear what I am about to reveal." She covered her face with her hands. The awful words leaked out one by one. "The Hessians are lawless men. Living in their presence is difficult."

Now it was he who did not understand. "If you are afraid, Sally, I'll post a guard here in the orchard and at the barn to insure your safety! I will not let the stinking Hessians lay one finger upon you!"

Her voice cracked suddenly in anguish. "Oh my John, they already have!" A sob shook her. She turned away from him, more at ease with the condemned trees of the orchard. "I am unclean! Please, for what I am about to say, do not hate me!" She straightened suddenly and recited in a dull monotone. "A Hessian died yesterday.... He tried to rape me." She squared her shoulders and trained her eyes on the fathomless waters of the bay. "I wish those black waters would swallow me up and erase the deed I committed. I fought the Hessian, John. I fought him and I won. I killed him." She added bravely, "With a rock and a vine." Now she looked back at him with the intensity of a bonfire. "I still love you, John Simcoe, I am yours to do with as your law intends." She stretched out her two hands as if she expected to be tied and led away.

The realization dawned slowly on John Graves Simcoe. His visage turned from surprise to shock to purple outrage. His eyes narrowed. The line of his jaw froze rigid in anger, but his anger was not for her. That the woman he loved had been provoked to kill, was repugnant and abominable. Minutes elapsed before he brought himself under rigid control and spoke. "It was Bayer, wasn't it?... How?"

She spoke flatly. Their eyes met and held. "The boy, Billy Youngs, the same you saved from the fire, hit him from behind... I finished by strangling him. I could not leave the youth thinking...." She watched the muscles of his neck contract and bulge as he swallowed, then continued bravely. "We hid his body. I did not want the boy to suffer." She ended with a lowering of her voice that spelled relief. "There, the evil is revealed. And now it is you who will withdraw your proposal and condemn me before your courts for a murderess."

"Never!" A fierceness swept over his face and he drew her slowly to him and cradled her head against his chest and cursed the heinous Hessians until the leaves shook on the trees, and buried his face in the tresses of her hair. She felt the muscles of his chest harden, his shoulders tighten and his heart pound in the cage of his ribs like a feral animal trying to get out. Finally, the beast in his breast howled in protest. "Hessians! They would soil the air we breathe with their lust and their greed! I could never condemn one so beautiful as you, but I will curse the Hessian! May he burn forever in the brimming bowels of hell!"

He pressed her to him with violence and passion and she clung there with every ounce of her strength. When he released her, she was trembling. Tears stained the white fear in her eyes. "He will be missed. They will find him."

"Let them. He will not be the first or last Hessian who has deserted."

37

Erect your batteries, engineers, in haste,
Mortars and cannons on the works be placed.

Construction of the fort began next day. Patrols of Hangar's Hessians descended on the village with axes, shovels and picks. They marched each morning in gangs, under guard, down the south road from Jericho and back to their barracks each night. John Simcoe assigned details to fell and haul, others to dig the redoubts, cut fascines and sink fleches, still others to prepare the thick bags of turf and fagots that would absorb the shock of assault. It was dirty, grueling work. The village resounded to the thud of broadaxe, the scrape of the pick and the crash of falling trees. Under strict guard, the promised guns arrived and lined the lane until their emplacements were ready.

John Simcoe positioned his Rangers along the south road to police the Hessians. He was tireless in his efforts. He rode back and forth along their ranks. He climbed the highest redoubt and descended the deepest pit. No detail of the rising fort escaped him. He enforced regulations to the letter from the conduct of every sapper to the delivery of guns and powder, from the emplacement of each cannon to the erection of the final flagpole. If he was not satisfied with a soldier's progress, he took up the axe or spade himself.

Samuel Townsend came frequently to watch. He would lean weakly on Sally's arm and shake his white head woefully. Sarah came out once struggling on her two canes, to the base of the hill and never came again. Her adamant support of Mother England never wavered and when she heard that Lieutenant Colonel Simcoe had proposed marriage to her Sally, he assumed the status of a god in her eyes. She dismissed the loss of the trees with a wave of her hand and upbraided Samuel for not agreeing to the match immediately. They did not tell her that, if the fortress' guns misfired, a stray ball could strike her home.

The orchard was the last to fall. Its loss caused Sarah Townsend minor concern because John Simcoe had already ordered new trees from England. In seven years, they would produce more and better fruit than the old. It was a biblical number - seven. Like the Jews in Egypt, Sarah would endure her seven years of famine until God and England would bestow an abundant harvest. But Samuel Townsend mourned, "I will not live to see their fruit..." There would be no leafy screen to shelter Robert or Caleb Brewster, or John Simcoe and Sally when they sought a quiet moment alone. The only shade would come from the shaggy locust, where Cob and other men had writhed and screamed to the strike of the cat. Sally, Audrey, Beulah and the slave children picked the remaining apples as the trees crashed down.

Hessians descended like soldier ants upon the hill. They hauled the apple trunks into position with their bare hands. They lay them around the perimeter of the fort, branches facing outward. It made assault through the tangle of branches, by foot or by horse, nearly impossible. The Hessians placed the last gun on the ramparts on October 16th and returned to their hovels in Jericho. The fort was finished; the village settled back for the winter into its peaceful routine. John Simcoe was exhausted.

He and Samuel Townsend and Sally toured the completed works. The old man climbed heavily with a cane and leaned on Simcoe's arm. Sally supported his other side. A nostalgia echoed in the old man's voice. He snapped off the twig of a dead tree. "It bends. The sap is still moist, but it will grow old and dry and dead and crack like me. God knows if I will survive to see the guns dismantled and this struggle ended and the young trees heavy with fruit." He added with a wistful glance at Sally, "...and my daughters fat with grandchildren." He kicked his toe into the packed-earth wall. Loose soil fell away revealing a soft basket of dirty decaying branches. "Your sturdy wall crumbles too easily."

"It absorbs the shock of the cannon. A solid wall would break up with the force of an exploding ball. There are many such baskets within the walls.

They are a French siege invention called *gabions*."

They walked on to inspect a cannon. The old man chuckled ironically, "They carve garlands on their caissons and cast angels into the brass muzzles of their guns! So much love and care to invent new and more powerful weapons! They would make an art of war! You have prepared well, Lieutenant Colonel, but you are tired like me. I see it in your eyes and the color of your skin. You worry because your leaders have forgotten us who must live here, all in the name of victory. But you worry for Sally beneath your stiff military reserve. You do love her, my son." They had reached the uppermost redoubt and looked out on the entire village. The scars in the land stood out in stark contrast to the autumn yellows and reds of the forests and fields and the blue of the bay. Where they had dug the earth, they had cut trees to stumps and dragged them over the turf. Ugly grey-brown swaths of mud lingered and froze hard into treacherous ruts. The snows of winter would cover them in sterile whiteness until the weeds could spread their ragged mantle the following spring. Samuel Townsend stretched out his arm like Moses with his staff, and declared. "It is devil's work. I cannot repair this devastation in my lifetime!" The old man's head wobbled and he muttered, "Robert will despise you for this... and others will condemn you secretly in their hearts."

It sounded like a curse. An aching dismay seized John Simcoe. It seemed to hollow out a piece of his chest and shake him from within. "I fear I have brought dissension to this home. I am sorry that you condemn me."

The old man smiled. "I do not condemn you. You are not to blame. You are an honest man and you have tried to preserve us. Don't apologize for what you are, Colonel....You cannot change that and she loves you for it! Come, my girl. Help me down." He took Sally's arm for support in descending the hill. John Simcoe followed wearily.

They reached the lane before John Simcoe raised his voice, "We are preparing a celebration to dedicate the Fort. I was going to name it after you."

"Oh no! You cannot create your monument to war and name it after me."

"I only meant to compliment...."

"I know you did." Samuel was growing tired, his eyes blinking with drowsiness. He leaned more heavily on Simcoe's arm.

Sally spoke up gently. "If it is to be dedicated, it needs a name. It is on a hill.... Call it Fort Hill!"

The dedication of Fort Hill was a grand celebration, the grandest party Oyster Bay had ever seen. They scheduled it for October 25th, with a rain date the first clear day after. Major John Andre, who had arranged the elaborate farewell ceremony for General Howe in Philadelphia, organized the dedication. He built a pavilion with a fringed marquis in the forward redoubt and emptied the Presbyterian Church of its pews. Steers and sheep were slaughtered and roasted. Ships arrived laden with wine and cheeses and sweet meats and rum and slaves to service the effort.

October 25th dawned bright and warm. General Clinton and General Pattison arrived in a coach and four with Lieutenant Colonel Tarleton and the handsome young Major John Andre. An escort from the British Legion accompanied them. Ships massed in the bay and cavalry deployed in the lane. Drums beat a fast tattoo. Flags whipped in the wind. There were foot races and horse races and a brief enactment of the medieval jousts. It was a display of military might such as Sally had never seen. John Simcoe rode proudly at the head of his rangers, then joined Sally Townsend and the generals in the forward redoubt, as in a loge at the theater, to watch the play unfold. Sally was chosen to place the laurel crown on the conqueror's lance.

When the games were over, the cannons fired a salute. Broadsides from the ships at their moorings thundered a deafening reply. The gunports flashed and the balls struck the water sending up walls of foam that glistened in the slanting rays of the autumn sun. When the smoke cleared, officers and landholders retired for feasting and dancing to the Presbyterian Church and Wright's Ordinary. Commoners danced on planks laid flat in the street, until the cool of evening made them seek warm hearthsides. Sally Townsend and John Graves Simcoe accompanied the generals to Wright's where the revelry resounded. About midnight, John Simcoe stumbled and fell. He could withstand the frantic pace no longer: the efforts of the past weeks had drained his strength. Sergeant Kelly and Sally assisted him home, but lecherous old Pattison and rakish little Tarleton twirled away until dawn.

It was noon the next day when they stopped at Townsend's to take their leave. Pattison paid cursory respects to Sarah Townsend, took two sips of tea and walked with John Simcoe and Banastre Tarleton to the gate. "An excellent fortification and capital celebration, Simcoe. Well done on all counts! I did not want to detract from the gaiety by giving you this too soon." He reached into his coat and handed John Simcoe a dispatch case.

John Simcoe opened the case and read the contents. The Queen's Rangers were instructed to make an incursion into the Jerseys at Brunswick. It was an order to action and an opportunity for promotion that every officer longed for. John Simcoe knew it came as a reward for his efforts of the last few months, but in his heart, he suspected it was really no more than a simple raid, the kind he would have expected from the ragged rebel saboteurs, not a precision cavalry corps of the British Army. But the probability of success was good. The exhilaration of a sea voyage would lift morale before the long cold seclusion of winter and the Gazette would ring with exaggerated praise. Promotion was assured. John Simcoe smiled his gratitude. "Thank you, General."

Pattison observed his reaction. "Then you accept. It is not an order, Simcoe. Rather it is an opportunity for greater honor and glory."

Tarleton clapped a hand on John Simcoe's shoulder, "I will volunteer my legion if you reject it."

"And let you claim my laurels! Never, Ban Tarleton!"

"Come then, walk with us to the ordinary. We'll raise a bumper to your success while I await my coach." They strolled off toward Wright's.

A wagon rumbled up beside them with Major Cochran on the box. He addressed Tarleton hesitantly, "Sir, if I may interrupt...."

Tarleton's frown evinced his annoyance. "What is it, Cochran? General Pattison is waiting."

"A dead man, sir, in the uniform of the Hesse-Hannau Corps under your command. The wolves scattered some bones. He has been missing from the muster for a while."

Tarleton wrinkled his nose impatiently. "Bury him and be done with it!"

Cochran would not leave. "His name was Bayer, sir, last seen on the day

Lieutenant Colonel Simcoe arrived. We thought him a deserter, sir!"

General Pattison interrupted, "I leave you to your local concerns, Lieutenant Colonels, but with a suggestion for you Ban Tarleton: that strict discipline and consistent punishment are the only ways to administer Hessians." Pattison nodded politely, but it was a rebuke. "I see my coach has arrived. Good day, gentlemen."

As the coach pulled away, Tarleton blasted Cochran. "You dare to interrupt a General with news of one more dead Hessian, Cochran! I should have you whipped!"

"Begging the Colonel's pardon sir, it was the way he died.... He was brained, sir. The animals had eaten the skull clean but you can see the hole yourself."

"Brained? There a precious few brains in a Hessian to leak! Perhaps less in your thick Irish skull!"

But Cochran persisted. "His skull was smashed with a hammer or perhaps a rock, sir. Captain Hangar's dog sniffed him out. Little more than a skeleton was left, on the road to Youngs' and the Neck."

Tarleton waved his gloved hand. "I repeat, Major. Bury the brute. We've no lack of shovels. Drive on."

"Yes sir." But Cochran did not drive on. "Sir...Captain Hangar says that if the English won't pursue the murderer and defend his countryman, that he will do it himself, and that this Bayer was family. He was red-faced, very angry, sir!"

Banastre Tarleton was not about to trouble himself over one Hessian more or less, especially after the admonition of General Pattison. "Captain Hangar be damned... Rum is what enhances his imagination." He slapped his riding crop across the palm of his hand. "Tell Captain Hangar that if an investigation is to be made, that I will commence it myself, and that I will squash any dissension within my ranks like a worm under the heel of my boot. I will not broach disobedience! Make that very clear, Cochran."

"Yes sir." Cochran drove on.

Tarleton added in deference to Simcoe, "Pattison is right. Hessians understand force and not much else." Then with a wry smile, "How fortunate you are, John, not to have to deal with these Germanic squabbles. This Bayer was a blathering brute. No doubt he was brawling drunk or up to his braces in debt. I envy you your obedient, civilized rangers... and you are housed at Raynham Hall with not one but two raving beauties! I dare say even Pattison is jealous!"

Simcoe smiled mildly. "I count my blessings."

As they entered the ordinary, Tarleton spoke, "You know why I have stayed, don't you?" John Simcoe shook his head. "Pattison left me with orders too. My legion will patrol Oyster Bay in your absence. I should be glad for your advice."

John Simcoe returned to Raynham Hall at six in the evening, slumped into the settle and sat holding his head and rubbing his eyes. Sally found him there. He heaved a sigh and looked up at her. "I am tired, my love, dreadfully tired, and I see no end to the struggle. Come, sit by me."

He took her hand, laid it upon his knee and traced the outline of her fingers. "Sally, I will assign a detail to remove the stumps from the orchard before winter, so the ground is fresh when the seedlings arrive in the spring." Lines of worry carved the fine structure of his face and sweat dripped from his brow although the house was cool.

Sally was shocked at his appearance. She put a hand to his cheek. "John, you are sick!"

He shook his head no. "I cannot sicken. A soldier cannot sicken. It is only the weight of command that exhausts me....Sally, they have found Bayer's body." He put a finger to her lips. "Say nothing and all will be well. Tarleton has blamed the Hessians and Hessians readily do this sort of thing."

She reached an arm around his shoulder. "I worry for the innocent soul who will pay for the crime that I have committed. And I worry for you, John. You don't sleep. You agonize over every detail. Other officers laugh and sing, drink away their troubles and sleep late into the morning."

"I will sleep late tomorrow my love! My mind is awash with conflict. They are so cheerful, so smug, these officers in command. But when I earn a command, it is snatched from me. When I would preserve decency and property, I must tear down. When I would sit by a quiet fire with my books and my love, I am assigned to battle. Worst of all, the woman I love must fend off the scum that my King in his infinite, misguided wisdom, has wished upon us." He patted her hand. "But do not fear. If Tarleton has his way, Bayer's death will go unpunished. Justice is too great an effort. But there is worse news..."

The look in his eyes warned her. "You are going away?"

He nodded, "This time, yes, but only for a few days, perhaps a week. General Pattison has assigned the Rangers to an action, as a reward." He suddenly burst out laughing, a breathless, hawking noise. "We will board the ships for Brunswick, Jersey, next week and raid the rebel storehouses near there. Sally, I confess to you, I do not want to go!"

"I will not betray you, John Simcoe, you know that."

"That's not what I fear, my Sally. I fear that there is no strategy or plan to support if the Rangers meet resistance, only a blind presumption of success."

"And you think there is danger? You think the rebels will resist?"

"Yes, I do. They have had the spring and the summer to regroup, to equip, to drill. The French are supplying them with viable weapons, muskets of uniform size and caliber, coats, shoes, stronger and longer bayonets. Monmouth was as much their victory as ours. Something has happened last winter or in the spring that has made them much fiercer opponents....The Rangers' incursion depends on surprise. If they discover us too soon, I cannot predict the consequences. My dear Sally, I should not have asked you to bear such dreadful uncertainty with me. A military life is a string puppet's dance to the beat of fife and drum. A faceless command controls what I do. Your father is right to consider. Know that I will retract my proposal if you change your mind."

"Don't think it, John Simcoe. I gave you my word. It is as sacred as yours... I cannot betray my own heart."

38

Short-sighted mortals! Catch the present joy!
'Tis all that heaven permits you to employ.

*R*obert Townsend came to bid his family good-bye before returning to New York ostensibly for business reasons, secretly to escape the growing British presence in Oyster Bay, to avoid John Graves Simcoe and to still the noise of scandal.

Samuel Townsend ushered his son to the upstairs chamber and sat behind his desk. Robert remained standing. The father had never approved his son's arrangement. Since the war, none of his children had formed an appropriate attachment. "You would do well to marry her, Robert, like John Simcoe, who wants to marry Sally."

"I've told you, father. That is not possible." His sharp eyes glared and his jaw set firmly. "I remind you, father, that you have not approved Sally's attachment for Simcoe either."

The old man turned his watery gaze on his own two clasped hands. "My son will not legitimize his love. My daughter will legitimize hers with a man who makes war his life's effort, and who, if I bestow an ample dower, will carry my Sally across an ocean!" His eye glazed as he looked back at his son. "Robert, am I a selfish man to want my beautiful Sally here? I want to see her red hair flying in the wind, like your mother's did when she was young, before she bore eight children and broke her hip." His voice was rising steadily in an eerie crescendo. "My Sally should live as she has always lived, freely, with the open sea and the shifting shore and good people who respect and love her!... I hear the dark accounts of the refugees in London. Americans are not welcome there." He met Robert's stolid stare with tears welling up. The old man pursed his wrinkled lips and blinked to hold the tears back. Great grey circles enveloped his eyes. "An old man worries, Robert, that the only inheritance he can give his daughter for her comfort and happiness, may end up in the hands of money-lenders in London, or squandered for uniforms for His Majesty's troops... for swords and guns or worse to feed these damnable Hessians." Samuel was nearly shouting in a hoarse, quaking voice, "He has outfitted his troops out of his own pocket, did you hear? It cost him dearly. He has dressed them in green to blend with the summer foliage, so they will be a less visible target." Suddenly he shook his head in despair. "And now he is going to the Jerseys with his Rangers on a raid after the green leaves have faded and gold is the color of the landscape. The sharpshooters are sure to find their marks."

Robert lifted an eyebrow. The irony was not lost on him. He stated blandly, "John Simcoe is a proud man. No doubt he will be successful."

The old man's head bobbed. "Yes, but I fear for him. I fear for her. I fear for you. I even fear for the lady you love, this Mary. I fear for all my children and I pray you are in God's hands."

"Yes, father." The interview had ended in meaningless agreement.

Before they left Oyster Bay, Robert and Mary walked to Youngs' to say good-bye. Robert was careful not to convey knowledge of John Simcoe's raid to Daniel Youngs.

Youngs was glad to see them. "The village has not treated you fairly, Rob. You will be happier in the city. If you go by coach, stop at Hempstead for the races. Austin is sure to be there, like old times."

"I hear Ban Tarleton is running a horse against DeLancey.

"You and Simcoe could run the bay!"

"Don't pair me with a Britisher, Daniel! I am sick of their pomp and reserve. The horse stays here, under the protection of the good Lieutenant Colonel. Mary and I will take old Horace."

"You'll kill the poor brute. Take my pacer. The foragers have left him. Take him as far as Hempstead, watch the races. There is a subscription race for ladies with a purse of 20 guineas!" He winked suggestively. "The whole British

Army will come out to see their backsides slap a saddle! You can catch the post for New York from there and leave my horse at Hagerman's. He'll keep the horse safely until I can pick him up next week."

Robert agreed. It would make a happy outing before the winter set in. The pacer's long stride sped them on their way south over the hill to Jericho, then across the empty plain to Hempstead. The grass was waist-high and yellow, the trees orange and red in the autumn sun. The air was warm. Rivulets of fresh water ran gently down toward the southern shore through a natural pasture where farmers had always grazed their stock. Today there was not an animal in sight. The foragers had appropriated all the animals to supply the vast army and they had not been replaced. The villagers had hidden away those few that were left.

Robert Townsend pulled Mary close to his side. The gig bumped and jangled over the ruts, the dry harness squeaked and they bounced together. They laughed and sang and arrived early at the racecourse, tired and happy.

Red coats were everywhere. Hempstead was the home of the 17th Light Dragoons, a fine, proud troop of horsemen, who loved the thrill of the race. They shouted and hooted and argued the odds. Money flowed like honey from a hive.

The first race was over when Austin Roe rode in an hour later. "Rob Townsend, what brings you here?"

"News of you, Austin, and a certainty that DeLancey's nag can be beaten." He laughed and Austin Roe almost thought he was drunk, "I shall bet 20 guineas, the price of the purse, on Tarleton's horse in the ladies subscription! Lieutenant Colonel Tarleton has a good eye for a horse!"

"And a good eye for a shapely wench! Who is his jockey?""

"One Molly Powell, a young maid from Bedford! Bet a guinea for me!" Roe tossed the piece into the air. Robert caught it on the fly and stalked off to find the tote.

Mary took Austin's arm as Robert disappeared into a crowd of soldiers. "I have good and timely news, Austin!" She smiled up at him.

"It's good news enough, Mary, to see you looking so well!"

"Serious news, Austin!" She winked teasingly. "For you to hand on to your friends in Connecticut. John Simcoe will lead a raid into New Jersey next week, to Brunswick."

Austin Roe whirled around in surprise. "Where did you hear that?"

"From Robert, from Samuel, from Sally... who heard it from Simcoe's own lips."

Austin smiled gleefully, "Say no more and I will see to it... And now, milady, shouldn't you bet on a rider of your own sex?"

"I do not risk money on spectacle, Austin." They laughed.

Tarleton's horse won and Robert returned with his pockets full. A jubilant Ban Tarleton accompanied him with his shapely jockey on his arm. They issued congratulations all around and broke open a bottle of madeira. Tarleton was already drunk and wove away on wobbly legs with the bottle and the girl.

They watched him go. Austin Roe noted a reserve in Robert. "What is it? You don't like Tarleton?"

Robert laughed. "No. Tarleton is sociable and predictable as the tick of a clock. It's Simcoe worries me. He's too honest a man and he wants to marry Sally. Simcoe is dangerous."

Austin winced. "You are against the marriage of course."

Robert stared icily at his friend. "I will do anything in my power to stop it." His words sliced like a razor through flesh and he sucked in his cheeks. It gave him a cruel, predatory look.

Austin Roe did not speak more. He put a hand on his friend's shoulder, squeezed, smacked his lips, "I am sorry, my friend! Perhaps the war will eliminate him." Then to Mary, "Fair lass, cheer the brooding man!" With a knowing wink, he leaped astride his own horse and waved his tricorn hat good-bye. Robert leaned back against the stiff seat of the cart and closed his eyes. The sun beat down. It was a warm day even now in November, probably the last warm day of the year. His eyelids drooped. He roused himself to transfer the baggage to the post and then drove with Mary to the Hagerman barn.

Mary teased him along the way. "Tell me how to cheer you, Rob. Money in your pocket should make you laugh, not frown."

"British money in my pocket jangles too loudly, Mary. I will rid myself of it at the first opportunity. Wouldn't you like a new frock, of fine silk? We could dress Stewart in kilts like his famous clansmen or buy a bone for his dog!"

She responded with teasing. "It would become you, Robert Townsend, to buy yourself something more colorful than Quaker grey!"

Robert protested. "Grey is a fine color!"

"For the aged and the dead. Grey is rain and smoke and gravestones. You should choose red, the color of the rose and the holly and the rooster's cock to offset the dark of your hair! Red is the color of Mars and passion!"

"And British coats." His voice was flat.

"Such is your role, Rob. You are young! You are handsome and virile! You keep me, a mistress! Your Quaker Meeting turned us out of their grey and white walls, or have you forgotten?"

Robert urged the horse on. They drove past the white-shingled Saint George's Church, over one hundred years old, one of the oldest houses of worship on Long Island. Mary's face turned serious, "The Anglicans would not cast us out and they dress in colors and fine silks. I should want to be married in an Anglican church."

She had never mentioned marriage before and Robert's heart skipped. He wanted to hug and kiss her all at once in front of the entire assemblage at the race course. But Youngs' pacer would not stand and he drove on.

Mary continued, "I would want to be married in a church, in silks and laces with sunlight shining through the stained-glass windows in a prism of colors. And I would want lilies and a carriage decked with flowers! Such dreams!" She laughed and shook her head.

But he was serious, "Was your first marriage in church?"

"It was in an orchard, in Tappan." She fell suddenly silent.

Robert pulled the wagon to a halt. "I will marry you in church, Mary Drake, today, tomorrow, next week...." His eyes spoke the emotion in his heart.

She patted his hand. "When I learn the fate of Thomas Drake." The haunting name fell like a curtain between them. The horse paced on to Hagerman's.

New York welcomed the young couple. Tory morals were more cosmopolitan and less stringent than those of Quaker, Oyster Bay. And Tory spirits ran high. A storm had devastated the French fleet off Newport and Count

D'Estaing, its Commander, had rounded up his ships and limped home to France. Rumor spread of a break between the French and the Continental Army. General Greene complained bitterly of French abandonment. Rivington's Gazette rang with British mockery of French cowardice.

Robert Townsend went dutifully to be measured by Hercules Mulligan at the sign of the Thimble and Shears. Mary chose for him a rich cherry velvet from France with a vest of pale yellow brocade. His new white shirt was ruffled and laced. Oliver DeLancey, the richest man in New York, had none better. She chose for herself a dress of rose satin with matching bonnet, and black velvet cape and for Stewart, a red plaid kilt.

The tailor's shop was crowded with prominent Tories. Mulligan catered only to the cream of society. Robert recognized Thomas Buchanan who had helped free Samuel but whose ship, the Glasgow, his brother Solomon had abandoned in Portsmouth. It was Buchanan who hailed Robert. "Your ship come in Robert? That's a handsome new outfit!" Robert was embarrassed. Mary answered for him. "He bet on Tarleton's horse!" His good luck brought a chorus of good wishes. Buchanan invited them both to dinner at Delmonico's, the finest tavern in New York, to celebrate the latest news from London. British victory was assured! The campaign was shifting south. Southern loyalists were flocking to defend the cause of righteousness and England, like crows to a cornfield!

Robert Townsend cut a fine figure in his new clothes, a figure that attracted envious glances when he appeared in the street. He felt eyes upon his back and recoiled. He felt himself too obvious, too flamboyant like the British dragoons in their gold braid and helmets. The ostentation irked his Quaker sensibilities. He covered his new clothes with a voluminous cape. He refused to wear a wig but continued to club his rich chestnut hair. Finally, he reserved his new clothes for Sundays and church service with Mary, and reverted to his comfortable Quaker grey.

But Mary loved her new finery and the attention it brought. She made the rounds of shops and coffeehouses with Robert and Stewart in tow like a princess with her retinue.

39

Each in his bowels, griping panic feels,
Each drops his haversack and trusts his heels.

John Simcoe sat astride his grey charger with Kelly standing stiffly in attendance at the horse's head beside him. Gangly Captain Thomas Sandford, second in command, stood his horse to his rear. The horse fidgeted with the pressure of Sandford's long legs that wrapped tighter than a girth around its belly. Now Simcoe and Sandford stood at attention while the Queen's Rangers and Buck's County Dragoons trooped by on their way to board the H.M.S. Panther. Lieutenants Ormond and Whitlock sat erect and assured. The horsemen advanced in ranks of twos, in perfect line. Their green coats were spotless, their boots polished to mirrors; their horses fat and clean. As each rank passed, they turned their heads in unison to face their commander and held their swords erect in salute. John Graves Simcoe sat immobile like a monarch accepting the homage that was his due. Here was the product of months of effort and he was very proud.

The whole Townsend family, the Weekes and the Barneys and the Underhills and the Youngs, had come out to watch the embarkation. Sally sat on the high seat in Simcoe's own phaeton, like a princess enthroned. But her heart was heavy. Consent to her marriage had not been forthcoming and her splendid lover was leaving on a dangerous mission. His green coat and those of his troops which should have blended softly with the green leaves of summer, would contrast starkly against the gold of autumn. The fattened horses were ready for winter, not fit for the exertion of battle. The men themselves were overconfident.

John Simcoe was the last to board. He rode a magnificent grey which stood out white amid the browns and bays. He swung the horse to face Sally and swept off his helmet to salute her. Their eyes met; her heart swelled. He replaced his helmet and thundered away up the gangplank. Sally watched as he dismounted, secured the horse and the ship unfurled her sails. A light southerly puffed, then blew; the sails filled; the ship edged away. John Graves Simcoe looked out over the stern. She waved. She saw him smile and nod, a discreet, elegant motion. The ship gathered speed slowly until it turned downwind and sped away under the guns of Fort Franklin. Then it was gone. Sally Townsend went home to wait.

Lieutenant Colonel Tarleton brought news of a safe landing in Jersey. General Pattison sent a courier and Tarleton had intercepted him because he wanted to convey the news to Sally himself. He sought her out, was polite and entertaining and inquired after Robert and the bay horse.

John Simcoe was not so fortunate. He disembarked at Somerset, New Jersey, drew up his corps: 300 strong dragoons, resplendent in their new green coats. He rode at their head, on the pale grey charger, over roads thick with mud, bordered by flooded, empty fields and swamps. When the land began to rise, a cold wind blew in his face. He led his corps along the course of a stream that wound through a fertile valley of tilled fields, past deserted farmhouses and pastures, to a wood. Here a stone fence defined the road which narrowed between gentle slopes of golden maples and reddening oaks. John Simcoe spied a clearing at the far end of the wood. The narrowing way worried him and he stopped to question, "Captain Sandford, have the guide come forward."

He came, a scruffy barefoot boy in a buckskin shirt. He waited for Simcoe to speak.

"We are north of our proper bearing by several miles."

The boy held his eyes cast down. He stuttered nervously. "Aye, sir. Ye cannot pass the other way. It was in the swamp, a sinkhole, sir." He lifted his eyes and stammered, "The road widens a bit, sir, after the wood."

John Simcoe met his gaze. He sat for a moment, signaled Sandford and thirty of his most trusted men to the head of the column. With his sword for his banner, motioning ahead, John Simcoe led the troop forward.

He never saw the men who shot the horse from under him. They wore grey skull caps. Their heads appeared like so many more rocks in the stone wall; their muskets were primed; their aim was true; they fired from a distance of only five yards. John Graves Simcoe heard the blast and smelled the powder. The flash blinded him as his horse's legs crumbled under him. He felt the animal roll as they both sank into the mud. He saw a hoof thrash like a war club close to his face. Then it was dark.

Captain Sandford's horse was hit too, but Sandford landed on his feet on solid ground and scampered back behind the charging animals of his comrades. A rain of grapeshot blasted from out of the trees - rebel artillery! Sandford called the retreat! The rebels surged over the wall like rats from a burning ship. The Rangers fell back. A second volley sounded, and a third and the Rangers withdrew in disorder. The body of their commander lay, presumed dead, in the road.

Rough men approached where John Simcoe lay, with bayonets at the ready, prodding the prone bodies for signs of life. John Simcoe felt the prick. His eyes came open stiffly in the mud. It blurred his vision and choked the air from his nostrils. He barely moved. He saw grimy toenails and callused feet, ankles caked with mud, grey threadbare pantaloons that hung midway down thick peasant calves! He felt the steel of the bayonet at his throat!

"This one's alive!" The words shimmered in the smoky air. Simcoe's head swam in a haze of pain. He rolled to one side.

Another voice grumbled, "Run 'im through to avenge Vorhees! Run 'im through afore he wakes!"

"No! He wears lace... He's a high-born, mighty officer for sure! We can sell 'im back for British gold!"

"I scorn the gold of men like 'im who starve their captives and force 'em to live like vermin in the holds of rotting ships!"

"Take 'im to Vorhees' grave to show 'im the cruelty of 'is race!"

"Run 'im through! He deserves no quarter!"

They hauled him up with brutal hands. There was blood on his brow where the hoof had struck. They pinned him against a tree and slapped him alert and questioned him and tied a rope around his neck and marched him off to Vorhees' grave and from there to the court of Elisha Budinot, Commander of Prisons in New Jersey, son of a Frenchman who kept an alehouse and hated all Englishmen. He sentenced John Simcoe to bread and water and secured him by the neck to a chain anchored in the floor. The cell was cold and damp, the cobbled floor where he lay to sleep, like a mat of sharp pebbles against his back. Days and nights passed. He passed out and awoke with unseeing eyes, he could not count how many times. In his delirium, he cried out for Sally.

Now a man stood over him, a callous hand lay on his brow and a voice whispered softly, "I am John Billop, Colonel, Staten Island militia and your fellow prisoner. I am a clergyman. I will pray with you."

"Will it do any good?"

"In this world or the next?"

John Simcoe beseeched God in heaven for justice and mercy and respect for the human kind. His eyes grew haggard and he lost weight. But John Simcoe was renowned, even among rebels, for fairness and right, and gradually news of Budinot's brutality seeped out. Letters of succor arrived from men of prominence. William Livingston, the rebellious governor of New Jersey, who had met Simcoe in New York, issued a special order of protection and sent a surgeon to attend his wounds.

The surgeon commanded release from his irons, clean food, clean bedding, and bandaged his wounds. He ate his first meat, a tough stringy mutton and it renewed a portion of his strength. But he brooded, like an angry hermit, in his prison cell. He had memorized the protocols for the treatment of prisoners-of-war. He knew his own treatment broke the accepted code. It was the thought of Sally that revived him and the simple prayers he invoked with the Reverend Billop. December came and the anticipation of Christmas and John Simcoe huddled in his cell in the damp and freezing swamps of New Jersey.

Sally Townsend awoke in the night to the steady patter of more rain. There had been no news. She arose with the cock's crow and went to the kitchen to eat. She was staring out at the jagged, raw stumps of the orchard when she heard horses trot up. Swords clanked and boots stomped. Her heart thumped louder than the oak door that resounded with the knocking. When she opened the door she recognized Sergeant Kelly who held the horses and gangling Captain Sandford. His long arms and bowlegs contrasted with the compact, muscular frame of Banastre Tarleton who stood in front, resplendent in his white uniform. Tarleton shifted his weight uneasily. Captain Sandford wore a bandage over his left cheek. They stepped through the open door in silence.

She glared cold-eyed at Tarleton. "Where is Lieutenant Colonel Simcoe?"

She already knew the answer. It was written in the solemnity of their gaze, but it seemed to hang in the air between them like an evil cloud. Tarleton bowed elegantly. Sandford's mouth dropped open, lengthening the droop of his eyes and the long oval gravity of his face.

Tarleton finally broke the silence. "Madame, Lieutenant Colonel Simcoe left instructions that you should be the first to be informed." He bowed his head. "Captain Sandford did all he could."

Sandford broke in, "He died a hero Madame, leading the advance guard in the face of withering fire." The bony chin quavered. "I was there. He rode in front, on his white horse. He fell gloriously, facing the enemy to the last. His horse went down. His body was pinned beneath. We could not reach him."

Tarleton broke in, "I offer you my condolences, Miss, and those of General Pattison. If I can be of service in any capacity, Miss, to ease your distress...."

Sally Townsend did not blink. Her eyes froze. She felt cold pincers wrap around her chest and squeeze the blood from her heart. Her eyes focussed on a dot of light that pierced the tiny glass window in the door. But she had ceased to see. Samuel Townsend came up beside her and put his arms around her. She buried her head in his frail shoulder and he stroked the rich red hair. The officers bowed and left. She roused and walked out through the kitchen to the raw, cold, dead stumps of the orchard. There she stood, a straight, lonely figure with the splinters of wood that were left from the graceful trees. Dry tears flowed from out of her soul into the deadness that enveloped her.

Audrey came to her in the freshening of the morning with a woolen shawl and Beulah came with a steaming mug of tea. They turned her gently and lead her to the kitchen where Sarah was waiting with something to eat. For the first time in many years, Sarah smiled on her daughter and offered words that she thought would bring solace. "There are other men my girl. You are young. Be cheerful that you chose so well! Let Colonel Tarleton or another distract you."

Sally blotted out the foolish words. To speak of another, to speak of little Tarleton as if he could compare with John Graves Simcoe, was sacrilege!

The days seeped by. Sally Townsend sickened with a strangling congestion that filled the cavities of her head and the passages of her lungs. Her red hair fell limp and damp from the sweat of fever. Her eyes were red and a hacking cough rattled her slim body. Then one day she awoke from a sleep refreshed, walked to the military hospital and resumed her old duties. When Audrey asked where she had found the strength, she answered, "John Simcoe always found the strength. He is alive. In my heart, I know."

Christmas passed like an irreverent cloud. On December 30th, it snowed. Sally sat stolidly by the fire with Audrey in the parlor, near the books that he had stacked carefully in the corner. Her fingers ran reverently over the pages, over the thoughts they recorded, thoughts that inspired his thoughts wherever he may be. She would study the stories of courage and prowess, and survive like him. She picked up a book and began to read. Audrey sat with her stitchery on the settle nearby. There were hoofbeats in the lane, then a knock at the door. It was a loud rapping like Tarleton's aggressive pound, not the kind that would bring welcome visitors. No one leaped up to answer it. The rapping increased and Audrey rose to answer. A familiar voice sounded. It had the lilt and ring of the Gaelic.

A gust of cold air made Sally shiver and blew the page from her grasp. She heard the tread of a man's boots. She heard Audrey gasp.

He came around the high back of the settle and stood before her in front of the fire. Still she did not look up. She pulled her shawl more tightly around her to stop the trembling of her limbs and smoothed back the printed page.

He said simply, "Sally," placed his hand under her chin and lifted her face to his. "Sally, don't you know me?"

John Graves Simcoe stood like a vision in front of her. She reached out to touch his hand to see if he was real. His grey eyes were haggard; his uniform hung in loose folds. He lifted her by the elbows, pulled her hard against him and buried his face in her hair. She hugged him back with every fiber of muscle and they cried together and he wiped the tears from her face, tears of unmitigated joy.

John Simcoe was now twice a hero. They prepared a feast to welcome him. The guns of Fort Hill blasted a salute and the tall ships anchored in the bay, answered with the deafening broadsides. Cob butchered a calf. Samuel Townsend summoned his neighbors. Lieutenant Colonel Tarleton and Major Cochran, Captain Sandford, Lieutenant Ormond, the Youngs, the Weekes, Captain Farley and the Captains of all the ships in the harbor, came to pay their respects. They served roast beef with Yorkshire pudding, squash and beans and Indian pumpkin sweetened with molasses. There was a punch made with aged Jamaica rum and pipes of madeira wines, chocolate and citron and fine coffee. General Pattison arrived in the Commander-in-Chief's own coach and General Henry Clinton himself sent best wishes. But Robert Townsend stayed away.

As winter progressed, it grew bitterly cold. The wood supply diminished and John Simcoe worried for the warmth and health of his men. The bay froze over and locked the ships in an icy vise. No new supplies would arrive by water. Foraging efforts doubled. Humans stayed indoors and took their animals with them to keep them warm and hide them from the British requisitions. A northwest wind from out of the Canadian Arctic rattled the walls of Raynham Hall, unprotected now by the break of apple trees. Hearth fires blazed. Sailors walked ashore over the ice to escape the howling wind that blasted exposed ships and turned sails and rigging into slippery strips of ice. They peopled the streets and taverns. Drunks froze to death beneath deadfalls and fences. And a gentle blanket of snow whitened over the corpses until the wolves performed their grizzly work.

But Sally Townsend did not see the suffering. She listened to the complaints of rebel cruelties from the lips of John Graves Simcoe. He was a changed man. A deep grief had come over him. For the first time, he despaired of ever reuniting the colonies with his beloved England. "They are British citizens. We have defended them from the French, from marauding Indians and where is their gratitude? They hate us Sally, from the soles of our boots, to the buttons of our coats, to the last grain of flour in our wigs....They make a mockery of the common laws of humanity. They beat our prisoners, deny them food and medicine... They are no true Englishmen, but a cruel, untutored mob, surly creatures from out of the wilds, like wolves and lions, fit only to bicker and fight!"

Sally listened attentively and consoled as best she could. "You have not lost the war, John. When the tide is lowest, is the time to redouble your efforts and man the oars so when the tide rises, it will carry you forward on its crest. You are a good and principled man. I love you in life. I loved you in death. Despair should have no place in your being!" But a fear had settled like a dormant seed in the pith of her heart. She feared the bitterness in him. She feared that their happiness on this earth would never come to pass. The fear heightened her passion and the exquisite pleasure of every moment in his presence.

They were always together. Sally Townsend accompanied John Simcoe when he walked out to inspect Fort Hill. She rode with him during the cold travels in his coach. She sat beside him in the evening when he poured over his books. After Sarah and Samuel went to bed and Audrey retired, she and Simcoe would talk long into the black of night.

There were brief moments of ecstasy. He took her once by sleigh to visit Joseph Cooper. He wrote a Valentine poem to her, three pages on sturdy parchment, penned in flowing black ink. He gave it to her the morning of February 14th as they drove out over the frozen ground to inspect the fortifications at Fort Franklin. It was the first time he had completely bared his soul. She read the verses aloud:

> *Victim of grief and deep despair;*
> *Say, must I all my joys forego,*
> *And still maintain this outward show?*

"Is your soul so bleak, John, that you must hide your sorrow? Is your love for me *an outward show?*"

"Not you, Sally. It is my position. I must flatter fools and suffer their advice... But read on. Read the ending."

She read almost in a whisper as if she were praying:

> *Shall no fair maid with equal fire*
> *Awake the flames of soft desire?*

"Fond youth" the God of Love replies,
"Your answer take from Sally's eyes."

Their eyes met and held. He moved toward her like a magnet to its pole and kissed her lightly and then more passionately and held her with a desperate violence in the silence of the coach. Finally, she lay her head on his breast and broke the sacred silence. "They are beautiful words, John. I shall treasure them forever."

"Know that I will love you always and forever, Sally. See here I have written..." He read the line. "*My heart was formed for constant love...* I am not a Howe or a Tarleton whose passion molts with every change of post and scene. You have there my pledge, my word of honor." He uttered her baptized name, "Miss Sarah Townsend." And he stared deep into her soul.

She bit her lip to hold back swelling tears.

Seconds lapsed before he kissed her again, first reverently and then with heat and fervor. They clung together with a passion inflamed by the months of denial and frustration.

When they came apart, she replied solemnly, "I will keep your words, John Graves Simcoe, here, next to my heart." She folded the parchment and slipped it beneath the bodice of her dress.

They awaited news from England that his family accepted her as suitable wife for their hero. Deep snow covered the ground. Ice choked the harbor. The weather held ships in port. The news did not arrive. Nor did Samuel Townsend accede to the intended match. He did not refuse outright; he simply ignored the possibility. Only Sarah laid her presumptuous plans.

When he was not with Sally, John Graves Simcoe smothered himself in work. He redoubled his efforts to perfect his Rangers. He visited his headquarters every day in Caleb Wright's tavern. There with Major Armstrong, Captains Shaw and Sandford, Lieutenants Ormond and Whitlock, he poured over maps, provisions, strategies. He drilled the Rangers himself, in horsemanship and musketry, in fair weather and blizzard. He proposed a winter campaign to General Clinton and was rebuffed. He conceived a plan to abduct General Washington by marching over the ice into Jersey. The high command did not think the plan practical. But his worst struggle was with his own passion, whenever he saw Sally. In his mind, he would undress and ravage her in wild flights of desire. Then he would castigate himself for his weakness. Finally, he requested an assignment in the south where London had now decreed the campaign was to be won, but his heart was heavy at the thought of leaving Sally. He did not immediately divulge his plans to her.

Sally Townsend watched him war with himself. Nightly, she knelt to pray at her bedside, not for herself but for him, for an end to this cruel conflict, for the reunion of colonies and motherland that would presage her own union with John Graves Simcoe and bring peace to her aching heart. Her prayers loomed like apparitions of some wonderful heavenly bower where she and John Simcoe could lay without guilt in fulfillment of all their earthly desires. She felt his eyes on her eyes, his mouth on her mouth, his hands on her breasts, his sweat mingling with her own. But when she awoke, he was not there.

40

They have not even Pantagruel's luck,
Who conquered two old women and a duck.

*R*obert and Mary squeezed into a rear pew for the midnight service at St. Ive's Anglican Chapel in Manhattan. Its tall gothic arches swept skyward. A pipe organ played. The bishop recited the sermon, a fervent eulogy of General Prevost, conqueror of Savannah in the Georgia Colony. Less avidly, he solicited help for the destitute refugees from Philadelphia. Trumpets blew as much to celebrate the victory at Savannah as to herald in the Christ child. General Clinton attended with Miss Blundell who was his mistress and daughter of his butler, the Lorings, Joshua and Elizabeth, DeLancey and Rivington, a bevy of officers in their finest raiment, and Provost Marshal William Cunningham. Coaches lined the street. Horses snorted in the blazing torchlight. The congregation had come to impress and to display.

There was a new group on the fringe of the crowd. They were dejected, shabby, former Philadelphians, merchants and craftsmen who had wagered their fortunes on British success, and lost. They had escaped with the clothes on their backs, a few pack animals, what they could carry and their lives. The wealthy among them were not here. They had boarded ships bound for England. These others had slogged through the Jersey mud behind Henry Clinton's retreating army while raiders sniped from the hedgerows. They looked upon the splendor and ritual of the Christmas service with haggard, sunken and envious eyes.

Robert Townsend felt their eyes on his back and writhed under the stare. He wished away his velvet coat, the lace and ruffles and manicured hands that held the gilt-edged pages of the hymnal. He preferred the white walls and grey shingles of a simple Quaker Meeting House. The tall spires of pipe organ resounded in his ears. Voices around him rose with the hymn. Mary was singing sweetly. He mouthed the words lest others think he was irreverent. What waste! What show! England had brought pain and poverty to these poor homeless for this! Robert clamped his mouth shut.

The sexton passed the collection plate. He placed his guinea on the velvet surface. His hand shook uncontrollably. He was sweating although the church was cold and damp. He mopped his brow with his handkerchief and wondered how many precious guineas would bring solace to a child whose home had burned, or meat to a man whose stomach ached with hunger and whose livelihood had vanished along with his property. And how many guineas would pay for the lace and beeswax, stained glass and carved kneelers that recreated this little piece of England?

Mary knelt beside him. Her hands were folded; her head was bowed. He clutched her hand and she smiled up at him. For what blessings did she pray? Did she ask the Lord to forgive their unlawful union? Did she beg freedom for Thomas Drake, or the repose of his immortal soul? Robert uttered his own prayer for physical safety, for release from fear and doubt, for a lifelong union with this strange little woman whom he loved so dearly. But he did not begrudge her the attachment to ritual and wealth. He pressed his arm to hers now to steady the pounding in his ribcage and he thanked God for sending him Mary.

In New York, refugees filled every available hovel and even like the babe on the first Christmas, some stables. They devoured food and fuel that would have been allotted to the army or to permanent citizens. Major General Robertson, Commander of the City of New York, instigated a lottery for the benefit of the refugees, but it was not enough and the refugees became scavengers who performed every kind of service for payment. Some were beggars on the streets. Some were thieves. New Yorkers treated them all like parasites and the British Army treated them like pus on a festering wound.

On the 26th, General Clinton departed with 3,000 troops for South Carolina. Rivington's Gazette reported how loyal Georgians had flocked to the British standard. South Carolina would be next to fall. An armada of ninety transports under Admiral Arbuthnot carried 8500 troops and sailors for a full scale assault on Charleston. New Yorkers crowded the piers to watch the embarkation as General Clinton tore himself from the clinging arms of his mistress and marched up the gangplank. He left General Wilhelm von Knyphausen, Commander-in-Chief of the German auxiliaries, a Hessian, in charge of New York. Robert Townsend watched the ceremony with foreboding.

By some miracle, January was mild. Still the poor suffered. They lingered at the entrance to the Townsend warehouse, arms outstretched, waiting for a meager handout. Robert sensed their jealous stares and hired guards. But Mary could not disguise her good fortune. She tossed coins and dispensed food freely to the unfortunates who swarmed like bees around her door.

Robert arrived home one evening in early January to find Mary serving tea to a ragged couple and two sickly children. "Rob, this is Francis and Abigail Hollet, Polly and Henry. I've invited them to stay in the upstairs room. They've had only a drafty tent 'til now."

Hat in hand, Francis Hollet bowed. "With your permission, Mr. Townsend." His voice rang clearly with only a hint of subservience. "We're honest loyalists. I was a shoemaker until General Clinton had to withdraw from Philadelphia. Yours and the kind lady's generosity will permit us shelter and warmth what with the winter setting in, and we will gladly work for our board."

It was so like Mary. Robert could not refuse, but he hesitated. How could Mary permit Tories to live under the same roof? It was inviting discovery! They would have to guard their every word and action. They would not be able to rest in their own home.

Mary filled the awkward void. "Francis will second Stewart in the warehouse and Abigail and the children will help with the household chores and cooking. It will free me to help you and Stewart."

A warning flashed in Robert's brain as he recalled how she had helped Stewart in the past. He stood by the door, still caped for the cold outside, without an acceptable alternative. He swallowed his fears and stammered, "Of course." His mind leaped ahead to practical arrangements. "We will take the upstairs room, Mary. There is more space for a family with children here below." It was a veiled rebuke, but Mary smiled. "And please Mrs. Hollet," he pointed to the children. "Scrub them first. We don't want vermin here."

Mary blanched at the criticism but Abigail Hollet curtsied politely. "By all means, sir."

It was settled. Like good Tories, the Townsends opened their doors to the refugees. Francis and Abigail Hollet boiled water and scrubbed until their skin itched and the children gleamed rosy pink. Robert herded them all to Mulligan the tailor for proper clothing. The food budget tripled and the house rang with children's laughter.

The winter continued mild. The harbor did not freeze. Two Townsend ships docked on the New Year: Farley's Katherine with limes, lemons and salt from Lisbon, 50 casks of Tobago rum and two hundred bottles of French brandy; and Captain Chadeyne's Weymouth, from Bermuda with 50 hogsheads of Virginia tobacco and casks of fine Liverpool beer.

The tobacco was welcome. Stewart filled his pipe and smacked his lips. First quality tobacco was rare in New York and had to be smuggled out of Virginia to Savannah, before a British ship could take it on. The fall of Savannah had been good for business. It had opened another port to Townsend ships. Seizure of Charleston would increase trade even more.

The warehouse was filled to the rafters and customers hammered daily on the doors. There was work enough for Stewart, Mary and the Hollets combined. Polly and Henry scampered up and down the aisles with Stewart's collie dog. The children cheered Robert Townsend and kindled in him a bedeviling desire for a child of his own and of Mary. Their love-making increased with wild abandon while Francis Hollet grumbled about the bumps and creaks that filtered down from the upstairs room and kept him awake at night.

Ship's captains, shipping agents, merchants, buyers and beggars, all flocked to Peck's Slip. Robert hurried from wharf to warehouse to keep pace with orders and check invoices and distribute the necessary bribes. He made presents of tobacco, to General Knyphausen, to Major John Andre, the new Adjutant General, and to his old friend, DeLancey. He delivered a case of French brandy to General Pattison, and to the captains of the Romulus and the Asia, two of the larger men-of-war. In return, he received convoy protection for Townsend ships, advance notice of proclamations, military postings, promotions and disbursements which he passed on to Brewster. Rivington as always, brimmed with information although his drinking increased with each passing day.

On January 22nd, when Robert arrived to deliver his copy, Rivington had gulped half a bottle of rum. Robert turned away in disgust from the stench of him but Rivington waved him forward with a breathless curse. The liquor had not affected his brain. "Headquarters has handed me a bit of tripe from the bowels of London, Rob. No room for your piece this week! Here, have a look."

Robert took the crumpled sheet and read, *"The Examination of Joseph Galloway?"* His voice rose, questioning. His blue eyes widened. *"The* Joseph Galloway of Philadelphia?"

"Precisely, the Lord High Commissioners are investigating Sir William Lord Howe and his foppish, laggard performance in the Colonies. Galloway will bear the blame. They will never accuse one of their own peers. It would smack of admitting their error." Rivington lay back his head, raised the bottle to his lips and gulped. "Enough frill and puff to fill my quarto for the next month! It's the stuff that snoring sleep is made of! I must feed my readers Britannic legalities when what they crave is smoke and battle! We need a writer like Tom Paine to champion our cause! Look here! They've spouted on for pages when a paragraph would do! I shall have to buy paper and add pages and swallow the cost of the paper myself." He shook his head sheepishly. "I am shy funds at present." Jack Rivington was always shy funds.

Robert took the hint. "How much do you need? I can have paper in trade from the Conklin Mill at Cold Spring." He set a bottle of brandy on the desk.

Rivington slapped down his bottle of rum as his eyes lighted upon the brandy. His lips spread in a wide grin. "Brandy, the warm, heart's blood of France! Enough paper for eight editions. I'll give you my note." Rivington wrote notes like clouds pour rain.

"No note. You already owe me for ten weeks' columns."

Rivington's rubbed his red eyes. "No, you say! Can't be that long? He rummaged through a pile of bills and jumped from his chair. "Wait here!"

He re-entered with a small velvet-covered box. "This will repay you and more!" He pushed the box into Robert's hands. "It's for Mary."

Robert lifted the lid. A strand of milk-white pearls glowed against rich burgundy satin. He was about to protest when Rivington interrupted. "You must accept it. It will square my debt. I won it at a cock fight. If I keep it, I'll lose it. I know myself too well. I've a foolish weakness for wagers and for the bottle both. I'll be happy knowing I have two friends who will not dun me for my debts or shun me for my drinking!" He clapped his hand on Robert's shoulder. "Come! We'll toast our friendship and Mary's fair neck that will glow like a queen's."

Rivington closed Robert's hands over the box and poured out more rum. His eyes blinked. His speech slurred. Robert backed away from the puff of his stinking breath and wondered if his friend understood what he was giving away. But Jack Rivington seemed perfectly lucid. Now his eye fell on the newly inked type. "This will interest you.... Your friend Simcoe has taken out an advertisement." He laughed until his shoulders shook. "He's offering forty guineas and a horse to any man who will enlist and two guineas to anyone who brings a recruit. He'll go bankrupt in a wink." He held up the copy for Robert.

"I heard he was in a rebel jail."

"No more. He was exchanged."

Robert read Simcoe's words. *All aspiring heroes...have now the opportunity of distinguishing themselves by joining the Queen's Rangers, Hussars...* Poor Simcoe, ever faithful to his king. Robert smiled wryly. "Loyal to the last farthing. How many do you think will join?"

"For forty guineas he'll fill his ranks. The dregs of the city will join and Simcoe will die in a debtor's prison!"

"If he does not die in battle first! He wants to marry my sister!"

"Sally? He'll not make her rich. I doubt he'll make her happy but you worry too much, Rob. Business is good. You have a beautiful mistress and precious pearls with which to woo her. Be merry! Sally is a resourceful woman." Robert smiled and remained silent. He lacked Rivington's carefree confidence.

Business was good. Another Townsend ship came in, the Promise. Stewart had to stack the new bales under tarpaulins in the alley because so many customers crammed the aisles, more than Robert and Mary and Stewart and the

Hollets could possibly serve. Some came for necessities. Some came to stare and chat and treat themselves to a small luxury, but others seemed too intently curious about shipments and prices, dates of arrival and payment of duties. Some were the legitimate appointees of the Admiralty. Still others were the eyes and ears of William Cunningham and Joshua Loring. Visits from Roe and Brewster halted. It was too dangerous. Contacts moved to Mulligan's, the Tailor's shop, under the sign of the Thimble and Shears.

In April, Robert called Mary and Stewart and the Hollets together. He had come to a decision. "I am closing the warehouse to customers from now on and moving our business to Smith Street. You both know the Oakum Store? I propose to take Henry Oakum as partner. 18 Smith Street is a large building and will accommodate the contents of Oakum's store and the overflow from our warehouse, and provide a more accessible market for our customers." He stopped to survey his listeners. The Hollets attended gravely. Mary smiled placidly. Stewart shook his head violently. "You object, Stewart?"

Stewart could not voice his objection in front of the Hollets. He mumbled, "Smith Street is very near military headquarters, sir."

"And it is nearer Broadway and only three blocks from Murray's Wharf where our ships unload." He continued, "Francis and Abigail will work with Oakum. Henry is old enough to help. As for little Polly...."

Abigail Hollet spoke up, "I would want her with me sir. She's small but she knows her place."

"Then she shall accompany you."

"You, Stewart, will stay here with me."

The move was made. A season of sunshine, warm rains, blossoms and greening followed. One early morning in May, Robert was surprised by a rumbling in the alley and a pounding on the warehouse door.

Stewart answered and summoned Robert. He was surprised to see Austin Roe standing in front of him, holding a scraggly bay horse. Robert ran out to clap his old friend on the back.

The little man smiled broadly. "Don't you recognize him, Rob?"

It was his own bay and Robert stroked the shaggy hair affectionately. The red shedding hairs came off on his hand. "He belongs to John Simcoe now whom thieves will respect more than me. He's lost weight."

Austin laughed. "Two holes on the girth. Feed is scarce and we had to change his appearance some when we borrowed him. There is none faster. Bring a bucket. He needs a drink."

The alley stank with the slops of the night before which had not yet been washed out into the river. They walked to the well. Roe raised the bucket and held it on his knee while the animal drank. Austin spoke, "Brewster will attack at Coram. He has been idle all winter and is itching for action before his Fairfield lovely can haul him to the altar."

Robert laughed. "Brewster! Married!"

"It won't happen. He would rather Sally!"

"Brewster is a better choice than a Britisher!

Robert looked away and Roe offered by way of consolation. "The swan does not mate with the duck, Rob.... We want to substitute your new shop as our point of delivery."

"But it is under their wriggling noses!"

"Exactly. The place is above suspicion. Our correspondence will be more secure. And you can write your dispatches freely with this." He pulled a package from his pocket. "It's invisible ink, the brainchild of a Mr. Jay from Boston!"

Robert opened the bottle and sniffed. "It reeks like Brewster in his whaler's coat or Jack Rivington in his cups!"

Austin Roe explained the new procedures. He would arrive weekly at the new shop in Smith Street with a written order for goods. On the reverse side, he would inscribe precise questions from the Continental command in the new ink. Robert would collect the responses and return them to Roe using the same ink to write the answers on the invoice that accompanied the goods. Roe would carry the goods back to Setauket, convey the information to Brewster who would carry it across the Sound to Benjamin Tallmadge in Connecticut. "Simple, ingenious, safe!" Roe continued with a warning. "I forgot to say that a coating of lemon juice will reveal the script. Tell no one, not even Mary! And you should know that the officer corps has deserted the Swan for Merchants' Coffee House. Drake is suspect."

Robert's eyes narrowed but his smile widened. "Does Oakum know?"

"Of course not. He's a true loyalist and good cover for you, as are the Hollets."

Silence. The two men eyed each other. Robert's brain clicked off advantages and drawbacks. Finally he nodded, "It's a fair plan."

"Thank you. I thought so!" The little man grinned impishly. Austin Roe departed shortly after but his enthusiasm lingered and Robert reentered the house with a new lightness in his step.

Mary sat in a tall chair in the parlor. A ray of sunshine brushed across the black curls that framed her face. She had drawn up a stool on which to rest her feet and she had fallen asleep. He did not disturb her but she sensed the intensity of his stare. Her eyelids fluttered.

Robert spoke to himself. "Mary, you sleep like the beauty in mid-morning!"

Her eyes flicked open impishly as she yawned and caught him by the hand. She arched her neck and squared her shoulders and held his hand to her waist. "Robert look now, I am trim and active. Soon I will be fat and lazy. Already my energy wanes. I am with child!" She stopped, hesitated to judge his response, then burst out laughing.

Her joy was infectious. He smiled, then laughed then shrieked for joy and buried his face in her black downy curls.

They rocked together in pure glee, kissed, came apart and together again until he moved away suddenly. "Mary, there is something that I've hesitated to give you, but you must have it this moment!" He ran upstairs and brought out the velvet box. "I would have given it to you sooner."

Her tiny hands gripped the box with reverence. "Rob, the feel of it is like silk." She raised the lid and stood for a moment in shock, then lifted out the pearls. She held them up to the sunlight and watched them shimmer like twinkling stars.

His heart swelled. "I've been saving them for you. I got them from Rivington in payment of a debt. Wear them and think of me!" He took them from her and clasped them reverently around her neck. "Mary, I am not good with words like Andre or Rivington." A choking sound echoed from his throat and he coughed, then his voice cleared. "Wear them forever, my Mary, as a sign of my love. Know that I will never forsake you. I pledge you my life. If that is what it means to be wed, then I take you, Mary Drake, as my wife. Love me in return as I love you."

He pulled her to him but she backed away and placed a hand on his cheek. She traced the line of his hair, his brow, his nose, the curve of his lip and angle of his chin. He closed his eyes and shuddered at her touch. Her words came in a soft whisper. "You are too good, my love. What can I give to you, that would be the equal?"

"Your love." He added wistfully, "There is no other who will love me." His even voice cracked. "My family does not love me...."

Mary placed her hands against his cheeks, "Always and forever, Robert Townsend. I will love you."

They did not speak more. Together they climbed the stairs to the bed with the feather mattress under the eaves. They fell together across the pillows into the ecstasy of their dreams.

An hour later, Stewart and his barking dog clambered at the front door but they had sealed their ears and barred the door. The bright morning sun streamed through the window. It was late May and the scent of the first roses lingered in the air.

41

Plunder's the Word, but plunder soon is o'er,
Rob folks of all, and you can rob no more.

*M*ay rolled into a brilliant June. News arrived of the siege of Charleston and the surrender of General Lincoln and his entire army. The Tories predicted a grand march north via Richmond and Philadelphia to New York!

Abigail Hollet voiced the Tory's praises. "Such a worthy General is Lord Cornwallis! He will sweep rebels before him as I sweep the mites of dust from off the floor. You've not long to wait, Mr. Townsend, and Francis and I and Henry and Polly will go back to our home!" Robert Townsend grit his teeth and sealed his ears.

More dire news arrived via Austin Roe. He knocked at the alley door and stood as before holding the bay horse. "I came myself, Rob, to apprise you.... Joseph Lloyd is dead."

Robert looked up quizzically and shrugged. "He's my father's friend, not mine." Joseph Lloyd of the Manor of Queens Village, was fellow merchant and friend to Samuel Townsend and a prominent citizen of Long Island, before the war. He was the father of John and Theo Lloyd with whom Robert and Sally had grown up, and he was the uncle of Elizabeth Lloyd Loring, the infamous wife of Commissary General Joshua Loring. "What has this to do with me? I thought he'd fled to Connecticut."

"Come walk and we'll talk." Austin lowered his eyes and turned to lead the horse toward the well. Robert descended the stairs walked with the horse between them stroking its neck. Austin continued, "There is worse.... He is dead by his own hand, Rob."

A revulsion seized Robert Townsend and he dropped his hand and jerked the rein. The horse threw up its head. "He killed himself? Why?"

Austin shrugged. "The fall of Charleston. He'd lost all hope, the hope we all struggle daily to maintain." The horse lowered his head and nuzzled his former master.

Robert stroked the soft muzzle and continued after a pause, "I could have read the obituary in the Gazette. You didn't have to come."

"I thought you should have the news from my own lips. Before he died, Joseph Lloyd named John Lloyd Jr. and you, Rob, as his executors." Austin met Robert's look of wide-eyed disbelief.

"I don't understand. Why me?"

"The son, John Jr., lives in exile and cannot set foot on the island... What is left of Joseph's lands is there at the Manor of Queen's Village. His uncle Henry, the only family member of consequence who stayed behind, is an old man and an avowed Tory. Joseph Lloyd must have felt that someone of less Tory persuasion, someone who could come and go without suspicion, who has shown talent in dealing with the British authorities, could best preserve what property he had left. He asked Tallmadge for a reference. Benjamin Tallmadge recommended you...."

"Why not my father?"

"Too old and Samuel is failing, Rob. You know it. You see it. You admit it." Robert was silent. He felt a piece of his life receding. They reached the well and lifted the bucket. Austin continued, "Joseph Lloyd felt you were like your father was, a man of your word, and you are young and strong."

Robert grimaced. The sucking of the horse as it drank punctuated the stillness. He did not like to imagine his father as an old man. It was like a finger of ice running down the length of his spine. The passage of time, the fleeting of his own youth, the passing away of the world as he once knew it, saddened him. He straightened and answered gravely, "I am overwhelmed and honored. The Lloyd lands are one of the largest family holdings on Long Island. The British have plundered the property, cut the timber and requisitioned the livestock. I do not know if the buildings still stand."

Austin prodded, "Do you accept?"

"How can I refuse? But I shall have to account to John Jr. for what property is left." He felt his voice wavering, gasping like a drowning man.

"That is all John Jr. asks, my friend?"

A silence ensued. Robert rubbed his eyes, refocussed and blurted, "Mary is with child."

The horse lifted its muzzle dripping water. Austin jumped back laughing. "Smile man! Shout for joy!"

But Robert was distraught. "How can I act the proud father when all you bring me is news of death. I fear for my child. I fear for Mary. I cannot put the dire possibilities out of my mind so easily as you. They are winning, Austin." He struck the stone wall of the well with a fist and repeated, "The bloody British are winning the war!" He shook his aching hand.

"They are stuffed cocks for all their crowing. The red is on their coats and not in their blood. Flatter them! Decoy them! Make them empty King George's coffers! The time alone will wear them to stubs." He lowered his eyes. Robert was not listening. Austin Roe gripped his friend's shoulder affectionately and shoved the week's dispatches into his hands. "It's good news, a baby! Let it inflame your spirit and bring you joy!"

Robert smiled wanly and nodded as if to reassure himself. "It does that. I gave you my word. Tell John Lloyd that I accept and thank you for bringing the news in person." He waved his friend away.

Austin mounted the horse. "He is a fine mount, Rob!" He added as an afterthought. "Rob, laugh a little!"

"Feed him more and run him less and bring me news to make me laugh!"

Austin shouted back, "Tomorrow, man, tomorrow!" and spurred the horse down the alley, the way he had come.

Robert Townsend scuffled back to the kitchen and slumped into a chair. It was a long while before he brushed lemon juice across the page and roused himself to read the message. Figures appeared unevenly. A ray of sunshine illuminated the faint grey letters. Robert squinted and could not read them. He closed his eyes. He felt his chest contract and his eyes water with an unmanly urge to weep. Joseph Lloyd's was an inglorious death. Lloyd had not died facing down the enemy or outwitting lazy Hessians. He had died by his own cowardly act. And he, Robert Townsend, was appointed to sort out what remained of the man's earthly possessions. There was little he could do to preserve the property of a known rebel without throwing suspicion on himself; little he could do even to communicate safely with John Jr.! Didn't Tallmadge know that? And how could Roe treat death so blithely? Robert thought of him as some freebooting cavalier parading around the countryside like the Robin Hood of legend. But he loved the little man and the little man still called him *friend*.

He roused himself with effort. Where was Mary? Mary would share the frightful news and cheer him. Mary would devise a way to appraise the ravaged estate without arousing suspicion. Mary would know how to restore his flagging resolve. Pregnancy had not slowed her as expected. She was more active, went out more frequently now that the Hollets lived with them. After the first month of discomfort, it was as if her energy had doubled, as if her pregnancy had insulated her from care and fatigue.

He applied more lemon juice and the figures of Austin's dispatch brightened into sharpness. Now he read them easily. It was an urgent request for news of the disposition of British troops. Did General Knyphausen plan a sortie into Jersey? When? Where? Any news of General Clinton's return to New York and did Clinton contemplate an attack up the Hudson toward West Point? Robert crumpled the paper, threw it into the fire and watched it crimp and blacken. His brows knit together over his long, straight nose.

He made his usual rounds to gather the requested news, to Rivington's offices, to the Oakum and Townsend store, to Merchants' Coffee House and Grace's Tavern. Knyphausen was already in Jersey, his troops drawn up before Springfield. Nothing Robert could report there. It was too late. He slogged to the warehouse and home again to Mary and Peck's Slip. Mary still had not returned home and it was late afternoon. The Hollets arrived with the children and the evening's exuberance erupted. The children ran, shouted, chased the dog that barked. Robert did not correct them. Exhaustion consumed him like a wave.

Mary bounced in smiling, just before curfew. His relief was obvious. She had seen a cabinet maker and ordered a cradle. He hugged her fiercely.

Days slipped by. Austin Roe came and went. Robert tended the ships' unloading and provisioning; he walked his rounds; he busied himself in the store. He was at home one warm afternoon in June, when Mary came running from the warehouse, red-faced and out of breath. "Rob, Stewart needs you immediately! Clinton's troops are on the move!"

For once, it was Robert who laughed. "And I am on the move, with you, to bed, before the children come home or you fall on your backside and harm the babe! He lifted her easily off her feet, but she kicked and shoved him away.

"Stewart will not wait, Rob! Be serious. You must come." She tugged him after her.

Stewart stood brooding in the doorway with the collared dog. His eyes were hooded, his voice, grave. "Two British Regiments of Colonel Fanning's Corps are at Whitestone, sir, at the Lewis mansion. My man says they have their eye on the Connecticut shore!"

Robert frowned. "How soon will Fanning attack?"

"One day. Two days...." Stewart shrugged.

"Roe has just been here. It's six more days until he comes again. We cannot deliver the news fast enough!"

Stewart shook his shaggy head. "The Britishers move like snails, sir. They do not sail except on a fair wind. We can wait for Roe."

But Fanning had already started and British troops plundered New Haven, Norwalk and Fairfield before Robert, Stewart or Austin Roe could relay warning. At Peck's Slip, they awaited Fanning's next move and watched as General Clinton returned the victor from Charleston. Robert Townsend's spirits sagged. He turned inward as his apprehension grew.

The main body of Clinton's army remained in New York, awaiting reinforcements which were overdue. Clinton had requested them long ago from London. He needed them to support garrisons on the Hudson and to attack West Point. Lord George Germain, His Majesty's Secretary of State for the Colonies, stalled. The reinforcements did not arrive.

July brought dense humidity and severe heat to New York. Steam rose from the harbor like wet smoke as the temperature climbed. The mere act of walking caused moisture to seep from a man's back and drip from his brow as if wrung from a sponge. Men and animals collapsed for lack of water. The air smelled heavy with decay and excrement, and the brutal sun glared down. Robert worried for Mary's health as she fattened and breathed in the fetid air. He longed for the fresh air of the country. He wrote Youngs who offered a small cottage near the shore on the Neck. This time, Mary was eager to go.

The journey was languid, by ship downwind on a light westerly to Oyster Bay. For a month, they lived an idyll by the edge of the bay that Robert loved. He drove to Cold Spring to inspect the Paper Mill on behalf of Jack Rivington and continued on to Lloyd's Neck and the lands of Joseph Lloyd. His heart sank. The devastation there was complete. Trees were leveled. Fields were burned. The Lloyd manor house still stood but it was in use as a stable and the feces of animals lay rotting on the floor. Fort Franklin commanded the cliff with its stiff stockade and looming canons.

Robert returned to Mary sickened by the sight and composed a letter of condolence to John Lloyd Jr. He delivered it to Roe for transfer to Connecticut via Caleb Brewster. The story of the devastation, he did not convert to writing, but related to Roe verbally. It was horrible news and lingered like an ugly scab on his mind. It was what he and Roe and Brewster must expect, if they lost the war.

Again Mary cheered him. She would place his hands upon her belly so he could feel the power of the new life within and laugh and banter on about the future. They spent the summer evenings sitting outside in the shade of the softwood sumac scrub that had escaped the foragers' axe and watching fireflies light the summer night. The faint pricks of light in the advancing darkness reminded Robert of the faintly flashing hopes of the Continental Army.

Samuel came to visit - he used a cane continually now - and Sally came several times on the way to Joseph Cooper's. Robert was shocked at the sight of her. Huge circles enveloped her eyes and she had pulled back her luxurious hair into a tight bun. Her cheekbones protruded and her lips pinched, but her eyes were still the deep cerulean blue that he remembered and she was still beautiful in a mature, ascetic way. He sensed a reservation that was not there before and questioned Audrey about it.

"She talks very little to me, Rob. She thinks me naive. But I know she sleeps fitfully and sometimes I hear her weeping in the night. You knew that Simcoe and his Rangers are in Carolina with Cornwallis? She sends him letters. Paul Dockery, Captain of the Jackal, delivers them and she carries John Simcoe's replies in a silk purse next to her heart."

Robert did not know. It was not good.

Audrey's thin face crinkled. "It was better for us when John Simcoe was here. He was a just and merciful man. Now we've ugly Hessians to contend with." She searched for something encouraging to say. "He left you your horse. We gave him to Austin." The bay horse mattered little now when life itself hung by so thin a thread. Robert frowned and Audrey continued aimlessly. "We've sent father's mare to Joseph Cooper who hides her from thieves." She placed a hand over her brother's and Robert felt a sympathy and a quiet strength in her angular bones where he had not encountered it before.

September brought news of another rebel defeat at Camden, a complete rout. Cornwallis' army had advanced on the Continental regulars who withstood the charge until the poorly led militia broke and ran like rats from a burning ship. The Americans threw down loaded muskets and fled in panic, leaving their dead and wounded on the ground. Brave Baron de Kalb died that day, trying to rally his troops, smeared with the blood of eleven wounds. Horatio Gates, the General in command, galloped precipitously to the rear, 180 miles in three short days. His troops scattered in all directions. Lord Charles Cornwallis was hero and conqueror. General Gates was condemned as a coward.

Gates' retreat could not escape the biting tongue of Jack Rivington. In the Gazette, he castigated the chubby general. His sarcasm stung.

Strayed, deserted, or stolen...on the 16th of August last, near Camden, in the state of South Carolina, a whole ARMY...A certain Charles, Earl Cornwallis, was principally concerned in carrying off the said ARMY....Nothing but the most speedy flight can ever save their Commander, Horatio Gates...

Robert read the report with a quaking heart to Daniel Youngs. He bit back his tongue to hide the quavering of his jaw.

Youngs spoke reassuringly, "If it's true, Rob, we must redouble our efforts if ever the rebellion is to succeed. You know who led the slaughter, don't you?" His piercing eyes flared in anger.

Robert shook his head.

"It was your gambling friend, Colonel Banastre Tarleton. He can ride, that one, like a demon god from hell. He makes no division between innocent and guilty and slaughters all alike. The lightly wounded, children, camp followers, he puts all to the sword! *Tarleton's quarter*, they call it." When Robert only stared immovably, he continued, "I dread to think what would have been the result if my Billy had killed a Britisher and not a Hessian! It was your sister, Sally, took the blame. Did you know? And Colonel Simcoe who shielded her from the Hessian's and Tarleton's wrath."

Robert did not know. He folded the Gazette and placed it securely under his arm. His deep voice shook as he met Youngs' earnest stare. "There is so much I do not know.... John Simcoe fights for the wrong cause." He stopped, swallowed his next words like a nut on the back of his tongue and choked. When his throat cleared, he remained silent and Youngs did not speak further. Finally, Robert Townsend bowed his head and ended the depressing conversation, "It is time Mary and I return to New York."

That afternoon, he paid a farewell visit to his family. He entered through the kitchen and sent Beulah to gather Samuel, Sally and Audrey. Sarah did not come.

Samuel hobbled in, stooped, wrinkled and old. Robert watched him lower himself painfully into the armchair. Sally and Audrey entered silently and Beulah called in Cob from the stable.

The deaf slave spoke first. A pink scar bridged his eye on the right side of his face where the whip had missed its mark. It pinched eye and nose together on that side of his face and gave him a crooked, ghoulish stare. Hatred flared up in Robert at the thought of the men who had inflicted such punishment on an innocent man. But the slave held no bitterness, "Your horse is well, Mr. Rob... with Mr. Roe, but Hessians have taken the three-year old that's hardly broke." That was a hardship for Cob who had raised the colt. Robert placed a hand in sympathy on the black man's shoulder but the memory of pain was still there and Cob winced at his touch.

Beulah passed mugs of cider. It had already fermented slightly and bore the bitter taste of vinegar.

Samuel congratulated Robert on the success of his business ventures and finally straightened rigidly and broached the inevitable reason for the interview. "Youngs tells me that you have begotten a child."

"Yes, father. He will be your grandson."

"You are not married. He will not bear the Townsend name."

Robert's blue eyes flashed. He confronted his father. "I am married, father, in my heart. If it is a boy, I will give him my name. I will name him Robert Townsend."

The old man leaned back. His eyes narrowed, dimmed and retreated into their sockets. New wrinkles etched downward in the crevices of his transparent cheeks. "You do not make the passage of years any easier." He rose then and gripped Robert's shoulder. "Do not tell me more. I do not want to deny you my love, my son. To you and yours is the future, and the fruits of this bitter rebellion. I pray for you, that God will make you happy. I am too old to understand you." He walked out.

Audrey turned to her brother. "You must forgive his age, Rob! Come back with Mary after the babe is born. Father's heart will soften."

Beulah took up a pitcher and refilled their mugs. The brown cider foamed up like the scum on the surface of a pond. Robert drank and licked the bitter sediment from his lips. He moved to the chair nearest Sally. "Do you want him to come back, Sal?" He could not bring himself to mention John Simcoe by name.

She hid her face against his shoulder and wept. When she finally spoke, he realized that she was not weeping for John Graves Simcoe but for herself. Her shoulders shook and her voice echoed the months of loneliness. "They stare at me, Rob, the eyes of the entire village! I feel their fingers pointing. They hate me, Rob. I never realized how viciously our neighbors could hate! They hate me for having loved! Say you warned me! Say you told me I would come to grief!" She covered her face with her hands. "But I do love him so, Rob." The tears seeped through her fingers. "I pray every night he will come back. I pray for patience to withstand their taunts. I pray for the strength and courage not to hate them back."

Robert Townsend stroked the tresses of her hair. "They don't hate you or him, Sal. They hate the devils who steal their cattle and requisition their crops, who take a colt from the stable before he is broken to ride or a cow from a family with children who need milk, who tell them how to bake a loaf of bread and how much they may sell it for. They hate the war that has impoverished them. They hate the curfew and the taxes and the insane allegiance to an uncaring and distant king." He held his sister out at arm's length. "I don't hate you, Sal."

She looked up suddenly dry-eyed, "You are a rebel, aren't you Rob?"

"You have said it, not I."

Beulah interrupted gently, "Mr. Robert is a brave man. And you are a fine lady, Miss Sally. Folks stare, Miss, because they are ignorant. They stare at me for my black face but they don't know the color of my heart. It doesn't mean they hate me! Look at my Cob, snatched from his homeland, chained, cuffed about the ears so he doesn't hear and now scarred in his face and on his back! Only God can judge the unravelling of our lives. Drink your cider, Miss Sally."

Sally lifted her head. Beulah had suffered more than she. "You are a comfort, Beulah. Thank you. You do not hate me either." She pushed back her chair, rose and walked out the door that led to the orchard.

Robert pushed his chair back to follow her.

"Not now, Rob." It was Audrey who spoke. "Only time will heal. Only God can sculpt the shape of a life."

"I'll send some Spanish sherry from the ship's stores. There may even be a bolt of silk and some French scent... to make your lives more cheerful." He stood up and declared, "I must go or Mary and I will miss the tide. The Katherine just weighed anchor. Farley will convey us to the city." He kissed Audrey's bony cheek.

It was September, 1780. An autumn southerly blew the Katherine swiftly on a wide reach out of the harbor and into the Sound. The crisp new wind banished the stench of summer. The sea was blue, the clouds white as combed cotton. The sun burned down brightly on the burgeoning city. From a distance, New York looked bright and beautiful.

From up close, New York looked squalid. Robert held Mary's arm tightly as they walked down the gangplank and climbed up the dusty, cobbled street the few yards to Peck's Slip. Mary trotted lightly on her feet. It was good to be home and Robert teased Mary happily, "You are pregnant and round as a billiard ball, my love. I shall hold you tightly lest you fall and roll back into the sea like a ball into its pocket!"

Word of their arrival preceded them. Jack Rivington held open the door to the house with a bouquet of goldenrod and a bottle of French brandy in his hand. Rivington noticed the pearls at Mary's neck. "I told you, Rob. She's prettier than Queen Charlotte! May she be as prolific!" He winked.

Stewart and the Hollets stood behind Rivington. Abigail Hollet had prepared sweetmeats and Stewart raided the warehouse for wine. Even the dog wagged its tail and did not bark.

42

Little children they may die,
Turn to their native dust,
Their souls shall leap beyond the skies,
And live among the just.
....Jupiter Hammon, slave

*S*eptember was dry and dusty. General Sir Henry Clinton sent ships up the Hudson for a planned attack on the rebel fortress at West Point. Then suddenly he withdrew them. Robert visited Grace's, the Dove Tavern and Merchant's Coffeehouse, Rivington's office, the Smith Street store, the tannery, the armory, even military headquarters itself and could discover no reason for Clinton's withdrawal. He was on his way back to Rivington's for one last inquiry before writing his missive for Austin Roe, scrambling nimbly over the cobbles of Queen Street in the rain, when an iron hand grabbed him from behind. The voice had a familiar ring. "Don't turn, Robert! You know it's me. Continue south over the bridge to the coffeehouse. I'll meet you at Murray's Wharf in an hour." Robert froze. The deep bass was Caleb Brewster's. His head spun as his thoughts juggled all the dreadful possibilities in the confines of his brain. He stood for a minute and turned his face to the rain. The cold drops pricked like bits of glass. Where was Mary? She would not accept confinement like proper pregnant women and went out often. Was she safe? Had the labor started? He pushed his way through the throng of vendors on the bridge and crashed through the doors of the Merchant's Coffeehouse into a huddle of officers.

They were both Hessian and British. Wet, breathless, glassy-eyed, he moved warily to a chair at the back, sat and ordered black ale. His hands shook and he folded them to stop the telltale shaking. He downed his drink. The liquid congealed in his throat like thick oil and he choked. He ordered another. He saw red-eyed Jack Rivington staggering toward him, sloshing his ale from a silver tankard, drunk as an oily whaler. Rivington took a seat across the table facing him. "Robert, my good friend, I've won my bet! A toast to my good luck! Ah but today, we do not cheer. We mourn! Our good Major Andre is dead, arrested at North Castle by infamous rogues and hanged by the neck like a scurrilous spy." He threw his head back and rubbed his red eyes. "We've got ourselves bloody Arnold, in the bargain!... A woeful story, makes me tremble for the injustice of it!"

Robert's mind raced. Arnold, a Brigadier General in the Continental Army, had betrayed the cause, had come over to the British. He stiffened and held his voice firm, "How much did you bet?"

Rivington waved a hand to order lunch and babbled on. "Bet? My shop, my press, the musings of this addled brain. I bet the Captain 100 guineas that they would hang Andre and not hold him for exchange. And that's precisely what the bloody rebels did! Now my British cohorts are doubly angry because their hero is dead and they have to pay me the wager. Then I must print the obituary, Robert! Some call me a traitor merely for printing bad news. Brave Andre executed! The toad, Arnold, exalted! West Point should have been ours for a generous price. Andre crossed the rebel lines to settle the sum with Benedict bloody Arnold." Rivington bowed his head like a tired horse and heaved a hefty sigh. "Poor Andre was arrested last Saturday and now he is dead."

Rivington paused for effect and Robert had the strange sensation that it was all an act. Everyone in the coffeehouse was listening and Rivington was playing to his Tory audience. Now his voice lowered to a feeble groan. "Arnold has joined our noble ranks! We have got the horse jockey while heaven has got the prince, God rest his soul!"

Robert lifted his gaze to stare Jack Rivington in the face. Rivington stared numbly at the dregs of his ale and did not meet his eye.

Robert forced his mind to focus on what Rivington was saying: Arnold, in New York, at British headquarters, relating all he knew to the high command. How much did Benedict Arnold know? Surely not Culper Jr.'s or Mary's or Brewster's identity as a spy. Arnold was a brigadier. He must know that intelligence flowed freely from New York to Washington's camp near Fort Lee and he probably knew its route via Setauket and Connecticut. Arnold himself had been on the receiving end! Robert's head spun. He gulped down his ale and got up and started for the door. Rivington's head slowly sank to the table like a wilting sail when a halyard breaks.

Robert Townsend walked out to the Murray's wharf. It was dark. The rain had diminished and a heavy mist hovered over the surface of the water. The water lapped eerily against the pilings and his nostrils flared in the tepid air. Brewster appeared like a soggy ghost. Robert knew him only by the deep voice. He was clean shaven, dressed in dirty Navy whites and crouched like a beggar with his hands upraised. "Listen carefully, Rob, listen to a poor beggar and look to the sea as if you do not know me." His hawklike eyes shifted from left to right. They were alone and he continued, "The Weymouth's launch is at the end of the wharf. Board her. Captain Chadeyne will weigh anchor with the tide. He is bound for Lisbon but he will stop in Oyster Bay to deposit you and Mary. Mary is already aboard."

Robert turned impulsively back toward Caleb Brewster. "But the babe is due soon! The midwife and all is readied here in the city! Am I to believe everything a drunken Rivington mutters?"

"Rivington tells the truth! Think first of your life and Mary's life, if there is to be a babe! We do not know how much knowledge Arnold has betrayed. We do not know to whom he has betrayed it. If news of our efforts has reached Provost Marshal Cunningham, greatest care is necessary. Give a few weeks, a month. Halt all activity. Leave no traces. The danger will play out in the next few weeks.... Washington himself commands we take care." He added with a shake of his shaggy head, "Youngs awaits you and Mary in Oyster Bay. Chadeyne must sail within the hour to join the convoy for Lisbon off Gardiner's Bay. Youngs will meet you in a whaleboat in the shallows off Plum Point at dusk. Youngs has already let it be known that you have been ill and at the farm for the last week."

"But I must apprise Stewart!"

"I told Stewart when I collected Mary. The Hollets think that Mary started to bleed prematurely and you have gone in search of a surgeon in Brooklyn. They will care for the warehouse in your absence."

Robert glared openly at the gaunt face of Caleb Brewster. There were crow's feet at the edges of his eyes and furrows in his brow and wisps of grey in the black of his beard. His fluid voice cracked when he spoke. The same fears were written in Robert's own tired visage.

Brewster repeated, "Rob, the sea is your salvation. Go now! Go!" Brewster pushed him toward the end of the wharf.

Robert Townsend jerked but did not move. Brewster who had avoided his gaze, turned his fierce eyes upon him. "One more precaution. Watch Mary closely. She tends to rashness.... Go now or you will be the loser."

Brewster left Robert Townsend standing on the crowded dock. The rain pelted harder than before. Water dripped from his chin and the lobes of his ears, as he stood puzzling out the events of the afternoon. He half expected to be arrested as he walked over the slick planks of the pier to the Weymouth's launch. Wind slapped his face and plastered his chestnut hair against his skull. His eyes scanned every cask, bale and coil of rope. Only a few scrawny dock workers were loading what looked like casks of salt pork for the Navy stores into a filthy wherry. They smelled like rotten fish. He followed with his eyes as they rowed the rancid meat in the direction of the prison hulks.

The launch was there at dockside, slapping against the pilings with hollow, deadening thuds. His foot slipped on the slimy wharf as he leaped to board her and a sailor's stout arm pulled him across. Only when he walked the length of the ship to the quarterdeck and saw Mary, did his tension ease. She was standing on the bridge with Jacob Chadeyne, windblown and wet and laughing like a banshee.

Chadeyne yelled jovially at the sight of Robert. "I told her to use my cabin but she would not go in until she knew you had joined us! She laughs at the rain! She laughs at discomfort! I wish my woman were as devoted and sanguine as she! Welcome aboard!" He held out a hand and shouted his orders aloft. Robert thought, *and she laughs at danger!*

Chadeyne was talking, describing the virtues of his saintly ship. Robert hardly heard him. His whole attention was for Mary.

"All's shipshape!" She patted her stomach, took him by the arm and pressed it against her heart. "I am swabbed and sparkling as Chadeyne's precious decks and grateful to the kind Captain here for his fine hospitality." She smiled exuberantly. "The rain is refreshing!"

Only when they were alone and dry, did she complain of her fate. She blamed Brewster. "Brewster is sending us to exile in Oyster Bay. Better a hut in the swamps than the welcome your family will give to me!"

"Exile is not forever."

"It is as long as I can endure it. The babe is due in a month! Promise me we'll be in the city for the birth."

He promised. Her confidence soothed him. He led her to the cabin which was warm and comfortable. She lay back on the bunk as they felt the boat sway out from the mooring and into the channel. It was a rough passage. The Weymouth tacked into an easterly wind on an incoming tide. Robert felt his stomach heave but Mary did not sicken. The steward served steaming tea and biscuits with butter. Mary enjoyed the roll of the waves as they watched the biscuits slide with the ship's movement from one end of the table to the other and the liquid in their cups slosh and spill. She weathered the motion as well as any able seamen who had spent his entire life at sea.

The whaleboat was waiting not at Plum Point but off the spit by Hog Island and they rowed against the suck of the ebbing tide, into the bay after dark. Billy Youngs was waiting with a lantern on the dock but he led them to the same Coe house where they had stayed the summer before. The widow Harmon occupied it now with her demented son who had suffered a head wound at Brandywine while serving with the Queen's Rangers. He had never completely recovered. It was a safe refuge. The widow Harmon blamed John Simcoe for her troubles.

The month of October arrived and with it the warmth of Indian summer and the last blooms of the year. Leaves fell and the effort of harvest progressed under a mild autumn sun. In the city, General Clinton introduced General Arnold to his officer corps with pomp and ceremony. They mounted Arnold on a powerful horse and dressed him in bright British red. It was thin a disguise for their disdain. In their hearts, the officers hated the rebel traitor-general, this low-born, colonial tradesman and newly proclaimed Tory. They remembered him, inciting the rebels to greater bravery, on his powerful steed, at Saratoga. They remembered the humiliation of their countryman, John Burgoyne. They would not listen to his counsels. Subordinates obeyed him lethargically or not at all. Pedestrians on the street avoided him. His hunched and limping form trod through the blustery streets of New York, alone, resentful and bitter.

But Provost Marshal William Cunningham conversed with Arnold on several occasions. Some of the Culper associates were arrested, notably Hercules Mulligan, the tailor, who was interrogated in Bridewell Prison, but the glib Irishman talked his way out. Robert and Mary remained in hiding and avoided all mention of the arrests.

As November approached, better news filtered slowly through to Oyster Bay. Mary was restless. The Coe House was cold and crowded. The widow Harmon complained incessantly while her son sat holding his senseless head and rocking interminably in an armchair. He was incontinent and dirty and hollered like a maniac if anyone touched him. Heavy with child, Mary had to meet Robert in the street to speak privately. "I cannot endure this any longer, Rob."

"Brewster has not deemed it safe for us to return."

"Six weeks have passed. I deem it safe. The child is due. It's time to go home!"

He wanted to protest. He wanted to grab her by the shoulders and shake her and make her admit the dangers, but he could not, and he buried his fears in the depths of his soul. He wanted to go home too. They left on the next available coach.

Abigail Hollet was not expecting them. She was at home when they arrived because Henry was sick with fever. "Mary should stay elsewhere lest the wee one she's carrying sicken! She is too close to labor!"

Elsewhere! Where in the city could they find a room? But Mary accepted the woman's thoughtless suggestion. "It is only for a few days, Rob.... We can find space in a boardinghouse."

"They are all full." His words were dry, like old straw.

"So many soldiers have departed for the Carolinas, we're sure to find something: Ask Rivington or DeLancey. Oliver DeLancey has been appointed to replace John Andre, I hear! You have friends in high places, my love! Use them."

"Too high, Mary! I should have to pass a herd of secretaries to be admitted to see them now. They would recognize me and sniff me out! And I don't incur debts that I cannot.or will not repay."

"Rivington will not betray us."

Jack Rivington found two tidy rooms in Queen Street, over the shop of a tinsmith. The banging of the smith's hammer echoed all day long, marking the passing of hours like the ticking of a clock. Mary stayed in the upstairs room or wandered into the tin shop for companionship.

Rivington visited often, always with a bottle under his arm, whose contents he consumed himself. But his concern was genuine. "Rob, tell me when her time arrives and I'll send for my surgeon. He's the best in New York."

Robert felt his hands shake and his eyes blink involuntarily from nervousness and lack of sleep. To distract himself, he resumed his rounds. Angus MacRae noticed the thinness of his frame and reacted. "Eat man or you'll faint away when you hear that she bore you a son."

On the 20th of November, Robert leaned over a table at Grace's with Jack Rivington. Rivington was talking and Robert's head was nodding from exhaustion. Angus MacRae was pouring more ale when a captain from headquarters sat in a corner and raised his drunken voice. "Just came from the Provost's office. They picked up a woman spy today. Caught her with the Naval Signal Code in her pocket! Right impudent lass, and sassy! Refused to name any of her cohorts. Should have seen old Cunningham gloat! Don't think he's ever had a pregnant one before! He'll invent some fiendish inducements to make her talk! His wolf's tongue was hanging out!"

Robert's head jerked up. His face went white. He felt the grip of Rivington's bony fingers on his arm. Rivington's careless monotone floated casually across the room, masking the horror of his words. "Won't they hang her like Andre?"

"If she won't inform, he'll put her aboard the good ship, Jersey!" The captain belched and chuckled irreverently. The Jersey was the discarded 64-gun ship of war and worst of the waterlogged hulks. Over a thousand prisoners were penned below her decks. Slime blanketed her sides and bearded her anchor chains. Filth covered her decks and fouled her hold. Plague, smallpox, flux and ague raged unchecked. Men died or went insane. As for women.... But women were not imprisoned there!

Robert's head swam. Rivington held him firmly by both arms. He could see his friend's mouth wrap around the syllables of meaningless words. An impulse to scream, to pound the walls, engulfed him. He opened his mouth. Angus MacRae came up behind, bumped his chair and fell over him, spilling a bumper of ale over his head and into his eyes. He blinked and blubbered. Angus whipped out his towel to wipe up the mess. He was rubbing his shoulders frantically with a towel when Robert heard Rivington's voice through the melee. "Surely they don't send women there!"

"The blackguard Cunningham sends them wherever he wants them!"

White-faced, Jack Rivington protested, "Not a woman! No civilized Englishman would do that!"

"Marshal Cunningham's no bloody Englishman! He's an Irish dog! And the guards who man the Jersey are fiends from hell!"

A trigger snapped in Robert's brain. His muscles contracted as if to tackle the captain and he lurched in his seat. But Jack Rivington and Angus MacRae held him down. Together they herded him to the back room, Angus brandishing the towel and babbling apologies for drowning him. They dried him, wrapped him in his cloak and bundled him into the street, where he struggled to free himself. They took him to the print shop where they tied him down to the heavy arm of the press until he calmed.

Robert Townsend half heard Jack Rivington trying to rationalize. "Don't act the madman, Rob. It's only the report of a junior officer, probably invention or drunken gossip. They don't torture pregnant women! Mary is most likely safe at home. Angus and I will take you there. We will find Mary, warm and happy, and you will fall asleep and forget the horror of this day like last night's nightmare. And tomorrow we'll go to headquarters and summon DeLancey to find out how the vicious rumor started."

They walked him to Queen Street to the tinsmith's shop. Mary was not there. She had complained of the banging noise, had gone out and had not returned. Night was falling and the smith was worried.

Robert turned back to the darkening street shaking in every limb. Jack Rivington's baritone sounded as if from a great distance. "We should check Peck's Slip."

Stewart answered the door. The little Scotsman's knowing eyes flashed at MacRae and Rivington, then settled on Robert. He closed the door and stepped outside. "She is not here, sir. She came 'round in the afternoon to see if Henry had recovered. I told her the lad was still abed with the fever. Since then I have not seen her." He closed the door behind him and stepped into the street with the others.

Robert flung his words like sharp daggers at the planks of the closed door. "I will kill the brutes! I will rub their noses in feces and gore! Vicious beasts! They encourage carnage! They are blind to torture, rapine, looting!" He raised his fists above his head and lowered them with a resounding clatter on the heavy planks of the door. It took three men to hold back the onrush of his anger.

Stewart spoke then with quiet authority. "Sir, I know where the wee lady went. We'll let ye go, if ye'll stand quietly while I explain.... It was her, sir, Mrs. Drake, your Mary, who enlisted Mr. Rivington for a fair price. Together they have deciphered the Naval Code and delivered the same to Tallmadge! 'Tis a great and valuable coup, sir, now with the French and a navy on our side! It will win us the war!" MacRae continued to hold Robert's arm while Stewart fell back. "Ye know Rivington, sir. He spends his funds freely, always juggles his debts. He needed money and they paid him well, the Frenchmen did, with gold and brandy! The wee lady was the contact. We thought a pregnant woman beyond suspicion. I am so very sorry, sir." Robert's fist struck out toward Stewart. Stewart stepped back to avoid the blow. His thin body seemed to crumble inwards and his steady voice cracked. "I... we all love Mrs. Drake, strictly purely that is, sir, in our own way. It's she who has saved us!"

Robert Townsend blinked back tears. His voice wrenched from somewhere in his groin. "And the baby? What is to become of her baby, my son?"

His face contracted as he looked wildly from one to the other, "Find me pistols, a sharp knife, a stout rope and I'll hunt down this Cunningham who nails down his prisoners to watch them die. I'll hunt him to the very bowels of hell."

"No, ye cannot, sir! Ye would only expose yourself and the others. Mary will have destroyed all evidence. Wait with us. Come to the print shop. We'll ask DeLancey, verify if the reports are true."

They waited. Rivington returned with DeLancey late the same evening. Oliver DeLancey's voice was bleak. "It is true, Rob. She has been taken! But she is not in the hulks. Headquarters says she was sent to Bridewell. I've just come from there and I could find no trace of her." He bowed his head and pursed his lips. "Please Rob, to think that an Englishman would do this! I am ashamed of my countrymen." It was a bald admission from DeLancey. They thanked him profusely and sent him away.

"He did not check the other prisons?" Stewart's eyes questioned.

"We'll go now." Rivington's long face frowned and signaled to MacRae.

"Sir, if I may suggest...." Stewart interrupted again. "We could take the dog, Laddie. Give him a mite of clothing to sniff and he will follow her trail."

Stewart collected the dog and a shawl that was Mary's and took Robert by the arm. Robert rose, but the ground seemed to give way under him and his knees reverberated with the shock of each footfall. They walked north toward the stench of the Sugar House, the Debtors' Jail and Bridwell Prison. A sentry stopped them but Rivington pulled out passes that allowed them passage. Night was falling. They ignored the curfew. Again Rivington produced forged authorizations and blustered his way in to question warders and keepers. They polished palms with guineas, to no avail. There was no reaction from the dog. Mary had left no trail. She had disappeared.

When they returned to Rivington's offices, DeLancey had returned. His white face betrayed his shocking news. "I have it from General Clinton himself. She was caught carrying the Naval Code. Such an horrendous breach of security and coming as it does after John Andre's recent execution in Tappan...." DeLancey's lip quivered. "Mercy was not a consideration. Cunningham himself has escorted her to the hulks... It is a barbaric act. Robert, I'm sorry. Such is war. There was nothing I could do."

Robert's muscles surged in protest. He ran from the building with a burst of speed and sought out the alleys and darkest crevices of the city. Like a hunted animal, he relished the darkness and welcomed its embrace. Hours later, he found himself on Murray's Wharf where Brewster had come to warn him and he leaned against a piling and stared at the dark lapping water. It tempted but he did not jump. She was alive! So his aching heart told him. He hunkered down behind the coils of cordage and looked out across the river. In the starlight he could make out the dull outline of the hulks, the Jersey, the Scorpion and the Good Hope. Their giant carcasses showed blacker still against the black moonlit water. His nostrils sniffed out their nauseating smell on the wind. How many lives were imprisoned there? How many good men and women? How many died a horrible death? His life, his love, the child of his flesh, was festering in one of them. No! His whole being protested. He crumpled to the slimy planks of the pier and beat them with his fists until his knuckles bled.

He was weeping when Stewart and the dog found him there. Robert saw their shadows approaching and sat up. The dog licked the tears from his face and the blood from his fingers. Stewart spoke but his voice filtered through the acrid air like a ghost's. "Wait for the dawn, sir. Wait until we can man a launch."

The dawn came, red like war. Robert sat in the armchair at Peck's Slip, a shrunken image of his former self. He did not sleep. He did not speak. He did not eat. Rivington came with news. He had called on John Simcoe's friend, Major John Montresor. Montresor was at first incredulous but promised to make inquiries of the Admiralty. As for the Provost's office and William Cunningham, that was a civilian arm of the military government and he was powerless.

At noon, Montresor himself came with the log of the Jersey under his arm and a list of all prisoners' names. "A woman was taken on board last night. Her name is Blanchard and she was brought back for exchange this morning. It is all some mistake." He shook his white-wigged head. "They do not imprison women. I cannot believe that British justice has come to this!" And he muttered under his breath, "I will personally look into the affairs of this Cunningham. I can make no apology for his actions."

Hercules Mulligan came. He insisted on talking with Robert alone. "I stand before you and accuse myself, Robert. I am partially to blame." He bowed his head, hat in hand. "There is more than one web of persons who spy on British doings. I have my own group of informants. Mary has been part of my ring since first she ordered dresses. She is a brave and daring lady. I will give my life, if it means we rescue her... at least if we can deliver the baby...."

The baby! At the thought, Robert shuddered, but the dog was licking his hand and he could hear Stewart again, talking as if from a great distance. "For the baby, sir, ye must rally. The wee lady would want that."

Stewart was right. There was still life to protect. But in his bones, Robert Townsend knew that his Mary, daring, overconfident, irrepressible, Mary whom he loved, was lost to him.

Stewart was babbling on. "Fiends of Englishmen, a fiend of a God who allows demons like Cunningham to inherit the earth!"

"Don't blame the lord. Blame the tyrant! Blame Mary for her rashness! Blame me for allowing it!" Mulligan pounded his breast and bowed his head. "Blame Howe! Blame Cunningham!"

Robert heaved a sigh. "I'm too tired to blame. I've had enough. They will come for me and I will be here to greet them." His voice trailed off. His muscles went limp. He ran his hand through the thick matted fur of the dog, and talked to the dumb animal. "You do not blame. Why cannot we humans be as guileless as you beasts?" He sank back. He could no longer stop the tears and he wept. The dog lay a comforting head on his knee.

Robert Townsend stayed on at Peck's Slip and awaited his own arrest. He was there on Christmas Eve, reviewing bills of lading, when there was a loud rap on the alley door. Abigail Hollet went to answer. Robert rose from his chair and walked haltingly forward, expecting to be lead away in irons. There was a hooded man at the door who held a tiny bundle. In the dark outside, Robert did not recognize the face. When he stepped into the soft interior candlelight, he saw it was Dennison, the strange doctor whom he had met in the swamps, years ago. Dennison held the package out to him. "Open it. It is Mary Drake who bid me come. Know she did not betray you or the courageous men with whom you work. She asked that I deliver this proof of her love and tell you that she has born you a son!" Dennison replaced his hood and turned to go.

"Where is she?" Robert moved to clutch the man's arm.

"I am not at liberty to say." He pulled his arm free and began to walk away. He was half way down the alley when Robert ran after him. "If she is alive, I'll go to her. I want to see my son!"

The black hood shook in denial. "No, you cannot. She and your son are safe. If you were ever to be seen together, they would arrest you on the spot or kidnap her for exchange. You are too valuable here. He placed a soft palm on Robert's arm. "Suffice to say that she is no longer in British occupied territory and she has assumed a new name. You must leave her be."

"No!" The word echoed back aimlessly from the walls of the alley as Dennison disappeared. He opened the package. It contained Mary's pearls.

Winter turned into spring. Robert Townsend rode back to Oyster Bay in April 1781, over the same route that he had traveled that ill-fated day five years ago. He mounted the heights at Brooklyn and looked down on the old battlefield. It was greening now in the warm spring sunshine. He remembered the smoke and the pounding blasts and the horrid, acrid smell of the powder. A farmer trod a nearby field, seed bag slung over his shoulder, toeing a hole for his seed and planting it with his bare hands. "Croswell!" Robert called out the name. The man looked up and shouted back, "He's gone these five years hence, to Connecticut!" The man resumed his labor, singing softly to himself. The tune carried to Robert Townsend's ears. It was Yankee Doodle, a catchy melody, popular with rebels and Tories alike. Robert could not distinguish the words and wondered whether the man sang the rebel or the Tory version or just some ditty that he made up himself.

He trotted the bay down the road to Jamaica, passed the race course and entered the deep woods of Queens County. He let the tired horse walk. The bay was only grass-fed now, no more oats to make him come alive and run like the wind. So many horses had died that he counted himself lucky. He leaned over to stroke the animal's neck. He had his horse. He had his life. But how much had he lost? He did not know if he still had the will to gain it back.

He missed Mary terribly. He missed his son whom he had never even seen. Every tree held thousands of buds, thousands of promises of new life but his own new life was absent. He rode past Manhasset and the Meeting House and gazed from the woods onto the Jericho encampment. It had grown like some ugly fungus. He turned into the road to Oyster Bay and passed through Pine Hollow by the farms of his neighbors, Underhill and Parrish. The farms were quiet now, sprouting shoots from out of winter's brown.

When he turned into the lane that led to Raynham Hall, he stopped. The stumps of the orchard marked the rows like gravestones. But Simcoe's seedlings had arrived and Beulah and Sally and Audrey had planted each one with their own hands. They were feeble stalks but they were laden with buds. He stabled the horse and walked out among them and sank onto a stump.

Sally found him there and sat beside him. "You are too melancholy, Rob. You would make a drudge of your son if he were here and mother would make his life miserable.... Mary is a good woman. She loved you. She loves him. Trust that she will bring him up with care."

"You are telling me to give him up, Sal, my own son! My heart is heavy." He turned away. She must not see him cry.

"I am telling you to let him live like you let his mother live, in his own way, in his own time. He would not be happy here. Let him seek happiness with his mother. Let Mary find comfort in that part of you that is in him."

He sat for a long while staring at the black earth where the sun's rays outlined the thin shadows of the seedlings. Sally stayed beside him. "I don't know if I can do it, Sal. It breaks my heart."

"Would you rather break hers?"

He faced her finally. The tears streamed down his face.

She put her arm around him for warmth and comfort. After a long while he roused and murmured softly. "And what of you Sal? Where is your Simcoe?

"I don't know. I receive his letters, all the news of marches and battles...." She huddled closer and her voice dropped to a whisper. "I don't want to hamper his career. I want him to be happy, to do what he thinks is right. His family has never given their consent to our marriage."

She smiled wanly and he was surprised at her fortitude. He questioned gently. "Even if what is right means letting him go?"

"His family has decided that I would be like an iron collar around his neck! These British have their peculiar notions. They cannot accept a love that is beyond their narrow scope. I've a mind to release him from his troth...." She did not finish the sentence. "At least that would end the unbearable uncertainty. You will stand by me, won't you, Rob?"

"Always, Sal. I am your brother."

"Good. And I will stand by you." She took his arm and they walked into the house.

John Graves Simcoe fought valiantly beside Lord Charles Cornwallis from Charleston, to Camden, to Yorktown. When General Clinton needed a trustworthy officer to oversee the actions of Benedict Arnold, he chose Lieutenant Colonel Simcoe. During the siege of Yorktown, Cornwallis assigned John Simcoe with Banastre Tarleton to Glouster Point, a dangerous position on the opposite shore. Simcoe was wounded there severely and hovered near death. After the surrender, he was evacuated to England on an invalid ship, never to return to New York.

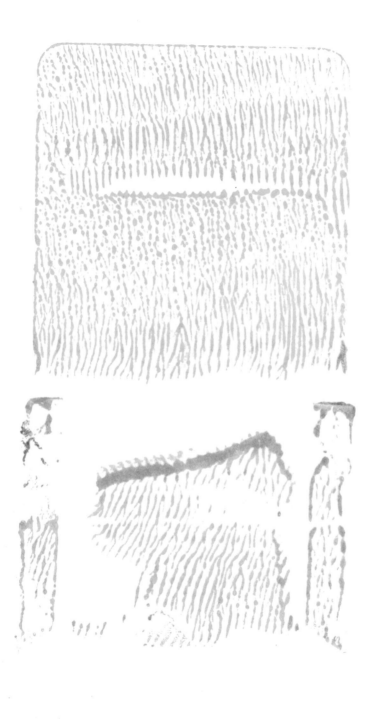